CREEP

CREEP

Jennifer Hillier

G

GALLERY BOOKS

New York London Toronto Sydney

Gallery Books
A Division of Simon & Schuster, Inc.
1230 Avenue of the Americas
New York, NY 10020

This book is a work of fiction. Names, characters, places, and incidents either
are products of the author's imagination or are used fictitiously. Any resemblance
to actual events or locales or persons, living or dead, is entirely coincidental.

Copyright © 2011 by Jennifer Hillier

All rights reserved, including the right to reproduce this book or portions thereof
in any form whatsoever. For information address Gallery Books Subsidiary Rights
Department, 1230 Avenue of the Americas, New York, NY 10020.

First Gallery Books hardcover edition July 2011

GALLERY BOOKS and colophon are registered trademarks of Simon & Schuster, Inc.

For information about special discounts for bulk purchases, please contact Simon &
Schuster Special Sales at 1-866-506-1949 or business@simonandschuster.com.

The Simon & Schuster Speakers Bureau can bring authors to your live event. For
more information or to book an event contact the Simon & Schuster Speakers Bureau
at 1-866-248-3049 or visit our website at www.simonspeakers.com.

Designed by Helene Berinsky

Manufactured in the United States of America

10 9 8 7 6 5 4 3 2 1

Library of Congress Cataloging-in-Publication Data
Hillier, Jennifer.
    Creep / Jennifer Hillier.—1st Gallery Books hardcover ed.
       p. cm.
    1. Women college teachers—Fiction. 2. Extortion—Fiction.
3. Psychological fiction. I. Title.
    PS3608.I446C74   2011
    813'.6—dc22   2010047864

ISBN 978-1-4516-2584-4
ISBN 978-1-4516-2689-6 (ebook)

For Steve Hillier,
    for so many reasons.

ACKNOWLEDGMENTS

So many people helped make my first novel a reality, and I'm very grateful for all the love and support I've received.

I'd like to thank my agent, Victoria Skurnick, for taking a chance on me, and for being relentless in helping me whip the manuscript into shape.

I'd also like to thank my editor, Kathy Sagan, and her assistant, Jessica Webb, for making the publishing process such a wonderful experience. Huge thanks to my copy editor, Steve Boldt, for all his hard work. And to Louise Burke, Jennifer Bergstrom, and everyone else at Gallery Books, thank you. I'm lucky to be part of such a great team.

I'm deeply grateful to my mother, Nida Allan, who always believes in everything I do, and to my father, Roberto Pestaño, for his gift of storytelling. And much love goes to my big brother, John Perez, who always has my back.

Big thanks to my best friends, Annabella Wong, Dawn May Robertson, and Winston Charles Jr., who don't write, but love that I do. You guys always said this would happen, and you were right (but please don't let it go to your heads).

Special thanks to my very first writing buddy, Gregory G. Griffin, for tearing apart my earliest chapters (rather obnoxiously, I might add), and then cheering me on as I put them back together again. May your inner dwarf always shine, my friend.

Numerous other writing pals also offered their feedback on this book long before I ever got an agent, and I'm so grateful for all your constructive criticism and encouragement.

Lastly, I'd like to thank my guardian angel, Helena Rosts, who was my first real fan and who blessed me early on with the confidence to chase my dreams.

CREEP

Three months. That's how long Dr. Sheila Tao had been sleeping with Ethan Wolfe. Three months, four days, and approximately six hours.

The problem wasn't the sixteen-year age difference. It wasn't even that she was his professor and he was her teaching assistant. The problem was that Sheila was engaged to Morris, and now the affair with Ethan had to stop. No more weekly "meetings" at the Ivy, the motel just off campus that rented rooms by the hour. No more sneaking around. No more lying. No more falling into that chasm of depression that consumed her for days after each of their trysts.

It had to end. All of it. Sheila and her therapist had been working hard on this. Yes, even psychologists had psychologists.

It wouldn't be easy. Ethan was good-looking and prone to getting his way. Hell, he had seduced her, though Sheila suspected not even her therapist believed that.

They were in her bright corner office on the fourth floor of the psychology building at Puget Sound State University. He was relaxed, casual, his jean-clad legs spread open in that cocky way he liked to sit. The desk between them was strewn with papers, an organized clutter that served as a makeshift barrier.

Observing him, she watched his full lips form words she only half-heard. There was nothing vague about Ethan's attractiveness, but he downplayed it by wearing ratty vintage T-shirts, worn jeans, tennis shoes. His hard, flat stomach wasn't evident through the loose-fitting shirt, but Sheila could damn well picture it.

She had no idea how he was going react to her news. She'd known him long enough to understand his propensity for structure, and she was about to upset the routine they'd established over the past three months.

Of her five teaching assistants, Ethan was the brightest and most ambitious. His intelligence and drive had been a big part of his appeal. They were discussing grades for her popular summer-session undergraduate social psychology class, and so far neither of them had commented as to why they were meeting here this morning, in her office, instead of room sixteen at the Ivy Motel. She knew he had to be thinking about it, because she was thinking about it, too.

She forced herself to focus on what he was saying.

"Danny Ambrose doesn't deserve a B," he said, fingers resting lightly on the arms of his chair. He never talked with his hands, even when he was passionate about something. "The similarities he drew between Milgram's experiment and the Nazis? Too obvious."

His brows were furrowed. Sheila was about to overrule the grade Ethan had assigned to one of her undergraduate students, and he didn't like it. He wasn't used to it. They didn't disagree often.

"He loses points for originality, but don't you think his argument is solid?" Sheila smiled to soften her words. "This is only a sophomore class. He did what was asked of him and it was better than average. I spoke to Danny personally the other day. He risks losing his scholarship if we give him that C. He's a good kid. I'd really hate to see that happen."

She could almost hear the wheels in Ethan's mind turning as he thought of a counterargument. Most of the time she encouraged healthy debate, but she wasn't in the mood this morning. There was a conversation they needed to have, and she was having a hard time steering them in that direction.

She waited, saying nothing. If she didn't push it, he'd come around. The key was to let him work through it on his own.

"Okay," Ethan said finally. "You win, Sheila. Danny gets a B. Lucky bastard. God, I hate it when you assert your authority over me." Lowering his voice, he glanced over his shoulder at the open door behind him. "You'll have to make it up to me later." He leaned forward and ran a finger down the back of her left hand, lips curled into the half-smile she liked so much.

His finger brushed over the band of her new diamond ring, turned inside out so the stone was tucked into her palm. His gaze dropped down to her hand.

She was surprised it had taken him this long to notice. *Here we go.*

Her first instinct was to yank her hand away, but that would only make things worse. Willing herself to appear relaxed, she twisted the platinum band around. Ethan's eyes widened at the sight of the four-carat diamond.

"What's this?" The lightness of his tone did not match his face. A flush emerged just above the neckline of his T-shirt. He touched a finger to the top of the stone, leaving a smudge.

She resisted the urge to wipe it off. The face of a diamond this size was like glass. Morris was a senior partner at Bindle Brothers, the largest investment bank in the Northwest, and he hadn't held back.

She withdrew her hand. "Could you close the door?" she

asked. "Just for a few minutes. There's something we need to discuss."

Ethan stiffened, as Sheila knew he would. He was fine in a lecture hall, but they both knew he didn't like closed doors in small spaces. Something to do with his childhood and getting locked in a closet for hours—she didn't really know, he'd always been vague. In their tiny motel room, the windows always had to be open, even if it was raining.

"Please?" she said. "Just for a bit so we can talk in private. I'll open the window."

He closed her office door reluctantly while she cranked open the casement behind her. A blast of August warmth entered the air-conditioned room. Ethan waited in silence, his expression betraying nothing.

There was no way around it except to be direct. "Morris and I are getting married."

Ethan leaned back in his chair and stared at her with unreadable light gray eyes. Again, she waited. The thrum of the air conditioner reverberated in the room.

"When did this happen?"

"Saturday." Five nights ago.

He looked around the office. He wasn't one to avoid eye contact, so she guessed he was digesting this information. His gaze focused briefly on a small, framed picture of Sheila and Morris on the window ledge before returning to her face. "Well, this is big news. But it doesn't change anything between you and me."

"It changes everything." The words were out before she could consider their impact. Biting her lip, she forged ahead anyway. "I can't be involved with you anymore outside of class."

He didn't blink. "Just like that?"

"I'm sorry."

He exhaled and she caught a whiff of the cinnamon gum he'd been chewing earlier. He always chewed cinnamon gum, and if she closed her eyes, she could almost taste it, could almost feel his sweet, spicy tongue in her mouth—

"Congratulations." The smile didn't quite touch his eyes.

"Thank you," she said.

"When's the wedding?"

"October tenth."

His smile turned into a grin she couldn't read. It wasn't amusement, or annoyance, or even a desire to please; it was something else entirely.

"So soon. Why the rush?"

She had prepared for this question, rehearsing the answer in her head during the drive to work that morning, and it rolled off her tongue. "I'm thirty-nine and I'm not getting any younger. I'm tired of living alone, Ethan. I love Morris. We want to start our life together. We—there might still be time for kids."

"What should I wear to the wedding?"

Shocked, she opened her mouth, but no words came out.

"I'm kidding," he said, his eyes finally showing a hint of amusement. "Joke, Sheila. I wouldn't come even if I was invited. Isn't there a rule about going to the weddings of people you used to fuck?"

She winced. She had no problem with cursing, but here, in this moment, it sounded unreasonably harsh.

"Ah, well. It's better that it's over anyway." He ran a hand through his short, mussed hair. "It really should have ended ages ago, now that I think about it. Remember when your father died? How messed up you were?"

Her stomach lurched. "Of course I remember." It had only been three months since her estranged father had passed away from liver cancer. Three days before the affair had started. She knew it had been the trigger.

His voice became low, accusing. "I never wanted this to be a long-term thing. But you were so goddamned needy. You kept telling me not to go."

It was a subtle but unmistakable slap in the face. *Please don't go.* Oh, yes, those had been her words exactly, words she'd whispered to Ethan the morning after her father's funeral while lying next to him naked under the scratchy motel bedsheets. It hurt to think he could bring it up now as if they were talking about the weather.

"The timing was bad," he said with a shrug. "I couldn't do it to you. But really, it should have ended right after it started."

"You said that already."

"Are you mad?" His face was open, interested. "Don't be mad, Sheila. I don't regret that it lasted as long as it did. But all good things must come to an end. This won't change anything professional between us. We still work really well together."

He sat back with a Cheshire-cat smile.

She was suddenly infuriated. Exactly who was dumping whom here? She had agonized over this conversation for days, wondering what to say to him and how to say it, alternating between supreme bliss at her new engagement and pangs of regret over the affair, worried about hurting Morris, hurting Ethan, hurting herself. Nothing about this had been simple. Nothing.

But here he was, easy like Sunday morning, his handsome face a mixture of pity and regret.

She arranged the papers on the desk into neat stacks to keep her hands from trembling, thinking hard about what she wanted to say next.

"All right, about that." Sheila's words were tight as she

forced herself to stay calm. "I don't think we should continue to work together. I'm going to recommend you work with Dr. Easton from now on."

This caught him off guard. "You're not fucking serious?"

"I am." She smiled, pleased at his reaction, then made a grand show of wiping her brow. "You know what, I need to close the window. It's really hot in here and the air-conditioning's escaping. You know how I get when it's stuffy."

"Sheila, don't close—"

She stood up quickly and cranked and latched the window. By the time she turned back to Ethan, his body had gone rigid. She sat down again and crossed her legs, not bothering to hide her own little smile.

"I promise you it'll be an easy transition. Dr. Easton was impressed with the work you did in his advanced personality theory class last term. His expertise on deviant behavior can only help your thesis." Sheila's smile widened. "Don't worry, the department won't have a problem with the switch. You can stay until the end of next term as my TA, but after Christmas—"

"I don't want to switch," he said. Beads of sweat appeared at his hairline even though the room was cooling. "I have less than a year to go. I don't want to work through the kinks of a new adviser."

"I'll do everything I can to help."

They sat staring at each other. It was awkward waiting out the silence, but she knew whoever spoke first would lose.

"You're trying to get rid of me," Ethan hissed. Circular sweat stains had formed at his armpits, soaking through the cloth of his gray T-shirt. "Well, guess what, I'm not switching. I've been working with you for going on three terms now. You're not passing me off to someone else because you're getting married and don't want a reminder you fucked the help. My thesis is nearly done." He was breathing hard. Perspiration trailed down his left temple.

She had about thirty seconds before he'd totally lose it; claustrophobia could be debilitating. "And I promise you nothing will change," she said again. "Dr. Easton's always admired you and—"

"Dr. Easton's a fucking fag!" Ethan slammed his hands down on the desk and the stack of term papers fell over. At that moment the air conditioner paused and the room was suddenly quiet. Pointing a finger at her, he stood up. "I am not working with him. You *are* going to finish what you started with me."

Sheila did her best to appear impassive. "You don't have a choice. I can reassign you anytime I like, for any reason."

"Really? And what would the dean say about that?" Ethan was towering over her desk. Little drops of sweat hit the term papers, blurring the ink into shapeless forms.

"Dean Simmons will back me up, of course," she said, looking up at him.

"Even after he sees you on the Internet taking it up the ass?"

"What? What are you—" She stopped. Her throat went dry and she swallowed. Her heart started thumping in her chest so hard she thought she could feel her silk blouse moving. "You deleted that off your phone. I watched you do it."

"Are you sure about that?" His eyes were flat, devoid of emotion. He was still sweating but his voice was once again controlled. "I didn't e-mail it to myself first? You're absolutely sure?"

Her temple began to throb. The fluorescent lights overhead were suddenly too bright, the walls too yellow, the air conditioner too loud. Her armpits tingled and she could smell onions. Ethan's body odor. Or was it her own?

"You wouldn't dare," she whispered.

"Wouldn't I?" He grinned triumphantly as he wiped his sweaty brow with his hand. Turning away from her, he finally yanked open the office door and stepped out, taking deep breaths of the semi-stale hallway air.

Sheila sat, dazed. There was a 99 percent chance he was bluffing—her gut told her there was no video anymore, he wouldn't have had time to send it somewhere else from his phone before she'd made him delete it—but goddamn it, it wasn't good enough. If anything like it ever showed up on CampusAnonymous.com, a website notorious for outrageous gossip and nasty comments about all things involving the university, she'd be ruined. The video would go viral before she could blink twice, and two decades of hard work would be snuffed out like a campfire in a thunderstorm.

Having an affair with a student was one thing. It happened all the time—she could think of three professors who'd been involved with students in the past, who'd gotten nothing more than slaps on the wrist. And Ethan was twenty-three and neither of them were married, which counted for something.

But a video? It wouldn't matter whom she was screwing—a video of her writhing naked on the Internet would get her fired. No hearing, no chance to defend herself, just an hour to collect her personal belongings and she'd be out the door on her ass. Do not pass Go, do not collect two hundred.

How could I have been so fucking stupid?

A voice broke into her thoughts, and she looked up. Valerie Kim, one of Sheila's other TAs, stood in the doorway just behind Ethan.

"One sec, Val," Ethan said to the petite young woman. His tone betrayed no hint of the tension that filled the office. "The professor and I are almost done here."

"That's cool." Valerie looked past Ethan into the office at Sheila. "I can come back in five."

"No need." Sheila's smile felt clownish. "Come in, Valerie."

Ethan stepped back into the office and made a show of bundling up the scattered term papers on the desk. Slinging his worn leather bag crosswise over his torso, he grinned at Sheila. "Dr. Tao, I'll see you next week. Thanks for your time."

"Sure," Sheila said. Her shoulders slumped and her back ached.

Ethan winked at Valerie as he left the office. "She's all yours."

She heard him whistling as he ambled down the hallway, not a care in the world, and her mind reeled. What the fuck had just happened?

"So, Professor Tao, did you hear?" Valerie's voice was breathy. The ponytailed teaching assistant plopped into the chair across from Sheila and rummaged in her bag for her own stack of papers to be reviewed. "Diana St. Clair's body was found this morning."

"Hmmm?" Sheila could not process what the graduate student was saying. Somehow, she had completely underestimated Ethan Wolfe. He had outsmarted her, and how was that possible? Damn him. *Damn her.* This was a disaster. Could he really still have that video? He'd made it several weeks ago, and maybe her memory was foggy, but she was certain she'd seen him delete it right afterward, could remember her relief when she saw it was gone . . .

"The swimmer? Diana St. Clair?" Valerie was saying.

"Yes, of course I know she disappeared," Sheila said, irritated. A drop of Ethan's sweat remained on the desk and she swiped at it. She forced herself to focus on Valerie's pretty face. "What's the update?"

"I don't know all the details yet." The grad student sounded appropriately somber, though her eyes were alight with morbid excitement. "She was found floating in Puget Sound early this morning. A ferry rider spotted her."

"She *drowned*?" Sheila's hand flew to her mouth. Valerie had her full attention now. "How is that even possible?"

Everyone was familiar with the story. It had been all over the news. Diana St. Clair was the pride and joy of PSSU, a champion Division I swimmer and Olympic hopeful. She'd gone missing after swim practice over a week before, and it was all anyone on campus could talk about. There'd been multiple theories about her disappearance: she'd eloped to Brazil with a guy she'd met online; she'd quit swimming but didn't have the heart to tell her parents; she was pregnant and hiding it from her sponsors . . .

"She didn't drown, that isn't how she died. I heard she was stabbed first." Valerie paused for dramatic effect. "Multiple times."

Sheila sat up straight. "Holy shit!"

Valerie looked pleased to hear her professor swear. "I heard they're going to be putting new security measures in place because of this." Clearly Valerie had heard a lot. "My boyfriend works part-time in the communications department. They're sending out a bulletin later today."

"Holy shit." Sheila felt disoriented as she tried to process the news.

Diana St. Clair had been her student. Sheila had never known someone who was murdered.

Until now.

CHAPTER : 2

The campus-wide e-mail sent out by the university's security department did a good job of outlining the new safety measures that all faculty, staff, and students were to follow. But ultimately, it was all for nothing, because nobody was taking the memo seriously. Nobody at the university was worried.

It had been almost a week since Diana St. Clair's body had turned up, and Seattle PD still couldn't confirm exactly where the swimmer had been when she was murdered. Her stabbed and decomposing body, bloated and gassy from days floating in Puget Sound, provided no evidence to suggest she was killed on university grounds or anywhere even near the university. Police had combed the campus and nothing had turned up. They had no idea whether she'd been stalked or snatched by someone she knew, or whether the killing was random. The only thing they could confirm was that Diana had engaged in sexual activity before she died, and that everyone close to her—including her boyfriend, fellow swimmer Donovan Langley—had airtight alibis for where they'd been at the time she was killed.

In short, Seattle PD had nothing. And other than her obituary and a long, gushy article in the *Puget Sound Village Voice* (the school newspaper), nothing further had been written about Diana once she'd been buried.

It was tragic. And to Sheila, the greatest tragedy wasn't just that Diana had been murdered, but how quickly the beautiful student had been forgotten. Everyone had moved on. Local news was now flooded with stories of a bomb scare at Sea-Tac airport. What had the world come to?

She sat alone in her office, trying to remember the last time she'd had contact with Diana. It had to have been about a year before, shortly before the social psych midterm during fall term. Diana had asked for an "early write," a common request for student athletes who had obligations within their sport. Sheila had received a supporting letter from Diana's coach so the swimmer could head to UC Irvine for the big Nike Cup Division I meet immediately afterward.

It was funny how Sheila could remember something so specific from a year ago that in itself wasn't memorable. But Diana herself had been an unforgettable person. Straight-A student, runway-model tall, long blond hair, focused. She'd had the world at her feet.

Come to think of it, wasn't it Ethan who'd proctored Diana's exam that semester? Sheila wondered now what he thought of her murder. She had meant to ask his opinion about Diana's disappearance after the swimmer was first reported missing. That was the morning she and Ethan had both come to work early. Without even saying hello, he'd kissed her neck and had reached under her skirt to pull down her panties, right here on the . . .

A knock startled her out of her thoughts, and she looked up to see all six foot four of her investment-banker fiancé standing in the doorway. She felt her face flush. *Christ.*

"I almost didn't want to knock, you looked so deep in thought," Morris Gardener said with a grin, his loud Texas twang filling her office. Morris used to play professional football, and his broad shoulders practically spanned the width of the doorway. "I hope you were thinking about me, darlin'."

"You don't want to know what I was thinking about," she said, the last word coming out a croak from her dry throat. Her water bottle was on the desk in front of her and she took a sip before getting up to give him a kiss.

His strong arms held her close for a few seconds. Resting her face against his burly chest, she breathed in his scent. Soap and water and spicy aftershave, a comforting combination. He kissed her again.

"This is a surprise. What brings you by?" She sat back down and smoothed her skirt, an excuse to dry her sweaty palms. She was breathless, though there was no physical cause for it. She looked at her fiancé, sitting across from her at the very desk she and Ethan had once . . .

Stop it.

Morris beamed at her, blue eyes twinkling. "I need a reason to see my future wife?"

"Never." She forced a smile. "But it's been awhile since you dropped by to see me at work."

And thank God for that, you stupid twat. You're going straight to hell.

"I forgot how nice your office is." Morris relaxed in his chair and looked up at the cheerful yellow walls and numerous potted plants. His eyes fixed on a framed photo of the two of them the night they got engaged. "I don't normally surprise you, do I?"

"Well—"

"That's why I brought you this." He pulled a skinny velvet box from his breast pocket and slid it across the desk. "Surprise, beautiful. One year ago we had our first official date. Happy anniversary."

She stared at it, the realization sinking in. "Oh, shit, it *is* our anniversary. It totally slipped my mind." She was horrified at yet another lapse.

He winked. "I figured as much. No worries. You've been busy with work and planning the wedding, and I've had my head up my ass with that Okinawa deal. I'm amazed I actually remembered."

"I'll make it up to you, I promise." She visualized slapping herself hard across the face. *Stupid bitch. You don't deserve him.*

"Well, don't just sit there looking like a bigmouth bass. Open it." Morris pushed the box closer to her.

"What is it?"

"Goddamn it, woman, open it," he said, laughing. "Only one way to find out."

She took the velvet box in her hands and turned the silver latch. Her breath caught as she lifted the lid. Nestled inside on a bed of dark blue satin lay a diamond tennis bracelet, glittering like little stars under the fluorescent lights of her office.

It was magnificent.

"Oh, wow," she breathed.

He was studying her face. "Do you like it?"

"Do I like it?" Her eyes were fixed on the bracelet in dazed awe. "Of course I like it, you crazy man. It's gorgeous!"

"If it's too long, I can have the jeweler take out a couple of the diamonds, maybe make you a pair of earrings." He was clearly delighted at her reaction, and his grin stretched ear to ear. And *he* was the one who'd done the giving.

She held the bracelet up to the light and stared at it in wonder. Her eyes welled with tears. "Morris . . . you really shouldn't have. This is too much."

"It's worth it just to see the look on your face," he said triumphantly. His expression was so loving she almost broke down. "It's an early wedding present. You deserve it, honey. You deserve everything I can give you."

No, I don't. I really don't. She wanted to crawl under her desk and die. The desk where she'd let Ethan put his dirty hands all over her.

She stuck her arm out toward him, her smile garish and fake. "Put it on me?"

He obliged. It was a perfect fit, complementing her platinum engagement ring beautifully.

"Damn, there go my earrings," she managed to joke.

Morris raised an eyebrow. "Good thing I put something on hold at the jewelry store then. Christmas is only a few months away."

The shame of it was too much. Struggling to compose herself, Sheila came around the desk and sat in Morris's lap, wrapping her arms around his thick neck. "I love you," she whispered, kissing his lips, his forehead, his chin, feeling the dampness in his hair from the rain outside. "Thank you. It's beautiful. Just like you."

"I love you, too," Morris said, returning the kisses. He stroked her hair. "You have no idea how happy you make me."

Sheila pulled back a few inches so she could see his face clearly. It was now or never. "Morris, there's something I need—"

A movement caught her eye.

Her words died when she saw Ethan standing in her open doorway, watching them. She hadn't seen him in days, not since their breakup and subsequent showdown. His face was hard, his eyes narrowed into slits. When he realized he'd been noticed, his features immediately arranged themselves into a more neutral expression.

"Sorry to interrupt, Dr. Tao." Ethan's words were polite but his voice was edgy. He held up the book he was carrying. "Just returning this to you."

Morris handed Sheila a tissue and she hurriedly wiped her eyes, getting up out of her fiancé's lap. "That's fine, Ethan. Go ahead and leave it there." She indicated the short, crammed bookshelf beside her door.

Ethan placed the book atop the pile of papers, his eyes darting toward Morris. The grad student's jaw worked tightly and his movements were stiff. He seemed unnaturally tense, but then again, Ethan had never met Morris. Maybe he'd assumed Sheila had broken off the engagement after his threats the other week. Threats that continued to hang like a noose around her cheating neck.

The graduate student finally stuck his hand in Morris's direction.

"You must be the lucky man who gets to marry Dr. Tao," Ethan said, his warm tone contradicting the coldness in his eyes. "I recognize you from the photos on the wall. Congratulations on your upcoming wedding."

Morris stood, his presence immediately dwarfing Ethan's. Grasping the younger man's hand, he pumped hard, his typical hearty handshake.

"Thanks, thanks a lot. I'm sorry, I didn't catch your name?"

"Ethan Wolfe. I'm one of the professor's teaching assistants." His eyes flicked toward Sheila. "How long have we been together now? Three months?"

"You mean three terms." Sheila's voice was strangled.

"Of course!" Morris said, too loudly for the modest-size office. "She's mentioned you several times."

Sheila bit her tongue. Always the polite Texan. Ethan's name had never once come up in conversation with Morris, she was certain as hell of that.

"So tell me, Ethan." Morris was wearing his wiseass grin. "What's it like working for this one? She as tough on you guys as she is on me?"

"Oh, she's definitely demanding." Ethan winked at Sheila, who was watching the whole exchange in dazed shock. "Never afraid to tell me what she needs. But it's all good. I've learned how to butter her up."

Don't vomit. "You mean the homemade oatmeal raisin cookies?" Sheila's stomach was in knots. "The ones your girlfriend makes?"

Ethan laughed and relaxed against the doorframe. "Right. The *cookies.* It's my girlfriend's grandmother's recipe," he said, addressing Morris. "Been in her family a long time. Whenever I need a special favor, I bring in a plate of Abby's freshly baked cookies for Dr. Tao. Never fails to get me what I want."

It took all of Sheila's self-restraint not to backhand the cockiness out of Ethan's pretty face.

Morris looked at Sheila, feigning scrutiny, and elbowed her good-naturedly. "Is that right? Interesting how you've never brought any cookies home for me."

"She eats them all at work," Ethan said. "She says they taste better than the ones she eats at home."

Sheila thought she might faint.

Morris laughed heartily, clearly missing the double entendre. Sheila's back and shoulders began to ache. Her office had never felt so small.

"You hit the nail on the head with that one." Morris clapped Ethan on the shoulder. "She does have a sweet tooth. Though I haven't seen her eating anything too sweet lately, what with the wedding coming up and all. She wants to be a skinny-minny in her wedding dress. You know women."

"I sure do." Ethan's eyes gleamed. "Dr. Tao, since I caught you, I do have a favor to ask. Unfortunately I didn't bring any cookies." His tone grew serious, and Sheila felt another wave of nausea roll over her.

"What is it, Ethan?" She forced what she hoped would pass for a natural smile.

His gaze zeroed in on her new diamond bracelet. "I was hoping you would let me out of my proctoring duties for next week's finals. I'm getting behind on my thesis and want to schedule some interviews down at the soup kitchen. Try as I might, I can't be in two places at once."

He's not serious. In all the years Sheila had supervised teaching assistants, she couldn't recall a single one asking to be let out of exam duty. It was part of the job.

She searched frantically for the right words, struggling to keep her voice composed. "This is rather short notice. I'll have to ask someone from Dr. Easton's class to cover for you. Midterms are next Tuesday. And don't you have several requests for early writes?"

Ethan shrugged. "Yep, I actually have four scheduled. But you know, you *have* been working me really hard lately, so I kind of think you owe me a favor." He stuck his hands in his pockets, head cocked to one side.

Motherfucking asshole bastard.

Sheila risked a glance at Morris and saw that his expression was one of wary politeness. Morris was big, and Morris was loud, but Morris wasn't stupid. She knew he'd picked up on the subtle tension that had suddenly dropped into the air.

"I guess I have been," Sheila said. "I'll see what I can do."

"Thank you." Ethan looked at Morris. "She really is fabulous to work for. All the grad students in psych request Dr. Tao.

I'm very lucky to have her as my adviser. Anyway, I should get home, but it was terrific meeting you, Morris." Ethan stuck his hand out again.

Morris shook it, but this time he didn't pump with quite the same enthusiasm as he had moments earlier. "Likewise. Be careful getting home, son. It's raining pretty hard out."

Ethan bristled at the word *son*, but he turned and left the office as quietly as he'd come. Sheila headed back around her desk and slumped into her chair, exhausted. Wiping her palms on her skirt again, she worked at controlling her emotions, keeping her hands under the desk so Morris wouldn't see them trembling. She listened for Ethan's footsteps and was relieved when they finally receded.

"What was that about?" Morris said, closing the door firmly. "Why do I get the distinct impression you just got lassoed?"

Sheila waved a hand. "Don't worry about it. He's a bit of a spoiled brat."

"Oh, I got that." Morris leaned forward, scrutinizing her face. It took every ounce of strength Sheila had not to look away. "Listen, darlin', it ain't my place to tell you how to do your job. Lord knows I wouldn't want you telling me how to do mine. But I think a little well-meaning advice is called for here, and trust me when I say that you need to rein that boy in. He works for *you,* remember. It ain't his place to tell you what his schedule's gonna be next week. You'd be smart to call him tomorrow and tell him he'd better be where he's supposed to be or he ain't gonna do so well on his next performance review."

"You're absolutely right, babe." Sheila's face was tight. "It isn't your place." She attempted a smile to soften her words. "Don't worry, I can handle my students."

It was a lie, of course, but she delivered it with ease.

CHAPTER: 3

Nothing was showing up on CampusAnonymous.com, or anywhere else on the Internet.

Sheila had been googling herself obsessively for almost two weeks, and she was now positive Ethan was bluffing. There was no video. If Ethan were really determined to destroy her life, certainly he'd have done it by now.

Thank God she hadn't said a word to Morris. What if she'd told him for nothing?

As far as she was concerned, it was over.

She picked at the seasoned nuts in front of her as she worked her way through her second cranberry lime. Her barstool seat at the Seafood Grille had a nice view of the waterfront, but her attention was focused on the young bartender serving her. Dark skin, dark eyes, tight black T-shirt, gold-plated name tag that read LUKE. Just good-looking enough for her to feel flattered every time he smiled at her, which was often. Bartenders had to make a living, too.

Sheila enjoyed the attention anyway, feeling rather celebratory, and watched as Luke deftly poured another martini for the sixtysomething man sitting three seats away. The older gentleman—a silver fox, as her students might have described him—was wearing a wedding band, but that hadn't stopped him from trying to catch Sheila's eye. He was appealing in a James Brolin kind of way, with maybe twenty extra pounds and a ruddiness to the cheeks. Not that she was interested. Those days were behind her, once and for all.

The new engagement ring flashed fire on her left hand. Sheila stared at it in that pretentious way women do when they're looking at their diamonds or their manicures. She couldn't help herself; it was a work of art. Morris had discreetly left the certificate of appraisal in the car when they'd stopped for gas the other day, and she'd peeked—a four-carat solitaire on a platinum, pavé-set diamond band, worth lots of zeros. She thought back to the night of the proposal and his earnest face when he handed her the blue Tiffany box. She'd stared at the ring in shock, and Morris had laughed and said, "You know me. Go big or go home." That was Morris, always a Texan at heart.

"Is it real?" Silver Fox from three barstools down finally said, interrupting her thoughts. She looked over to see him grinning at her. He was chewing an olive, a toothpick dangling out the side of his mouth. "Or do you just wear it to keep the guys from hounding you?"

His voice was nasal and higher than Sheila expected. She didn't answer.

"He must think the world of you to get you a rock that size," the man said, trying again. "It's blinding me from here."

Sheila relented. "Thanks. We just got engaged."

"Congratulations. Buy you a drink to celebrate?" Silver Fox's body language told her he was ready to slide over at the slightest hint of interest. He downed the last of his martini and winked at her, his lips still working the toothpick.

Sheila glanced at his wedding ring. "Won't your wife mind?"

"Not if you don't tell her."

"My fiancé would."

"Not if you don't tell him." He grinned, the toothpick bobbing up and down between his unnaturally white teeth.

Sheila smiled sweetly. "Why don't you tell him yourself. He'll be here in a few minutes."

"Ah. I assumed you were in town on business." Silver Fox's tone was polite but his face had turned a shade ruddier. "Enjoy your evening." He eased up from his barstool and strolled away, leaving a twenty for the bartender.

"Ouch," Luke said, stuffing the bill into the pocket of his apron. "Guess he doesn't take rejection well."

"I thought I was pretty nice about it." Sheila's laugh was sheepish. "I feel sorry for his wife, wherever she may be. Tacky guy."

"You'd be amazed how many tacky people come into this place. And God bless 'em," Luke said with a grin. "I wouldn't be able to pay my rent otherwise."

He was polishing the inside of a wineglass with a clean white cloth, his biceps flexing as he turned the glass back and forth in a rhythmic motion. He was close enough for her to smell his musky cologne, and she suddenly imagined what Luke's lips would feel like on her nipples.

She mentally slapped herself. "You must see everything working here."

"You'd be surprised."

"Nothing surprises me anymore. What about you?"

Luke laughed, and something about it sounded forced, reminding her of Ethan. Her thoughts sobered instantly. He tapped her glass. "Another?"

He fixed her drink, then left to tend to a couple at the end of the bar who'd just arrived but already looked bored with each other. Not even Frank Sinatra over the loudspeakers could seem to cheer them up, and Sheila wondered how long they'd been married. As she watched Luke work, her thoughts turned to Ethan once again.

Three good years in Sex Addicts Anonymous and she'd slipped. With one of her *students,* no less. *Christ.* And not only that, she'd let it continue for three months. Father's death or no, she'd fucked up, plain and simple.

She would never have thought she could treat someone as badly as her first husband had treated her, but here she was, scrambling to cover up her infidelity so Morris would never find out. He deserved better. He was a kind and decent man— unlike Bill, who had been cruel and distant for most of their marriage. And it had taken her years to figure out why.

Bill Chancellor was a prominent heart surgeon, two decades her senior. The age difference had never bothered her, and she knew it had everything to do with her father.

They had met at a university benefit. Bill was handsome and charismatic, and it hadn't taken long for Sheila to fall in love with him. He made it easy, courting her with a single-mindedness that swept her off her feet. After only a few months of dating, they were married. Shortly after the wedding, he was appointed chief of surgery at Seattle Pacific, one of the best teaching hospitals in the Northwest. The early months of their marriage were blissful, a happy whirlwind of late mornings in bed, fund-raising dinners, and weekends spent at Bill's family's lake house.

But after their first anniversary, things began to sour. Bill worked all the time and was spending less and less time at home. Early-morning rounds of golf replaced their lazy weekends, and poker nights with the guys kept him out late. When he was home, he was distant, impatient, and often distracted.

Much the way her strict Chinese father used to be. And just as with her father, Sheila had to work diligently to get

Bill's attention. She cooked romantic dinners, planned week-end getaways, couple's nights out, day trips to quirky places she read about in travel magazines. Despite her best efforts, he continued to withdraw. And the less interest he showed in her, the harder she tried.

She knew the marriage was in trouble. She was working on her Ph.D. in social psychology by this time, and it wasn't hard to identify the basic problems. Still, she didn't have the courage to leave him. Not even when she began to suspect Bill was cheating on her.

Instead, she threw herself into her work. Made full professor. Her work gave her so much joy and fulfillment, she could almost convince herself it was enough.

Almost.

Her marriage came to an end one weekend in April, nearly a decade after her wedding day. She came home two days early from a psychology conference because her pesky cold had turned into bronchitis.

Bill's Jaguar was in the driveway when she pulled up to the house in her taxi, exhausted and dizzy from the long flight and too much cold medication. At 3:00 p.m. on a Wednesday, this was unheard of. She'd never known him to blow off a weekday afternoon. Beside the Jag sat a cute little Toyota hybrid, a car she'd never seen before. It was then she knew.

She paid the driver and stood at her front door, light-headed and sweaty, wondering if she was ready for this. Leaving her suitcase on the front steps in case she had to spend the night at a hotel, she let herself into her house. She tiptoed up the staircase, taking care to avoid the steps she knew would creak.

The door to their bedroom was closed. She paused, ear cocked. Somewhere behind the door, Bill groaned in ecstasy.

It was a sound she hadn't personally heard in over four years, and it stabbed her.

Finally, she was going to come face-to-face with her husband and his mistress, a woman who'd been stealing his heart away, piece by piece, for God only knew how long.

She opened the door in a trance. If she thought she was prepared, she was wrong.

That Bill was doing it doggy-style with his favorite surgical scrub nurse was not surprising.

That the scrub nurse was a forty-two-year-old man named Norm floored her.

In all the years they'd been married—despite all of Sheila's work in social behavior and perception—it had never once occurred to her that her domineering, bullying, brilliant heart-surgeon husband was gay.

A full minute passed before either man noticed she was there. Then all hell broke loose.

Yelping in surprise, the two men jumped off the bed, penises still hard but wilting fast. They knocked into each other in their search for pants, shirts, anything to throw over their naked bodies, cursing and red-faced, watching her with furtive eyes, wanting to slam the bedroom door in her face. Neither did.

She watched them for a few more seconds before she turned and walked slowly back down the stairs. She was seated on the sofa as Norm the surgical scrub nurse flew by, missing the last step and almost wiping out on the hardwood floors. He was out the front door and into his little car with scarcely a backward glance. Through the window she watched as he pulled away, flattening the recycling bin from next door, which their ornery old neighbor Mr. Zeminski never brought in on time.

Bill didn't come downstairs for another ten minutes. When he did, shirt buttoned haphazardly, hair in messy tufts, he was shaking, his face a mask of shame and self-loathing. She had never seen him look anything but confident, and it was almost as unsettling to her as the gay sex act she'd just caught him in.

The silence between them was like dead space. She waited for him to speak, having no clue how to begin this conversation.

"Promise you won't tell," he finally said, his voice choked.

She watched as her man-of-steel husband burst into tears. He dropped onto their sofa, sobbing like a child in the pale afternoon light.

"Oh, Bill." At that moment, her genuine pity for him outweighed his betrayal. It didn't make up for the years of emotional neglect and abandonment she'd suffered for most of their marriage, but she couldn't deny there was relief.

The story tumbled out. He had known since before they met. He'd had a long string of affairs before their marriage, most anonymous and taking place in the basements of gay clubs that Sheila had never heard of. When rumors began to swirl, he'd married Sheila quickly to secure his appointment as Seattle Pacific's chief of surgery. The longer they stayed married, though, the more he'd come to resent her. She reminded him every day of the man he only pretended to be.

He was at the height of his career and didn't want to be labeled a gay man. Sure, Seattle was a progressive city, but the hospital still ran on a good old boys' network and nobody wanted a homosexual as their chief. He'd found love with Norm, and Norm wanted them to come out, but Bill would rather have died.

The divorce was quick. The settlement was exceptionally generous once Sheila agreed to sign the confidentiality agreement. She bought a brownstone townhouse in cash in the prestigious Harvard-Belmont area of Seattle. Shortly after, she was granted tenure at the university. It was time to make a fresh start, but surprisingly, there were no feelings of liberation. Just a broken heart. She had loved a man who had never truly loved her back.

At thirty-five, she was divorced, childless, too tired to start over with someone new, but much too young *not* to. It was a shitty, weird, in-between place to be.

Luke the bartender interrupted her thoughts. "Your man's late, huh?"

Sheila smiled. "If it's his worst habit, I'm a lucky woman."

"I'm pretty sure he's the lucky one," Luke said with a grin.

Three years ago his smile would have been a proposition. She would have invited him home in a heartbeat.

It had started off with a couple of glasses of wine late at night to help her sleep and, when that stopped working, late-night Internet games to replace the social life she'd once had. Bill had not been much of a husband, but being married did have its perks—there were dinner parties to go to, work functions, couple's nights out. As a divorcée, the invites dried up. She realized that most of her friends were actually Bill's friends, and they'd chosen sides.

The loneliness ate her up.

On a lark, she joined a dating website, and within a few months she had profiles posted on half a dozen sites. The thrill of meeting new men was exhilarating. Finally, she was getting the attention she'd craved her entire life. She felt beautiful. Wanted. Sex made her feel powerful and in control, something she'd never felt before around men. Every man she met presented an opportunity to erase the insecurity and unworthiness she'd felt during her marriage. Before long, she was sleeping with just about everyone she met.

It didn't occur to Sheila then that she had a problem. Sure, she met a lot of guys. Sure, she ended up in bed with most of them (or in the backseats of their cars, or in the bathrooms of the bars, or in the bushes behind the nightclubs). So the hell what? How was it any different from the women on *Sex and the City*, who drank Cosmopolitans every night and screwed every cute guy they saw? She was a liberated woman, completely in charge of her sexuality. Wasn't she?

Wasn't she?

Never mind that she sometimes mixed Ecstasy with her wine and that sometimes it led to blackouts. Never mind that sometimes she'd wake up in a strange room, unable to remember where she was or why she was there.

She couldn't help herself. She couldn't seem to stop it. She couldn't temper her need for the warmth of another man's body on top of her, beside her, inside her. The excitement of meeting someone new, the rush she felt when she saw the desire in his eyes, the adrenaline pumping through her veins as they had sex—it all seemed to be a perfectly satisfactory replacement for love. Even if he didn't remember her name.

Even if it didn't last.

She finally hit rock bottom when she woke up in her car early one Sunday morning, scared and alone, wearing nothing but her skirt, shoes, and someone else's leather jacket. Her forehead was cut and she ached all over. She reeked of sweat and men's cologne and was so bruised she could barely drive herself home.

It was one hell of a wake-up call.

That night, after a hot bath and a long sleep, Sheila went online and found a Sex Addicts Anonymous group in Renton, a city south of Seattle where she hoped she wouldn't run into anyone from the university. Luckily, she never did. She started meeting with an old colleague, Marianne Chang, for therapy shortly after. Though she didn't join AA, Sheila gave up drinking along with sex.

A year later she was twelve months sober, nobody the wiser, and thriving. And that's when she met a tall, strapping investment banker named Morris Gardener.

They'd ordered the same drink at Starbucks, Grande caramel lattes. Though he'd paid for his first, he let her take his coffee, and a witty banter ensued. He gave her his card. She discussed phoning him with Marianne, and the therapist gave her approval. Dating was fine, so long as they built a solid foundation of friendship first. And definitely no sex, not until the relationship was serious.

It wasn't long before she recognized that he was an alcoholic, but it didn't turn her off. If anything, she made it her mission to help him get clean. She got him into AA, helped him through the same twelve steps she'd been through in SAA, and was there for him the many times he was tempted to slip. It was rewarding to be part of the reason he pulled his life back together, and they became genuinely good friends. Close to a year after they met, they started dating.

The early days of their courtship were a fairy tale. Morris was kind, sweet, generous, funny. Sheila's life was finally on an upswing, and it stayed that way for the better part of a year.

Until she found out her father was dying of cancer.

The news was devastating. Though they hadn't talked in years, Sheila had gone to her father's bedside, only to have her heart broken when he demanded she leave.

When he died, Ethan Wolfe provided the perfect distraction. One indiscretion with him led to another, then another. It was almost chilling how quickly she fell back into her old ways. But this time there was guilt, lots and lots of guilt, because Morris was a good man who deserved better.

That Ethan had pursued Sheila relentlessly for months didn't matter—she'd known it was wrong from the beginning.

But the problem with addicts is *not* that they don't know the difference between right and wrong. The problem with addicts is that they do it anyway.

A familiar voice interrupted her reverie and she looked up into the handsome face of the man she was going to marry.

"This seat taken?"

The devilish glint in Morris Gardener's blue eyes matched his grin. He gazed at her, taking in the details of her face. She loved the way he looked at her, as if she were the only woman in the room. She slipped off the barstool and kissed him, snuggling into the warmth of his thick arms.

Sheila's knight in shining armor might be six foot four and 240 pounds with bad knees, but he was all hers.

And to think she'd almost thrown it all away.

She would never tell him she was a sex addict. The shame was too great. That part of her life would stay secret even if it meant handing Ethan Wolfe his master's degree on a silver platter to keep him quiet about the affair. She'd be damned if she was going to lose her job, her reputation, and her fiancé because of a stupid mistake with a self-centered, arrogant grad student.

Morris's large hand rested protectively on her lower back as they made their way through the restaurant. She caught a glimpse of the two of them in the decorative wall mirrors as the maître d' led them to their table. They made a fine couple, she sleek in her black dress and heels, he in his custom suit and Armani tie. This should have been the happiest time of her life.

She'd never been so miserable.

than entered the offices of Bindle Brothers at Fifth Avenue and Virginia, brand-new briefcase in hand, shoes polished to a spit-shine. Dressed in a navy pin-striped suit and paisley tie, he looked every inch the young, confident businessman he was pretending to be.

The dark blond wig he wore itched, as did the fake blond goatee, but he didn't think the interview would take long. Colored contact lenses had changed his eyes from their natural light gray to hazel. A small amount of latex, carefully applied around his nose in thin layers and blended into his real skin with professional movie makeup, added width to his nostrils and bridge, transforming his face in a more dramatic way than anyone would ever expect. Slight changes to the nose could have a major impact on the look of the face—ask any one of the millions of people who'd had rhinoplasty.

Expertly applied bronzing powder completed the look— not too much, just enough to give him the illusion of a tan without looking powdery. He'd scrutinized himself under harsh lighting before he left home and knew he looked perfectly natural. This was one of his lighter disguises; anything heavier was unnecessary. He'd only met Morris for a few moments, and enough time had passed that he doubted the big man would remember.

But it was better to be safe than sorry. Ethan pulled out a pair of nonprescription eyeglasses from his breast pocket and casually slipped them on. The trendy black, rectangular frames were just thick enough to create shadows across his eyes, obscuring their shape a little.

He caught a glimpse of himself in the lobby mirror. Perfect. Disguises were so much fun.

He strode through the impressive lobby of the investment bank, all high ceilings and cornice moldings and marble. Well-dressed employees rushed around looking important, their BlackBerrys glued to their hands, creating an aura of tempered frenzy.

The round mahogany desk in the center of it all had two receptionists. The one with the frizzy hair and fifteen extra pounds smiled at him first. At his approach she sat up straighter, quickly taking her glasses off and primping her permed hair.

"Good morning." Another big smile showcased a poppy seed stuck dead between her uneven front teeth. "Can I help you?"

Ethan smiled down at her, taking a long look at her freckled cleavage before meeting her eyes. "Good morning, Stacey," he said, reading the name off the tag pinned to her shiny blouse. "I have an appointment on the tenth floor. I'm Tom Young."

Stacey's pale cheeks flushed. "I'll call up and let them know you're here," she said, slightly breathless. "Just a moment."

He thanked her and stepped away while she murmured into the phone. He was dying to scratch his head but couldn't risk shifting the wig. Instead he grinned at Stacey, who blushed and pointed the way to the elevators.

The bank hummed with activity. Ethan weaved his way to the back of the lobby and to the elevator doors. An attractive woman followed him in, giving him an appreciative once-over before taking her place in front of him. He took a moment to enjoy the view from behind. Bare legs, no panty lines. Either she was going commando or she was wearing a thong. He chuckled. Both scenarios were acceptable. She exited on the eighth floor, her ass cheeks flexing like two well-oiled pistons underneath her tight business-length skirt.

On the tenth floor, he exited the elevator and another woman at another mahogany desk greeted him.

"Mr. Young?" she said, her voice crisp. Her gray hair was fashionably cut and her suit looked more expensive than his. "Please have a seat. He'll be with you in a moment. He's just finishing up a call."

Ethan walked over to the waiting area but did not sit. The tenth floor was not the highest in the building, but the view of Puget Sound was still incredible, thanks to the floor-to-ceiling windows lining one wall.

The beautiful blue-green ripples of the Sound glistened brightly under the morning sunshine. He wondered absently if Diana St. Clair had ever swum in those waters. He'd never asked her. If he closed his eyes, he could still picture her beautiful body, toned and tight from years of training. . . .

A hearty laugh made him turn. Striding down the hallway was a big man, well over six feet tall with a belly that stretched firmly over his belt. He was flanked on both sides by women who had to jog to keep up with him. A cerulean silk tie complemented a custom charcoal suit, and Ferragamo shoes encased what had to be size fourteen feet. His graying temples did nothing to detract from his handsome features and a charming smile. In fact, the man looked much better than Ethan remembered.

Morris Gardener. In the flesh.

The women tittered with laughter. Ethan didn't catch what was said, but clearly Morris was a funny guy because both ladies smacked his thick arm and cackled in amusement before walking away.

"Tom Young?" An outstretched hand came toward Ethan, sausage fingers swallowing his palm in a vise grip. "Morris Gardener. Glad you could make it on such short notice. Come on in. Beautiful day, isn't it? Bet you'd rather be out there than in here. God knows these days are few and far between in the Northwest. Perfect day to throw the pigskin around. You like football, Tom? Used to play back in the day until my knees gave out. Two years with the Packers, Longhorns before that. Right this way. My office is just down the hall. You want coffee, water, muffin, anything? Theresa! We need sustenance, please!" The big man's voice boomed loudly in the hallway and another woman appeared out of nowhere, smiling cheerfully at them as she passed.

He called, they came. He joked, they laughed. There was no doubting who the big swinging dick was around here. Morris Gardener's presence seemed to shrink everything around him, including Ethan, who suddenly felt very insignificant.

He forced himself to stand straighter. This was no time to buckle. He was here to scope out the competition and figure out what, exactly, Morris had that he didn't.

If he couldn't have her, then neither could Morris. He'd rather see Sheila dead.

All he needed was an excuse.

: : : :

There was a small stain on Morris's tie, likely a remnant of whatever he'd eaten for breakfast. It pleased Ethan.

The big man was on the phone again. Ethan took the time to look around the large office, noting the abundance of natural light and the thick carpet that matched the creamy walls and ceiling. Against one wall, two football jerseys were framed and hung. Both were number 75—one in rusty orange for the Texas Longhorns, and one in forest green for the Green Bay Packers. On Morris's huge mahogany desk sat a football encased in Lucite. The furnishings were surprisingly modern, all clean lines, steel, and dark wood, a contrast to the more traditional décor in the public areas of the bank.

Ethan wondered if Morris had decorated the office himself. The man certainly had great taste in clothes. And he was wearing monogrammed cuff links, for fuck's sake. A man would only wear monogrammed cuff links if that same man had monogrammed French-cuffed shirts to go with them. Which Morris did. Ethan's own suit, bought off-the-rack the day before at Macy's, seemed cheap and bland in comparison.

He fingered Morris's business card, noting both the thickness and whiteness of the paper. The lettering was raised and glossy, expensive: MORRIS GARDENER, SENIOR PARTNER, BINDLE BROTHERS. How much did a senior partner at an investment firm make? There was no way to ask without sounding like a total asshole.

A framed photo of Sheila was resting on Morris's desk, turned slightly outward so that visitors could see her pretty face. She was smiling, her dark Asian eyes alight with amusement, full red lips parted to reveal straight white teeth.

She was laughing at him.

Phone still glued to his ear, Morris turned his back for a moment as he reached for something on the bookshelf behind him. In one smooth motion, Ethan turned the photo toward Morris so he could no longer see Sheila's face. *Better.*

Morris finally put the phone down and jotted a quick note on his yellow memo pad. "My apologies, Tom. I'm working on a deal with Japanese investors over the phone—not the easiest thing to do even with all our technology."

"Not a problem, Mr. Gardener." Ethan slipped the business card into the breast pocket of his suit jacket. "I'm just glad you could fit me in."

"Call me Morris." Bits of boisterous conversation drifted into the office from the hallway. "Whoa, I'd better close the door. My team is a chatty bunch and it can be distracting."

Ethan's heart rate quickened. "Uh, would you mind terribly if we left it open? I have a tendency to get a bit claustrophobic."

Morris raised an eyebrow. "Is that right?"

"Only during interviews." Ethan's grin was sheepish and he hoped it hid his burgeoning panic.

Morris relaxed in his seat. "No problem, we'll leave it open."

"Thank you, sir."

"Call me Morris," he said again, waving a hand dismissively and turning to face his computer. Large fingers clicked on the mouse. He scrolled until he found what he was looking for. "There's the e-mail. You know, Tom, I'm glad to meet you because Randall says you'd be a tremendous asset to our organization. He says the two of you know each other from Stanford and you moved here to get married. What did you study?"

"I majored in economics at Stanford, then went to Wharton for my MBA. Specialized in strategic investments for global industries, particularly those based in the Middle East." The story rolled smoothly off Ethan's tongue. He'd practiced reciting it for days. "Met my fiancée here when I did an internship at Microsoft in their business development division. Decided Seattle might be a nice place to raise a family."

"Where you from originally?"

"I grew up in Texas. Austin." Same place as Morris.

"You're kidding. What area?"

"Tarrytown."

"Clarksville!" The hearty laugh again. It hurt Ethan's ears. "Small world. How long were you there?"

"I graduated from Steve Austin High in '99. Left for Stanford after that."

"I graduated in '78. Go Hawks!" Morris seemed pleased. "Christ, we're practically family. Does Randall know that you and his old man are from the same hometown?"

"He didn't mention it? I thought for sure that's why you agreed to meet me."

"Well now, he might have, maybe it slipped my mind." Morris's grin didn't waver, but his eyes changed ever so slightly.

Interesting. Morris Gardener wasn't a half-bad liar. Ethan tucked this tidbit away for future reference. He knew for a fact that Morris hadn't talked to his oldest son, Randall, in years. Sheila had confided this little piece of gossip to Ethan months ago in bed, after a particularly sweaty romp involving her silk scarf and a jar of chocolate body paint.

It had been the easiest thing in the world to make up an e-mail address for Randall and contact Morris, asking dear old Dad if he could make time to meet with his good buddy Tom from college, who was in town and job hunting.

Ethan said, "Randy told me you've been here at Bindle for over ten years, used to work at LoneStar Capital." He'd actually read this off the man's bio that was posted on the firm's website.

"That's right, Tom. Transferred over in '99 and never looked back."

"So you're clearly happy with your career here. How would you describe the corporate culture?"

"I thought I was supposed to be the one asking the questions."

A well-timed self-conscious laugh. "Right. Sorry."

Morris grinned. "Don't be. Determining whether this job is the right fit for you goes both ways. Let's see . . . corporate culture . . ." A rambling five-minute explanation followed, then, "Now, let me tell you more about the job."

For the next twenty minutes, Ethan sat politely while Morris droned on about the responsibilities of being a junior account manager, interjecting with questions when appropriate. If he'd really been Tom Young, the job might have sounded okay. Morris was probably a decent boss. Ethan kept his face composed, nodding in the right places and forcing himself to take in as many details as he could—one never knew what might be useful later.

It was clear Morris was a smart man. This didn't surprise Ethan. Sheila wouldn't waste her time on someone who didn't match her own intelligence. But everything about her fiancé was *large*. Big body, big voice, big hands, big feet. He made Ethan feel . . . small.

Ethan hated him.

"Based on your qualifications, Tom, I think you'd be a great fit for this division."

"I'm glad you think so, Morris."

The big man cleared his throat. "Now, I gotta confess that we've done things a bit backwards here. Obviously I wanted to meet you since my—Randall—spoke so highly of you, but you'll need to submit a résumé with Human Resources and be interviewed by our hiring committee before an official offer can be made. Though with your background, I don't foresee any problems."

"I understand. I'll send them the information today."

Morris stood up. Ethan followed suit.

"Great meeting you, Tom. I'll be putting in a strong recommendation."

"Thank you. I really appreciate that, Morris."

The older man hesitated. "Listen, any chance you'll be talking to Randall over the next day or two?"

"Probably. He'll be curious to know how our meeting went."

"Uh . . ." Morris's face flushed. A bead of sweat appeared at his graying hairline. "Maybe you could tell him to give his old man a call. I'm getting married in a few weeks and he, uh . . . never officially confirmed whether he's bringing his girlfriend . . . uh . . ."

"Donna."

"Right, Donna." Morris paused, then threw a hand up in the air. "Ah hell. You've been friends with Randy for what, eight, ten years? You must know we've hardly spoken. Not since his mother and I divorced. I'm a recovering alcoholic. Wasn't exactly the best husband and father back then."

Ethan gave a sympathetic nod. "He told me. We've talked about it quite a bit, actually. But I think—" He stopped. "You know what? It's not my place to say."

"Please, speak freely."

Ethan counted to five, hoping for just the right amount of hesitation to seem uncomfortable but also concerned. "Well, he's been doing some thinking. He and Donna have been going through some difficulties of their own, and I think it's given him some perspective on you and his mom divorcing."

"Really?" Morris's round face was so filled with hope that Ethan almost felt a pang of pity. Almost. "He told you that?"

"Pretty much. And he also said that you and he—"

A loud beep shrilled from the phone. Pained, Morris held up a chunky finger and pressed the speaker button.

"Yes, Darcy," he barked.

Her crisp, no-nonsense voice chirped, "Mr. Evers and Mr. Chan are here. Waiting for you in the boardroom."

"Be right there." Morris pressed the button again. "I'm sorry, Tom, what were you saying?"

The timing was perfect. "You know, Morris, it would be better if you talked to Randy directly. I'll let him know our meeting went well and pass along the message that you'd like him to get in touch. I really appreciate your time."

Ethan shook Morris's hand firmly and headed toward the doorway. He was just outside the glass door when Morris stopped him. A few employees were milling around in the hallway, chatting, and they looked over curiously.

"Hey, Tom, wait a minute there." Morris leaned in close, well beyond the boundaries of personal space. Immediately Ethan felt trapped. The big man's voice was low, out of earshot of the other employees. "I know you're a good friend of Randall's. I'm ashamed to say I think I need some help here. I understand if you're not comfortable, but he's my son . . ."

"What can I do?"

"If you're free for dinner tonight, maybe you'd let me buy you a steak and pick your brain about the best way to approach him. The last few times I've tried, he's shot me down."

It wasn't hard for Ethan to feign discomfort with Morris standing so close to him. "I don't know, sir. I'm not sure how Randy would feel about that."

"No, no." Morris looked around and moved in even closer. Ethan fought the urge to step away. "I'm not asking you to give away any of his confidences. You're his buddy, that wouldn't be right. But I could use some help figuring out what to say. And how to say it. I need to find common ground. He's my son. He's never even met Sheila, my fiancée."

Ethan pretended to think it over. "Sure. Okay. I'd be glad to help."

Morris rewarded him with a huge grin and clapped him on the shoulder. He finally took a step back and Ethan stifled a sigh of relief.

"Wonderful. That's wonderful. There's a great steakhouse on Olive Way, just two blocks from here. Why don't we meet there at six? And we can also talk strategy about how to get you into this place. You would love working here, Tom, you really would."

Tom might, but Ethan definitely wouldn't.

: : : :

Pleasantly stuffed after an expensive dinner of porterhouse and sourdough bread (no wine for the recovering alcoholic Morris), Ethan sat alone in front of the TV at home, mindlessly watching a rerun of *Friends*. Abby was at work, the midnight shift at Safeway. It was a crummy job, but it paid more than being a teaching assistant.

He rolled the platinum cuff link between his fingers, looking at it in the soft glow of the TV light. The initials MG were engraved into the square face in italics. Had this been a present from Sheila? Ethan had pretended to stumble on the sidewalk after dinner, and he'd slipped it off Morris after reflexively grabbing the man's arm. No special reason for taking it, other than the pleasing thought of Morris looking for it later and realizing he'd lost it.

The dinner with Sheila's fiancé had been enlightening, though Ethan's blond wig had itched the entire time. He'd had to excuse himself several times to go to the restroom to scratch his head. Damn cheap wig.

It was clear Morris had liked "Tom." They'd spent the first half of dinner discussing the elusive Randall, and Ethan had pretended to know exactly why the younger Gardener still held a grudge against his old man after all this time. As a psych major, it wasn't rocket science to guess what most of Randall's issues might be. Neglect, guilt, blame, feelings of helplessness watching his father on a downward spiral, anger at the family being torn apart. Blah blah blah, all very text-book and mundane. No doubt Morris had discussed it all with Sheila already.

As the evening progressed, Ethan had been able to steer the conversation toward Morris's impending marriage, and therein lay the real reason Ethan had agreed to dinner. He wanted to know who Sheila was through Morris's eyes. Thanks to the ca-maraderie that the charming and sensitive Tom had been able to build with Sheila's fiancé, the older man hadn't hesitated to drop a bomb.

Morris had been dating Sheila for an entire year and *they had never once had sex.*

It had taken all of Ethan's willpower to contain himself, though he continued to listen with polite interest. Sheila had never slept with the man she was engaged to marry, but she'd been fucking Ethan regularly for the past three months. That meant something, right? It made him superior somehow, right?

A porterhouse had never tasted so good.

"Are you sure you should be telling me all this, Morris?" Ethan had said to the older man, then chewing his steak and feeling like the cat who'd swallowed the canary. "It's been my experience that women don't like it when you talk about your sex life. Or in this case, lack thereof."

Morris chuckled. "You're probably right, Tom, but it's no secret. She was pretty up-front with me when we first met. She wanted to wait till marriage. I actually really liked that about her. It made me want to get to know her."

"So she's old-fashioned."

Morris speared a sautéed mushroom. "That's the thing. She's not. She's a very modern woman in most ways. But we had an instant connection. We met in a Starbucks, you know. She's the one who convinced me to go to AA."

Ethan put down his fork. "Really." His stomach churned. He hadn't known they'd met in a Starbucks. What else had Sheila kept from him?

"Yeah." Morris squeezed more lemon into his sparkling water and looked ruefully at Ethan's beer. "It took me a year to get up the guts to ask her out on a real date. Look at me. I'm a buffoon. Everything about me's oversized. Sheila's beautiful. Everybody who's met her thinks so. What would she want with me?"

Ethan almost agreed with him but remembered he wasn't supposed to know Sheila. "I thought they discouraged dating in AA," he said instead.

"They do. That's why I waited a year. And it was clearly worth it, because I'm sober and getting married." Morris grinned.

Ethan thought about that now. Married? Not if he could help it.

The episode of *Friends* he was watching ended and a rerun

of *Seinfeld* came on. He switched off the TV and sat in the quiet room.

Fuck if he was going to sit back and let them live happily ever after.

Morris's cuff link was warm in his palm and Ethan held it up to the light once again, wondering.

If they autopsied this out of Sheila's stomach, would they arrest Morris for the murder?

CHAPTER : 5

Calvin Klein shirt, Gucci tie, and Armani suit, tailored to perfection. But going by Morris's crestfallen expression in the full-length mirror at Romano's Formal Wear, it still wasn't perfect enough.

"I look like a jumbo-sized jelly bean."

"Shush." Sheila smoothed the lapels of Morris's jacket and smiled up at him. Her neck muscles were strong. He was thirteen inches taller and she'd had lots of practice looking up at him over the past two years. "It looks great."

Morris stared at his reflection, the space between his thick eyebrows creasing. He clearly didn't agree.

Sheila sighed. "You look so handsome. I wish you could see yourself as I see you."

The small Italian tailor who was fitting Morris's jacket watched them intently, thin lips pursed. "You don't like it?" Pietro's eyes were microscopic behind his thick glasses. "Tell me what you don't like and I fix."

"We like it." Sheila gave her fiancé a look, but Morris said nothing. She smiled warmly at the anxious tailor. "Would you mind giving us a minute?"

Pietro disappeared into the next room.

Sheila faced the mirror beside Morris, linking her arm

through his. "Come on, babe. What's the problem? It fits you perfectly."

"I look nine months pregnant."

"You've lost forty pounds! Why can't you be proud of that?" Sheila couldn't keep the dismay out of her voice. "You've been working so hard."

"Yeah, well, I need to lose forty more." Morris unbuttoned the suit jacket, exposing the crisp white tuxedo shirt underneath. "Be honest. Would I look thinner with a vest or a cummerbund?"

He was joking, but it wasn't funny. Sheila touched his hand and his fingers closed reflexively around her palm. Big, capable man though he was, he still struggled with his body image. He might be a bulldog walking into a boardroom filled with millionaire investors, but inside, he was a giant marshmallow.

She loved him for this paradox. It made him real. Human.

Cupping her chin, he tilted her face upward and kissed her.

"Hey, ever done it in a change room?" he stage-whispered.

A zingy reply was on the tip of her tongue, but a discreet cough interrupted her thoughts. They pulled apart to see Pietro standing in the corner of the change area looking completely uncomfortable. Morris's face flushed a deep red, and Sheila put a hand over her mouth to stifle a laugh.

"Excuse me, I don't mean to bother you beautiful couple, but my shift end in five minute. You want I fix something or is everything okay?" The tailor fidgeted, tape measure in hand, ready to act quickly at the slightest indication of dissatisfaction.

Sheila glanced at Morris. He was still flushed. "The tuxedo is wonderful, Pietro. Perfect the way it is."

The little man beamed. "Excellent. That make me very

happy. You need handkerchief? Cuff links? You want I fit you for cummerbund?"

Morris frowned slightly, touching the French cuffs of the shirt he was wearing. "I don't think so, my friend. I'm kind of partial to the James Bond look, no cummerbund, no vest. But I'll come back if I change my mind."

Pietro's smile grew wider. "Okay. I give final price to cashier. Thank you for your business, and, please, you tell everyone who needs good suit that your friend Pietro is the best."

Sheila thanked him. Morris was still fingering the empty holes at the end of his sleeves where his cuff links should go.

"You didn't bring any with you?" Sheila pointed to the naked French cuffs. "You must have a dozen."

"Yeah, but there's only one pair I would've worn for the wedding." Morris's face was glum. "I lost one of the cuff links Randall gave me. I looked everywhere—I don't know what the hell happened. I know I had them on last week. I would've worn them for the Okinawa conference call this morning, but I could only find one."

Morris always wore his monogrammed platinum cuff links when he was working on a particularly difficult business transaction. They'd been a Christmas gift from all three of his sons, back when he was still drinking and married to their mother. The cuff links were special. Shortly after that Christmas, Lenore had filed for divorce and his oldest son, Randall, had stopped speaking to him.

That had been over five years ago.

"I'm sure it's somewhere at your house." Sheila squeezed his arm. "It probably rolled under the bed or behind the bureau or something. I'll help you look tonight."

She shooed him back into the changing room to undress.

When he pulled the curtain closed, she dug into her purse and fished out her BlackBerry.

No new e-mails. Damn. Nothing from Randall.

She'd been trying to get hold of Morris's estranged son for weeks. But he hadn't lived in the United States for years and wasn't an easy man to track down. Randall Gardener's work with Amnesty International had taken him to seven different countries in the past decade, and while Amnesty kept solid records of where their people were at all times, they were stingy about giving out that information. Sheila had been forced to get creative, sneaking into Morris's address book to contact his other two sons—Stephen, a high school football coach in Orlando, and Phillip, a grad student in San Francisco—to see if maybe they could help. Neither brother had heard from Randall in months.

Frustrated, Sheila stuck her phone back in her purse. While she was fine spending her Sunday helping Morris search for his missing cuff link, the best wedding present she could give him was Randall. The wedding was four weeks away and she was running out of time—and ideas. The thought of speaking to Lenore, Randall's mother and Morris's ex-wife, wasn't too appealing.

She left Morris in the changing area and headed toward the cashier's counter at the front of the store. Angling her way past the racks of men's suits and tuxedos, she took her place in line behind a young couple complaining loudly to the frazzled clerk.

Trying to tune them out, Sheila mentally strategized her next move. Dammit, she had no choice but to call Lenore in Texas. She shuddered; that was bound to be an awkward conversation. Morris and his ex hadn't parted amicably, and Sheila wasn't even sure if the woman was aware her ex-husband was getting remarried.

Her thoughts were disrupted by a movement at the store window. Through the fancily dressed mannequin displays, Sheila caught a glimpse of a face, blurry through the rain-streaked glass. The little hairs at the back of her neck suddenly pricked.

Someone was watching her.

She strode to the double glass doors where there was a clear view of the street. The man was already walking away. The rain made it difficult to see clearly, but something about him was familiar. Her breath caught in her throat.

She watched through the watery glass as the man sauntered down the wet sidewalk toward his green and chrome motor-cycle, hands stuck casually in the pockets of his worn jeans. Zipping up his leather jacket, he threw a leg over the bike and slid a shiny black helmet over his short, mussed hair.

That walk. Those jeans. The scuffed leather jacket bought used from a secondhand shop on Howell Street. Somewhere on the sleeve of that jacket was a streak of red permanent marker where she'd accidentally bumped his arm while grad-ing papers.

She'd know him anywhere.

Her BlackBerry pinged at that moment, but she kept her eyes focused on Ethan as he sped away. When he was com-pletely out of sight, she pulled out her phone and saw she had one new text message.

He must have sent it while he was at the window. There were no words, only an attachment. She clicked on it, waiting the three seconds it took for it to download, her heart beating so hard she could feel her pulse throbbing in her temple.

The photo was small and grainy, but it was irrefutable. Her

back was to the camera, as was her naked ass, but there was no doubt it was Sheila on all fours, looking back with a smile as Ethan took her from behind.

A still shot from their sex video. The one she'd been so sure he didn't have.

Her life, as she knew it, was over.

CHAPTER : 6

St. Mary's Helping Hands looked and smelled like a shithole because it was a shithole. Overcooked vegetables, salty gravy, and the body odor of eighty or so homeless human beings combined to form a vomit-inducing aroma not unlike that of a garbage dump.

Then there were the sounds. The constant thrum of voices, metal forks clanging against metal plates, the scraping of cheap chairs on scarred pine floors, the occasional outbursts of laughter or shouting.

It was an assault on the senses.

Volunteering here had been Abby's idea. In theory it was brilliant. What better place to study the psychological consequences of poverty than at Seattle's premier soup kitchen?

St. Mary's was a cesspool of living, breathing human beings representing almost every behavioral, mental, and societal issue Ethan had read about in books. These were the forgotten folks, the dregs of society, the people you didn't notice and made a point not to see while you stood in line wearing your $300 boots waiting to order your $5 latte. These were the people you believed you'd never become, despite the fact that at some point in the past, they'd all had normal lives.

Someone whose name Ethan couldn't remember now had

once described it as Before and After. Before was when they were normal, when they had jobs and homes and loved ones, before the financial devastation, drug abuse, or mental illness had overpowered them and taken everything away. This was the After. And there was nothing after the After, just this, every day, until the end.

It made for a great thesis.

He slopped another portion of green beans onto someone's plate, managing to avoid eye contact even though the person murmured a polite thank-you. On another night he might have engaged this person in small talk, and if that had been interesting, the small talk might have led to a deeper conversation. But not tonight. Tonight Ethan was in a foul mood, because Dr. Sheila Tao had dumped him. For Morris. An oversize gorilla who'd somehow managed to make him feel tiny and inconsequential.

He wanted to kill them both.

Her lovely face appeared again in his mind, all dark eyes and red velvet lips. Delicate Asian bone structure. The curve of her slender white neck and the sweet spot above her collarbone he liked to kiss. He'd chased her for the better part of a year . . . only to have it end as if it never even started. Did she really think he would let it go that easily?

It was never supposed to be anything more than a convenient affair. Screwing the professor had yielded some nice perks. Flexible deadlines, a reduced workload, more one-on-one help with his thesis. Plus she could hoover him senseless.

It had never once occurred to him that it would end this way, on *her* terms. That she'd try to get rid of him, as if she were taking out the trash. She'd caught him off guard, and it was his fault for being surprised. He was normally never surprised.

He normally couldn't *feel* surprise.

He might have been able to accept the sexual relationship ending, but trying to pawn him off onto another professor? Unacceptable. She was flexing her muscles, and that was not okay. And then that gaudy display with Morris and the brace-let, sitting on his lap, batting her eyelashes like a lovesick teen-ager? Making wedding plans as if everything were all right with the world?

That was very *not* okay.

Ethan thought of the picture he'd e-mailed her—the one with her ass in the air—and finally allowed himself to feel a twinge of satisfaction. It was Photoshopped, but she didn't need to know that. Hopefully it had done its job.

Okay, he needed to think of something else. Anything else. Forcing Sheila out of his thoughts, he surveyed the large room.

Dozens of dirty heads were bent over plates of hot food, open mouths consuming whatever slop St. Mary's was serving tonight. The room was filled with skin diseases, lice, and respi-ratory infections he was sure you could catch just by breath-ing. His skin itched thinking about it and he pulled a small bottle of hand sanitizer out of his pocket. The ventilation sys-tem worked well and air fresheners were scattered everywhere, but the smell of filth was never completely masked.

A few feet away, Abby was at her station handing out cups of apple juice and milk. Ethan watched her mouth form words he couldn't make out over the constant din of chatter and eating. Even wearing an apron stained from the grease of a thousand meals past, Abby looked beautiful, her un-made-up complex-ion making her look even younger than her twenty-three years.

Abby Maddox was Ethan's live-in girlfriend. He adored Abby. But he craved Sheila. Nothing in life was ever simple.

A guffaw of laughter drew Ethan's attention to the corner of the room, and he saw that Marlon was here tonight, looking no better or worse than normal. The old black man sat in his usual spot by the window, under the sign that read BELIEVE IN MARY BECAUSE SHE BELIEVES IN YOU. He was muttering to himself as he scanned the newspaper. Ethan hadn't seen Marlon in a month, but knew the schizophrenic man wouldn't be able to explain where he'd been. Even if he could articulate it, he wouldn't, because Marlon believed himself to be a spy for a supersecret government agency disguised as a homeless man, right down to the feces- and urine-stained clothes. His job was to find old newspapers and circle code words. During one brief hour of clarity a few months back, Ethan learned that Marlon had once been a high school custodian in Portland with a wife and daughter. But as far as the volunteers could ascertain, Marlon had been off his meds for at least a year. And nobody was looking for him anymore.

The young woman with the old face sat at the table nearest the restroom. Her name was Marie, and she was a prostitute, thief, and crystal meth addict. For twenty bucks, Marie would tell you anything you wanted to know about her life, and for another twenty, she'd throw in a blow job. She'd been pretty once, a runner-up in the Miss Teen New Mexico pageant when she was sixteen, but looking at her in this place, her hair greasy and sticking to her pimply forehead, it was hard to believe.

Ethan had talked to Marie every week for the last four weeks and she'd agreed to be one of his long-term case studies. He was planning to follow her progress—or lack thereof—over the next year as he finished his master's thesis. Assuming she stuck around St. Mary's long enough. You never knew where these people would be from one week to the next.

Marie's eyes finally shifted toward Ethan and he locked his gaze on hers. It was hard for her to stay focused for more than a few seconds. The meth made her twitchy. Ethan jerked his head in the direction of the shelter's side door. She sighed, but made no move to get up. Finally she nodded.

Glancing at Abby, Ethan asked another volunteer to man his green bean station. His girlfriend was engrossed in conversation with the head coordinator, but she favored Ethan with a smile as he passed. Abby knew all about his interviews with Marie, and it didn't matter to her that he was here for reasons unrelated to any sense of humanitarianism.

Ethan smirked inwardly. Humanitarianism. *Please*. He didn't give a rat's ass what happened to anyone at this shithole beyond the scope of his thesis. But he admired Abby's enthusiasm—it set her apart from Sheila. He couldn't imagine his professor ever showing up and getting her pretty little hands dirty. Especially now that she had a massive fucking diamond hanging off it.

Marie. Focus on Marie. The homeless woman was inside his circle of control. Sheila, at least for the time being, was not. There was plenty of time to deal with his former lover later.

He watched as Marie exited the room through the back door. Really, who would notice if Marie disappeared off the face of the earth? She had no permanent home, no job, no skills. Both her parents were dead and her brother in Albuquerque wanted nothing to do with her. If she went missing, if she was kidnapped and murdered and cut up into little pieces and buried in a place where nobody would ever find her, who would care?

Nobody.

The thought excited him.

He found her standing several feet into the alleyway between St. Mary's and the army surplus store next door, which was closed for the night. The air was warm but Marie looked cold. A fresh cigarette dangled between stained fingers, and one skinny arm was wrapped around her body for warmth. The light was dim and kind to her. She almost passed for pretty.

"What now?" Marie's voice was flat. "I told you everything last week."

"That's the point, Marie," Ethan said patiently. He glanced up and down the alleyway. They were alone. "We're supposed to talk every week, remember? That's the deal."

"Fuck that."

"You don't want the money?" Ethan reached into his pocket and took out a thin wad of cash. He peeled off a crisp $20 bill, waving it in her face. "All you have to do is talk. A lot easier than some of the other shit people ask you to do."

She snatched the money and stuck it into the pocket of her jeans.

"What did you do this week?" he asked.

"Scored, got high, scored, got high . . ."

"What about your kid?" Ethan's eyes searched her face. "Did you call him like you said you were going to?"

"I was high when I said that." Marie flicked ashes onto the cement. They burned orange a moment before dying out. "I got no business calling him."

"I'm sure he'd love to hear from you."

"He don't want to talk to me. Trust me."

"Which is why you should call him," Ethan said with a sigh. "So eventually he will want to talk to you, so he knows you care."

"It don't work like that. And besides, my brother would never give him the phone." Marie's voice was hard.

"So you still haven't contacted anybody?" Ethan watched her face carefully. "No family, no friends, nobody from Albuquerque?"

"Nope."

"So nobody knows where you are?"

"They can all go fuck themselves." She fingered her necklace. It was a silver amulet on a black leather string. She'd told him last week that it was the only thing she'd brought with her from New Mexico, other than the clothes on her back. Something to ward off evil spirits. It glinted in the dim light of the alley.

Ethan nodded, satisfied.

Marie crushed her cigarette out with her running shoe. She stepped closer to him, tracing one skinny, nicotine-stained finger down the front of his shirt. "So, listen." Her voice was suddenly husky. "I could use another twenty."

Her breath was foul from poor hygiene and too many cigarettes. Ethan moved away. "My girlfriend's inside."

"So what? For forty I'll let you do that thing you like, only this time don't squeeze so—"

"Not tonight."

"Since when?" Marie sighed and her voice returned to normal. "You're a piece of shit, you know that?"

"Some other time." Ethan glanced down the alley.

"When? When are—"

A voice interrupted them. "Ethan? You there?"

It was Abby. Ethan could make out the shape of her head peeking around the corner of the building and into the alleyway.

"I'm here," he called out.

"We need you back inside, babe. We can't get the dishwasher working and we could use your magic hands."

"Be right there." Abby's head disappeared and Ethan turned his attention back to Marie. "Sunday. Meet me here, late. Midnight. But don't tell anyone—nobody—or you don't get paid."

"Midnight? For another twenty bucks?"

"A hundred."

Marie's eyes narrowed and she fished into her pocket for another cigarette. "A hundred for what?"

"You'll find out next Sunday." He looked at her hard in the dim light. "You don't show, we're done. I'll find someone else for my case study."

He started walking back down the alley toward the entrance of the shelter, leaving Marie standing alone. He heard the flick of her lighter somewhere behind him.

Enjoy the cigarettes, darling. There are only so many left in your future.

CHAPTER : 7

Her skirt was too tight.

Sheila could feel the waistband cutting into her stomach, but there was nothing she could do about it now except suck it in and act natural. Two hundred pairs of eyes were on her, and they were unforgiving. They caught every mistake, every stumble, every inconsistency.

Especially Ethan, whose gaze was unwavering from the front row. The picture he'd sent her flashed through her mind for the umpteenth time.

Pacing the lecture hall slowly, she forced herself to focus. The small mike pinned to her silk blouse picked up every word with perfect clarity and transmitted it to the speakers overhead. She looked up at the rows of expectant faces watching her in the auditorium, organizing her thoughts before speaking.

"I want you all to think about your own relationships, the people in your own lives. Your parents, for instance. How alike are they to each other? If you have brothers and sisters, which ones are you closest to, and why? And your friends. Why are they your friends? Is it because you have similar interests? Similar ways of thinking? Similar patterns of behavior?

"Or do you enjoy being around people who are different from you? If you're an introvert, do you gravitate toward people who are outgoing? Chatty? Social? If you're an extrovert, is your partner an extrovert as well? Or does he or she complement you by being perfectly content to sit in the background and let you shine?

"What do you think, people? Like attracts like, or opposites attract?"

Sheila stopped and scanned the room. Several hands were raised. She pointed to a young man in a plaid shirt and horn-rimmed glasses. "Mark. What do you think?"

"My girlfriend is the exact opposite of me." Mark's lazy voice barely carried through the large lecture hall. "She's short, I'm tall. She's smart, I'm not." The class laughed appreciatively. "She questions everything, whereas I mostly take things at face value."

"Very good," Sheila said with a smile. "So opposites attract as far as you're concerned, at least in terms of personality. I'll come back to you in a second. Anyone else? Priya?"

"I don't have a boyfriend, but I know I'm drawn to people who are like me." Priya was a pretty girl with jet-black braids who always sat in the third row. "I don't know if that makes me boring, but I always have a lot in common with my friends and tend to shy away from people who seem too different."

"Which is a common thing, actually." Sheila clicked the small remote control in her hand. The large screen changed to show a picture of smiling, similar-looking people attending church. "Think about all the social groups out there. School clubs. Organizations. We're drawn to people who are like ourselves, people who have the same beliefs, because most of us just want to belong. It's human nature."

Her eyes passed over Ethan's face. He was smirking. Suddenly her throat felt a bit dry. Sheila paused to take a sip of water from the stainless steel bottle she always kept on the desk in the lecture hall and forced him out of her mind. "Now let's talk about appearance. Mark, you said your girlfriend is short and you're tall. But what does she look like? Facially?"

Mark's eyebrows furrowed in thought behind his glasses. "Um . . . she has blue eyes, like me. People say we have the same coloring. And both our noses are crooked."

"How about you, Michelle?" Sheila looked directly at a student in the front row. "What does your boyfriend look like? Does he sort of look like you?"

Michelle, a blonde with huge blue eyes, giggled and blushed slightly. "Yeah. People think we're brother and sister."

"Gross!" said a male student from somewhere in the middle of the lecture hall. The class erupted in good-natured laughter.

"Folks, this is not uncommon." Sheila forced a smile. "So here's your homework assignment for the week. I want you to think about all the couples you know—could be your parents, grandparents, even celebrity couples—and consider their appearances. Think about what they look like, and conclude whether these couples look more the *same* than they do different, or more *different* than they do the same. Also, think about the people you find yourself attracted to. Girls and guys you've had crushes on, or dated. What did they look like compared to you? Similarities? Differences? Next week we'll compare notes. I'll be interested to know what you've discovered. Thanks, everyone."

Time was up. The room grew loud as students shut laptops, shoved books into backpacks, and flipped open cell phones.

Sheila downed the rest of her water and stuck the hard steel bottle into her leather bag. Valerie Kim and Caroline Stevens immediately approached her to ask if she needed help getting prepared for next week's class, something her TAs typically did before leaving the lecture hall. She assured them they were clear, and they left Sheila alone to pack up her briefcase.

She was painfully aware of Ethan's eyes on her. He'd made no attempt to leave the room and was still seated in the same spot he always occupied during her lectures—front row, right side, the desk closest to the podium. The last couple of weeks had been torturous. Having to stand in front of two hundred students knowing that one of them had a video of her naked, writhing, and covered in sweat? Forget painful. It was humiliating.

A student approached as Sheila was snapping her briefcase shut. She smiled to hide her annoyance. Leanne had been peppering her with questions lately, clearly a type A student who needed clarification on every test and assignment.

"Of course everything we talk about in class is subject to examination," Sheila said to the gangly student again, who had her pen and notebook ready in case she needed to jot something down. "As I said last week, Leanne, everything is testable. Class discussions, assigned reading. Even the footnotes."

"The footnotes, too?" Panic filled Leanne's brown eyes, which were already comically wide. "Oh my God."

"I'm kidding." Sheila placed a hand on the sophomore's skinny arm. "A little professorial humor. Of course not the footnotes. Leanne, don't fret so much. If you've done all the assigned readings and haven't missed any lectures, you'll be fine. And don't forget to talk to your TA. What's your last name again?"

"Armstrong."

Sheila's reassuring smile wavered slightly. "Then your teaching assistant is Ethan Wolfe. He's your first source of information. Don't be afraid to call or e-mail him, or drop by during his office hours to ask him questions. That's what he's there for."

She pointed to Ethan, who appeared to be having an intense discussion with a doe-eyed female student who'd taken a seat next to him. Another coed hovered nearby, waiting her turn. Ethan had always been good with the girls.

"Um, Dr. Tao?" Leanne leaned closer and lowered her voice. "I did e-mail Ethan last week. Twice. And I called. And when I went by his office yesterday, he wasn't there. I haven't been able to get ahold of him for over a week. And I'm not the only one." Leanne looked over her shoulder. "I'm not trying to get him in trouble. I know he's supposed to handle these types of questions. But he hasn't been available. Otherwise I'd never bother you with it."

Sheila thought for a moment, then patted Leanne's arm again. "Of course it's not a bother. You can come to me anytime. I'll check with Ethan today and see what's up, maybe his schedule's out of whack somehow. I trust everything's going well otherwise?" The brightness in Sheila's tone was forced.

"Everything's fine." Leanne's dark ponytail bobbed up and down. "Great class, Professor. See you next week."

Sheila started shutting down her laptop. The PowerPoint presentation on the screen behind her disappeared. Slinging her bags over her shoulders, she risked one more glance at Ethan, only to find him staring at her again. He was alone now, books in hand, about to pack up his own bag.

A trio of students still lingered in the lecture hall, chattering loudly in one of the aisles. Hesitating, Sheila walked toward Ethan, her insides tight.

She couldn't put it off any longer. It was time.

"Professor Tao," Ethan said as she approached. His light

gray eyes crawled over her face, missing nothing. "Great lecture today. Very engaging. Even learned something new, though of course I took this class as an undergrad. You have such a refreshing take on classic theories."

Always the terrific bullshitter. He usually got away with it because of his good looks and cocky demeanor. But today, the very sound of his voice made her want to throw up.

"We need to talk." Her voice was low. She was hyperaware of the three students still chatting about twenty feet away in the otherwise empty hall.

"Oh?" He continued to study her. "About anything in particular?"

"You know exactly what this is about."

"Let me guess. Leanne Armstrong tattled on me." He finally broke eye contact to glance at his watch. "Can this wait?"

Unbelievable. He knew damn well this wasn't about Leanne. Fine, he wanted to play it that way, so be it.

"No, it can't." Her voice was still quiet, but she spoke with authority. "Whatever the hell's going on between us, you still work for me, and you still need to do your job."

Ethan laughed, and the sound echoed in the large auditorium. He didn't care who might be listening. "You're ballsy. I always liked that about you. Always so professional."

"Ethan—"

"So why don't you do my job as well? From now on, I'll redirect all student concerns to you. You can handle that, can't you?" He cocked his head to one side. "I know how much you care about your students, Dr. Tao. You'd never let them down. Especially me."

The three students still chatting in the lecture hall were watching them, perplexed looks on their faces. Sheila didn't think they could hear anything from where they were standing, but there was no way to know.

Ethan leaned in closer and she could smell his cinnamon breath. "I watched our video again last night, Sheila, and I am *this close* to making you famous. Go ahead. Push me."

CHAPTER : 8

Normally Sheila would complain about spending all day Saturday watching college football in Morris's gigantic living room. She had nothing against football, but it wasn't her idea of a fun time.

However, she couldn't bear to protest. Her days with Morris were numbered. Any moment now, it would all come crashing down, and she wanted to enjoy what happy times they had left. Watching football with him was the least she could do.

He was yelling at the TV, clutching an old football in his hands as he always did when the Longhorns played. He had no idea how beautiful he was. She loved everything about him—his thick brown hair with a touch of gray at the temples, the crinkles around his blue eyes that gave him character. He was dressed in jeans and a half-unbuttoned white shirt, the sleeves rolled up to expose his strong forearms. He caught her staring at him and winked.

The game went to commercial. Putting the football down, Morris leaned toward her, cupped her face in his big hands, and kissed her deeply. He smelled the way he always smelled—a blend of fabric softener, soap, and spicy citrus aftershave.

Butterflies fluttered in her stomach—they always did when

he kissed her like that. She parted her lips, slipping her tongue inside his mouth, and let her hands wander down to his belt.

From somewhere nearby, wherever she had dropped her purse, her BlackBerry chimed. She had a new e-mail.

"Don't you even think about checking that." Morris's hands were under her shirt.

"Wouldn't dream of it."

She continued to kiss him, but then it occurred to her the e-mail might be from Randall. She'd been in contact that morning with a sweet-sounding woman from the New York branch of Amnesty International who'd promised to get back to her with new contact info for Morris's long-lost son.

The game came back on and a moment later a loud cheer erupted from the TV. Morris turned his face toward the screen midkiss.

"Yes!" he barked in her ear. "He makes the extra kick and they're going into overtime. Are you excited?"

"Oh, hell." She pushed him away and stood up, looking around for her purse. "I can't check my phone while we're making out, but you can watch football?"

"Aw, honey, it was just one quick look." He feigned sorrow but his eyes were still on the TV.

"Where's my purse?"

"Kitchen."

She found it sitting on the shiny black granite of the large center island. She loved this kitchen. Morris had designed it himself because he loved to cook. It was one of the things they often did together. Like the rest of the house, the kitchen was huge, with cabinets that stretched up to the ceiling, sleek stainless steel appliances, a chef's cooktop and double wall oven, even a pot rack hanging over the island. She wouldn't miss her townhouse.

Scrolling through her BlackBerry, she saw that she actually had two new messages. The first was an e-mail from Katrina Lebert, the nice Amnesty woman. The other was a text message from Ethan. She ignored the text and clicked on Katrina's e-mail first.

Subject: Randall Gardener

Hi Sheila,

Good news. Randall and his team should be passing through the AI office in Honduras sometime this week and my sister just happens to work there. I've let her know you urgently need Randall to contact you and will have her pass along your info.

Hope this helps!
Katrina

Damn. It didn't really help. She'd been told before that Randall would be passing through one of the Amnesty offices, but if he'd gotten her messages, he'd never contacted her. Every phone number she had for him was disconnected, every e-mail address was either inactive or he just wasn't checking. Time was running out. The wedding was in three weeks.

She could understand the issues Randall had with his father. Morris had admitted he'd been a distant parent to all three of his sons, and unfortunately Randall, as the oldest, had taken the brunt of it. Morris's drinking had damaged his son deeply. All Sheila wanted to do was help—first, by reuniting the two of them, and later, by helping Randall work through his issues, whatever they might be.

Sheila poked her head into the living room. Morris was

yelling at the television, lost in the world of football. After a second of hesitation, she clicked on the text message from Ethan. It only took one second to read what he wrote.

What do u see in that fat fuck anyway?

Sheila gasped, then looked up quickly to make sure Morris was still in the other room. She took several deep breaths in an effort to stem the rage building inside her.

The goddamned son of a bitch! Who the hell did he think he was?

Suddenly she didn't give a rat's ass about the sex video that could destroy her career. Ethan wanted time off and a reduced workload? Fine, whatever. But nobody talked about Morris that way. *Nobody.* Careers weren't everything. If Ethan was determined to get her fired, there was nothing she could do about it. But there was still a chance she could protect what she had with Morris, and that mattered more to her than anything. She had let this scumbag into their lives and *it had to stop.*

Shaking with anger, Sheila's thumbs flew over the keyboard of her BlackBerry.

He's 1000 times the man you will ever be. Go fuck
yourself.

She pressed SEND before she could change her mind.

A sense of utter satisfaction washed over her. God, it felt good to stand up to this asshole once and for all. Closing her eyes, she allowed herself a small smile, picturing the shock on Ethan's face when he got her reply.

It was a full minute before panic set in.

Oh, no. What have I done?

Morris came into the kitchen and Sheila looked up, wondering if her burgeoning hysteria was written all over her face. She stuck her phone back into her purse as Morris opened his enormous Sub-Zero fridge to peruse its contents. He selected a can of Diet Coke and popped the tab.

"Anything important?" he asked, taking a long sip.

It was time to tell him everything. Her e-mail had just cemented her demise, and if she didn't tell Morris now, Ethan certainly would. She had to explain before the bastard splashed her naked body all over the Internet. She had to prepare Morris.

"Not sure yet. We'll see." She came toward him with her arms outstretched. He accepted her embrace as he always did, resting his chin comfortably on the top of her head. She burrowed her face in his chest. "Is the game still on?" she asked, her voice muffled. *There's something I need to tell you. . . .*

"Done. Longhorns lost."

"I'm sorry, babe. They're just not as good without you, huh?" It was a sad attempt to be lighthearted and she hoped he wouldn't notice her abrupt mood swing.

He kissed the top of her head. "You sure know how to butter me up."

How do I tell you what I've done? "I know you miss being a superstar hotshot college football player," she said, still muffled.

"I do, can't lie. Best days of my life. Till I met you, that is."

The anxiety was too much. It was seeping into every pore, right to her bones. She pulled back and looked up into his face. "Hey. I think I know of a way to make you feel better." It was really a way to make herself feel better, a surefire way, but Morris didn't need to know that.

He grinned at her, putting the soda down on the granite

island behind them. His hands moved down to her butt and squeezed. "Oh, yeah? How's that?"

She took him by the hand and pulled him toward the stairs. "Come and see." *I need you,* she thought, but couldn't say it.

Morris followed a few paces, then stopped. "Wait. Are you teasing me?"

"Not this time," Sheila said, pulling him close. Her hand went to his crotch, and she massaged him purposefully through his jeans.

He pulled back, breathing hard. "What about the wedding? I thought you wanted to wait."

"I changed my mind."

"Out of the blue?"

No. I'm panicking and I need to feel close to you before I lose you. She swallowed and managed a smile. "What can I say, I'm ready."

He took her face in his hands, looking intently into her eyes. "Honey, I've waited a whole year. I can wait another three weeks. I know how important it is to you."

His sincerity almost broke her heart. *Goddamn you, Ethan Wolfe.* "Are you turning me down?" she whispered.

Morris stared at her, the realization spreading over his face. Yes, she was completely serious. "Hell no!" he said.

Despite her turmoil, she couldn't help but laugh. He picked her up and slung her over his shoulder, heading toward the stairs. "Let's go before you change your mind. Hoo-ah!"

: : : :

He carried her all the way up the stairs, and while it was exhilarating to know that her fiancé was strong enough to haul her weight over his shoulder, Sheila couldn't help but worry he was going to drop her. After all, Morris was fifty, no spring chicken.

They got to the bedroom and he placed Sheila gently on the bed, out of breath but still grinning. The exertion on his red face didn't stop him from reaching for his belt buckle immediately. Sheila touched his arm to slow him down.

"Take it easy, big guy. We have all day." She gave him her most seductive smile, not wanting him to know that her real reason for slowing down was because she was worried about his health.

She'd never had to worry about Ethan's health, but she pushed that stupid thought out of her mind. She needed to focus on the man in front of her. The man she loved with all her heart. The man she was finally ready to make love to.

She reached for his belt buckle, unfastened it, and pulled down his jeans. Through the thin fabric of his boxer shorts, she could see he was already hard.

He gazed down at her with an expression full of wonder. "You are something else."

"I'm just getting started." Her voice was throaty. "Take off your shirt."

He immediately began to undress, his large fingers fumbling with the small buttons on his shirt. A few buttons in, he yanked it over his head, impatient. Underneath he was wearing a thin, white, sleeveless undershirt, but he made no move to take it off. Sheila didn't ask him to, either—she knew he was self-conscious about his stomach. His jeans stayed bunched around his ankles and he stood like a statue, waiting to see what she'd do next.

She slid off the bed and got on her knees. After pulling his boxers down, she took him into her mouth with a passion that felt totally natural even though she'd never performed oral sex on him before. Hell, she'd never seen him this *naked* before. She'd never let him get past second base.

Her mouth worked on him expertly. The carpet in the bedroom was plush with thick underpadding, and Sheila could have stayed on her knees all day. But then something happened. She noticed it right away, and her heart sank.

Despite her expertise, Morris was starting to get soft.

Oh, God. She tried not to panic.

Pretending not to notice his softening erection, she worked him harder, moaning from the back of her throat like a porn star and looking up at him with big brown eyes. At first he met her gaze, but then he squeezed his eyes shut, putting his hands on her head to urge her on faster.

But it was no use. He couldn't get hard again. She knew it, he knew it, and worst of all, *he knew that she knew it.*

She couldn't imagine what the problem might be. Morris had never mentioned having difficulties maintaining erections before.

Sheila stopped what she was doing and he slid out of her mouth. She looked up at him. "Are you okay, babe? What's the matter? Am I doing it wrong?"

"No, it's fine. I guess I'm just a little nervous." Morris attempted a laugh. It came out harsh and desperate. "I thought I'd be watching football today. Maybe go slower?"

She did, taking her time. But it didn't help. Her hands, which were resting on his buttocks while she worked, were beginning to feel clammy. She wasn't sure if it was her own cold sweat or his.

The key was not to panic. If she panicked, he would panic, which would only make things worse.

Standing up, she pushed him back on the bed. "Get comfortable," she said, favoring him with what she hoped was a natural smile. Flicking on the stereo behind her, she found a station that played soft jazz. She waited till he had kicked off his jeans and removed his socks and was lying down on the bed. The white undershirt stayed put.

She turned her back to him and unzipped her own jeans slowly. Wriggling out of them, she bent forward so he could have a good, close view of her ass. She was thankful she'd thought to put on nice pink bikini panties that morning. She slid out of them slowly, looking over her shoulder at him and winking. Locking her eyes on his, she pulled her sweater up over her head and unfastened her bra. She tossed it to him. He caught it, smiling.

Cupping a generous breast in each hand, she licked one of her own nipples, exaggerating the movements with her tongue, which she knew drove most men nuts. Morris watched her steadily, his eyes flicking up and down her body. But still, he stayed soft. She hiked a leg up on the bed to give him a better view. Moving her hands down to her crotch, she touched herself. It never failed to work.

Not even a twitch.

She climbed on top of him, sitting in his lap, writhing her hips as she kissed his neck and nuzzled his earlobes, something that usually drove him crazy. He kissed her back passionately, his tongue aggressive and searching, but when her fingers wandered down to his penis, it was still soft. He moved her hand away.

"Why don't you let me work on *you*," he said.

Sheila smiled, secretly relieved. They switched positions and she lay back on the bed, placing her arms behind her head on the pillow.

Starting from her neck, Morris worked his way down her body with his lips. A moment later he was between her legs. Sheila moaned, thrusting her hips into his face, and he worked with her rhythm until she climaxed a few minutes later.

She caught her breath and sat up, noting happily that he was semihard again.

"My turn now." She rolled him on his back and went down for the second time. He seemed more relaxed.

Five minutes later, he had a full erection and she stopped what she was doing with her mouth so she could straddle him. For a while, everything seemed fine, but a few moments later, it happened again. He was going soft.

Stifling her frustration, she asked him once more while she was still sitting on him. "Seriously, babe, is there something wrong with what I'm doing?"

"Nothing's wrong." Morris's tone was curt. He turned his face away. "I think I'm just tired."

"Have you ever . . ." Sheila paused, searching for the right words. She had to tread very, very carefully here. "Have you ever had problems before?"

He still wouldn't look her, but his face flushed a deep red. "No, I've never had problems. Not even when I was drinking. I told you, I think I'm just tired."

Sheila glanced at the clock on the nightstand. "At . . . three o'clock on a Saturday afternoon?"

His maroon face went purple. "Maybe I just need a nap."

"Okay." She climbed off and pulled the covers up over her naked body, lying beside him. "Me, too."

"Fine."

But it wasn't fine. It really wasn't. This was an almost exact replay of her sex life with her ex-husband, Bill, and she couldn't—wouldn't—go through that again.

She refused to let it go. Sitting up, she touched Morris's face. "Honey, please, if I'm doing something wrong, just tell me."

He jerked away from her caress as if stung and said nothing. He still wouldn't look at her, instead staring at the TV on the dresser, which wasn't even turned on.

She sat up straighter, her heart plummeting. "So it is me." She pulled the covers tighter around herself and swallowed her pride. "Okay, tell me. I don't mind. Tell me what you like and I'll do it. Or what you don't like. Or what I did wrong. Just *please* talk to me."

He didn't answer for a full minute, and it was agony not to repeat the questions again. She didn't want to push him, although somehow she felt as if she already had. Finally he said, "It's not what you're doing. I usually like everything you're doing. What guy wouldn't? It's . . . the *way* you're doing it."

Sheila was taken aback. That was not the response she'd been expecting. "What do you mean? Is it my technique?"

Morris shook his head, his jaw clenching. He finally turned and looked directly at her. "No, nothing's wrong with your *technique*," he said, his words slow and controlled and enunciated. "Your *technique* is perfect. Especially for someone who said she didn't like sex and shouldn't even have a *technique*."

"What?" Sheila's mouth dropped open. "I never said I didn't like sex."

"Maybe not in so many words, but that's damn well the impression you've been giving me for the past year. Why else would a woman in her thirties not want sex? I honestly thought you didn't know how. And then, out of nowhere, *this*?"

Sheila stared at him and saw for the first time that he wasn't just embarrassed, if he was even embarrassed at all. Morris was *angry*. Really, really angry. Red-faced, struggling-for-control *enraged*. And for the life of her she couldn't figure out why.

He wasn't nearly finished. "Your mouth, your tongue, your hands, that striptease . . . it's like you've gone from a prude to a porn star overnight. I mean, what the hell? Who *are* you?"

Sheila felt her face go hot with shame and fury. She glared at the side of his face because once again he wasn't looking at her. "I'm me," she snapped. "And I love you. Just because you can't get it up doesn't give you the right to insult me and call me names, you self-righteous son of a bitch."

He turned over on his side without another word. Sheila sat beside him, still naked, staring at his broad back. What the hell just happened?

Forty minutes ago they'd been giggling and teasing each other while watching a football game. They loved each other. She was wearing his engagement ring. But their first real attempt at making love?

Complete and utter disaster.

The wedding was three weeks away.

CHAPTER : 9

The Seattle Seahawks bobblehead had come with the office. Ethan was tempted to throw the ugly thing out just to piss everyone off. All five of Sheila's teaching assistants shared this office, all with different hours, and sticking Post-it notes on Sonny (as the stupid toy was affectionately nicknamed) was someone's fun idea for keeping the TAs posted on important matters.

Currently Sonny was asking Sheila's assistants for twenty bucks to put toward her wedding gift. Valerie Kim was planning to purchase a set of wineglasses from Williams-Sonoma. *Fancy schmancy.* So far Ethan hadn't contributed anything— and had no plans to.

There wasn't going to be a wedding; he'd made up his mind. Her text message telling him to go fuck himself had been the nail in her coffin.

It had been fun for a while, watching her squirm. The picture he'd sent her had given him great leverage for the past couple of weeks. She'd been handling all his e-mails and taking his student calls, but he couldn't play that card forever. Sooner or later she'd realize there really was no video, and she'd allow herself to be happy.

And that was unacceptable.

The question was, just how much damage could he do? Should he go right for the jugular? Or find some other way to torment her until she cracked?

Voices drifted in from the hallway and Ethan straightened up. Through the open doorway he could see Sheila in her red Donna Karan suit as she passed, animated, chatting with another professor. No pause, not even an apprehensive glance into his office even though she knew he'd still be there.

The only thing worse than being insulted was being ignored.

Ethan waited sixty seconds, mentally picturing the length of time it would take for her to catch the elevator to the first floor. Then he bolted out of his chair and followed suit.

He made it to the parking lot in time to see Sheila drive away in her white Volvo sedan. He was on his Triumph ten seconds later.

It was barely 6:00 p.m. but the skies were already darkening, the road slick with the light rain that seemed to torture Seattleites from September to June every year. Motorcycles on wet roads were never a great idea, but Ethan wasn't planning to do anything stupid. He was getting pretty good at tailing her. Making sure to stay a few cars back, he kept one eye on Sheila's car and the other on the vehicles around him. Traffic on I-5 South was bumper-to-bumper, something he'd normally weave around, but he couldn't if he wanted to keep pace with Sheila.

He'd been following her a lot the last couple of weeks. One never knew what information might be useful. Besides, everybody had secrets. If he was going to ruin her life, it would help to know everything about it first.

A little over an hour later, in a city called Renton, Ethan parked at the curb outside the Front Street Methodist Church. Sheila's car was parked in the lot. She had entered the church through a side door a few minutes before, and Ethan, still in his helmet, was frowning, trying to figure out why the hell she was here. She wasn't religious. If she'd suddenly found God, it was news to him.

Over the next few minutes, he watched as more cars pulled into the parking lot. Adults of all ages, races, and attire entered the church the same way Sheila had, through the side door rather than the front entrance. Ethan checked his watch. Were there normally church services at seven fifteen on a Thursday night? Wasn't that a Sunday thing?

Ethan had never been to church, so he didn't know. But even in his limited experience, something seemed off.

If this was a regular church thing, or maybe an evening wedding or memorial service of some kind, why weren't people entering the church through the front door? And why weren't people in *pairs*? Most people didn't go to church alone, right?

He finally locked his bike and headed toward the side entrance, keeping his helmet on. He didn't think this would seem weird since it was raining and the lower half of his face was completely exposed anyway. The door was sticky and it took a good yank to get it open. Stepping into a small landing, he had the choice of taking the stairs up or down, or he could walk straight through. A glass door was six feet away, leading to what he assumed was the main area of the church.

He wasn't sure which way to go.

He peered at a bulletin board to his left, hoping it would tell him what was going on here tonight. Scores of notices on colored paper were stapled to the corkboard—bake sales, yard sales, Sunday-school updates, walking and exercise groups, offers for free Avon makeovers. He squinted to read them through his tinted visor, his scalp beginning to feel hot under the helmet.

The door in front of him swung open and a man with red hair and a wiry, ginger beard stepped through. He passed Ethan, eyeing him curiously as he headed toward the stairs leading to the basement. About two steps down he stopped and turned around.

"Are you looking for the SAA meeting?"

"Uh, yes, I am," Ethan answered quickly. *Essay meeting? What the fuck's that?*

The man sighed and shook his head. "They don't post it on the bulletin board. It's such crap. The church lets us use the room in the basement, and we pay a fee to use it, but they refuse to let us post even a small notice, which would clearly"—he gestured dramatically to Ethan—"help new members like yourself figure out where to go. And yet they have no problem advertising the AA and NA meetings that go on here three times a week, *each*. But sex addicts? Forget it. We only get the room once a week, no bulletin board, and we're supposed to be grateful." The man pursed his lips. "Sorry, didn't mean to rant. It just irritates me. The meeting room's downstairs and we start in ten minutes. I'm Dennis if you have any questions."

Sex addicts? This was Sex Addicts Anonymous?

"Thank you." Ethan's mind reeled. "I'll be right there. I just need to use the restroom first. Say, Dennis?"

The man glanced at him.

Ethan cleared his throat. "Do you guys hire professional therapists or psychologists to do some sort of counseling at these meetings?"

Dennis looked confused. "Of course not. It's a twelve-step program like any other. Addicts helping addicts. Why?"

Ethan grinned under his visor. "Just wondering. First time and all."

Dennis returned the smile. "You should know that today's the first day of the rest of your life. You took an important step by coming here tonight, and you should be proud of yourself. See you inside."

Ethan waited until Dennis was out of sight, then exited the church. He could barely contain his exhilaration as he headed back toward his bike.

The infallible Sheila Tao was a sex addict.

He wondered if Sheila's fiancé knew and thought there was a helluva good chance the big Texan might just be as clueless as Ethan had been five minutes ago.

It was too delicious for words.

: : : :

Abby looked up from her station at St. Mary's Helping Hands. The brown hairnet might have looked ugly on anyone else, but she still managed to look gorgeous. Large blue-violet eyes searched Ethan's face.

"Where have you been?"

He stiffened at her tone. Her voice was reproachful so he didn't respond, just watched as she dropped a helping of mashed potatoes onto the plate in front of her. The recipient, an older woman with two missing teeth, smiled and moved on to the next station.

"You totally blew off tonight's shift," Abby said, wiping a drop of rehydrated potato from the side of the large tin. "We've been really swamped and Maxine's pissed you didn't call in. I didn't know what to tell her." Maxine was the head volunteer, in charge of scheduling.

"I'm sorry." Ethan touched Abby's arm. "My cell phone died. I had a last-minute meeting that took longer than expected."

"With Dr. Tao?" Abby's gaze was cool.

Ethan blinked. "No, with a student. A guy named Dennis." The lie rolled off his tongue.

Abby turned back to her mashed potatoes.

Ethan couldn't read her body language and a ripple of fear went through him. "Is there anything you need me to do now?"

"Start cleanup." His girlfriend's voice was clipped. "Or wait for me outside. Or go home. I don't care."

He touched her arm again. "You're that mad at me?"

She shrugged off his hand. "We'll talk later."

He was dismissed. Chastised, he slunk into the kitchen, where another volunteer named Horace was loading the dishwasher.

"Look who decided to show up." Horace grunted, his pockmarked face shiny under the harsh kitchen lights. "We have a schedule for a reason, rock star." Horace jerked his head in the direction of three black garbage bags piled in the corner, bursting at the seams. "Take those out for me. Least you could do."

Ethan's skin immediately itched at the thought of touching garbage, but he managed a weak smile. "Sure thing, H."

He grabbed two of the bags, his nose wrinkling at the smell. Pushing open the back door with his hip, he stepped out into the alleyway where the large metal trash bin sat. It was already overflowing with garbage, but he heaved the bags up and into the bin anyway.

One missed. Swearing under his breath, he heaved it again.

The alleyway smelled like piss and shit. It made him think of Marie, the former beauty queen from Albuquerque turned meth addict and whore. He took out his small bottle of hand sanitizer from his jacket pocket and liberally doused his hands with the clear liquid, savoring the memories of the last time he'd seen her.

Marie. Who had twisted and writhed under him, helpless,

while his hands were around her throat. Who had looked at him with terrified eyes, just as he liked it . . .

His groin twitched. Hands clean, he reached into his jeans to adjust himself, his fingers lingering down there a little longer than necessary. She never did get her hundred bucks. What for? *Dead people don't need money.*

A voice spoke suddenly and Ethan jumped, his hand flying out of his pants.

"You a bad man," the voice said softly, seeming to come from nowhere.

Ethan whipped around, almost dropping his hand sanitizer. The alleyway was completely dark. Only the spot he stood in was lit, thanks to the dim bulb above the soup kitchen's back door.

"Who's there?"

"You do bad things." The voice was deep. It had to be a man's. And he sounded forlorn, as if things weren't strange enough. "Very bad things."

Ethan's heart thumped. He stepped away from the trash bin and closer to the door, his posture rigid.

Was it his imagination, or was the voice vaguely familiar?

"Who's there?" Ethan hardened his voice. "Speak, motherfucker, before I call the cops."

"Bad things happen to bad people," the voice said, drifting away.

Ethan looked down the alleyway, first left, then right, but there was nothing but blackness.

Shaken, he pulled open the door to St. Mary's and stepped inside quickly.

And came face-to-face with his very pissed-off girlfriend.

CHAPTER: 10

The sun was still low across the sky, and the light in the room was golden against the plush white décor. Very soothing. Sheila would have killed for an office like this, but only those in private practice were entitled to such luxury. She was an educator at heart, though at the rate she was going, not for much longer.

She sipped her coffee and stared out the window.

"Did you finish that book on grieving I gave you?" Marianne Chang asked.

"I did. It helped."

"Want to talk about it?"

"My father's death?" Sheila shook her head and grimaced. "No thanks. Not today."

"I think it's important we open up a dialogue about this again. We've gotten sidetracked with all this Ethan business, but we've been neglecting the reasons that led you here." The therapist's voice was soft. "The things your father did to you, his categorical denial when you confronted him—"

Sheila put up a hand. "Not today, okay?"

It was seven thirty in the morning and Marianne had agreed to meet for an early session. Not that their sessions were really sessions—Marianne was a friend first, and their conversations didn't mirror that of a typical therapist-patient relationship.

Sheila's anxiety was through the roof. After several days of icy, monosyllabic communication, Morris had disappeared. Sheila hadn't heard from her fiancé in forty-eight hours, and after leaving numerous messages on Morris's cell phone and direct line at the bank, she had finally caved and called his executive assistant directly. She was flabbergasted to learn Morris was out of town on business. Darcy wouldn't tell her where and would only say that she'd have her boss call when he returned. Morris had never gone away without telling her.

And was it Sheila's imagination, or had his secretary's tone been a bit snippy?

Marianne didn't think it was anything to be concerned about. Sheila had told her about their failed attempt at love-making, and Marianne was convinced that Morris was just taking some time to lick his wounds.

In any case, the last thing Sheila wanted to talk about was her dead father.

"Okay, then." Marianne folded her hands in her lap. "Moving on. There's something new I want to discuss with you. And I want you to hear me out before you say no."

The therapist's tone was ominous and Sheila looked at her in surprise. She'd never seen her friend look so serious. "You're scaring me," Sheila said, half-joking. "What is it?"

Marianne took a deep breath. "Do you consider me a friend?"

"You know I do."

"You remember I had reservations about being your therapist in the beginning?"

"Yes, and we're past all that." Sheila had no idea where

Marianne was going with this. "Clearly it's worked out. You've retained your objectivity—"

"Have I?" Marianne said, her brow furrowed. "I don't think so. I'm starting to think I've let our friendship get in the way of our therapy. I think I might be doing you a disservice by being your therapist. I'm not nearly as objective as I should be, and I think if you'd been treated by someone else, you might not have ended up in this mess in the first place."

Sheila's mouth dropped open. It was the last thing she'd expected to hear. She thought she was going to get another lecture about Ethan, or another list of reasons why Morris should have been told everything up front. She would never have guessed Marianne was doubting her own abilities as a therapist.

"What are you talking about?" Sheila was shocked. "It's because of you I've been doing so well—"

Marianne put up a hand, looking tired even though the day had barely started. "No, you haven't been doing well. If you were truly doing well, you wouldn't have relapsed. And you did relapse, Sheila. Badly. On my watch."

Sheila stared at her in disbelief. "You and I both know a psychologist can do only so much. Therapy only works if you make it work. I screwed up. I own that. It would have happened whether you were my therapist or not."

"I'm not so sure. Which is why I want you to consider this." Marianne leaned over, reaching for something on the side table. Apparently it had been there the entire time, but Sheila hadn't noticed. "Here, take it."

Sheila looked down at the brochure in her hand. Glossy color trifold. Serene faces pictured against a beautiful backdrop of green trees and blue sky. An italicized slogan across the bottom that read, *You don't have to do it alone. We're here for you.*

It was a pamphlet for the New Trails Treatment Center for Addiction in Roseburg, Oregon.

Sheila didn't bother to unfold the pamphlet. "You're kidding me, right?"

"Do I look like I'm kidding?"

"You want me to go to rehab? In Oregon?"

Her friend nodded.

Sheila opened the brochure and read it quickly, the hysteria rising in her gut. She jabbed at the page with a hard finger. "Marianne, it says this an *eight-week, in-facility* program. I can't do this. I have a job. I'm getting married in two weeks. I haven't even talked to Morris yet."

"Then the timing is perfect." Marianne spoke calmly, unfazed by Sheila's anxiety. "When he finds out you're a sex addict, you can show him that brochure. It will help him to know you're serious about getting help."

"You've got to be shitting me!" Sheila's voice was only a few decibels shy of a shriek. "You seriously want me to go to rehab? Now?"

"I didn't say that. But I think it should be part of the discussion, yes." Marianne pinched the space between her eyes and sighed. "I'm not trying to make your life more complicated, Sheila. I'm trying to help you *uncomplicate* it. I've been thinking about this a lot, and I believe you need more intensive treatment. I don't think Sex Addicts Anonymous is helping you enough. You need more."

"I have you."

"I'm not enough either." Marianne's smile was sad. "I'm your friend, right? You trust me, don't you?"

Sheila slumped. "I can't believe you're springing this on me now."

"Well, that's where I screwed up," Marianne said bluntly. "I wasn't separating your therapy from our friendship. I'm trying to now, and I should have said this a long time ago." She leaned forward. "Listen to me. I want you to go to New Trails. Before the wedding, after the wedding, no matter so long as you discuss it with Morris *before* you get married. He deserves to have the option of backing out. If you want your relationship to survive this, you have to let him feel he has a choice in the matter. Otherwise he'll feel like you trapped him. But regardless of what he decides, you need to go."

Sheila took a deep breath, trying to stay calm. She felt like a rabbit caught in a trap. "I'm already committed to telling Morris everything, Marianne. As soon as I see him. But I can't go to rehab. You don't know what you're asking. I don't want the university to find out about my addiction. Ethan hasn't released the video, and if he's bluffing, there's no need to—"

"I understand your logic. I agree Ethan could be blowing smoke. But that has nothing to do with this. I don't care what you tell the university. You still need to go, whether the university knows the truth or not."

It hurt to breathe. "I'd have to take a leave of absence. What am I supposed to say?"

"We'll figure something out."

Sheila stared at the plush carpet for a full minute before looking back up at Marianne, feeling more helpless than she ever thought possible. She knew Marianne was right. If their positions had been reversed, she'd be saying the exact same things. "Fine, I'll consider it. I'll talk to Morris, see what he thinks." But she already knew what Morris would say. Morris would tell her to go. Without a doubt.

The question was, would he still marry her?

Sheila put her head in her hands, tears welling in her eyes. How had it come to this? She was a smart woman, a trained psychologist, an excellent teacher. How could she have made so many mistakes? "Ethan Wolfe. *Jesus Christ*. What was I thinking?"

Marianne, her face filled with a mixture of compassion and relief, reached across the coffee table and touched Sheila's arm. "Not that I've met him, but I'd guess he's a textbook antisocial personality. He'd have to be to take it this far."

Sheila plucked a Kleenex from the box on the table and dabbed her eyes. "He's a sociopath, Marianne. How did I not see it till now?"

"Sociopaths are beautiful liars."

"Still. I should have seen this coming." Sheila laughed bitterly. "I'm supposed to be an expert on human behavior. And I missed this?"

"You're also *human*."

The soft lighting in Marianne's office suddenly seemed too bright. Sheila rubbed her eyes. "Is this what rock bottom feels like?"

"Yes," the therapist said. "I won't bullshit you. And there's only one way out."

"Maybe I should just leave now." Sheila sniffled. "You want me to go to Oregon? Why don't I take off now? And write Morris a letter when I get there? Because honestly, whatever courage I thought I had just dissolved. I don't know how I'm going to face him with all this."

Marianne's voice was careful. "That would be cowardly, Sheila. It would really hurt Morris if you left without telling him. I think your fiancé deserves better."

"It will hurt him anyway when he finds out the truth."

"There's no easy answer, is there?" Marianne's face was filled with regret. "Except to say that no matter what happens, I promise I won't let you down again."

Sheila managed a small smile. "What would I do without you?"

Her friend reached over to give her a hug. "You'll never have to find out."

: : : :

The entire conversation was worked out in her head by the end of the day, but Sheila honestly had no idea if she'd actually be able to say the words. Assuming she even got the chance.

The little red light on the cordless extension in her kitchen was flashing. Setting her purse on the counter, she grabbed the phone. She had messages—just one, as it turned out, but it was the one she was waiting for.

"I'm home," Morris's recorded voice said through the speaker. *Finally.* "Sorry I didn't tell you I was going out of town. It came up pretty quick. The Japanese investors wanted to meet in Vancouver—oh, hell, you don't give a horse's ass about that. Call me back, let me know if it's all right to come over."

It was more than all right. Twenty minutes later, Morris was ringing her doorbell.

She opened the door to see him standing there with the rain at his back, his dark hair plastered to his scalp, face haggard from a long day. But his smile was genuine and, to Sheila, he looked like Christmas morning.

He stayed on the porch, not moving. Without hesitating, Sheila stepped outside in her bare feet. He met her halfway, wrapping his arms around her and nuzzling her hair.

"Hi, darlin'," he said softly in her ear. It was the best sound in the world. "I'm sorry I went AWOL on you. I've been an ass."

Sheila pulled back and looked up at him. His blue eyes were kind. She stood on her tiptoes to kiss him. "Let's talk in the kitchen. I ordered Thai food but it'll be another thirty minutes."

They sat across from each other at Sheila's round kitchen table. His shoes were kicked off, his jacket thrown carelessly over the back of his chair. He had taken both her hands in his and was massaging her palms gently with his thumbs.

As she looked at him now, even though he was disheveled and tired, Sheila's heart swelled. "Should we talk about what happened Saturday afternoon?"

Morris's gaze dropped to the table. He withdrew his hands quickly, placing them in his lap. Something he did when he was nervous. "Of course we should."

"It was my fault." She was glad her voice didn't waver. "You were right about me."

"Oh, darlin', I shouldn't have—"

"Let me speak for a moment." Sheila took a deep breath. "I was aggressive. You were right. You hit it on the head. I was aggressive because . . ." She paused, searching for the right words. "Because that's what I can be. In bed. Not always, but sometimes."

"Well, so am I!" Morris said, incredulous. "Most of the time, anyway. I don't know what the hell happened. I've been waiting a year to get into your panties and the moment you drop them, I fold like a burrito. I think I was just nervous."

"But I made you that way." She kept her eyes steady on his face. "Because I held out for so long. Of course you think I'm shy about sex. The truth is, I'm not."

"Okay, then. Well, that's good to know. I'm relieved, actually."

"Don't be. There's more."

Morris sat back in his chair, his eyes searching her face. "What is it? You trying to tell me something?"

He had the gift of reading people, which made him so good at his job. "Yes. But I don't know how to say it."

The phone at Morris's hip rang.

"Shit," he said, detaching it from his belt and checking the call display. "Honey, I'm sorry, I gotta take this. It's one of the Japanese investors—he's so goddamned squirrelly. I'll just be a minute. Okay if I use your office?" She nodded, and he ducked out of the kitchen and into her study, closing the door behind him.

He was gone for exactly eighteen minutes. It felt more like eighteen years. When he finally came back into the room, she hadn't moved from her chair. She saw the amused look on his face.

"Hey, I can't believe how big Mercury is!" Morris said, chuckling. He was referring to the goldfish that lived in an oversize bowl on her desk. "I gave him some food because he's looking a little skinny. You might want to get him a bigger bowl, because he's—"

Sheila couldn't hold back any longer. "Morris, I'm a sex addict." The words, once unleashed, came out in a rabbity rush she couldn't control. "I've been in therapy to deal with it. And for the most part, I was doing okay. But then I messed up. I had an affair with one of my students. I'm so sorry. I love you."

Morris stood in stunned silence, his phone still in his hand. The grin faded from his face, so slowly it was almost comical. He reached out, placing a beefy hand on the counter to steady himself.

"Hoo-ah." Morris's voice was heavy in the silence of the kitchen. "Well now. That's a big problem."

As if to punctuate his words, the doorbell chimed. The food had arrived.

CHAPTER: 11

The documentary chronicling Yale psychologist Stanley Milgram's experiment on obedience to authority figures was at the halfway point. The video was part of Sheila's undergraduate social psych course, and she always found it interesting to observe her students' faces in the dim lights of the lecture hall as they watched it. A handful of kids snoozed; nothing could be done about that. But most were fascinated by the evidence that so many normal, morally conscious people could be coerced into severely electroshocking another human being simply because a person in authority told them to.

It was endlessly fascinating what people would do under pressure.

Ethan was in his usual seat in the first row, his face calm as he watched the giant screen above Sheila's head. The son of a bitch looked well rested, as if he'd slept twelve hours the night before without a single disturbing dream. If only Sheila could say the same. She was horrified to see the bags under her eyes when she woke up that morning. She knew she looked like hell, because it was exactly how she felt.

She hated Ethan Wolfe. If she could hook him up to a machine and electroshock him with a thousand volts, she would. She had no doubt that he was a sociopath, a classic antisocial personality just as Marianne Chang had suggested. His superficial charm and extreme sense of entitlement mirrored Ted Bundy's. Looking at him now, the comparison to the infamous serial killer didn't seem at all absurd.

The student with the long, blond ponytail sitting next to Ethan murmured something in his ear, and he favored her with a smile. Even in the darkened room, Sheila could make out the faint blush that spread across the girl's apple cheeks. Her resemblance to the late Diana St. Clair was striking.

Sheila was struck by a creepy sense of déjà vu. As she thought back on it now, hadn't Ethan had a thing with the swimmer? He'd never mentioned it, and Sheila had never asked him, but hadn't she picked up on something back then? Overheard something, maybe? With a familiar pang the memory flitted out of her consciousness as quickly as it had entered.

Not that Sheila thought Ethan was capable of murder. Or did she? Did the police even talk to him? He'd been Diana's TA, after all. They'd spent a lot of time alone together. He'd proctored at least two of her early writes and had provided extra tutoring at the swimmer's request. . . .

Sheila shook the thought out of her head. The last thing she needed was to become paranoid on top of everything else.

Checking her watch, Sheila walked over to the blackboard and jotted down the chapters to be read for next week's class. Drowsy heads popped up immediately at the sounds of her chalk squeaking, and a few of the faces showed panic. Sheila smiled reassuringly at no one in particular. The smile would make the students feel better, even if there was nothing behind it.

Ethan caught her smile and grinned.

She shuddered.

: : : :

Morris's car was in her driveway when she pulled up to her townhouse. Her heart soared, though her stomach knotted like a ball of twine. She hadn't seen or spoken to him in five days, not since the conversation where she'd finally told him everything. Were they still getting married? She was about to find out.

He was sitting on her porch steps, his long legs stretched out in front of him. The front door was locked. He'd never had a key because most of the time they went to his place. He was dressed for work, his wool overcoat unbuttoned even though it was chilly. Thrilled to see him, Sheila went to greet him with a kiss. But he turned his face away at the last moment and her lips only brushed his cheek, prickly with a day-old beard. He hadn't bothered to shave that morning. A bad sign. Normally he was fastidious about his grooming.

His eyes matched hers—red and puffy from lack of sleep. Before she could open her mouth to say something, he beat her to the punch.

"I can't do this," he said.

Pausing only for a split second, Sheila walked past him and unlocked the front door. Dropping her purse and briefcase on the foyer tile, she kept her voice calm. "Will you come inside? I'll make coffee." She paused. "I also have to feed Mercury."

It was a calculated move on her part to mention the goldfish. Morris had won him for her at the Puyallup Fair the year before, on their first official date. It was a subtle reminder of their history and all the beautiful moments they'd had before she'd infected their relationship with her lies and unfaithfulness.

Morris did as she asked, closing the door behind him. But he made no move to take off his coat and he wouldn't enter the house past the foyer. "I don't want coffee. I need to sleep on the plane tonight. I'm flying back to Okinawa to try and get the Taganaki deal closed." His voice was filled with exhaustion.

The house felt unbearably hot and she realized she was still wearing her coat. She took it off and hung it in the hall closet, then bent down to zip off her stiletto boots. She moved slowly, wondering what to say, what to do.

She felt Morris's eyes on her. Other than his obvious fatigue, his face was impassive. Unreadable.

"I can't do this," he repeated.

"Can't do what?" she asked, standing in front of him in her stocking feet. Her voice was shaking. She could lecture in front of hundreds of students without one slip, but now, in front of her fiancé, her whole body was quivering. "You need to be more specific. You can't do *us*? This relationship?"

Morris was quiet. The seconds ticked by like hours while she waited for him to respond. When he finally spoke, his voice was steady.

"When I met you, I was in trouble. You helped me. You got me through AA and the twelve steps, you helped me see what I had to lose if I didn't get sober. Because of you I was able to salvage my relationship with two of my sons. That's more than anyone else could ever have done for me." He paused, his eyes gazing past her to some invisible spot on the wall. "I admired your strength, your confidence, and not just in yourself, but also in me. You believed in me. You somehow helped me put my life back together. You helped me save my job. You reminded me that I'm a decent person. For that, I owe you everything."

His face hardened. "But that doesn't change the fact that everything I thought I knew about you is a goddamned lie."

It was over. Sheila could feel it in every bone in her body. He was ending it. She was losing him, and the pain was so excruciating she thought she might vomit. "Morris—"

He held up a large hand. "I'm not finished."

Sheila nodded weakly and took a seat on the stairs.

"You're a sex addict." His voice was heavy. "I did a little reading on it—gotta love the Internet—and I get that it's a viable addiction. Like alcohol. Like drugs. Like gambling. There's even twelve-step meetings you can go to. Do you go to those?"

Sheila nodded again, afraid to speak.

"As an addict, I get the shame. I get the desire to keep the addiction a secret, to not want to admit it to yourself or to anyone, to keep that part of you compartmentalized so that you can try and have some semblance of a normal life." He took a breath. "But what I don't get is how you could have kept this from *me*. We're supposed to get married."

His voice began to tremble. The next words to come out of his mouth were at a volume a hundred times louder than the words before. "Did you not think, somewhere in that large, intelligent, sensible brain of yours, *that I had a goddamned right to know?*" The boom of his voice echoed throughout the quiet townhouse, and Sheila cringed.

"I'm sorry," she whispered. "I'm so sorry, Morris. Oh, God, I'm so sorry." Her words caught in her throat. She could barely look at him. His face was full of accusation and loathing. "Sex addiction . . . it isn't like drinking, Morris. You tell people you're an alcoholic, they get it. They won't hate you, or think you're gross. But you tell people you're a sex addict, and suddenly you're sick. You're a pervert. Or they want to take you out back and fuck you. It's not an easy thing to tell people."

"I'm not *people*."

"I know. I'm just trying to explain." In frustration, she ran her fingers through her hair and her diamond bracelet tangled up in the strands. She yanked, ripping out two glossy black hairs. "I wanted to tell you, I did. But I couldn't."

"What's your specific addiction anyway?" Morris's gaze never left her face. "Porn? Chat rooms? Multiple partners? What?"

"Yes." Never had a word tasted so poisonous. "All of it."

"That's great. Just fucking great." Morris rubbed his head. "And how many men since we've been together?"

"Just one." Sheila's voice shook. "I swear. I was celibate for a long time before we met."

He raised an eyebrow. "Until the affair with your student."

"Yes."

"What's his name?"

"Does it matter?"

Morris's face was expressionless. "All those things we did last Saturday. Did you do them with him?"

Sheila kept her eyes glued to the floor and refused to answer.

"Look at me. I want to know." Morris was eerily calm. "Did you?"

Reluctantly, she nodded.

"Other stuff, too?"

She didn't move, didn't speak. Which she knew would be answer enough.

"Fuck!" he yelled, punching the wall beside him hard. A fist-size dent appeared in the drywall. White powder flew everywhere. He hit the wall two more times, adding to the damage. Sheila cowered. Glaring at her, he rubbed his raw knuckles, chest heaving. "Was he of legal age at least?"

"Of course!"

"Should I get tested for STDs?"

It was a low blow, but she had no right to be offended. "We used protection."

"Can't blame me for asking."

"I don't."

Morris massaged his red knuckles and spoke carefully. "Here's the thing, darlin'. Even if I could get past your addiction to sex—which I'm not sure I can—I still don't understand why you weren't having any kind of sex at all with *me*. You told me you wanted to wait till marriage. I respected that. In fact, even though there were times I thought I'd pass out from blue balls, I'll admit I liked that about you. But now I look back at all of it and realize it was a goddamned joke. You weren't saving yourself for me. *You cheated on me.* You had an affair with your *student*. You were willing to put your career in jeopardy, which has always meant more to you than anything, to have sex with some goddamned kid, rather than be with me. So tell me, how am I supposed to get past that? How am I supposed to forgive you? And how in the hell can you expect that we'll get married in *ten fucking days?*"

Sheila wiped the tears from her face, trying not to appear as pathetic as she felt. "I don't know." It was the only thing she could think to say.

"I don't either." He turned and opened the door. "I don't know anything anymore."

"Don't go." She stood up in alarm. "Please, don't go. I am so, so sorry. More than you could ever imagine." She was unable to hold it in anymore; her chest racked with sobs.

Morris looked at her. Beyond the anger and betrayal and broken trust, she saw the pity in his face. That was the worst thing of all. She cried harder, barely able to breathe.

Softening slightly, he finally came to her, pulling her close. She clung to him like a drowning rat, which she pretty much was.

"I know you're sorry. I do," he whispered, kissing the top of her head just once.

"Tell me we're going to be okay," Sheila said into the soft wool of his overcoat. "Tell me we can get past this."

Morris broke away. He didn't answer, but his jaw was working tightly. Finally he sighed. "I don't know. Give me a few days."

A glimmer of hope blossomed in her heart, so small she thought it might dissolve if she took another breath. She nodded before he could take it back. "Whatever you need."

"I'll be back from Japan on Sunday morning and we can talk again then. I don't . . ." He paused, and his face showed a sudden tenderness that killed her. "I don't want to make any hasty decisions. Because I do think it says something that you told me after all. You didn't have to. You could have waited till after the wedding, or not told me ever. Truth be told, I wish . . ." His voice trailed off and he sighed again, the weight of it all bearing down on him.

The sentence hung in the air. Sheila didn't ask him to finish it.

"We have an appointment at the Fairmont on Sunday at two," she said quietly. "To finalize arrangements for the reception. Should I cancel?"

Morris ran a hand over his face. "No. Wait till I get back from Japan and then we'll decide. In fact, let's meet there, at the Fairmont on Sunday. At noon. We'll have lunch, talk, decide what we want to do. If we decide to postpone, at least we're there to tell the caterer in person. We'd lose a lot of money, though," he said with a grimace.

"I'll pay you back. I will."

She felt almost dizzy with relief. He'd said *postpone*, not *cancel*, and *if we decide*, not *if I decide*, and that meant things might still be okay. Things weren't irreparably broken if he was using those words. Morris would never say anything to her he didn't mean.

Another tear fell freely down her cheek. He reached out and wiped it away. She grabbed his hand and kissed it.

"I do love you." His smile was faint and sad. "Maybe it's not enough."

"Morris—"

He pulled his hand away. "I gotta go," he said, the words catching in his throat. "Sorry about your wall."

He didn't look at her as he stepped past her into the chilly afternoon air.

Sheila watched him get him into his car and drive away. She had no idea whether she'd done the right thing. Maybe all she'd done was transfer her terrible burden over to Morris.

But, incredibly, it wasn't over yet. There was still a chance she and Morris could work this out. Sunday at noon at the Fairmont. There was still hope.

Her BlackBerry pinged from the floor where she'd dropped her purse. Reaching down to pull it out, she checked and saw that she had one new e-mail, sent to her personal account. She halfheartedly clicked on it. Her eyes widened in surprise when she saw whom it was from. The message was simple.

Subject: (None)

Dr. Tao—I'm told you are looking for me?

Randall Gardener

Sheila's heart leapt and she smiled for the first time in days. She might not be able to fix her relationship with Morris right now, but she might be able to help him out with his son. That she could definitely do.

She headed down the hallway to her study and opened her e-mail program. She had a lot to tell Randall Gardener.

CHAPTER : 12

Kidnapping Sheila, Ethan knew from experience, would be the easy part. It was what came after that was always difficult. There were so many ways to get caught—DNA, trace evidence, eyewitnesses . . .

The mind-fucking was officially over. It had been fun while it lasted. It was time to get to work.

He stood naked in front of the full-length mirror inside his walk-in closet, wearing only a nylon skullcap. His face, neck, and shoulders had been dusted with talcum powder, an absolute necessity for keeping his skin dry under the silicone mask.

The inner wall of the closet showcased a dozen masks on wooden busts, lined up precisely along a wide metal shelf. He allowed himself a moment to admire his collection. He'd amassed quite a few over the years, and special memories were attached to each of them.

He already knew which one he would use tonight. With dexterous fingers, he peeled the chosen mask from its stand. Good-quality silicone masks—the kind used in movies and by hard-core costume lovers at Halloween—could be bought on the Internet for about $600, and they looked surprisingly real. In contrast, this mask had cost him $6,000.

It was a work of art, custom-made to fit his face, and constructed out of the thinnest silicone money could buy. He'd worked closely with the owner of Professional EF/X Masks in Hollywood to design one that looked so real that the owner's wife herself couldn't tell it was fake from six inches away. Even its surface felt like real skin. Unlike makeup, it wouldn't melt under hot lights or from excessive sweating.

Facing another full-length mirror, he placed both arms inside the mask all the way up to the elbow. He stretched it gently, width-wise, as far as he dared go, careful not to stress the delicate facial features. Ducking his head, he slipped it over his skullcap, pulling it down over his nose and mouth. When it was properly positioned under his chin, he slid his arms out, allowing the mask to close snugly around his neck and shoulders.

Watching his reflection, he pressed the silicone into his cheeks with clean fingers, smoothing away every bump and crinkle. He took extra care around the openings of his nostrils, where the product was very thin. The mask fit him so well, the silicone actually wrapped around his nostrils, extending a few millimeters into his nose to brush up against the tiny hairs inside.

He did the same around his eyes, pressing the whisper-thin silicone into the skin below his eyebrows and underneath his lower eyelashes. His natural lids would remain exposed.

It was common for masks of this quality to include lips, which would wrap around the wearer's own. But he couldn't stand the way those masks felt. Or tasted, for that matter. This mask had been specially made without lips, with the silicone thinning to almost nothing as it neared his mouth.

Stepping back, he appraised himself. He looked incredible. The sight of a face that wasn't his own never failed to thrill him.

But the face staring back at him wasn't perfect yet. Peering at himself closely under the harsh lights of his workroom, he could detect a subtle color difference around each eye where the silicone rested next to his real skin. No problem. Selecting the correct shade of foundation from his makeup kit, he blended his real skin with his fake skin.

His lips posed a different problem. Because they were exposed, even the best-fitting silicone would separate a tiny bit if he smiled or spoke.

No worries, he had a solution for this as well. A small amount of skin adhesive, purchased at any store that sold wigs, worked well to keep the latex tight around the mouth. And, to be on the safe side, facial hair was always a good idea.

Picking through another box of supplies, he selected a thick, dark goatee made of real human hair that matched the coarse texture of the mask's hair and eyebrows. He studied himself for a moment, then applied a small amount of lip stain to better match his lips to his new complexion.

Concentrating on his reflection, he started to make a variety of different facial expressions. This exercise was critical—one should never assume that everything was in place until one had tested it properly. He lifted his eyebrows, and the skin of his forehead wrinkled naturally. He grinned, and his cheeks moved with him. He opened his mouth wide, and the silicone around his lips stayed put.

The mask was perfect, right down to the last detail. His left earlobe even had a hole, in case he wanted to wear an earring. And just under his right eye was a small but discernible scar, which added a bit of edginess to his face.

From his collection of colored contact lenses, he selected the darkest pair he owned. They were almost black and had been very difficult to find, as most manufacturers didn't make lenses this dark. But any color other than this deep chocolate shade would draw too much attention. While he wanted attention—he needed to be noticed tonight—he certainly didn't want to be scrutinized.

Blinking the lenses into place, his face was complete. Now it was time for the rest of him.

He padded his midsection with soft foam that added ten pounds, securing the pads around his abdomen with thin Velcro straps. It softened his lean frame into the body of someone who wasn't fat, but who probably didn't hit the gym often enough to be considered fit.

A light application of skin stain darkened the backs of his hands and forearms, enough for the long sleeves he planned to wear.

Time to get dressed.

The outfit, like the mask, had been selected well in advance. Dark blue denim jeans and a fitted black dress shirt highlighted his new love handles perfectly. Because he was a stickler for details, he'd even bought new underwear. Normally he wore boxers, but tonight he was donning tight black cotton briefs. The soft material so close to his skin made him feel very aware down there, and he knew Sheila would pick up on that.

To complete the ensemble, he slipped on a black corduroy blazer and scuffed leather boots. The left boot had a three-quarter-inch-thick rubber insole—just high enough to change his gait as he walked, but not so uncomfortable that he couldn't run if he needed to. From a drawer, he chose a pair of eyeglasses with thick black rectangular frames and tinted lenses. Tinted glasses could draw suspicion, but tonight they'd be fine. He wouldn't be surprised if several people—Sheila included—showed up to this meeting in sunglasses.

And now for the finishing touch: a light spray of Burberry cologne. It had taken him two hours in the department store to figure out the right one. He spritzed it lightly on his neck, inhaling the clean, masculine scent. Citrus and musk. Morris had been wearing this exact cologne during the fake interview. Which meant Sheila liked it. Perhaps she'd even picked it out.

Ethan assessed his appearance one last time. Such a full disguise was probably unnecessary—he could certainly have planned this night differently and done away with the mask altogether—but he wanted to indulge himself. Why not? Disguises made him feel omnipotent.

Tonight, though, there was another reason: he wanted Sheila to know *just how fucking good he was.*

He smiled at his reflection. He'd transformed himself from a twenty-three-year-old white male into a light-skinned black man, late thirties, with clean-cut bone structure and soulful, knowing eyes.

Handsome, strong, confident. The perfect bait.

: : : :

Ethan jogged up his basement steps and moved quickly through the main level of his home. The four-thousand-square-foot rambler was nothing like the dingy apartment he shared with Abby in Seattle's university district. For one thing, this house, nestled in the sleepy suburb of Lake Stevens, was all his.

He'd bought it two years before, shortly after he and Abby had settled in at PSSU. It was the best decision he'd ever made. The house made it possible to separate his university life from his *other* life, as he sometimes thought of it. It had a huge, airy basement—hard to find in the Northwest—which was perfect for his needs. And the thick forest of trees behind the house made it easy to slip in and out of the neighborhood undetected.

Flicking off all the lights, he opened his back door slowly and peeked outside. Houses were on either side of him, but they were separated by at least fifty feet of trees. Thankfully, interaction among the neighbors was low—Briar Woods residents were just snooty enough to avoid each other unless it couldn't be helped.

It was almost six o'clock. The McClellans, the workaholic neighbors to his left, still weren't home. She was an attorney with her own practice in Everett, he was an orthodontist here in Lake Stevens. No kids. They almost never made it in before 8:00 p.m.

Simon and Elizabeth Hoffer lived on the right. He could see Mrs. Hoffer bustling around the kitchen while her three young children sat around the large table doing homework. Simon Hoffer was in town this week, which meant Mrs. Hoffer's lover would not be coming over once the kids were asleep.

A quick streak across his backyard and he was on his way, heading toward the forest behind. Briar Woods was technically a gated community, but the only actual gate was at its front entrance, which was manned by a security guard at night. The small forest was the only thing separating the homes from the rest of Lake Stevens. The Homeowners' Association had polled the residents earlier that year, asking if they were willing to pay to have twenty-four-hour security. Ethan, of course, had voted no. So had most of the other residents, which wasn't surprising. Rich people were notoriously cheap.

Once immersed in the trees, he moved through the forest at a quicker pace. It was completely dark, but the small, thin flashlight he'd stuck in his back pocket provided just enough light to keep him from stumbling.

Ten minutes later, he popped out on the other side of the forest, into the small community park. It was dinnertime and empty now, so nobody noticed the dark figure with the slightly off-center walk making his way past the monkey bars toward the big black Chevy Suburban parked near the sidewalk.

The SUV was a rental. He'd paid for it up front in cash using a fake driver's license and phony insurance card in the name of James Smith. He never used the same ID twice.

Coming back home he would have no choice but to drive the Suburban through the main entrance, but he'd already planned for that. It was all in the timing.

Heading south on I-5, he had forty minutes until he reached Seattle. His first stop: the Safeway where Abby worked.

No better place to test out his disguise.

: : : :

Standing in line under the harsh lights, Ethan held a carton of milk in one hand and a box of Fiber One cereal in the other. Once he got to the express checkout, he picked up a copy of *People* and placed it on top of the conveyor belt beside his groceries.

Abby stood at the cash register wearing her green Safeway smock. The bluish tinge under her eyes told him she was tired. Her shift wasn't over for another four hours and she'd already been on her feet awhile. With a brief smile that didn't quite touch her eyes, she pressed the large button near her hip, sending his items down the conveyor belt toward her.

"How's it going?" Her tone was terse, disinterested. She scanned the items and placed them into the plastic grocery bag stretched open in front of her.

"Great." He smiled. "It's a beautiful evening. How about you? Long day?"

"Aren't they all?" Finally she glanced up at him. "You're Australian?"

"I'm from New Zealand, actually. Been here for ten years. Can't seem to get rid of the accent."

"Why would you want to get rid of it?"

He shrugged. "To blend in, I suppose."

She punched the buttons on her cash register and frowned. "What's so amazing about blending in." It came out a statement, not a question. "That'll be nine fifty-two, please."

He paid with a ten. She made change, putting it right into his hand. Their fingers brushed.

"Sometimes it's good not to stand out," he said.

Their eyes met briefly. He held his breath. Her eyes moved away.

"Thanks and have a good night," she said, then added, "Enjoy your *People*."

The words would have sounded sincere to anyone but him. Abby had no interest in celebrity gossip.

He grinned. "Thanks. Don't work too hard."

Nodding, he picked up his bag and headed for the exit.

He couldn't resist glancing back at her just once before he reached the automatic doors, but she was on to the next customer.

He'd passed with flying colors.

: : : :

The Sex Addicts Anonymous meeting started at eight. Ethan made it with five minutes to spare. He parked his SUV in the parking lot of the Front Street Methodist Church and entered through the side like everyone else, bypassing the doors to the chapel and heading straight down to the basement.

The windowless room was large and surprisingly cheerful. Colorful biblical murals were painted on the walls, and he wondered if this was the same room they used to teach Sunday school. Rows of folding chairs filled the space, all facing a shabby wood podium. Most everyone was seated, and only a handful of empty chairs were left.

He felt several curious pairs of eyes on him as he took his seat and was relieved the room was dimly lit. Ethan was confident he looked normal, but soft lighting always helped.

Sitting quietly, he avoided making eye contact with anyone and instead listened carefully to the limited conversations around him. Traffic. Movies. Weather. Last night's episode of some reality show he'd never heard of. Small talk. Nobody seemed particularly close to anyone else.

He took a moment to turn and scan the room. A good ten seconds passed before he spotted her, five rows back, her makeup minimal except for her trademark red velvet lips. He was a bit jarred by her appearance—he'd only seen Sheila in professional attire. Or naked. Tonight, in a sweater and jeans, you'd never know she was a distinguished professor and board member of the American Psychological Association. Sex Addicts *Anonymous,* indeed.

Their eyes met for a brief moment. He felt a tingle go through him. Then her eyes moved to the front of the room, no trace of recognition on her face.

"Welcome, everyone." The man at the podium was the same ginger-haired guy Ethan had met in the stairwell the first time he'd followed Sheila here. "Happy Thursday to all."

Voices murmured around him.

"My name is Dennis, and I'm a sex addict."

"Hi, Dennis," the group chorused on cue.

"I see we have some new faces here tonight." The meeting leader's smile was warm. "Welcome, so happy to have you. For the benefit of our new members, I'll quickly go over the rules.

"First and foremost, we are anonymous. We're a twelve-step program whose purpose is to support and encourage our members. We aim to achieve sexual and emotional health and stop the compulsive sexual behavior that has hurt ourselves and the people in our lives, using these twelve steps. You're all encouraged to share as much as you can, but for now you may simply choose to listen until you're ready. When we're listening to other members' stories, we do not judge and we do not interrupt." Dennis smiled encouragingly and scanned the room. "Who'd like to begin?"

A hand shot up in the front row, belonging to a bald man wearing a denim jacket. Dennis nodded and stepped aside. The man positioned himself in front of the podium, his scalp shiny and pink under the dim spotlight above him.

His large Adam's apple bobbed as he spoke. "My name is Kenneth and I'm a sex addict."

"Hi, Kenneth," the room responded in unison.

"It's been a tough week. I got caught masturbating again at work. I thought I was doing so well, but I was searching for something on the Internet my boss needed and one of those ads for free porn popped up. I don't know why they don't block those! Anyway, that's all it took. Next thing I know, my hand is down my pants and I'm . . ."

Ethan listened with great interest as Kenneth the Masturbator relayed his embarrassing story, concluding with the look on his poor supervisor's face when she walked into Kenneth's office and caught him spanking the monkey.

Ethan bit back his laughter. And to think, the fun was just beginning.

CHAPTER: 13

The first half of the meeting was over and they were given a fifteen-minute break. Eight people had shared their stories so far, and Sheila hoped this part was finished for the evening. In her three years attending Sex Addicts Anonymous meetings, she'd just about heard it all. Nothing really surprised her anymore, but it could be pretty depressing.

Kenneth was on the verge of being fired from his third job in two years due to his uncontrollable urges to masturbate in public places. Christina suffered from blackouts during sex and often woke up unable to remember where she was or why she was there. Curt was addicted to online pornography and had spent over $40,000 on membership fees to various websites. His wife and kids had left him after the house was taken by the bank.

These stories might have been interesting, funny even, if Sheila didn't have to count herself as part of this group of addicts struggling day in and day out for control.

Her butt sore from sitting on the hard metal folding chair, she welcomed the opportunity to stand up and stretch. She followed the herd to the back of the room where the coffee and doughnuts were and watched as people began to pair off or stand in small groups. She murmured a few hellos, but she had no desire to bond with anyone here. If anybody asked, she always said her name was Stella.

She waited patiently for her turn at the free coffee dispenser, which produced mild but not horrible-tasting coffee. A corduroy-clad arm reached out from behind her to drop a $50 bill into the large donation jar. She turned, curious to see who'd donate such a high amount, and a man about her age with smooth caramel skin and tinted glasses met her glance. A newbie. His eyes stayed on her face for only a second before darting away, which happened a lot in SAA. Nobody wanted to be recognized here.

"Fifty bucks." Sheila couldn't resist commenting as she reached the coffee dispenser. "Generous. I think the average contribution tends to run about five dollars. You must be planning to stick around."

"Depends on what happens in the second half of the meeting."

The man had an accent she couldn't quite place. "Enjoyed the sharing, did you?"

He shrugged but his expression was serious. "It was interesting. I can't get past the size of this group. Back in Ohio we had only seven people. There's got to be forty here tonight."

He didn't sound as if he was from Ohio.

"I wonder what that says about the Pacific Northwest," Sheila said.

He finally laughed, pushing his glasses farther up on the bridge of his nose. He wasn't bad looking. "Right."

"Affirmations and visualizations are next. Have fun."

She glanced at him one last time before she walked away. Something about him seemed vaguely familiar, but that often happened. She taught hundreds of students every year, of all ages, races, and backgrounds. She hoped he hadn't been one of them.

::::

At Tony's Tavern an hour later, Sheila ate her mushroom-and-Swiss burger. Greasy food had become a ritual for her after her weekly SAA meetings. Something about all the sex-addict talk made her crave comfort food, and Tony's burgers fit the bill. The tavern was only a five-minute drive from the church, and the dim lighting and classic rock booming over the loudspeakers made it the perfect place to pig out unnoticed.

Taking a big bite of her burger, she observed two women sitting at the bar. One sported a miniskirt and high heels; the other wore a top so low her red lace bra was showing. They were attracting a lot of attention from the workingmen who frequented Tony's, all of whom they shot down with sarcastic barbs.

Sheila understood what they were doing all too well. Whatever their stories might be, these women were here for validation. They weren't necessarily looking to get laid, though someday that might change.

A tall, well-dressed man took a seat beside them at the bar. Sheila recognized him immediately from the SAA meeting—Fifty Bucks Guy. The two women stopped talking long enough to check him out while he ordered a drink. The blonde with the low-cut top puffed out her chest and gave him an obvious once-over, but he didn't even glance her way.

Sheila took another bite of her burger and three slices of greasy mushroom fell into her lap. Swearing under her breath, she picked them out of her napkin, popping them quickly into her mouth. She looked up to see Fifty Bucks Guy watching her from the bar with a sardonic grin. He gave her a small wave.

Reflexively, she lifted a hand in response. Instantly she regretted it. She watched in dismay as he hopped off his barstool to make his way over to her. Miniskirt and Tight Top watched with disappointment.

Despite herself, Sheila couldn't help but feel a tiny thrill at his approach. *Validation.*

He was better looking than she remembered. A little paunchy around the middle perhaps, but she liked his hip, stylish look. He walked with a slight limp and she wondered what was up with that. Not that she was interested, of course.

"I didn't get a chance to introduce myself earlier," the man said when he reached her table. He leaned down so she could hear him over the loud din. She caught a whiff of his cologne. Expensive. "I'm James. I was just at the meeting."

She wiped her mouth with her napkin. "I remember. Fifty bucks."

"I didn't catch your name." He held his hand out.

She shook it, not bothering to hide her reluctance. "Stella."

"Nice to officially meet you, Stella. Mind if I join you? There don't seem to be any empty tables and—" He turned to look at the seat he'd just vacated, now occupied by an older man trying to pick up the two loud women. "It looks like I've lost my seat."

Sheila looked around the room. He wasn't lying, every single table was full except hers. Forcing a smile, she acquiesced.

"Don't worry, I have no desire to talk about the meeting." He sat down heavily in the rickety wooden chair. "In fact, we don't have to talk at all if you don't want to. I just need to get some food in me and I'll be on my way." He signaled the waitress.

Sheila felt bad. Was she being bitchy? Maybe a little small talk wouldn't hurt.

"Where are you from?" She attempted a more natural smile. "I can't place your accent, but it doesn't sound like Ohio."

Up close, James was handsome. Nice, even features. She wasn't a fan of facial hair, but the goatee suited him, and something about his presence was very masculine. He sat with his legs apart, leaning away from her. It made her want to move closer. A small scar was under his eye, and she had a sudden urge to take off his glasses and run her finger over it. She forced the thought from her head.

James grinned and took a long sip of his beer. "You remembered. Damned accent gives me away every time."

"Australia?"

"New Zealand."

"A Kiwi. Very cool." Sheila took a bite of her burger and lost a few more mushrooms. "Damn. This burger is good but so messy."

The middle-aged waitress approached, harried, her bright red hair frozen to her head under what looked like three coats of cheap hairspray. "Another Sam Adams? Or something to eat?" She was addressing James, her voice hoarse from either too many years of smoking or too many years of shouting in loud bars. Probably both. "Make it quick, I'm on break in two minutes."

"Hi, Jean," James said, reading the name off her tag. He gave her a winning smile. "I can be quick, but I thought you gals liked a guy to take his time."

Jean's eyes widened in surprise. Finally, she burst out laughing. "Okay, you got me."

James pointed to Sheila's plate. "I'll have what she's having. And another beer."

"Mushroom Swiss." Jean scribbled on her little notepad. "Good call, it's the tastiest thing in the joint. Except for you, maybe." She winked at him. Still smiling, she said to Sheila, "Another Diet Coke for you?"

"Please, with lime," Sheila replied, amused.

"Diet Coke with lime?" James said once the waitress had left. "You sure go for the hard stuff."

"I don't drink," Sheila said, refraining from adding *anymore*.

"Ah." His gaze moved to the large TV screen behind her, one of the many that were bolted to the walls. ESPN was showing football highlights, and Sheila couldn't help but think that if Morris were in town, he'd be watching the exact same thing.

James didn't seem particularly interested in conversation, but the silence felt awkward to Sheila.

"So, James." She leaned in toward him, catching another whiff of his cologne. Without meaning to, she inhaled deeply. Damn, he smelled good. It was a little unsettling—she'd always been a sucker for great-smelling men. Morris always wore cologne when they were together. Come to think of it, something about James's scent reminded her of her fiancé. Assuming there was still a wedding, of course. "How long have you been in SAA?"

James raised an eyebrow. "Thought we weren't going to talk shop."

Sheila smiled. "You said that, not me."

"Fourteen months. What about you?"

"Longer than that." She pushed her plate away. "Is it helping you so far?"

He started to answer but was interrupted by Jean.

"Thank you. That was quick," he said, then winked at the older woman as she set down his food and beer. She winked back, a blush seeping into her wrinkles.

When she left, he said to Sheila, "I think so. Maybe not in

the traditional sense. It hasn't been easy. But I'm better than I was."

"Better in what sense?"

"For starters, I no longer pay for sex."

She wasn't surprised. She figured it was something like that.

"I had a problem with prostitutes," he continued, dumping ketchup onto his burger.

He had long fingers, artist's fingers, and they reminded her of Ethan's. She felt a tingle go up her spine, thinking about what fingers like that could do. *Stop it.*

"It pretty much ended my marriage," he said.

"Not too many wives can handle that." Sheila's smile was sympathetic. "Good for you for getting help."

"Can I be honest?" James munched on a fry. "I don't think I would have stopped. Not even after Cheryl—that's my ex—left me. It was the money that did me in. I was seeing two, three women a week who charged three hundred bucks a pop. I don't make enough money to afford that indefinitely."

Jean came back, paying particular attention to James. Sheila watched with amusement as the waitress batted her well-coated eyelashes, giggling like a schoolgirl. Apparently Sheila wasn't the only one who found James attractive.

"Excuse me, Jean, I never got my Diet Coke with lime." Sheila favored the waitress with her brightest smile.

Jean pursed her lips, clearly annoyed that Sheila had dared to remind her. "I told the bar. I'll check on it. And then I'm definitely going on break, so make sure you's don't need anything else for a few minutes." She flashed a smile at James before she stomped away.

"So what about you?" he asked. "What was your problem?"

Sheila waved a hand. "Oh, you know, the usual. Poor impulse control, sex with strangers, blackouts."

"Pardon? Did you say blackouts? It's hard to hear in here." James leaned forward, his dark eyes on hers. "I've never heard of that."

"They're hard to explain," Sheila said, then paused.

Why was she discussing this? What was it about strangers that made it so easy to talk about personal, painful things? Was it because they had no stake in it and weren't emotionally invested in anything that happened to you?

"It's like I become someone else," she finally said. "The next day, I can't remember where I was, who he was, or what we did." She sipped her soda, mostly ice at this point, and craned her neck to see if Jean was coming with a fresh beverage.

"Do they still happen?" His intense gaze dropped to her lips for a split second before meeting her eyes again.

She felt self-conscious. She'd wiped her mouth while eating and was painfully aware of how washed out she looked without her favorite red lipstick. Not that it should matter whether James thought she looked good or not.

"I don't engage in those types of activities anymore," she said.

"So you're celibate?"

Sheila sucked in a breath at the pointed question.

Instantly his face was troubled. "I'm sorry. Much too personal. Forget I asked."

"It's all right." She licked her lips, fidgeting with her paper napkin. "Let's just say it's complicated."

"Isn't it always?"

"I'll be right back." She stood up and reached for her purse. "Ladies' room."

"Sure. I'll see if I can find out what happened to your Diet Coke."

"I'll bet if you sweet-talk Jean, it'll be here by the time I get back," Sheila said with a wink.

James laughed. "She does seem to like me, doesn't she?"

In the restroom, Sheila washed the grease off her hands and applied a fresh coat of lipstick. The color brightened her face instantly and she felt better. On a whim, she dug into her purse and pulled out a small sample of perfume she'd picked up at the mall a few days before. She dabbed a little on her neck, then stood back, appraising herself in the bathroom's sallow light.

What the hell was she doing putting on perfume?

She knew she could go home with James if she wanted to. Two sex addicts meeting at a bar? It was a no-brainer.

The question was, did she want to?

Back at the table a minute later, she saw that her plate was gone and a fresh Diet Coke—with a perfect wedge of lime—was sitting in its place, condensation covering the sides of the glass like sweat.

"Magic," James said with a grin.

"Finally." She slid into her chair. "Thank you."

"You won't believe what I had to do to get her to bring it."

"I don't think I want to know." Sheila laughed and took a long sip, feeling his eyes on her once again. She was beginning to like it. *Christ*. She sipped her soda again to avoid meeting his gaze.

"So, do you have a sponsor?" he asked, picking up where they'd left off.

"I have a therapist."

"Are you dating anyone?"

His question came out of left field and she felt her eyes widen. He laughed at her reaction. "I'm not asking for me. It's the sex-addiction issue. I'm wondering if it's really possible for any of us to have normal relationships."

She relaxed, but she couldn't ignore the twinge of disappointment that he hadn't asked for himself. "I'm engaged, actually."

The words embarrassed her for some reason. She couldn't bring herself to add that the wedding was in a little over a week.

"Is that right?" He looked surprised. "Congratulations."

Was it her imagination, or did he also seem disappointed? She couldn't be sure. She smiled, but it felt forced as thoughts of Morris clouded her mind. "All the plans are made. I just have to get my dress fitted one last time." She rubbed her temple. Her head was feeling a bit heavy, no doubt from the greasy burger and fries she'd just eaten. "It's not a big wedding, but I want to look good. I probably shouldn't have eaten here tonight."

"I'm sure your fiancé thinks you look beautiful no matter what." James's dark eyes bored into hers. "You're a gorgeous woman. He's a lucky man."

She took another long sip of soda, suddenly feeling as if she needed the caffeine. "I'm the one who's lucky."

She pictured Morris's face. He was on a plane to Japan now and she wondered if he'd made any decisions. Her heart panged thinking about him.

A yawn escaped her lips before she could put a hand over her mouth. Aghast, she took another sip of her soda. "Yikes," she said to James, who was watching her intently. "Guess it's been a long day."

"Don't apologize." He favored her with a charming smile. "I'm beat myself. Maybe you should get going before you get too sleepy to drive. How far do you have to go?"

"I live in Seattle. Capitol Hill."

"So, thirty minutes?" James said. "That's a long drive if you're tired. I'll ask our friend Jean for the checks."

"Ha. *Your* friend Jean."

He waved and the waitress came over quickly with their bills. Sheila noticed a little happy face was drawn on James's ticket, and that Jean's large, gnarled hand rested on his arm a little longer than necessary. If it bothered him, he didn't show it.

"I should get going, too." He put some cash on the table and stood up. "Early day tomorrow."

They left the tavern together. The waitress looked disappointed as they passed. So did the two loud women at the bar. Sheila allowed herself a small smile. They all probably thought she was leaving with James.

It wasn't a terrible thought.

The night air was crisp and refreshing, but it didn't do much to clear Sheila's sudden brain fog. She yawned again as she approached her white Volvo, staggering a little as she tried to fish out her keys. Despite the brightly lit parking lot, her vision was going blurry.

"God, I'm so exhausted all of a sudden." She rooted around in her purse with a hand that felt like rubber. Her eyelids were heavy and she blinked rapidly a few times to try to wake herself up. Where the hell were her car keys? "That burger really did a number on me. I might have to go back inside for some coffee to go."

"You'll be up all night if you do that," he said.

"Where are you parked? Don't wait for me . . ." The words came out slurred. She blinked again, feeling dizzy, and put a hand on the car to steady herself.

"I'm just a few spots down." He pointed to a large black SUV and then looked back at Sheila with concern. She began to feel embarrassed despite her fatigue. "Maybe I should give you a lift home. It's on the way."

"No, no." She lifted a hand that weighed fifty pounds. "I'll be fine." *Holy shit, I can't be this tired. . . .*

It was her last thought as her head rushed to meet pavement.

than's hand rested casually on Sheila's denim-clad thigh, a small smile on his face as he headed back to Lake Stevens. This was the first time they'd been in a car together. It might have passed for a date had she not been unconscious.

The radio was tuned to a classic-rock station and the Rolling Stones "Sympathy for the Devil" was booming out of the loudspeakers. Sheila had once told him about the summer she and her girlfriends drove cross-country to catch the opening of the Stones' American tour. The story included a car breakdown, hitchhiking, some bad pot, and a zany stop at a truckers-only diner. She'd barely been out of her teens. He wished he could have known her then.

She breathed evenly beside him, her face peaceful. He figured she'd be out for about three hours—just enough time to get her into the house and make preparations for the next phase.

The Stones' song ended and he switched the stereo to MP3 mode. Fiddling with his iPod, he found the song he was looking for. After all these years, Radiohead's "Creep" still gave him shivers. The first time he'd heard it, he'd been in love. And having sex. And strangling someone.

All at the same time.

He smiled as the memories overtook him. The late-afternoon sunlight streaming across his bedroom walls. Books and backpacks strewn across the floor. The smell of her skin, slick with her musky sweat. Her voice in his ear as she whispered his name.

The way her face looked, pale and slack and immobile, a few seconds after she stopped breathing. Her hair tickling his bare arms as he shook her, trying to revive her.

The small line of saliva that ran from her bloodless lips and down her chin as she lay heavy and unmoving in his arms.

You never forget your first time.

: : : :

Upon reaching the gate at Briar Woods, Ethan punched in his code, noting with satisfaction that the guard booth was empty.

He'd timed it perfectly, same as always. The ancient security guard hired by the Homeowners' Association was predictable—Henry always left at midnight to take a dump. Every shift, without fail, the old rent-a-cop drove to the twenty-four-hour doughnut shop two streets away, did his business, and returned to the guard booth with a large coffee and French cruller. Not that Ethan couldn't have handled Henry if for some reason the geezer's bathroom habits suddenly changed. But why take the risk?

He looked up at the security camera mounted above the booth. It was broken and had been for a year. He was sure of this because he was the one who'd broken it.

He was nothing if not careful.

In under a minute he was in his driveway, pressing the button on the remote garage-door opener he'd stuck on the visor of the Chevy Suburban. His street was dimly lit, with no movement anywhere. In the bedroom community of Briar Woods in Lake Stevens, everybody was tucked in for the night.

He parked right in the middle of the large garage so there'd be ample space on either side of him. His vintage Triumph was gassed and ready to go. Once he got Sheila settled in, he'd be taking the bike and going back out to Renton to get her car out of Tony's Tavern's parking lot.

As for her Volvo, that was easy. He was going to park it back at Sheila's place.

He pressed the button to close the garage door, got out of the car, and walked around to the passenger side. He opened the door and unfastened Sheila's seat belt.

Hoisting her over his shoulders, he carried her inside the house through the connecting door. There was no alarm to disengage. He'd never had a system installed because he didn't want the headache of a security company snooping around, should the alarm go off by accident. Besides, security systems were designed to keep the bad guys out . . . and *he* was the bad guy. The thought made him grin.

Inside the house, he took an immediate right, heading through the basement door, which he'd propped open before he'd left that evening. The door behind him closed and locked automatically, and it had a keypad. Nobody could enter or exit the lower level of the house without the code.

It hadn't been easy to find a house with a basement in the greater Seattle area. The basement mirrored the upper level— huge and sprawling. He felt no claustrophobia here. As he navigated down the stairs, the lights turned on automatically.

It would only take a few minutes to get Sheila prepared. He hummed, almost giddy with anticipation.

He placed her gently on the bed and her head rolled to the side. Her mouth was slightly open and a line of saliva trailed down her chin and under her jaw.

She looked dead.

Lovingly, Ethan traced the saliva with his finger and tasted it, remembering.

CHAPTER : 15

The room smelled pleasant, like the grass after a good rain, reminding Sheila of summers spent on Fox Island as a girl, running around barefoot in the backyard of the house she'd lived in until her mother died.

That was so long ago, decades really. But, at this moment, it felt as if she were there. The cool breeze kissed her damp skin like a lover. Inhaling deeply, the fresh, clean air expanded her lungs, and it felt good.

She sensed movement behind her closed eyes and tried to open them, but the eyelashes on her right lid stuck together and it stung as they ripped apart.

This was not Fox Island.

Her vision was blurry and her head was thick with the brain fog that only happened after nights of serious drinking or one of her blackouts. Is this what happened? Had she fucked up again? Her mouth was cotton dry, and when she tried to swallow, she gagged.

The shadow in front of her danced around. She tried to follow its movements, but it wasn't easy. She heard voices in the background, low voices, chuckling voices, familiar voices. Her breath came faster as she fought back panic. She must have passed out in a public place. What if she was at the university somewhere? What if one of her students saw her?

She struggled to stand up, but couldn't. Her arms were lead and her legs wouldn't respond.

"Just relax," a man said in a kind voice. "Nobody's here but you and me. It's just the TV. I put it to CNN because you're an avid CNN watcher, aren't you?"

She tried to speak but her parched throat refused to comply.

"Now listen carefully and try to relax. I know it's difficult because you don't know yet where you are, but you have to try. I'm going to put a straw to your lips. I'm going to give you some water. Okay? Here it comes."

Something must have happened. She must be at a hospital somewhere, and any minute, the kindly voice was going to explain to her what the hell was going on. Wherever she was, Morris was on his way. He had to be.

Sheila felt the plastic touch her lips. She puckered in reflex, sucking in the cool water. She took five long sips before he took it away.

"There. Better?"

She tried to nod but her head felt heavy.

"Now, I want you to listen to me. I want you to focus. Can you see me?"

She looked straight at him. Gradually, the abstract colors started taking shape and her vision began to fill out, transforming him from a two-dimensional picture into real life.

"Do you remember me from last night?" he asked, smiling.

She kept staring at him, struggling to focus as his features continued to sharpen. Tawny skin, dark hair, dark eyes appraising her behind thick-framed glasses, tall and confident. It came back to her quickly. Tony's Tavern. Swiss-mushroom burger and a Diet Coke with lime. Yes, she remembered.

"James," she said, her voice hoarse. "You're James. Where am I?"

"At my house." His voice was reassuring. "In a room in the basement, my most favorite room actually, a room only very few people get to see. You're very lucky."

"I don't understand. Why can't I move?" Her voice felt a little stronger now. She tried to look around the room but her head felt like rubber, lolling on her chest like a rag doll's. It was bright in here. From somewhere in the room, a fan blew cool air into her face.

"Because I tied you down," he said. "Look."

She followed his direction and was shocked to see he was telling the truth. She was propped upright in a queen-size bed, pillows at her back. Her wrists and ankles were encased in thick steel bracelets attached to chains that were handcuffed to the wrought-iron headboard and footboard. A thick wool blanket covered her from the waist down. She couldn't see or feel her feet.

"I don't understand," she said, again fighting the panic that started to churn in her belly. "I—"

"Are you going to throw up? Tell me now so I can get you a bin."

She nodded. In a flash something metallic and shiny was in front of her and she vomited into it.

"Feel better?" He wiped her face with a moist paper napkin. Scented, like roses and vanilla, nauseating. A baby wipe. The straw touched her lips again. "Here, have more water."

Her mouth tasted awful but she sucked anyway.

"Now, Sheila, I know you feel terrible right now, but that feeling will pass soon enough. It will change into something else, something worse I think, but I promise you that in a little while you'll be able to think very, very clearly. Because in a minute your body is going to produce a surge of adrenaline and it's going to help wake you up. Are you listening?"

She nodded. The voices coming from the TV were distracting. Democrats arguing with Republicans. It was difficult to concentrate. As if reading her mind, he muted the sound and stepped closer to her.

"Here's the situation. We had dinner last night. I slipped something into your soda when you went to use the restroom. I'm sure you can guess what it was, because you always discuss date rape in week four of your social psych course. No need to panic, I didn't rape you. With me so far?"

She nodded again.

"But I did bring you here to kill you. And I think it's important you know this, that you understand this very clearly, because when you understand it, it makes my job a lot easier. And then other people don't have to get hurt. Do you follow me so far? Do you understand everything I'm saying?" His voice was reasonable, soothing, and familiar.

She opened her mouth to say yes, but the sound that came out was no more than a squeak. Staring at him, she was helpless, frozen in the bed, her vision alternating between blurry and normal. Bile burned at the back of her throat. She vomited again and the bin was there to catch it. Once more he offered her the bottle of Evian with the white bendy straw, but this time she turned her face away.

"I need you to say that you understand me, Sheila."

"But I don't understand. I don't understand any of this. Please, James . . ." Her vision blurred. She squeezed her eyes shut, then opened them again, trying to focus.

"Oops." He sighed. "I forgot, forgive me. My name isn't James."

With a grin, his fingers reached into his shirt. It was a full minute before Sheila realized the screaming in the room was her own.

The man was peeling his face off.

: : : :

Five minutes passed. Or five hours. She didn't know. She had passed out, and when she woke up, the lights were off and the room was pitch-black.

From somewhere nearby, the man laughed, delighted. "Never fails to shock."

Sheila heard panting in the room and wondered if there was a dog here. But, no, she was the one breathing hard. She couldn't seem to get enough oxygen. A thousand questions flooded through her brain.

Who are you? Why are you doing this?

But the words wouldn't come. All she could do was scream again in primal fear.

"You know, if I hadn't prepared for this reaction, it'd be rather annoying," the man said. "I turned off the lights to give you a minute to relax. Are you relaxed?"

Was he crazy? How could anyone relax in a situation like this?

"Silicone, darling. Just a little silicone. And some fake hair. You'll see."

She screamed again. It turned into a gag. In the darkness, she felt the water bottle touch her lips. She turned her head away, her breath coming faster. The last time she could remember breathing this hard was when she'd signed up for a spinning class at the university athletic club two months ago.

"Come on, drink," he said, his voice gentle.

Sheila shook her head.

None of this was happening. It couldn't be.

He sighed and she heard him place the water bottle on the nightstand. "Let me know if you want it."

"Who are you?" she managed to croak. Her eyes were not adjusting to the absence of light and she couldn't see anything. "What the hell is this?"

"I already explained that to you. Do you want me to go over it again?"

"Are you going to kill me?"

A momentary silence. Then she heard him walk away.

An instant later, the lights were on, sending streams of pain into Sheila's eyes.

He smiled at her from the foot of the bed. At the sight of him, the room spun and the bile in her stomach rose.

Taking her hand in his, he sat down next to her and caressed her fingers. "Hello, Sheila."

"*Ethan.*"

It was the only word Sheila managed to say before she vomited all over him.

CHAPTER : 16

Morris's first-class seat on Japan Airlines was reclined all the way back, but he still couldn't get comfortable. No matter how he sat, he felt as if he were pinching a nerve. He was a big guy, and the only chair he really liked was his oversize Barcalounger at home.

Glum, he rubbed the hole in his sleeve where one of his lucky cuff links should have been. He still couldn't seem to pinpoint when, exactly, he'd lost it, and it was driving him nuts. He should have known that losing it was a sign of more bad things to come, because everything had gone to shit afterward. The Okinawa deal had taken longer than normal to finalize, he hadn't been able to make love to his fiancée, and he'd had to listen to Sheila's painful confession about her sex addiction . . . which, as it turned out, wasn't even the worst of it.

She'd had an affair with her student. She'd cheated on him. It wasn't as if she were addicted to porn, or a compulsive masturbator. Yeah, he'd read all about those types, and he might have been able to handle something like that. But she'd had sex with another guy under his nose.

She had broken his heart.

Morris pushed the call button above his head. In an instant, a pixie-faced flight attendant appeared.

"Everything okay, sir?"

Her English was flawless and he wondered where she'd gone to school. Morris had been out of Texas for more than ten years and his damned accent was still as strong as ever.

"Suki, my back's killin' me. Do you have any ibuprofen?"

"Certainly. I'll be right back."

In a flash, she returned with a two-pack of Extra Strength Advil and a minibottle of Aquafina. Morris accepted the painkillers, but shook his head at the water.

"Bloody Caesar, please, Suki," he said, holding out his glass, which was still red from the other Bloody Caesar he'd just downed. He'd already had two.

The flight attendant's lovely Asian features showed concern. "I don't think it's a good idea to drink if you're taking—"

Morris held up a beefy hand. "I'll be fine, darlin'."

Suki looked doubtful but didn't argue. They never did in first class.

Morris leaned back and tried to get comfortable. His seatmate, a small Japanese man, was curled against the window and snoring softly. They'd chatted earlier and the man told him he'd been married for almost thirty years. Morris had shaken his head in wonder—long-lasting marriages seemed almost as impossible as finding love in the first place.

Morris had loved Lenore, his first wife, but not the way he loved Sheila. He would never have married his college girlfriend if she hadn't gotten pregnant during their sophomore year at the University of Texas. Sure, they'd been dating for a year and it was somewhat steady, but, hell, Morris was gunning for the NFL. He was an All-American offensive lineman and had a promising career as a pro football player—the last thing he wanted was to settle down.

But he couldn't turn his back on Lenore and the baby. They'd had a quick civil ceremony, and four months later Randall was born.

Things were all right at first. Both their parents helped with the baby, and Morris was drafted by the Green Bay Packers after his junior year. Lenore was happy to get out of Texas. There were good times in those early days.

But barely two years later, the ligaments in his right knee were torn apart by a badly timed tackle in practice. Despite a year of rehab, his knee never fully recovered. At the age of twenty-three, his career in the NFL was over.

They moved back to Texas, where Lenore encouraged him to finish his degree in finance. After graduation, his father, a VP at LoneStar Capital, hired him. Morris liked the job well enough, but the resentment of losing his football life never went away. The death of his dream ate at him constantly, gnawing in his gut like a rat stuck in a cardboard box, and some days it took all his willpower just to get out of bed. Drinking was the only thing that dulled the bitterness.

Stephen was born two years later. The marriage was already in shambles, but that didn't stop their third son, Phillip, from arriving three years after that. By then, Morris was a full-blown alcoholic.

He managed to hide it, at least at work. He was hardworking and affable, and the bank's clients enjoyed his football stories and loud sense of humor. He moved up through the ranks with relative ease, thanks in part to his father.

But life at home was a different story. Morris was filled with an anger he couldn't control, and the drinking only made it worse. He was a distant, impatient father, and a harsh, resentful husband. The littlest thing would set him off. Every argument with Lenore seemed to end with something in the house—a vase, a stack of dishes, their framed wedding photo—being smashed to pieces.

Like many alcoholics, Morris refused to acknowledge he had a drinking problem. Lenore, codependent and terrified to raise three boys by herself, stuck it out despite the marriage being a farce. Eventually she found a support group, who made her realize she'd never change him and that she could, and would, survive without him.

They were both better off now, though Morris wouldn't exactly consider them friends. Lenore was still living in Texas, happily remarried to a lawyer who apparently hated football.

A few years after the divorce, Morris accepted a job at Bindle Brothers in Seattle, and he moved out of Texas for the second time in his life. The boys were finally out of high school and it seemed like a good time for a fresh start.

The job was satisfying, but it was lonely being in a new place. It was hard to meet women his age, and most of the guys at work were married. So he didn't have much of a social life. The pounds began to creep on—too much television, beer, and takeout. As he gained weight, his bad knee began to hurt again. Then the other knee began to creak. Exercise became torturous.

When he met Sheila, he was still in denial about his drinking. Even when it began to affect his work—so much so that he was told by Bob Bindle Jr., the managing partner of the investment bank, to start Alcoholics Anonymous or lose his job—he still thought it wasn't that big a deal.

It was Sheila Tao who gave him the kick in the ass he needed. He'd had a crush on her long before anything romantic happened between them, but the thought that something *might* happen if he cleaned up his act was enough to spur him on. A few weeks after meeting her, he joined AA.

When he'd completed all twelve steps a year later, Sheila was the first person he called. By then he was completely in love with her and determined to win her heart. He was over the moon to discover she felt the same way. When he kissed her for the first time, just before midnight at the end of their first date, holding the bag with the goldfish he'd won for her, he'd felt sixteen again. They'd been inseparable ever since . . . she was his whole world.

As clichéd as it was, Morris was a better man because of her.

His Bloody Caesar arrived. Before he even took the first sip, he asked Suki to bring him another. He ignored the look on the flight attendant's face—yes, he was sure he wanted it, and, no, he didn't need a lecture.

He'd never had a problem making decisions. But he did have a problem with quitting.

Halfway through his fifth drink, Morris made up his mind. He was going to stay with Sheila. He would marry her on Saturday, as planned. They could work everything out after the wedding. Every addict deserved a second chance, and he was damn well going to bet on her the way she'd bet on him. He was in it for the long haul.

But goddammit if he wasn't gonna get good and drunk first.

CHAPTER : 17

Sheila's wrists and ankles burned from the handcuffs. After three days of being chained to the bed, her skin was raw, her back and shoulders ached, and she was constantly disoriented from whatever sedative Ethan was mixing into her water.

He'd left the TV on, tuned to a channel that played old sitcoms. Sheila couldn't stay awake long enough to watch an entire episode of anything, so she stared up at the white ceiling instead. Her greasy hair was sticking to her cheeks and forehead in itchy clumps she couldn't swipe away. Her teeth—unbrushed since she'd been here—felt coated in wet cotton. She tried not to think about her full bladder. The adult diaper Ethan was making her wear was dry because she refused to pee in it.

She wiggled the fingers on her left hand to keep the blood flowing. Her engagement ring was gone. She knew Ethan had taken it and wondered abstractly if he was planning to pawn it or keep it as a trophy of some sort. She'd never ask him. Her questions aggravated him. He'd talk when he was ready.

The room was large and sterile, with a ceiling that appeared to stretch up forever. From her position on the bed, she couldn't see any windows or doors, though a vent directly above her head funneled in fresh air. The only light in the room came from the overhead lights, which Ethan kept dimmed. A bottle of water and the remote control for the television sat on the bedside table next to her, but she couldn't quite reach either. Against the wall across from her was a brown leather sofa where Ethan usually sat when he came to feed her. He never stayed long.

Sheila decided it was good he was keeping her tired. It helped pass the time. If not for the sedatives, the hours would have been agonizing. She didn't have an appetite so she couldn't eat much, though she did try. It angered him if she didn't at least take a few bites—it was as if he thought her rude for not eating the food he brought.

So far, unless the chafed wrists and ankles counted, Ethan hadn't hurt her. But she had no doubt he was going to. The anticipation of what was to come was the worst part of all.

Sheila considered herself to be a pretty good judge of character—most psychologists were—so how was it possible she'd been involved with Ethan sexually for three months without having the slightest clue as to who he really was? Never in her wildest, darkest dreams could she have envisioned she'd be locked up here, that any of this could happen. She and Marianne had pegged Ethan as a sociopath, yes, and blackmail had come as naturally to him as breathing . . . but kidnapping and murder?

Diana St. Clair's face flitted through her mind. Ethan had killed the beautiful young woman—Sheila was certain of this now. To think, the comparison to Ted Bundy hadn't been so absurd after all.

A door slammed from somewhere on the other side of the wall, jolting her. She whimpered as her wrists rubbed painfully against the cuffs once again.

Footsteps approached, and every muscle in her body tensed.

"How are we doing today?" Ethan's head popped into view. "Miss me?"

Just the sight of him filled her with fear. But there was no point in screaming—the room was soundproofed and her shrieks were absorbed into the walls.

"I have to use the bathroom." Her voice was hoarse. She cleared her throat, but didn't ask for water. She wanted to keep a clear head long enough to try to talk to him. "I really have to go."

"So go."

She couldn't. Not in front of him. Not in a diaper. It was too humiliating. She'd have to wait and let it happen in her sleep, as she had the last couple of times, so he could change it while she slept.

He smiled. It was the first time she'd seen him smile in the past couple of days. Something had shifted.

"Can I ask you a question?" she said.

"That in itself is a question."

Sarcasm. Decidedly normal for him. He was in a better mood. A good sign.

"How come you're not claustrophobic in this room? No natural light, no windows. Why aren't you a basket case?"

Ethan snorted. "That's what you've been lying here thinking about?"

"Yes." It wasn't, but she needed to get him talking.

Ethan looked around the sterile room and shrugged. "I'm home."

Home. This huge white room with no windows was home? But of course she knew that all phobias stemmed from fear— fear of losing control. And Ethan was in complete control here.

He would decide if she lived or died. It was a terrible thought.

"You can change the channel on the TV, you know." He frowned at the flickering screen. "You don't have to watch re-runs all day."

Maybe it was the banality of his words, or the casual tone of his voice, or the sedative that had worn off, but something inside her snapped. "I can't reach the remote, you piece of shit."

He smiled. "Aren't we in a winning mood?"

"Fuck you." She sounded like a petulant teenager, but she didn't care.

He chuckled and reached toward the bedside table. "Here," he said, putting the remote control directly into her cuffed hand. "Now you can watch whatever you want. CNN is channel forty-four. Didn't you once tell me you had a crush on Anderson Cooper? Hey, do you think I'll look like him when I'm his age?"

Sheila opened her fingers and the remote control slipped to the floor, landing soundlessly on the industrial carpet. She spoke slowly, enunciating every word. "News. Flash. You. Are. A. Fucking. Psychopath."

Ethan's face went still. "Watch yourself," he said, staring at her.

A chill went up her spine. He maintained eye contact for a few seconds as she held her breath.

"Okay, time to make some calls," Ethan said, oddly cheerful. He pulled her BlackBerry out of his pants pocket.

Sheila let out a breath at the sudden change of direction. "It won't work," she said, staring at her small black phone with sudden longing. "The battery was already low on Thursday night at the meeting."

Ethan smiled, pressing the button on the phone to turn it on. "Don't you worry your pretty little head about that. It's got enough juice, and we'll only keep it on for a minute or two. Don't want anybody trying to triangulate your signal."

"So you do realize people are looking for me?" The desperation in her voice overpowered the confidence she was trying to fake. "Which means you know this is stupid. Have you thought about this at all? It's Sunday, and I've been here for three days. Everybody knows I'm missing by now."

"Aren't we arrogant," he said without looking up. His thumb moved across the trackpad as he scrolled through her data. "I'm sorry to inform you, my dear, but nobody is looking for you. You weren't scheduled to work Friday, and Morris has been away in Japan. You're not much of a social butterfly, so I doubt you missed any parties. And you have no living family. Ergo, if someone has indeed called you, it hasn't been long enough for them to think anything's wrong." He chuckled again. "Sorry to burst your bubble."

"You son of a bitch."

He looked up, his gray eyes cold. "I'm not going to tell you again. Easy with the names. Why do you want to piss me off? I'm in a good mood today." He found what he was looking for and held up the phone so she could see the screen. "Morris's home number. You're going to call him and leave a detailed message on his answering machine. Then you're going to call Dean Simmons at the university."

"What?"

"We don't want people to worry, do we?" He waved the phone in her face. "I checked your schedule. You have an appointment today at the Fairmont with the wedding planner. But you're having lunch with your fat fuck of a fiancé first. Thank you for being so detailed in your appointment calendar, by the way. And as a matter of fact," he said, checking the time on the phone, "it appears you're running late. Morris is there waiting for you right now, no doubt starving even though his body fat alone could sustain a small African tribe. So you're going to give him a call at home—where's he's not—and leave a message there. Don't you fret about finding the right words. I'll tell you exactly what to say. We'll rehearse it first."

Sheila stared at him in disbelief. "No way. I'm not doing it." She shook her head. "I'll scream. I'll tell him to call the police."

Ethan sighed. "I was afraid of that. I see a little incentive is necessary."

He set the phone down on the sofa and disappeared behind the wall. Sheila guessed another room was there and wondered how big this place was. She heard a faint beeping sound—was he punching numbers into a keypad?

Her BlackBerry lay on the sofa just a few feet away. She couldn't take her eyes off it—she'd never wanted anything so badly. But there was no way to reach it. The bastard had left it there to taunt her.

He was back a moment later with two items and a cocky swagger.

"Gun to your head, or knife to your throat?" Ethan's tone was boisterous, his eyes full of mischief.

He held up one, then the other, letting her get a good look at both. The knife was slim, a surgeon's blade. The gun was small and silver.

They were equally horrifying.

Ethan smiled. "I'll let you pick. Though personally, I'd go with the gun. The knife's super sharp, and I wouldn't want to slice you by accident."

Sheila opened her mouth to speak, but all that came out was another whimper.

Ethan sat on the edge of the bed. "Now, I want you to listen carefully because I'm going to tell you exactly what you need to say. If you do it right, I'll let you live a little while longer." His laughter sounded completely genuine. He was enjoying every second of this. "I know, right? You're never getting out of here anyway, so why should you make the call?"

Sticking the gun in the waistband of his pants, he moved closer with the knife outstretched until the delicate point rested against the spot just above her carotid artery. "Because if you don't," he said, answering his own question, "I won't just kill you. I'll kill Morris, too. *Capiche?*"

The point of the knife dug into the thin skin at Sheila's throat. She froze.

"Want to see something else?" Ethan changed gears yet again. He tossed the knife onto the sofa and Sheila slumped, her body a rag doll of relief.

Reaching into his pocket, he pulled out something small and shiny. He held it until it was just inches from her face inside his upturned palm. Sheila recognized it instantly. Her stomach did a somersault.

"Do you know what this is?" he asked.

Of course she did. It was Morris's cuff link. The one he thought he'd lost, the Christmas gift from his sons. There was no mistaking it.

"Yes," she said, choking.

"I thought you would." Ethan looked satisfied. "I'll leave it here, on top of the TV, where you can look at it. Hopefully it will serve as a reminder that if you try and fuck with me, you and your fat fuck of a fiancé will die. Painfully."

He leaned in close, and she could smell his cinnamon breath. "Because this is how close I've been to him, Sheila. *I took it right off his fucking wrist, Sheila.*"

The thought of his being so close to Morris made her want to throw up.

Ethan smiled. "So, do we have an understanding?"

She nodded.

"Good. Now pay attention. Here's what I want you to say."

CHAPTER: 18

She was running late. Or she wasn't coming. Morris didn't know what to think.

He was standing in the plush, formally decorated Garden Room of the Fairmont Olympic Hotel, BlackBerry in hand. He'd tried calling Sheila three times, and all three times it had gone to voice mail. She'd missed lunch and it was now thirty minutes past their scheduled appointment time.

He was starting to worry. She was never late. That was *his* flaw.

Beside him stood Carmen Khan, the hotel's assistant director of catering and events, also known as the wedding planner. Though her demeanor was pleasant, he knew the woman was annoyed because she'd checked her watch four times in the last ten minutes.

Morris had only been in the Garden Room once before, and it was grander and more elegant than he remembered. The room was filled with natural light. The thirty-foot-high Palladian windows offered breathtaking views of downtown Seattle, but it still felt warm and inviting. White table linens offset the luxuriously patterned teal carpet, and the tropical trees that framed the windows added a lush and exotic ambience. As usual, Sheila's taste was impeccable.

He faked a smile as the woman checked her watch one more time. "I'm really sorry about this, Ms. Khan. She's never late. I can only guess that something held her up."

Carmen Khan returned his smile, but her shiny lips were pressed together too tightly for it to be genuine. "I understand, things happen. I'm available for another thirty minutes, but I do have another appointment at three. Did you want to try calling Dr. Tao again? Or do you want to go ahead and sign off on the preparations? There are only a few minor things left to be decided, and I'm sure between the two of us we can handle it. Worse comes to worst, she can call me tomorrow and make changes."

Morris didn't know what to do. Sheila had planned everything and he had no idea what she wanted or didn't want. Other than the fittings for his tuxedo, he'd been content to sign the checks and let her do all the work.

"I'll try her again," he said. "Though I don't think her phone's even on."

"Would she have left a message with you somewhere else?" The woman's tone was polite, but her unnatural smile remained.

"I'm not usually at the office on Sundays." Morris thought for a moment. "But I suppose it's possible."

Carmen Khan stifled a sigh. "Well, I have to make a call myself anyhow. Why don't I meet you back here in five minutes? If you can't reach her, I suppose we could reschedule for Tuesday, though that really is cutting it close."

Morris agreed, and Ms. Khan walked away briskly. When she was out of sight, he pressed speed dial number two on his phone to call Sheila's BlackBerry. But just as the previous three tries, it went straight to voice mail. He had no choice but to leave another message.

"Honey, it's me again. It's two thirty-three now. The wedding woman is getting pissy. She's got a stick up her ass something awful, and I'm scared she's gonna combust if you don't get here soon. We can reschedule for Tuesday, so if I don't hear from you in the next five minutes, that's what I'm gonna do. Call me." He hesitated, then added, "I love you. If you're scared to see me, don't be. We're gonna be okay."

He paced the room with his phone clutched in his fist, willing it to ring. It didn't. He called her house one more time, then checked his voice mail at the bank. Nothing.

He saw Carmen Khan striding toward him and decided he might as well make one last call to his own house. Maybe there'd be something on his answering machine there. Not likely, because Sheila knew he'd be here at the Fairmont, but it was worth a shot.

It took a second to remember what buttons to push. He was surprised to find there were two messages. The first was from Pietro, the Italian tailor, letting him know his suit was ready.

As it turned out, the second message was from Sheila. It was time-stamped—she'd left it ten minutes ago. Morris breathed a sigh of relief at the sound of her voice. She'd probably pressed the wrong speed-dial button on her BlackBerry. But his relief evaporated instantly when he realized she was crying, sobbing so hard he could barely understand her.

"Morris. It's me. I . . . I'm so sorry. I'm not coming. You and I both know this marriage would be a huge mistake."

Morris stopped breathing. Had he heard her right? There was a long pause before she continued.

"We both know I need to get help. There's a treatment center I can go to. It's out of state, and I'll be gone for a couple of months. Or longer, I'm not sure. Morris, I might not come back to Seattle. I need you to . . . cancel the wedding. I'm sorry to leave it to you, but I just can't bear to deal with it right now."

Another crackling pause. Where the hell was she calling from, a cave? Morris's heart was beating so hard he felt dizzy.

"In time I hope you can . . . forgive me." She was full out sobbing by this point. "I'm taking a leave of absence from the university. Please don't follow me or look for me. Respect my decision. If you ever loved me, you'll let me go and move on with your life. I'm sorry, Morris. Take care of yourself."

Her last words were barely a whisper and he could hardly hear them over the blood pulsing in his temples. He couldn't have heard her right. He replayed the message again, unable to process that she was, indeed, leaving him.

"Everything okay, Mr. Gardener?" Carmen Khan said at his elbow. Her face was a picture of concern, but her dark, perfectly made-up eyes revealed her impatience.

Morris turned to face the woman, scarcely able to believe the words he was about to say.

"The wedding's off," he said hoarsely. "It's canceled."

The wedding planner's eyes widened in alarm. "I—I'm sorry to hear that. Are you certain?" She placed a hand on his arm.

Morris moved away from her. He didn't want to be touched. "Truth be told, I'm not sure." He felt deranged. "We're having . . . problems." He couldn't think of how else to phrase it.

Carmen stared at him a moment longer before consulting her clipboard. "The wedding's not till Saturday. We can sign off today assuming it's a go and give it a couple days." She hesitated. "The thing is, Mr. Gardener, everything's already been reserved. You've already paid the deposit for the room and the food, and it can't be refunded. Same goes for the DJ and the photographer. If there's any chance you two might . . ." She noticed Morris wasn't listening.

"Mr. Gardener." She touched his arm again.

He jerked his arm away and looked down at her. She instinctively stepped back.

"Mr. Gardener, if you cancel the wedding today, you'll lose a lot of money. I don't know if you realize how much—"

"Cancel it."

"But I really think—"

"Cancel it."

Carmen Khan pressed her clipboard to her chest and nodded. "I'm very sorry."

Morris watched her walk away, her four-inch heels soundless on the thick carpet. "So am I," he said quietly to no one.

CHAPTER : 19

Something was around her neck that hadn't been there when she'd fallen asleep. Reflexively, Sheila pawed at it.

"Easy," Ethan said. "You'll break it."

She opened her eyes. Ethan was sitting on the edge of the bed, blocking her view of the TV, but she could hear Anderson Cooper's voice recounting the day's top stories. She had no idea how long Ethan had been here. Her captor was watching her, a thoughtful expression on his face.

Her head groggy, Sheila touched her neck again, rattling her chains. He'd put some kind of necklace on her while she was sleeping, and she pulled it away from her so she could see it better. It took a few seconds for her vision to clear, and when it did, she saw a silver amulet on a leather string. Engraved on it were symbols she didn't recognize.

"It's Apache," he said. "From New Mexico. Something to ward off evil spirits. I got it from a friend."

She stared at him through her brain fog. "Are you being ironic?"

"It doesn't quite match the diamond bracelet Morris gave you," Ethan said, his voice sly. "But it looks good on you still."

He was thinking about the tennis bracelet Morris had given her? Why in the world would he be thinking about that? The bracelet was at home, locked up in the small vault in her bedroom closet, safe and sound. Unlike her engagement ring. She was still too scared to ask what he'd done with it.

Her bare legs felt cold. He'd taken her jeans off a couple of days before, and all she was wearing was her sweater, stained and rank from her own body odor and covered in dried particles of food. As if sensing her discomfort, Ethan pulled the blanket over her legs. He looked tired. His eyes were rimmed with red, and new lines were on his forehead and around his mouth. A small red pimple on his cheek marred his complexion, and he'd cut himself shaving.

It confused her. If he'd kidnapped women before—and of course he had, this entire room was built for it—then what was he stressing about?

She needed him to talk to her. She had so many questions and they were gnawing at her the same way the steel handcuffs were eating into her wrists.

"So. What's going on at the university?" Sheila's tone was casual. She could have been asking what movies were coming out next weekend, or whether it was cold outside. "Have they replaced me?"

"Not permanently. Dean Simmons sent out a department-wide memo the Monday after you left him the voice mail. It said you were taking an indefinite leave of absence due to stress, just as you told him in your message. But there are some weird rumors floating around." There was a smirk on Ethan's face. "Rumors that you're going to rehab for sex addiction. Heard it from the dean's secretary herself, the gossipy little twat."

Sheila stopped breathing. "That's not possible. How could she know? Nobody could know, unless you . . ." She saw the glint in Ethan's eyes. He was messing with her. "You asshole."

His laugh was cruel. "I'm amazed you'd even care."

She did care. It might seem trivial to worry about her reputation, but she didn't want to die with people knowing her secret. It was the absolute last way she wanted to be remembered. She blinked back tears, not wanting to show weakness around him.

At least he was talking. That was the important thing.

He smiled. "Nobody's looking for you, if that's what you're wondering. Nobody's even talking about you."

"Why are you doing this?" she said softly. "Ethan, talk to me. Whatever it is you're going through, whatever's caused you to do this, I can help. You know I can. There's still time to fix this."

She had tried this tactic several times over the past few days, using her best psychologist voice to varying degrees of failure. Individual therapy wasn't Sheila's specialty and she was running out of ideas.

Ethan looked away, his jaw tightening. Then he stood up and began pacing the room.

She had agitated him with her question. She watched him pace, waiting. When he slowed down, that would be the time to ask another question.

His pace slowed, and she pounced.

"Have you thought about the consequences of this?" she asked.

Ethan didn't quite break stride, but he did glance her way.

"Like after I'm dead, what will you do with my body? You can't just get rid of a dead body, Ethan. There are a million ways to get caught."

He looked surprised at the question, one she hadn't asked before. "You don't think I have a plan? I'm very good at what I do."

"I believe you." She did believe him. She'd been here for days, which wasn't a feat any amateur could pull off. "I just want to know what you're thinking. Do you have impulses? Urges? Do you hear voices?" He didn't reply, so she tried again. "Are you acting out a revenge fantasy? Do I fit some kind of . . . profile? Were you abused as a child?"

Ethan's eyes glinted with amusement. "What else? Any more theories?"

Her mind working fast, Sheila said, "Do you care about me at all anymore?"

He looked away again.

She'd touched a nerve. She leaned forward, her chains clanking against the side of the bed. "If you care about me, you wouldn't do this to me. You'd let me go. It's the right thing to do, and you're a decent person—"

"Don't talk to me like I'm a nut job." He turned back to her, glaring. "You don't think I know what I'm doing? If I let you go, I get arrested. I go to jail. For life."

So he understood that his actions had consequences. He didn't want to get caught. Which meant he wasn't completely psychopathic. He knew there were rules.

"Bet you'd like that, wouldn't you?" His tone was scathing. "I'm sure you'd love to see me locked in a tiny little cell, away from civilization. Wouldn't you just love to get me out of the way, so you can go and live your happy little life with Morris?"

Morris again. Sheila watched his jaw work in anger. Such irony in his words, considering he'd locked *her* away from civilization. "I'm sorry I implied that, Ethan. I don't believe you should be locked away." The lie almost stuck in her throat. "I'm just scared. You can understand that, can't you? And if it makes you feel any better, Morris knows everything. I told him about my sex addiction, and the affair. There won't be any happy little life, even if you do let me go."

Ethan looked genuinely surprised. He hadn't expected that. "Yeah, but you had an appointment to finalize wedding plans. He was still going to marry you."

"I don't know if the wedding would have happened." She was being truthful now. "He was so disgusted. It would be a miracle if he forgave me."

"Did you tell him it was me?"

"Of course not. I didn't want him to be able to picture it. I've already ruined everything."

Ethan's jaw finally relaxed. "I'd tell you I'm sorry, but I'm not. The thought of you and him together—" He turned his head away again.

Sheila stared at him, incredulous. She waited a moment but he didn't continue. "Ethan, you don't want me to be with him? Is that what this is about?" She tried to process this new revelation. "I'm here because you're *jealous*?"

He pulled something small and silver from the back waistband of his jeans and walked toward her. It was the gun. She flinched at the sight of it. She hadn't realized that he'd been armed this whole time. Her wrists burned as she reflexively strained against the cuffs.

He frowned at her reaction. "Relax. I'm just taking it out so you don't try anything stupid. You want answers, right?"

She nodded, afraid where this was going. "Yes."

Ethan clicked the gun. "There. I just took the safety off. This gun has a particularly sensitive trigger. I'm going to uncuff one of your hands, so I suggest you don't do anything to make me shake or jerk."

"I'm not stupid."

"No, but you're desperate." Ethan leaned in toward her,

his face only inches from hers. "I'll tell you what you want to know. Hell, I'll *show* you. But to do that, I'm going to have to take the handcuffs off. Don't do anything stupid. I won't think twice about shooting you in the face." His cinnamon breath wafted over her. To think she'd once found that alluring. Now it made her nauseous. "Do you believe me, Sheila?"

She nodded. He put the gun to her temple gently. The cold steel felt like fire.

"This is how we're going to do it. I'm going to unlock your right hand first. Don't move until I tell you. You do, and your brains will be splattered all over Anderson Cooper's pretty face. Still with me?"

She was afraid to nod under the pressure of the gun, so she simply said, "Yes."

"If you're good, I might even let you take a bath and brush your teeth. Wouldn't that be nice?"

There was a *bathroom* here? Then why the fuck was she in this diaper?

"Now where was I?" Ethan said. "Oh, right. After I uncuff your hand, you can do the other one, then you can do your legs. Once that's done, we'll walk over to the next room, and I'll show you what it is you're so eager to know. *Capiche?*"

"*Capiche.*" She was beginning to wonder whether she even wanted to see what was in the next room, but she sure as hell wanted to get out of this awful bed.

He pulled a key out of his jacket pocket, the gun never leaving her forehead. Leaning over her, he unlocked the cuff of her right hand. She could smell the cologne he always wore and couldn't stop herself from shuddering.

Was it really only a few weeks ago she'd had fantasies about being draped in his scent?

"Take the key," Ethan said. "Move slowly. No sudden movements."

"As if I could overpower you."

"The gun keeps you from trying. Which makes it easier for both of us." He held out the key. "This ain't my first time at the rodeo."

It was something Morris would have said.

She took the key from him with an arm that was practically numb. Her shoulder muscles screamed when she moved her left arm toward her right. She bit her lip in pain.

"I guess I could give you longer chains." Ethan had a funny expression on his face. He looked almost sympathetic.

"How about no chains?" Sheila wanted to cry. "It's not as if I can beat you up."

She finally got her left hand free, then attempted to bend forward to her ankles. Every muscle and nerve in her back was instantly on fire.

"Does it hurt?" His concern seemed genuine. "Your back?"

"Yes," she said through gritted teeth.

"Take your time, then. After you've unlocked yourself, I'll let you stand up. You can stretch, get the blood flowing. It's about time we did this, anyway."

She managed to get her ankles free, sweating from the exertion. He offered her his hand, and she moved her bare legs carefully over the edge of the bed so her feet dangled.

Taking a deep breath, she stood. A million burning needles flooded through her body. In desperation, she gripped Ethan's arm for support.

"Take your time," he said again.

After what seemed like a lifetime, relief set in. She put her arms over her head and stretched. The bones in her back cracked and the sound was like microwave popcorn.

"Better?"

"A little." She had never before despised another human being this way in her life.

"Walk over there." He pointed to the far wall she'd spent almost every waking hour staring at. A doorway was to the left, but no door. "Remember, you move funny and I'll have no choice but to blow your head off."

The gun looked too small to blow anyone's head off, but she wasn't going to argue semantics with a murderer. She didn't doubt the little gun could punch a nice, neat hole in her skull, the bullet bouncing around, shredding the very essence of who she was into pulp.

She shuffled toward the wall, feeling the blood rush through her legs and feet. The pain was finally subsiding and it felt good to move. They passed through the doorway, and she wasn't entirely surprised to find a long corridor behind it.

She couldn't believe how large this place was. She'd come to assume she was in a basement, but now that she was getting a better idea of the size, it seemed too big for that. The house above them would have to be huge. Maybe a warehouse of some sort?

Two doors were at the end of the corridor, one with a keypad bolted beside it, and one without. Sheila wondered if the door without the keypad was the bathroom.

"Stop," Ethan commanded. With the gun trained on her head, he reached past her and punched a code into the keypad. His arm was in the way and she couldn't tell what he'd entered. After a short beep, the door popped open.

"Go on," he said, nudging her lower back. "Go see. Everything you wanted to know is inside."

Sheila shuffled forward.

The room was dark and Ethan reached past her again. The lights came on suddenly, glaringly. It took her a moment to focus on what she was looking at. Even then, she didn't know what to make of it.

It was a room wrapped entirely in plastic.

She blinked, trying to take it all in. The space was large, approximately twenty by twenty feet, about the same size as the area where her bed was. In the middle sat a folding table resembling something a traveling massage therapist would tote, only it was wrapped snugly in some kind of cellophane. The walls were also covered in plastic and, through the transparency, she could see stained concrete cinder blocks underneath.

Against the wall to the right, a six-foot-tall stainless steel cabinet showcased a bevy of weaponry. It was mostly guns and knives, but she could also see a small ax, an ice pick, and a sledgehammer. A large freezer sat beside it. Leaning against that was a chain saw, and a few feet away was something that looked like a mini-forklift.

Her bare feet felt cold, and she looked down. Unlike the wall, the cement floor was exposed and pristine. He followed her gaze.

"You're right, I have to remember to lay down fresh plastic." He sounded pleasant and matter-of-fact. "You can't get blood out of concrete."

Though she hadn't entirely processed what she was seeing, she felt faint. Her knees buckled and Ethan placed an arm around her waist to keep her steady.

"Welcome to my workroom." His lips were at her ear. "This is where I get rid of the mess."

Sheila tried to speak, but no words came.

"That's Marie." Ethan looked directly at the concrete wall. "Say hello, Marie."

Only two of them were in the room.

"Who's Marie?" Sheila whispered, dazed.

He took a few steps forward, gesturing with the gun for Sheila to follow. He stared at the wall, eye level. "If you look close enough, you can see part of her hand."

Sheila followed his gaze to the plastic covering the concrete. What the hell was he talking about?

Then, suddenly, like one of those 3-D stereogram pictures you had to stare at cross-eyed for the image to appear, she saw it.

A hand. Small, with long fingernails, clearly belonging to a woman. The fingertips jutted out about an inch from the concrete, brushing up against the plastic covering. The skin had a bluish tint.

With her eyes now knowing what to look for, the scene in front of her unfolded all at once.

She saw a foot. Several feet actually, spread out over the wall. Pink toenail polish. Gold toenail polish. Blue toenail polish.

A hand with short red fingernails. An elbow. A knee.

A swatch of brown hair.

It was a wall full of dead bodies.

"Guess the evil spirits thing doesn't work after all." Ethan's voice was detached.

She hadn't noticed that he was behind her once again.

"It didn't work for Marie, and you're wearing her amulet. Do you see them, Sheila?"

She managed to nod.

"You asked me if I was jealous. That, my darling, that isn't jealousy." She felt his hot breath on her cheek. "That's *rage*.

That's what I've been filled with every day, since the day you ended it with me." He pointed to the wall. "And *that,* my love, is what you have to look forward to."

His fingers touched her throat, and the last thing Sheila heard before she passed out was the sound of her own screaming.

Sheila was really gone.

She wasn't returning his calls. She wasn't at home. She wasn't at work. Morris had staked out every place he could think of and there was no sign of her. She had meant every word in that awful message she'd left.

He'd never gotten the chance to tell her what he'd decided. Or to wish her well. Or to say good-bye. Now she was out there somewhere, trying to get better, with no idea that he still loved her and wanted to make it work. She was all alone, probably terrified, and whatever she'd done, she didn't deserve that.

It was all his fault. If he hadn't been so goddamned judgmental . . .

He sat in his office, staring at a dark computer screen, his door shut tight. He was finally back at Bindle after taking a day off, but he couldn't seem to remember his user name or password to log on to his computer. All he could think about was the locked drawer in his desk where a brand-new bottle of Johnnie Walker Red was hiding. He'd sneaked it in that morning, which hadn't been too difficult—everybody was avoiding him thanks to Darcy's strict instructions to the staff not to mention the canceled wedding.

He could only imagine the rumors swirling around the office like a flu virus. After all, it wasn't every day that a senior partner got dumped a week before his own wedding. Hell, if this hadn't been his life, he'd be titillated by it, too.

His gaze shifted to the framed photograph sitting beside his computer. The picture had been taken the night he proposed, at the restaurant at the top of the Space Needle. Sheila in a low-cut black dress, red velvet lips, gorgeous and glowing; he in his favorite pin-striped suit and the tie Sheila had picked out.

He touched the glass. She looked beautiful and he looked happy.

Someone cleared a throat discreetly. Morris looked up to see Trevor Baker standing there, one of his many account managers. Goddammit, he'd forgotten to lock the door.

"Good morning, Trevor." His usually hearty voice sounded flat and deflated even to him. "What can I do for you?"

Trevor stood staring at his boss, not bothering to hide the shock on his angular face. It wasn't hard to guess what the younger man was thinking—Morris knew how he looked. He'd slept only two hours the night before, and his eyes were puffy and bloodshot, his face ruddy from too much whiskey. Oh, yeah. He knew exactly what he looked like. And he didn't give a shit.

Trevor eased his twig-thin frame into the office. His salmon shirt clashed with his coral tie, the combination too bright for Morris's dry eyes. The man's bony fingers clutched a thick manila folder.

"Sorry to bother you, sir, but I need your signature on these documents for the Glasgow account—"

"Leave the file with me."

"Thanks." Trevor placed the folder on the edge of Morris's desk, then hesitated.

"Anything else?"

The younger man shifted his weight. "Just, uh, wondering how you're doing."

Morris grunted and leaned back in his chair. Cracking his knuckles, he glared at his account manager, suddenly unable to think of a single reason why he'd hired the twerp in the first place. "Well, let's see. How do I *look,* Trevor?"

The younger man swallowed and backed away. "It's just . . . I met your fiancée at last year's Christmas party and she was so lovely, very down-to-earth. I honestly can't believe—"

"For God's sake, Trevor, she's not dead. She dumped me." Morris could see the spittle flying from his lips as he spoke. He kept his fingers firmly on the armrests of his chair so he wouldn't spring up and detach Trevor's pretty little head from his twiggy little body. "Thanks for your condolences, but if I'm not talking about it, why are you?"

Trevor opened his mouth to speak, then closed it again.

Morris stared him down. "Shut the door on your way out."

The account manager scurried out without another word.

Morris got up and locked his office door, then sat back down, not sure what to do next. He stared at the football that always sat on his desk, preserved in Lucite. Game ball from his last college game with the Longhorns. He wished it weren't boxed up in plastic—he wanted to hold it, squeeze it, smell the leather. Football used to be such a great outlet. He missed it almost as much as he missed Sheila.

Suddenly he felt her eyes on him. He turned back to the framed photo of the two of them. Restraining himself from hurling it against the wall, he instead shoved it into his top drawer, facedown.

It seemed like a real good time for the Red.

Unlocking his bottom cabinet, he poured a shot into the empty coffee mug. It went down like fire. He poured another, glancing at the clock. It was ten thirty in the morning. He poured one more.

It was gonna be a long day.

Feeling marginally better, at least for the meantime, he locked the bottle back up and turned to his computer. Mellowed from the booze, his password came back to him and he finally logged on.

Morris's e-mail program informed him that he had twenty-one new e-mails, not terrible for a Tuesday morning and a day off from work. Darcy was good about screening his messages. He scrolled through them quickly. There weren't any e-mails from Sheila. He hadn't expected any, but he was disappointed anyway.

An e-mail buried in the middle of the list caught his eye and he scrolled back up. It was from Brenda Walcott, a woman in Human Resources. The subject line read: *Tom Young.*

Oh, yeah. Tom Young. He'd forgotten all about his son Randall's old friend. They'd had dinner after the interview. Had that really only been a few weeks ago? It felt as if a decade had passed. Morris's eyebrows furrowed as he read Brenda's message.

Subject: Tom Young

Morris,

I got your e-mail last week about Tom Young applying for position #M-39003. I have not yet received his formal application. Just a reminder that the position closes Tuesday and interviews are next week if he's still interested.

Brenda

p.s. Sorry about your wedding.

Morris felt his face flush. Well, fuck, if the news had made it all the way to HR eight floors down, then clearly the entire company knew that he had been stood up at the altar. Humiliating.

He pushed away the mental picture of his colleagues whispering behind his back and forced himself to concentrate. At least now he had something to distract him.

What the hell *had* happened to Tom Young? He was surprised that the paperwork hadn't arrived—the kid had seemed bright. Morris had been impressed by him, had liked him because he'd made him feel one step closer to his estranged son.

He scrolled through his e-mails until he found the one Randall had sent him a few weeks before. Not giving himself a chance to chicken out this time, he hit REPLY and started typing.

Subject: Re: Favor

Dear Randall,

Hope this e-mail finds you well, wherever you are in the world. I was thrilled to hear from you, even if it was due to a business matter. I was going to respond earlier but I kept overanalyzing what I would say (you know me).

By the way, I gave your friend Tom a hearty recommendation. HR hasn't received his résumé yet, so would you remind him to send it in no later than tomorrow?

My home and office numbers are the same. Your old man would love to hear from you.

I miss you very much.

Love,
Dad

Morris hit SEND.

Exactly three minutes later, he received a reply. That was quick. Excited, he clicked on the new e-mail.

Subject: Re: Favor

We're sorry, but this e-mail is undeliverable for the following reason(s):

SENDER ADDRESS UNKNOWN.

than couldn't stop staring at the woman with the flaming-red hair.

He'd served her chicken and peas twenty minutes ago and hadn't been able to get her out of his mind since. Her disheveled appearance did nothing to minimize her beauty. Petite, with creamy skin and a spatter of freckles across her nose, she was distracting as hell. The irritated homeless man waiting for his chicken sighed impatiently. Ethan slopped a thigh and a drumstick onto his plate to get rid of him.

Ethan's groin stirred just watching her eat. He could only imagine what that fiery hair would feel like bunched up in his fists. If only he weren't so tired. Abby wasn't volunteering tonight, and it would be a shame not to take advantage of the opportunity. With Sheila locked away from the world and Abby at work . . .

Oh, the possibilities.

A small boy approached Ethan's station clutching a clean metal plate with dirty fingers. The kid's short hair was unevenly cut and there were hollows under his eyes. Stopping in front of the food, he held his plate out. His eyes wouldn't rest on Ethan's face longer than a second before darting away.

Ethan scooped up a chicken thigh and dropped it onto the kid's plate. Across the room, the redhead was picking something out of her teeth. She caught Ethan looking and blushed. Interesting. She couldn't have been homeless for long if she still cared about her table manners. The deep rose in her cheeks made her look prettier, sending a ripple of desire through Ethan's body.

The boy was still standing in front of him, so Ethan ladled up a portion of peas.

"Actually, could I just have some extra chicken instead?"

Ethan put the spoon down and eyed the kid in disapproval. Skinny, with big teeth that would need braces in another year or two, he looked as if he hadn't eaten in days. "Didn't your mother tell you beggars can't be choosers?"

The boy's ears colored. "My mom's dead, but thanks for the words of wisdom."

Ethan grinned. Spunky little shit. He couldn't have been older than ten, but it was hard to tell because he was skeletal under his stained sweatshirt and jeans. He might very well have been a malnourished twelve.

Ethan placed a chicken drumstick on the boy's plate. "That enough or you want more?"

"More, please." The boy's voice was quiet and he seemed to be thinking hard about what he was going to say next. Finally his chin jutted out. "And I'm not a beggar. The food is free for anyone who's hungry. At least that's what your sign says out front."

"Does it, now?" Ethan said, amused. He gave the kid two more drumsticks. Reaching over to the other station, he grabbed a plastic cup full of cherry Jell-O. "Here, dessert. So what's your name?"

"Why do you want to know?"

"Just making conversation. Don't get your panties in a twist."

"Is that another old-man saying?"

Ethan couldn't help but laugh. "Yeah, it is, wise guy. And my name's Ethan."

"Ben," the kid said finally. "The chicken's for my dad. He didn't want to come up and ask for a second helping." Ben pointed to a table where a man who looked old enough to be his grandfather was sitting. He was slumped in the chair. His deeply lined face was haggard and his cheeks sagged where there'd once been fat to fill them out. "We're on our way to Alaska."

"Yeah? What the hell for?" Ethan wasn't particularly interested, but the dinner rush had passed and the kid was cool. Also, the redhead was watching them, smiling. Ethan stood up straighter and looked at Ben, continuing to keep one eye on her.

"My dad got a job on a fishing boat." The boy looked glum. "We have to go because he lost his job and he says we have to go where the money is. But I don't want to. Our room will be, like, the size of a closet. And I heard that it's dark all the time in the winter. I saw that movie, *30 Days of Night*? All these vampires came out and killed everybody."

"Good movie, though, wasn't it?" Ethan said. The redhead had finished eating and was looking around for a spot to leave her tray. "Here, Ben, take another Jell-O."

"Thanks. So, do you think it's true?"

"Do I think what's true?"

The redhead had stacked her tray on the table with the others and was buttoning up her sweater. It was impossible not to notice her breasts. High and firm.

"About the thirty days of night," Ben said, exasperated.

"Oh, yeah, that's true. Absolutely." The redhead was near the door. Shit. *Don't leave yet.*

"For real?" The boy's eyes were round. "I thought it was just a movie!"

"Yeah, but don't worry about it," Ethan said, his mind in two places at once. "All you need to do is get one of those laser pointers. You know the kind you get on a key chain from the dollar store? You just flash it at the vampires' eyes. It blinds them."

"For real? That works?"

"Little-known secret. And if they can't see you, no way they can catch you."

"Awesome." Ben grinned. "Thanks, Ethan."

"Anytime. Now go eat."

The redhead was gone.

Next time, then. Probably best not to complicate things, anyway. Sheila was enough for now.

Ethan watched as the boy passed the older man his plate of chicken and got a halfhearted hair ruffle in return.

Ethan wondered briefly what would become of them in Alaska and knew he'd never find out. Maybe they'd be okay, maybe they wouldn't. People passed through St. Mary's all the time. But at least father and son had each other, which was more than Ethan had ever had. His old man had split when he was five, leaving him alone with his crazy bitch of a mother.

On the surface, a really sweet woman, and he'd loved her. Until she tried to kill him on his tenth birthday.

: : : :

At first, he hadn't minded being locked in the closet. In the darkness of the closet, with its narrow walls and the smell of mothballs, there was comfort.

Ever since Dad had gone away, Mom had become forgetful

and easily frazzled. She couldn't work, so she had boyfriends instead. Lots of boyfriends. And when one of them visited, Ethan would be locked away in the closet. Grown men didn't like little boys hanging around.

The closet was in Mom's bedroom. It had a little keyhole that he could peek through. At first, he felt guilty watching her with them, seeing the things she'd let the men do to her. The handcuffs, the straps, the different positions. Eventually he came to understand that she must not mind his watching. After all, she could have sent him to the park. Or to the mall with ten bucks for a movie. But, no, she chose to put him in the closet, where he could see everything. . . .

So he watched.

But, sometimes, she'd forget about him. One time, he'd been cooped up for thirteen hours. She'd forgotten about him and had gone downstairs to the living room to watch television, where she'd fallen asleep until the next morning.

He hoped he wouldn't be stuck here that long tonight. It was his birthday, and he really wanted to open his presents. He really wanted some birthday cake.

Unfortunately, Michael was coming over. Michael was his Mom's favorite boyfriend. Even though Michael knew today was a special day, he'd insisted on seeing Ethan's mother anyway. So Ethan was put in the closet, his birthday celebration on hold until they were done.

He hated Michael. He hated all these men because they came into his house and took his mother away from him and did things to her he couldn't.

Tonight her bedroom was filled with candles. They were everywhere, on the dresser, on the window ledges, on the nightstands. Mom said candlelight made women look more beautiful.

And she did look beautiful. The sex thing went on for a few hours, maybe longer. Ethan had finally fallen asleep, his head pressed against one of his mother's long winter coats.

It was the smell of smoke that woke him.

In the dark, he sat up straight, confused at first by the intense but unmistakable odor, his nostrils working like a rabbit's. He felt the closet door.

It was hot. Very hot.

Panic washed over him like a rogue wave. He looked through the keyhole. His mother's bedroom was awash in bright orange flames. He scrambled to his feet, pounding on the door, screams pouring out of him.

"Mom! Mom! Mom!"

Nobody answered. The closet was locked as it always was. The house was burning down, and she had locked him in a closet.

He was trapped.

: : : :

"Bye, Ethan."

He looked up to see Ben waving at him from a few feet away. He waved back. "See you, buddy. Best of luck." He forced himself to sound enthusiastic. "Remember what I told you about the laser," he added, and nodded to the boy's father.

Ben grinned. "I will. Anything else I should know?"

Ethan smiled. "Yeah. Don't get locked in any closets."

CHAPTER : 22

Morris missed Sheila the most in the evenings.

On a night like tonight, with the television tuned to CNN, it was hard not to see her sitting in her usual spot near the fireplace, her small feet curled under her, marking papers or skimming a magazine while keeping her ears pricked toward the TV.

Morris sat in his leather Barcalounger, his tired feet stuck in the wool house slippers he'd had for ten years. His whiskey— not the blended Johnnie Walker Red but a more expensive single-malt Macallan—sat beside him on the side table. Remnants of cold pizza were hardening on the plate next to the bottle.

He'd fallen off the wagon all the way. Back to drinking, back to junk food. So much for all the weight he'd lost last year. Not that it made much of a difference. Losing forty pounds on a body his size was like brushing a long-haired cat—some fur might come out, but there was still a whole lot more where that came from.

The phone rang, disrupting his gloom. At first he thought it was the television; it took him a second to realize it was his home phone line. Hardly anybody ever called him at home anymore save for telemarketers and a couple of golf acquaintances.

He checked the number on the call display. Private name,

Seattle number. Likely a telemarketer. Should he even bother? Then again, it might be Sheila.

He picked up on the fifth ring. "Hello."

"May I speak with Sheila Tao, please." The woman's voice was crisp and unfamiliar.

Morris muted the TV. "Who's calling?"

"It's Dr. Chang, her therapist. Am I speaking with Morris?"

"Yes." He was totally caught off guard, and it took him a second to find his voice again. "I'm sorry, I didn't know Sheila had a therapist."

There was a pause on the other line. "She listed you as her emergency contact. I normally wouldn't phone, but she missed her last appointment and hasn't returned my calls. Would you put her on the phone, please?"

"She's not here." Morris rubbed his head, trying to process that his psychologist fiancée had been in therapy. Another thing she hadn't mentioned.

"Would you tell her to call me?" The woman's tone was careful. "I need to know she's all right."

"I . . ." Morris was confused. "Can't *you* call her? She went to the treatment facility."

"I'm sorry?"

Maybe he'd had too much whiskey. He rubbed his head again. "What did you say your name was?"

"Marianne Chang."

He finally placed her name. "You were invited to our wedding. I didn't realize you two were—"

"Yes." The woman paused. "I received the note about the cancellation your assistant sent."

"If you're her therapist, you must know what happened. She called off the wedding. Over voice mail. I haven't heard from her since Sunday."

There was a long silence on the other end. Finally Dr. Chang spoke. "What else can you tell me?"

Morris shrugged even though he was alone in the room. "Well, she's taken leave from her job. She said she was going to some treatment center for two months, and she might not come back to Seattle." He stopped. "But shouldn't you know this already?"

Dr. Chang didn't respond.

"Listen, I think . . ." His voice finally cracked. "I think I'm the reason she left. She finally told me about her sex addiction. I reacted badly."

"I see." Dr. Chang's voice was carefully neutral.

He stood up and started pacing. "I'm probably not supposed to ask, but did she give you any indication she was planning to do this?" He sounded desperate and hated it, but he couldn't help himself.

"I can't speak about what Sheila and I discussed, Morris. I'm sorry."

"Can you at least tell me what rehab facility she went to?"

Dr. Chang's voice remained professional. "Again, I'm sorry. I wish I could help."

"Please. Just tell me where she went. I need to tell her . . ." He took a breath. "She needs to know I love her."

The therapist was quiet. Finally she sighed. "Morris, listen. We both know Sheila's a smart woman. We have to trust she's made the best decision for herself. Please don't worry. I'm sure she's fine."

:::::

It was a twenty-five-minute drive to the Harvard-Belmont district in the historical Capitol Hill neighborhood of Seattle.

Morris drove slowly down Sheila's street, parking his fat

Cadillac in her skinny driveway. He looked up at the three-story home for the third time that week, breathing in the chilly night air. A few lights were on inside, but they were the same lights that had been on all week. A thick wad of mail was sticking out of her mailbox.

"Can I help you?" a voice behind him said.

Morris was startled. A spritely woman in her early seventies was standing behind him, holding a leash attached to a small, hairy dog. The dog eyed him suspiciously under a mop of rusty bangs.

"Hi," he said, feeling foolish. "I'm Morris Gardener. I—"

"Oh, you're Sheila's fiancé." Recognition lit the woman's wrinkled face. "We met once, last summer, at Sheila's barbecue. Julia Shelby."

"Hello again."

The woman was only vaguely familiar, but Sheila had spoken of her often.

"Sheila with you?" Mrs. Shelby said, peering into the Cadillac's tinted windows. "I haven't seen her around for a few days."

"Neither have I."

The woman blinked.

Morris softened his tone. "Sorry, I guess you haven't heard. The wedding was canceled and Sheila's . . . left town." He was beginning to sound like a broken record. If he had to explain what happened one more time, his head might explode.

"Yes, I got the note. I was sorry to hear that. I was looking forward to seeing you two get married." Mrs. Shelby frowned and the dog at her heels barked. She bent down to pick it up, scratching its auburn hair thoughtfully. "So she's away? Where'd she go?"

"I'm not sure." He couldn't meet Mrs. Shelby's eyes. "She didn't tell me."

"I thought maybe the two of you decided to elope at the last minute. I was wondering if I should bring in her mail." She spoke openly, no trace of awkwardness. "Guess not, huh?"

He held up his left hand and wiggled his bare ring finger. "No such luck. Still single."

"Well, I'm very sorry to hear that," Mrs. Shelby said again, her kind eyes filled with concern. "I didn't realize you two were having problems."

Morris stuffed his hands into his pockets. "We were working on it."

"When will she be back?"

"Seven weeks." Morris hesitated. "Maybe longer."

"So I suppose you're coming by to feed the fish and water the plants." Mrs. Shelby put her dog back down on the lawn. It barked and nipped at his pants. "She should have asked me—it must have been terribly inconvenient for you to drive all this way. You live on the East Side, don't you?"

Morris stared at her. Jesus Christ, he hadn't even thought of that. "She didn't ask me, actually. I—I lost my key."

"That's odd." Mrs. Shelby's gray hair was blowing in the chilly night wind. "If she didn't ask you and she didn't ask me . . ." Her voice trailed off and she looked toward Sheila's house. "You want to go in and look around?"

: : : :

It took a minute of jiggling before Morris got the door open. The alarm was beeping and he stepped inside quickly to enter the code the neighbor had given him, 0–6–1–5 for Sheila's birthday. The beeping stopped, and he pocketed the key. The sudden silence was jarring.

It was ridiculous to think they were engaged and he didn't have a key to her house, nor did he know the code to her security system. He'd asked Sheila a few times over the past year, but she'd always joked that she didn't want him walking in on her with her *other* boyfriend.

In the end, it hadn't really been a joke, had it? She'd always been a private person, and now he knew why.

He stepped farther into the house. Immediately, something didn't feel right. And it wasn't because she'd covered the holes he'd made in her wall with an old mirror she'd been meaning to donate to Goodwill.

The throw pillows on the living room sofa were in disarray. A minor thing, but it wasn't like her—she hated to leave the house messy if she was going to be away for an extended period. Once, before a weekend trip to Las Vegas, she'd made him wait an hour while she straightened and vacuumed the entire house.

In the kitchen, the sink was filled with dirty dishes. One even had a chunk of dried chicken still stuck to it. Sheila would never have left those dishes to sit overnight, let alone for eight weeks while she was in rehab.

Something was very wrong here.

He crossed through the kitchen into her study. The desk lamp was bright and the computer was still on. The screen saver was flickering, and when Morris hit the ENTER key, he was prompted to enter a password. She had locked her computer—no surprise there.

His eyes gravitated to the little fishbowl that always sat on her desk. His heart sank.

The water in the bowl was cloudy. Mercury, the goldfish he'd won for her on their first date, was floating belly up, his bright orange color faded to a dull yellow.

Sheila would have never let that little fish die.

He pulled out his cell phone and dialed 911.

CHAPTER : 23

There was no immediate danger, the desk sergeant on the phone informed Morris, so it would be forty-five minutes to an hour before somebody from Seattle PD would be at the house to take his statement. Or he was welcome to come in and file a missing-person report. Neither choice sat well with Morris, but he opted to stay at Sheila's house and wait for an officer to arrive.

He rifled through her desk drawers while he waited. Everything was meticulously organized, and he found nothing unusual amid the pens and Post-it pads.

A small stack of invoices lay beside the computer, waiting to be paid. Electricity bill, gas bill, mortgage statement; all were unpaid for the month. He noticed her gas bill payment was due five days ago. He wasn't intimately familiar with Sheila's bill-paying habits, but it seemed odd that she wouldn't have taken care of these things before she left. In the stack he'd grabbed from her mailbox there were more bills—why hadn't she forwarded these to the rehab facility? Or arranged to make the payments some other way?

He took one last look at the lifeless little goldfish, then headed down the hallway and up the long, straight staircase.

Two bedrooms and a bathroom were on the second level.

One bedroom was done up as a guest room, and the other was bare except for a treadmill and an old TV. He checked both rooms and the bathroom, even looked inside the closets, but nothing of note was in any of them.

Turning down the hallway, he took the final set of stairs up to the third floor, which was entirely Sheila's bedroom. By the time he reached the top, his knees were aching from carrying his big body up so many steps.

Her bedside reading lamp was still on. The bed, though made, was slightly rumpled, as if she'd just been lying on top of it. A novel was lying open and facedown next to the indent left by her body. Her reading glasses were beside the book.

It was all so peculiar—it didn't even look as if Sheila had left in a hurry. It was as if she'd left knowing she'd be back right away. He was certain the police officers, if they ever arrived, would agree.

He felt every inch the intruder as he sat on the edge of her queen-size bed. He was invading the wall of privacy she'd so carefully constructed, and it made him uncomfortable. He had been in her bedroom only half a dozen times, if that. They weren't having sex and she had no television here, so there'd never been much reason for him to come upstairs. Now he was alone in her room, trying desperately to get inside her head. He picked up the novel she was reading. The latest thriller from Jeffery Deaver. Morris had never heard of the guy.

He opened the top drawer of her nightstand and pawed through it. Hand lotion, another book by another author he'd never heard of, a few pens, receipts from various clothing stores. No recent purchases. He opened the second drawer.

And stared into it, his jaw dropping open.

It was a box of condoms. Jumbo pack. Trojans. And ribbed . . . for her pleasure.

The box was open. Morris looked inside, knowing damn well what he was going to find but needing to see it anyway.

A jumbo pack came with twenty-four condoms. In this box, only six remained.

The doorbell chimed three floors down and he jumped.

: : : :

Morris gave his statement to the Seattle PD officers, trying hard to maintain a sense of professionalism. But in between every sentence was the nearly empty box of condoms, glowing like a fluorescent beacon in his head.

It didn't help to know that she had at least practiced safe sex. No, sir, not one bit.

"So you don't live here?" The younger detective was a petite woman named Kim Kellogg. Dressed smartly in a tailored pantsuit, she'd been making notes the entire time using a small black leather notepad she kept clipped to her belt. Her partner, Detective Mike Torrance, was wearing a shirt that needed ironing and a tie that looked outdated. He had been listening to most of the exchange without comment, his hawk eyes missing nothing.

"No," Morris said. "But I am—was—her fiancé. I haven't seen or heard from her since she left a message calling off our wedding."

"When were you supposed to get married?"

"This Saturday."

"And she called you from where?"

"I don't know. She didn't say."

"She called you on your cell phone?"

"No, the home phone."

"Did you check the call display?"

"I can't remember. I was upset when I got home."

"Can you check it when you get home and give me the number she called from?"

"Certainly."

Torrance cleared his throat, interrupting them. He had a jawline full of razor bumps, and his short black hair stuck straight up from his scalp like he'd been electrocuted. "So, Mr. Gardener, if you don't live here, you must have a key to get in."

Morris suddenly wondered if he was going to be arrested for trespassing. "I do," he lied. "We were engaged, after all."

Detective Torrance's face was expressionless. "And why is it you think something's happened to your fiancée?"

Morris hesitated. "Truth be told, I don't know what to think."

Torrance stared at him. "Then why are we here, Mr. Gardener? Either you're reporting her missing or you're not."

Kellogg was jotting everything down furiously, her pencil making loud scratching noises against the paper. Torrance frowned at her as if he wanted her to stop.

Morris rubbed his head. "It feels like something's not right. Her house is messy. She wouldn't leave it like this if she knew she was going away for a while. It would have bothered her. And her fish is dead."

"Fish?"

"Her pet goldfish. It's dead."

Torrance and Kellogg exchanged a look Morris couldn't decipher. "Let's go see," Torrance said, and Morris led the way to Sheila's study.

Detective Kellogg looked closely into the fishbowl, her blond ponytail bobbing. "It's dead all right," she confirmed, jotting it down in her notebook.

Torrance grimaced. "Thank you, Kim." He looked around the office before directing his gaze back to Morris. "So you're saying it's out of character for her to leave so suddenly, but she did call you to say she was going away for a while."

"Yes, she did."

"Have you tried looking for her?"

"She asked me not to."

Torrance frowned. "You still have that message on tape?"

"I didn't erase it."

"Can you drop it by the station tomorrow?"

Morris stifled a sigh. "I can do it tonight."

"What were the problems between you and your fiancée?" Torrance asked.

"I beg your pardon?"

"The problems between you and Ms. Tao." Torrance's voice was patient, as if he were explaining something to a five-year-old child. "Obviously things weren't going well between you if she decided to blow town a week before your wedding."

Kellogg looked up, her pencil paused midair.

"It's *Doctor* Tao." Morris felt his jaw tighten, and he forced himself to relax. "We did have an argument, yes."

"What about?"

"It's personal. But we were still getting married."

"Sir." Torrance's voice was flat. "Everything's personal. We can't help her if you don't tell us everything you can."

Morris stared at him. The detective stared back.

"Relationship stuff," Morris said finally. "Nothing we wouldn't have gotten past." He didn't want this man to know about Sheila's sex addiction. He couldn't bring himself to say the words.

Torrance sighed. Kellogg's pencil scratched into the silence.

"And tell us again when the last time was you saw her?"

"A week ago. Wednesday."

They were treating him like a goddamned suspect.

"But she was okay when you left her." Torrance's voice was breezy, but there was no denying the ice behind it.

"Are you kidding me? Why the hell wouldn't she be?"

Torrance raised a hand. "Just doing my job, Mr. Gardener."

Morris seethed in silence.

"So you said you got Ms. Tao's message—sorry, *Dr.* Tao's message—on Sunday while you were waiting for her at the hotel. What time did she leave the message?"

"I told you I don't remember the exact time she called." Morris was exasperated. "I can check my call display when I get home. And if you're gonna ask me every question three different ways, Detective, we're gonna be here awhile." Morris glared at them.

"Do you have a cell phone?" Torrance was unfazed.

"Of course."

"Why wouldn't she call you on your cell? Didn't you think it was strange that she called you on your home phone knowing you weren't going to be there?"

"It was strange, yes. But she might have pressed the wrong button on her phone. Or she didn't want to actually speak to me. Considering what she told me, I can't blame her."

"But when you got the message, you weren't alarmed. You didn't go looking for her?"

"Of course I did," Morris said, the heat building in his neck. "I came here first thing, she wasn't home. I called, she didn't answer. What else could I have done?"

"Is it a normal pattern of behavior for her to just take off?"

"No. We've been dating for a year and nothing like this has ever happened."

"You must have been pretty angry with her for dumping you over voice mail a week before your wedding day. Must've been pretty embarrassing for you to have to make all those phone calls to your guests."

"It was the worst day of my life, yes." Morris hated how defiant he sounded.

"So you still have that message on your answering machine?"

"For God's sake, Detectives. Yes. I will bring it by tonight."

"It would be good if you could," Kellogg piped in sweetly.

Morris felt like ripping her ponytail from her pretty little head.

"All right then, I think we have everything we need for now." Torrance nodded to his partner, who was still writing in her notebook. "Thanks for calling us, Mr. Gardener. We'll get her missing person's report on file."

"And then what?" Morris was relieved that the questioning was over, but he was still pissed off. "What's your plan?"

"Our plan?" Torrance was barely able to keep the condescension out of his voice. "Well, we'll pop around the university and see if her colleagues know anything. We'll chat up her neighbors. Does she have close friends? Family?"

Morris thought of giving them Marianne Chang's name, but then he shook his head. Sheila's therapist obviously didn't think anything was wrong, and he didn't want the detectives contacting her and deciding they agreed before they conducted a thorough investigation. "Both parents are dead and she's an only child. The only friends she ever talked about are from work."

Torrance nodded, then glanced at Kellogg again. They seemed to have a wordless way of communicating with each other. It was irritating. "Listen, Mr. Gardener—"

"Call me Morris."

"Morris. For what it's worth, it doesn't sound to me like

anything bad's happened to your fiancée. What she did may be unusual, maybe even out of character, but it's not necessarily cause for concern. She's an adult, and she left a very specific message telling you that she was leaving town. If we don't find evidence of foul play, we won't be able to pursue this. People have the right to up and walk out of their lives." Torrance paused. "It's shitty, but it happens every day."

"She wouldn't have let her fish die," Morris said stubbornly. "How long can a goldfish go without being fed?"

"Five days," Kellogg answered. She smiled, sheepish, when the men turned to stare at her. "I had one when I was a kid. Never remembered to feed it on time."

Torrance gave her a look and her grin faded.

"Okay then." Torrance stuck out his hand. Morris shook it halfheartedly. "We'll be in touch. Don't forget to bring that tape. And also the time of the call and the number she called from."

"Got it," Morris said, tired. He couldn't have forgotten if he'd wanted to.

"You leaving with us?"

Morris shook his head. "I need to lock up."

He saw them back to the door and watched them drive away, just as his BlackBerry rang. Private name, Seattle number. He answered the call.

"Morris?" a voice said.

His heart deflated. It wasn't Sheila. "Yes?"

"This is Dr. Chang." Her voice was more anxious than the last time they'd spoken. "I tried you at home first. I thought I would let you know that I called the treatment facility I thought Sheila might have checked into. They have no record of her. Neither do a dozen other places I've tried." The therapist paused. "It was an in-patient program?"

"That's what she said."

"I thought so." Dr. Chang was quiet for a moment. "Listen, I'm concerned."

"I am, too. I'm at Sheila's place now and the police were just here. I've filed a missing person's report."

"That's good." The therapist sounded relieved. "I think that's best. Not that I think anything's wrong," she added quickly. "But it would be good to know she hasn't been in an accident of some kind."

"That's pretty much what the police said. Should I give them your name?"

Dr. Chang was silent for a moment. "There's really nothing I can tell them. If I knew something that could help, I would say so, but only if I thought she were a danger to herself or others. She's not."

"That's what I figured." Morris hesitated. "Listen, the detective on the case thinks Sheila probably flipped out. He said that people walk away from their lives all the time. Do you think that's what she did?"

Dr. Chang answered carefully. "In my experience, I've seen people walk away for all kinds of reasons."

His heart sank.

Finally, the therapist sighed. "I shouldn't say this, but she loved you very much, Morris. You mean the world to her. Once she's worked through everything she needs to, I really believe she'll come back."

He closed his eyes. "Thank you. You don't know how badly I needed to hear that."

CHAPTER : 24

It wasn't even twenty-four hours before Detective Torrance called.

Morris was working late at the bank, running numbers for a new deal he was working on. He'd been at it all afternoon and was irritated to be interrupted, but the minute Darcy told him who was on the line, he forgot about his spreadsheets.

"Yes, Detective." He didn't know what he was expecting to hear, and his stomach had that acidic feeling again, now a daily occurrence. He reached for the bottle of antacid in his top drawer.

Was Sheila dead? Or had they found her, shacked up with some guy on the other side of the country?

"Hello, Mr. Gardener," Torrance said. "I have an update for you."

"I'm listening." Morris shook out three antacid tablets and popped them into his mouth. They tasted like sweetened chalk. He took a sip of the coffee that Darcy had brought in an hour before and grimaced. It was cold.

"Thought you'd like to know we conducted a thorough investigation into the disappearance of your fiancée. The good news is, we found no evidence or sign of foul play."

"That is good news," Morris said, relief washing over him. "What's the bad news?"

"We have no idea where she is."

"Okay. But you're gonna keep looking, right? She's still missing."

"Yeah." Torrance cleared his throat. "But the thing is, sir, she *wants* to be. So we're closing her file."

"You're kidding." Morris's mouth hung open in shock. "I only filed the report yesterday. What about her fish? She wouldn't have let the goddamned thing die."

"Goldfish die all the time, sir." Morris could practically hear the detective's smirk right through the phone line. "Perhaps it died before she left, and she was in a hurry to get out of town and didn't think to . . . flush it."

Asshole. "What if she leaves the country? Couldn't you flag her passport?"

"Sure we could," Torrance replied, "but it was sitting on the kitchen counter. I saw it when I was there the other night." The detective lowered his voice. "Look, I know this is hard for you. But as I said before, this isn't that uncommon. She's taking a break from her life. It happens. It's not what you want to hear, but you're going to have to accept it one way or another."

"I still think this is wrong." Morris's stomach churned. "The woman had a life here, Detective. She had a job. Responsibilities. I can deal with the fact that she changed her mind about me, but you don't know Sheila. I'm telling you. None of this makes sense."

"She's an adult, Mr. Gardener. She's free to come and go as she chooses. I listened to her phone message several times and she was pretty adamant about her decision."

A headache started in Morris's left temple. "So what should I do?"

"You want my advice? Let it go. She's probably having a midlife crisis. She freaked out, left town, needs space. Like you said yourself, she has a life here. She'll come home eventually."

Morris pounded his fist into the desk, rocking his mug of cold coffee. "And in the meantime, I'm supposed to just . . . what? Sit around and wait for her?"

"Get on with your life."

"Yeah? And how do I do that?"

"There is another option. You could hire a private investigator." Torrance's voice was so low, Morris could barely hear him.

"Come again?"

"Write this number down." It sounded as if the detective was cupping the phone to his mouth. Morris grabbed a pen and copied down the number Torrance recited. "His name is Jerry Isaac. Retired cop. Not saying it'll go anywhere, but you want to keep digging into this, he's the man for the job. That's my best advice." Torrance's voice returned to normal. "Seattle PD can't take it any further."

Morris mumbled his thanks and hung up. He rubbed his temples, trying to process what he'd just been told. By all accounts, Sheila had left him. Really and truly. Whether it made sense or not, she was gone, and he was going to have to find a way to deal with it.

He looked at the spreadsheet he'd been working on before Torrance called and couldn't remember a damn thing about it. Then he reached for his bottom desk drawer and pulled out the bottle of Johnnie Walker Red.

He was surprised to find it was almost empty.

CHAPTER : 25

M orris hated Fremont.

Jerry Isaac's office was located in the heart of the quirky Seattle neighborhood, made popular by the young professionals who wanted to stay in the city and didn't mind living in old houses that needed work. Fremont was filled with independently owned coffee shops, secondhand clothing stores, and ethnic restaurants Morris had never heard of. Its residents were environmentally conscious, and most of them had no need for a car.

In other words, it was hip. And he could count on two fingers the number of times he'd been here.

He trudged up the sidewalk, the black leather bag on his shoulder getting heavier by the second. He was sweating profusely. The Cadillac was parked three blocks down in the only spot he could find. For a neighborhood that prided itself on its nondependence on automobiles, it was interesting how every available parking space within a two-block radius was taken.

He consulted the slip of paper in his hand where he'd written down Jerry Isaac's address, finally stopping in front of a store called Bead World. Confused for a moment, he looked straight up and was relieved to see a sign in the second-floor window that read ISAAC AND ASSOCIATES, PRIVATE INVESTI-GATORS.

He looked around but saw no entrance to the second level of the building. Dismayed, he pushed open the doors to the bead store. The bells that were attached to the door's frame chimed his entrance. Loudly.

Four ladies were sitting around a large, square white table, all working on projects of some kind—necklaces, bracelets, God knew what else—and they all glanced up as he entered. The room reeked of musky sweetness and he tried not to gag. The only thing he hated more than beads was incense. Plinky New Age music played in the background to complete the experience.

This was Morris's version of hell.

"Can I help you?" the oldest lady said in a singsong voice. In her hands was a long rope of red and silver beads that matched the sari she wore.

Morris was afraid to venture in farther. Beads of all colors, shapes, and sizes surrounded him, in boxes, in bins, in little plastic bags hooked onto the walls. The smell of patchouli assailed his nostrils. His eyes began to water.

"Uh, yeah, can you tell me how I can get up to the second floor?" His throat was getting sore.

Four pairs of eyes scrutinized him from his tie to his shoes. He was much too dressed up for Bead World, and for Fremont in general.

"The entrance is at the back," the lady said, the space between her eyebrows wrinkling in disapproval. "If I've told Jerry once, I've told him a thousand times, put something on that darn sign that tells people to *go around back*. Is that so hard?"

Morris didn't think she wanted an answer, so he didn't offer one.

"You *are* looking for Jerry, right? It's either him or Rosemary the psychic. Not that it's any of my business."

"Thanks." Morris turned quickly back toward the door.

"Come through this way!" the lady called. "It'll save you from walking all the way around the building. Don't worry, we don't bite. Unless you ask us to."

The other three ladies tittered.

Plastering on an uncomfortable smile and trying not to breathe through his nose, he made his way through the aisles of all things bead. He passed the table where the ladies sat and nodded politely.

"He's cute," one of them said out loud. "And burly. I like 'em burly."

He felt his face turn red.

"Straight through, exit out the back, entrance to the second floor is on your right." The oldest lady appraised him through spectacles perched low on her nose. The glasses were, of course, attached to a long string of shiny black beads that draped around her shoulders and neck. "Stop back in afterwards if you have time. I have an introductory necklace workshop starting in half an hour."

Morris's smile was strained. "I'll try."

They all tittered again.

He exited and another tinkling of chimes announced his departure. Stepping out into the dreary gray day, he found himself in the building's parking lot. Half a dozen parking spots were free, of course. Swearing under his breath, he thought of his beloved Cadillac parked three streets away. At least the October chill was refreshing. The incense had left him with a headache.

He took one last breath of fresh air, then headed for the back-door entrance. He was dismayed but not surprised to see that there was no elevator. Adjusting the bag on his shoulder, he started up the long, narrow staircase to Jerry Isaac's office. And, of course, Rosemary the psychic.

Hell, if the private investigator couldn't get him any answers, maybe Rosemary could.

Morris's knees were creaking in protest by the time he reached the top step, and he had to stop and wait for the burning sensation to subside. Looking down the long corridor, he saw that quite a few offices were up here. Most seemed unoccupied, and the flowery, colorful sign to Rosemary's office said CLOSED. No psychic reading for Morris today.

The door to Jerry Isaac's office was open and Morris stepped into the small, dingy waiting room. A dark-skinned young woman—presumably the one he'd spoken with the day before—looked up at him. Some type of rap music played softly through the speakers of her computer.

"Can I help you?" She was pleasant enough, but after giving him a quick once-over, her eyes were back on her computer screen. Before he could answer, she was already typing.

"Morris Gardener for Jerry Isaac." His tone was brisk. If she'd worked at the bank, he'd have fired her ass for not telling a client about the parking lot at the back. Okay, he wouldn't, but the thought was comforting. "I have an appointment."

"I'll let him know you're here."

She typed something else into the computer, giggled, then typed something else. He glared into the side of her face, but she was oblivious. After a full minute, she finally yelled, "Uncle Jerry!"

A man about the same height as Morris but with about fifty pounds less on his lanky frame popped out from the doorway just behind her. He had a close-cut Afro and ebony skin, which made his teeth look startlingly white. He saw Morris and grinned.

"Jerry Isaac," he said with an outstretched hand.

"Morris Gardener."

"This is my receptionist, Keisha. She's also my niece." Jerry gave the young woman a stern look. "Keisha, you'd better not be chatting online with that old guy in Idaho. I already told you."

"He's not old, he's twenty-six."

"So *he* says." Jerry rolled his eyes, leading Morris through another door and closing it behind them.

"These kids today." Jerry gestured for Morris to have a seat. "They have no sense of danger. It was hard enough staying out of trouble when we were young, but with the Internet, it's a whole other thing. They go into these online chat rooms and they meet these people, and you have no idea who anybody really is. It's a scary world out there, I tell you. You got kids?"

"Three boys," Morris said. "But they're grown. And when they were Keisha's age, the Internet wasn't the juggernaut it is now."

The private investigator had his back to the window. Facing him, Morris was surprised to see that the office had a rather nice view of downtown Fremont. If Fremont could be considered nice.

"Exactly." Jerry nodded. "I tell my sister—Keisha's mother— to put the computer out in a central area in the house so she can monitor where the girl goes, what she does online. Keisha's a bright kid, but she's got no street smarts."

Morris nodded politely.

The private investigator suddenly sniffed the air. "Did you pass through Bead World?"

"Unfortunately."

Jerry threw his head back and laughed. "Miss Gwendolyn and her crew are harmless. Bet you made their day."

Morris managed a smile.

Jerry cracked his knuckles. The popping sound was loud in the small office. "Anyway, you didn't come here to talk about the Internet or beads, you came here to discuss your fiancée. She's missing?"

"The cops don't seem to think so."

"Ah." Jerry grinned. "Mike Torrance sent you? He's a good guy. We were partners up till I retired last year."

Morris looked at Jerry doubtfully. "You don't look old enough to be retired."

Jerry laughed. "I'm fifty-two. It's the West Indies blood that keeps me looking so young. I started working for Seattle PD fresh out of college at twenty-one, put in my thirty years. Got a full pension, so this is a nice side business, something to keep my mind occupied until I figure out what to do with the rest of my life. Get a lot of referrals from Mike—Detective Torrance. I owe that guy a steak dinner and a few beers. But enough about me. How far did he get in the investigation?"

"According to him, all the way. But I'm thinking he wouldn't have suggested you if something more couldn't be done."

"Maybe, maybe not." Jerry's face was neutral. "Sometimes the case is closed but you have this inkling there's more to it. Sometimes Mike recommends me just to put the client's mind at ease. What was his official conclusion?"

Morris cleared his throat. "That Sheila—that's my fiancée—left town voluntarily. She's been gone over a week now. He thinks she'll be back when she's ready."

Jerry reached for a notepad and pen. "And you don't think this is normal behavior for her?"

"Blowing off our wedding? No, I don't. She's a meticulous person. Every hour of her day is planned. Even if she changed her mind about getting married, I can't imagine she'd take off the way she did. She's a tenured professor at PSSU. It's hard to imagine her leaving before the end of the term." Morris described the phone message Sheila had left. "Her therapist said she didn't check into any of the better-known treatment centers. I'm worried about her. I need to make sure she's okay."

"Puget Sound State professor? What did you say her name was?"

"Sheila Tao. She teaches psychology."

"Huh. I took a behavioral psych course through PSSU about seven, eight years back. But the professor's name was Sheila Chancellor, I think."

Morris nodded. "That's her. She was married then."

"Get the hell out." Genuine shock spread over Jerry's features. "The world just gets smaller and smaller. She was a helluva lecturer. She even gave me some one-on-one help with my final paper. She's your fiancée?"

Morris nodded again.

Jerry was quiet, clearly perturbed. "Well, shit, this puts it all in a different light, knowing who she is and all. I was upgrading to a bachelor's degree in criminology back then, through night school, which wasn't exactly easy, being a cop and keeping crazy hours. She helped me write a paper that focused on criminal behavior patterns. Nice lady." Jerry was thoughtful for another moment, then jotted something down on the notepad. "How old is she now?"

"Thirty-nine."

The private investigator looked up. "I hate to suggest it, but maybe she's going through some kind of midlife crisis. I went through it with my wife when she turned forty a few years back."

"That's what your former partner said."

"It does happen." Jerry saw the look on Morris's face. "But you don't think that's it."

"She was having an affair. She admitted it."

Jerry didn't blink. "She say who?"

Morris shook his head. "And there . . . might have been others. I'm not sure." He couldn't bring himself to say she was a sex addict. The words were too ugly. And this guy was a former student—Sheila wouldn't have wanted someone like him knowing her secret.

Jerry's expression was hard to read. "Did Mike explain to you that most of the time adults go missing because they *want* to? Forget what you see on TV. The majority of people who disappear do so on purpose. Considering she left you a message, it sounds like this is the case here."

"Torrance made a point to tell me all that, yes. Twice, actually." Morris didn't bother to mention that he also thought Torrance was a jackass. "But I need answers, Jerry. Isn't that why people hire you? Because, unlike the police, you can find people who don't want to be found?"

Jerry smiled.

"I can't force her to come home, but I need to see for myself that she's all right. I've invested too much of . . . my time to let it go like this." Morris had almost said *of myself.*

Jerry didn't look happy. For a moment Morris thought he might have offended the former cop. Or maybe he had second thoughts about investigating someone he knew.

But then the PI reached into his drawer and pulled out a stack of yellow forms. He peeled one off the top. "All right then. These are my fees. I need two thousand as a nonrefundable retainer up front, and then I bill a hundred per hour plus expenses—"

Morris put up a hand. "That's fine, whatever. But I have something else to show you."

"What's that?"

Morris reached into his leather bag and pulled out Sheila's laptop. "Can you hack into this? I'm sure if you do, it will tell us a lot. This is her personal computer. It's password-protected."

"Whoa." Jerry leaned back in his chair again, appraising Morris with narrow eyes. "Computer hacking? That's illegal, man."

Morris's gaze did not waver.

Jerry cracked his knuckles again. "No wonder you want to hire a civilian. All right, I'll see what I can do. Computers aren't my specialty, but I know a guy."

Morris smiled his first genuine smile in days. "I thought you might."

CHAPTER: 26

Sheila's nipple was on fire.

She opened her eyes and found Ethan staring at her. Her left breast throbbed painfully. Looking down, she saw why. Ethan was squeezing her left nipple hard, pinching it between his thumb and forefinger like a stale gumdrop he was trying to soften.

"Stop it," Sheila said, her voice hoarse. She moved her arms as if to hit him, but the movement only caused her chains to rattle. "That hurts, you asshole."

"You were really out." Ethan tweaked her nipple again. "What were you dreaming about? Were you imagining Morris fondling you in your sleep?"

She had been lying in bed all day—or was it night?—and her back ached. With great effort, she managed to sit up, and he adjusted the pillows to support her lower back. It was becoming routine. The bones in her spine cracked rapidly as she attempted to stretch, one pop right after another.

"I wasn't dreaming." Her throat was sore and dry. It was always sore and dry. Between her muscle aches, headaches, and fatigue, she felt as if she constantly had a mild case of the flu. "If Morris were touching me, it wouldn't hurt."

"He's moving on, you know." Ethan stuck a straw in an

opened bottle of Evian and put it to her lips. "You were just a little blip in his predictable little life. Happy wedding day, by the way."

Oh, God. He was right. Today would have been her wedding day. Sheila took a deep breath, trying to control the stampede of emotions that had just been unleashed. She felt as if she'd been stabbed in the heart.

She wondered what Morris was doing right this moment, and her eyes began to moisten. She blinked before Ethan could notice.

Her captor was obviously trying to antagonize her. He knew her fiancé was her most sensitive button. But Morris was a giant sore spot for him, too. For now, Sheila refused to engage. She hadn't yet figured out how to use Ethan's jealousy to her advantage, but she sensed it could be a valuable weapon.

Her mouth closed around the straw and she sucked in the cool water. She was still being sedated, but it was all right. Sleep was her only measure of relief in this never-ending nightmare.

"Did you pee?" he asked.

Sheila flexed her abdominal muscles reflexively at the word *pee* and winced at her full bladder. Her diaper was dry. "No. But I do have to go. Really badly." It was awful to have to say those words, but she had no choice. "What do you want to do?"

It wasn't a strange question under the circumstances. Ethan usually changed her diaper when she was sleeping. She shifted in the bed, thinking about how great it would be to sit on a toilet seat like a normal adult. God, the things she'd taken for granted. Now that she was thinking about it, it was starting to hurt. She looked at him, desperate. "I can't wait for the sedative to kick in."

"You really have to go, huh?" Ethan's hand went to the small silver gun in the waistband of his jeans.

"Yes." She winced again. "Do you think . . . could I use the bathroom this time? Please?"

"No way."

"Ethan, please. I won't try anything. I'm too tired. I've barely stood up since I've been here." She rattled her chains again to emphasize her plight. "Just this once, let me use the bathroom like a regular person."

She knew from his expression that he was seriously considering her request. She opened her mouth to plead her case further, but then closed it again when she remembered he didn't like to be pushed.

Finally he nodded. "Okay. We'll try it. You've been good."

Good? What a fucking joke. How was it possible to be *bad* chained to a bed twenty-four hours a day? "Thank you."

Ethan took the gun out of his waistband. "You fuck with me—"

"I won't. I don't have the energy. Trust me on that." She meant every word. She was in no shape for a fight.

Ethan fished a key out of his pocket. She caught a whiff of his clean scent as he leaned over and unlocked her right wrist, then her left. When she brought her arms together to rub her wrists, her shoulders tingled with pins and needles.

"Here." He handed her the key. "Do your ankles. Like last time."

Sheila bent forward, and her back was instantly on fire from the sudden movement. It took all her willpower not to shriek. She was dizzy from the exertion when she finally got her legs free.

Handing the key back to Ethan, she moved her legs slowly over the edge of the bed, pausing a moment to let the blood circulate. Using small, deliberate movements, she stood up and began shuffling toward the bathroom. Her muscles felt like

Jell-O. Looking down, she could see the angry welts on her bare ankles that matched her chafed wrists.

If she could have walked faster, she would have, the urge to urinate was so strong. Ethan followed behind her, the gun in his hand. As she turned down the hallway toward the bathroom, she couldn't help but wonder what would happen if she suddenly whipped around. Could she disarm Ethan if she took him by surprise? If she did, then what? She'd have no trouble putting a bullet in his head, but what good would that do? She'd still be stuck in this modern-day dungeon. The door had a keypad and she didn't know the code to get out.

Maybe she could use the gun to torture it out of him. Shoot one limb at a time. It was a lovely thought.

"Holy slow, Batman," Ethan drawled behind her.

She made it to the bathroom. Like the rest of the basement, the small room had no windows and was completely done in white—white toilet, white sink, white walls, white floors, white tub, everything perfectly clean. The smell of disinfectant was strong, which didn't surprise her. Ethan was a germaphobe.

Sheila pulled her dry diaper down to her ankles. She lifted the toilet lid and sat down. Almost instantly, the bathroom filled with the pungent odor of urine that had been marinating far too long.

Ethan watched from the doorway, amused. Sheila couldn't have cared less. She sighed. This was the closest to contentment she'd felt in a long time. After a full minute, her bladder finally flexed out the last drop.

Then, as if to punctuate being finished, she farted.

The sound echoed loudly in the ceramic bowl. She felt her face grow hot.

"Jesus Christ." Ethan laughed, his face a blend of amusement and mild disgust. "Excuse you."

"Sorry." Her hands flew to her face. It was ridiculous to be embarrassed about a fart—after all, she was being kept here against her will, and what could be worse than having to urinate in adult diapers?—but she was ashamed nonetheless.

And when the smell hit, she was mortified.

"Holy fuck." Ethan clapped a hand over his nose. "Don't tell me you're about to take a shit."

As if on cue, her bowels cramped.

"Yes," she said, doubling over. She couldn't look at him. There seemed to be no limit to how much humiliation a person could take.

The thing was, she hadn't pooped since she'd been here. It was no surprise; she was hardly eating anything. She wondered now if Ethan had been slipping something else into her water along with the sedatives. This was the first time she'd felt the urge.

"This is so gross." Ethan's T-shirt was pulled up over his nose, exposing an inch of flat, hard stomach. His muffled voice was filled with glee under the fabric of the shirt. She knew he was laughing at her.

"Can you get out of here, please?" The cramping was becoming painful and urgent. She didn't think she could hold it in much longer.

He moved back a few inches. "I'll leave for a minute, but the door stays open and I'm right outside."

"No, please." Sheila had to go so badly she was shaking. Her hands were clammy on her naked thighs. "Close the door, Ethan. Please."

While he stood there contemplating her request, her bowels spasmed painfully, and she had no choice but to let it out. The room filled with the stench of fresh shit.

"Jesus Christ!" Ethan jumped back so quickly he almost fell over. "You fucking disgusting cunt!" Holding one hand over his nose, he reached into the bathroom to turn on the overhead fan.

Sheila stared up at him from the toilet seat, her hair hanging over her face. Rivulets of sweat ran down her temples. Her bowels continued to cramp and she knew it was far from over. He was looking at her with such shock and disgust that, despite her abdominal pain, she couldn't resist a chuckle.

"Well, what did you expect? I've been here for days, you cocksucker." Sheila grunted again. "I'm not done. I suggest you get the fuck out."

The door slammed shut. Sheila was finally alone in the bathroom.

It was a small victory, but a victory nonetheless. How strange, she thought, that someone who was perfectly capable of killing people and hacking their corpses into little pieces could be disgusted by something like pooping. After all, everybody had an asshole. It made no sense.

"Flush the fucking toilet!" Ethan yelled from behind the door.

"I'm not fucking done!" she yelled back, even though she was.

"Courtesy flush! And hurry the fuck up!"

Quite possibly the world's stupidest conversation. What did he think she was going to do? There was nowhere to go, no way to escape. She wiped herself and flushed, then flushed again for good measure. Feeling almost 100 percent better, she put her diaper back on.

Turning on the faucets, Sheila let the water run into the

small sink. She quickly opened the cabinet doors of the vanity, looking for anything that could be used as a weapon. There was a roll of toilet paper and a hotel-size bar of soap. Nothing that could kill Ethan.

She ran her hands and wrists under the warm water, sucking in a breath as her welts began to sting. She lathered them with the soap, gritting her teeth as they burned, then rinsed and washed her face. Grabbing a paper towel, she patted her face dry and caught a glimpse of herself in the vanity mirror.

And almost fell over. The face staring back at her was barely recognizable.

Her hair was stringy with oil and dried sweat. The strands hung limply in uneven waves. Her complexion, normally flaw-less thanks to a militant skin-care regimen, was ashy, a shade she couldn't totally attribute to the harsh bathroom lighting. Dark hollows under her eyes looked an inch deep, and her forehead had grooves she'd never seen before. Her full lips were dry and cracked and covered in small brown scabs. Dried white spittle had congregated at the corners of her mouth. Her eyebrows were unplucked and messy.

She'd aged twenty years since she'd last seen herself.

The door swung open.

"Are you finished?" Ethan stood in the doorway, his face turned to the side. He didn't seem to want to look at her. He was rubbing his hands with the liquid sanitizer he always kept in his pocket, and she rolled her eyes. He hadn't even touched her and already he felt dirty. "Get the fuck out already."

"Can I take a shower?" She turned away from the mirror, unable to look at her reflection. "Please?"

Judging by the look on his face, he clearly thought her question was insane.

"Ethan, come on. I haven't bathed in a week. There's soap here. Please."

"I'll think about it. But right now, come the fuck out."

She wiped her hands once more with the paper towel and tossed it into the trash, then stepped out of the bathroom. He took her by the elbow, gun in hand, and yanked her back toward the bed.

She cringed at the sight of the chains and handcuffs.

"Don't strap me in." She twisted around to try to get away from him. "Please, Ethan. Look at my wrists. I'm not going anywhere. Don't strap me in."

He pushed her onto the bed. "No. I don't need the headache."

"Where am I going to go?" She held out her wounded wrists. "This place is a jail cell. Do you think I can hurt you? You outweigh me by at least fifty pounds, and you have a gun."

He pointed the barrel at her. "Put the cuffs on."

Sheila picked up a handcuff but didn't fasten it. The steel felt cold against her bare leg. "Come on, even if I could hurt you, how am I going to get out? You've got this place locked up like Fort Knox. I can't get out without the codes."

His face was like stone. She softened her voice and tried a different tactic. "Ethan, you're in control here. You're the boss. I'm not going anywhere. Let me at least sit on the sofa when you're not here and use the bathroom when I need to. Let me have some measure of dignity. What difference does it make? Let me feel human before I die."

His face twitched. She contained her jubilation. She'd gotten through to him.

"Fine." He kept the gun trained on her. "We'll give it a try. But if you—"

"I won't."

He leaned over her, cupping her chin with his free hand, his eyes boring deeply into hers. He spoke with perfect enunciation. "If you piss me off, Sheila, I'll end you. Without hesitation. I'm getting as tired of this as you are."

She nodded, her chin still in his hand. "So let me go." She said it quietly, keeping her eyes focused on his face. "I'll walk out of here and hitch a ride home and never tell anyone what happened. You can leave town. I'll say I freaked out, started drinking again, passed out, and didn't know where I was. I'll say anything you want me to. Just let me go."

"So you can go back to Morris?"

Morris again. Her mind raced as she tried to think of what to say.

Before she could respond, Ethan shook his head. "Never mind. Shut up. I don't want to talk about him."

"But—"

"I said shut up."

"Do you actually think I'm in love with him?"

That got his attention. "Aren't you?"

She gazed back, hoping her calm demeanor concealed her increasing heart rate. "I have love for Morris, yes. But I think you've misunderstood what it is I feel for him."

A moment of silence passed before he sat down beside her on the bed. The gun rested comfortably in his hand. "Explain it to me."

She was ready. "I'm thirty-nine. I'll be forty in a few months. I'm divorced. I don't have children. Morris was my chance to have the family I've always wanted."

She reached out and placed her palm lightly on Ethan's knee. He jerked in surprise, but didn't pull away. It was the first time since she'd been here that she'd willingly touched him. "You're twenty-three and still in grad school. Can you tell me you're ready for that? You said it yourself the day we broke up—our affair was never destined to go anywhere."

"I was angry."

"So you didn't mean it? You wanted to be with me? Long term?" The words were ridiculous. He would see right through them. But her eyes stayed steady on his face.

"What difference does it make now?" Ethan's face was impassive. "Look around. It's too late."

"It's not too late." Sheila tucked her bare legs underneath her, a girly move that would make her seem more vulnerable. Her right hand was still on his knee, and she used her left hand to smooth her straggly hair behind her ears in an effort to look less unattractive. "This situation is extremely unconventional, yes, and I'll be honest when I say you have serious issues we'll need to work on. You know that. But if the reason you brought me here is because deep down you want to be with me and can't stand to see me marry someone else, then that's normal. That's human." She paused for effect. "Ethan, you should have told me how you felt. You should have fought for me. You would have won."

She moved her hand from his knee to his palm. Squeezed. He looked at her, studying her features closely. "Don't bullshit me."

Was that *hope* she heard in his tone?

"You think that's what I'm doing?" She unfolded her legs. "I'm going to take a shower if that's okay with you. Stay right here. Don't leave, okay?" She squeezed his hand once more before letting it go.

He made no move to stop her when she slipped off the bed and headed back toward the bathroom.

When she finished showering fifteen minutes later, he was gone.

CHAPTER : 27

The doorbell rang at seven thirty, and Morris's subconscious promptly implanted it into his dream.

He was in his kitchen cooking up a huge breakfast. Bacon, eggs over easy, sausage links, and French toast topped with his mama's famous strawberry preserves (even though his mama had been dead for fifteen years).

Sheila was there, playful and affectionate, her arms around his slim waist.

In Morris's dreams he was always thin.

He and Sheila started teasing each other about who should answer the door, and neither of them could because he was cooking and she was naked.

The doorbell ringing turned to banging, and Morris woke with a jolt.

He sat up, a new crick in his neck from yet another night in the Barcalounger. The doorbell rang again. Someone really *was* at the door, and the person was damned persistent. Goddamn Jehovah's Witnesses. Third time this month they'd come around.

Swearing under his breath, he heaved himself out of his chair and padded toward the front door, pausing briefly to check his appearance in the hallway mirror. His thick hair was standing up in crazy tufts. His old terry-cloth robe hung open to reveal a stained undershirt and wrinkled pajama pants. Booze was on his breath from the night before. He was guessing he wouldn't smell too good to a clean and brightly smiling messenger of God. He tousled his hair once more for good measure. He looked deranged.

Perfect. Maybe he'd scare them away once and for all.

Not bothering to check the peephole, he swung the door open with a flourish, prepared to lambaste the unfortunate soul standing there. The sudden insurgence of sunlight into Morris's eyes temporarily blinded him and he couldn't make out the shape standing on his porch. He shielded his eyes, trying to focus.

Then the shape spoke. "Hi, Dad."

At the sound of the voice, Morris's mouth dropped open.

Blinking through the sunny haze, he found himself face-to-face with a man in his late twenties. Dark hair, six feet four, maybe two hundred pounds. White button-down shirt and jeans. Tanned, fit, and healthy. An almost exact replica of Morris at that age.

He stared into the young man's blue eyes, identical to his own. "Randall?"

"I see you're off the wagon," his son said with a sad smile. He reached over and grabbed Morris in a tight embrace. "Looks like I got here just in time. Hey, what's up with your hair? How come you look crazy?"

: : : :

Fifteen minutes later, father and son were sitting in the kitchen. His hair still wet from the world's fastest shower, Morris brought over two cups of freshly brewed coffee and marveled at the handsome man who was his eldest son.

"I figured I could catch you before you went to work." Randall looked around the kitchen, then out the window at the golf course behind the house. "Beautiful place, Dad."

Morris stared at him. "I can't believe you're here."

Randall grinned and took a sip of coffee. He took it black, just as Morris did. "Flew in late last night. Been in Austin with Mom the last couple of days. She and Bob just bought a new place. Needs some work, but it's nice."

Morris wasn't interested in news of his ex-wife. "Where have you been?"

"Well, I—" Randall stopped, then laughed. It was a sound that warmed Morris to the core. "Dad, it's been six years. How do I sum up?"

"Don't. Tell me everything. How's Donna?"

"Who?"

"Your girlfriend. It is Donna, isn't it?"

Randall shook his head. "I don't have a girlfriend, Dad."

"Oh." Morris was confused. "Sorry, I don't know why I thought . . ."

Randall waved a dismissive hand. "It's okay. It's my own fault for not doing a better job keeping in touch. Where do I start? I guess after you and I . . . ." Randall hesitated. "After I left Stanford, I went backpacking in Europe for about a year. Met a bunch of people. One guy, Dave, convinced me to go with him to the Philippines to volunteer for a youth organization. Our goal was to help impoverished communities achieve greater independence. It was hard work, but unbelievably rewarding. Then I hooked up with Amnesty and went to India, Burma, the Sudan, Borneo, Honduras . . . and here I am. Ten-second update."

"Wow." Morris didn't know what else to say.

Randall had been twenty-two when they'd last spoken, and

he certainly hadn't been anywhere near as composed and articulate as he was now. Of course, he wasn't hurling insults at the moment.

"Are you planning to visit long? When do you have to get back?"

"I'm not going back," Randall said, and Morris's heart leapt. "I've had my fill of sleeping in tents and pissing in the dirt for a while. Don't get me wrong, it's been an amazing experience, but I'm burned out."

"That's understandable." Morris felt an immense sense of pride, and a thought popped into his head. "Hey, why don't you come work for me? I can find you something. You could start next week. I've got lots of room here and—"

"Dad."

Morris stopped. "Sorry."

Randall chuckled. "Some things never change."

Morris settled into his chair. "Okay, no more talk of that. So what brings you to Seattle?"

"Well, you, of course."

Morris grinned.

"And I do have friends here, believe it or not. One in particular."

"Of course." Morris's grin widened. "What's her name, and is she cute?"

"His name is Kyle, and, yes, I think so." His son's gaze was steady.

Morris blinked. "Oh. Wow. Okay." He paused, searching for the right words. There weren't any. "So, you'll stay awhile?"

Randall let out a breath and smiled. "That's the plan. I'm going to see about an apartment today. Seattle has a great vibe and I thought it would be a nice place to settle down. And good for us. You and me, I mean. What do you think?"

"I think that's the best news I've heard in weeks."

Randall touched his arm. "Listen, Dad, I heard about your fiancée. I'm really sorry. I heard you got sober but . . ." Randall sighed. "I'm not here to bust your balls. Been there, done that."

Two identical grins lit the room.

"Phillip told Mom you haven't heard from Sheila in a while? What happened?"

Morris rubbed his head. His ex-wife had heard? Great. "I don't know where she is. And frankly, I'm really worried."

"Are the cops looking for her?"

"They were. But they don't think anything's happened to her and they closed the case. I hired a PI to look into it. Sheila told me things were over, but she had some, uh, personal problems I only recently found out about. I need to make sure she's okay."

"At the very least you need closure." Randall sipped the last of his coffee. "Funny, I wouldn't have predicted this in a million years. She seemed so committed to you."

"I thought she was," Morris said, then looked up. "But how would you know that?"

"Because we've been in touch. She tracked me down to invite me to your wedding. Was pretty relentless about it, actually. She got me thinking about things." Randall frowned. "If it weren't for her, I wouldn't be here. I thought you knew."

Morris was stunned. "I had no idea."

"Maybe she wanted it to be a surprise. She was trying to find me for weeks. But I couldn't get to a phone or a computer all that often, couldn't even remember what my e-mail address was half the time."

Morris nodded. "That's what I'd heard. Though it was good of you to send me that e-mail about your friend Tom."

"Who?"

"Your friend? Tom Young? From Stanford. I interviewed him for a position at the bank."

A look of concern spread over Randall's clean-cut features. "Dad, I have no idea what you're talking about. First Donna, now Tom? Are you sure you don't have another son out there named Randall who knows these people?"

Morris was bewildered.

Randall seemed equally confused. "Maybe I'd know him if I saw him—I'm better with faces than I am with names. Or maybe he just really wanted the job at the bank and dropped my name to score an 'in' with you. Did you hire him?"

"He never came back." An uneasy feeling swept over Morris. "Never mind. I'll sort it out." He smiled, but something wasn't right. His mind flew back to the night he'd had dinner with the guy. Tom Young had known too much about his family problems for a guy who'd just wanted an interview.

Someone was fucking with Morris and he didn't like it one bit.

His son stood up. "I should get going. I have to see that apartment in half an hour. It's downtown, near the fish market. You still make a mean grilled salmon? If I get the apartment, you should come over, show me your secret recipe."

Morris resisted the urge to rumple Randall's hair. He wasn't a kid anymore. "You bet," he said instead. "What about football? You still play?"

"Not since I left Stanford. You?"

"Does it look like it?" Morris rubbed his belly and grinned. "Nah. Knees are shot. Not even a weekend warrior anymore."

"I can't remember the last time I saw a game."

"I have Seahawks season tickets. What are you doing next Sunday?"

"Going to the game with you."

For only the second time in six years, Morris embraced his son. "I'm glad you stopped by." Morris's voice was choked with emotion. "And that you're doing so well, despite all the things I put you through as a kid. You deserved a much better father than you got."

"It's okay, Dad." Randall's voice cracked, too. "It was my choice to disappear. But we can deal with it later. I just want to move forward."

Morris waved as his son drove off in the dented Jeep, feeling the best he'd had in weeks. Then he headed back into the house to call Jerry Isaac.

Happy day or not, who the hell was Tom Young?

CHAPTER : 28

Jerry had some information of his own to share with Morris. The two men met for lunch at the Golden Monkey, a dive in the heart of the International District that was cheap and funky smelling even going by dive Chinese-restaurant standards. The place was packed. Men and women in business suits filled the room, happy to take advantage of the lunch specials.

"I love this place," Jerry crowed, digging into a small plate of Cantonese chow mein. "It closed down last summer due to health-code violations, but it just reopened. Thank God." Using his chopsticks, he scooped up a mouthful of noodles and chewed contentedly.

"Was it necessary to tell me that?" Morris stirred his wonton soup and suddenly wondered if the wontons were really wontons. His mind flashed back to the scene in the second *Indiana Jones* movie where the queasy actress asked for soup and they brought her a big bowl of steaming eyeballs.

Jerry belly-laughed. "I'm kidding. Really. The food here's excellent. I know the owners."

"I'm glad they put their money into the food, since they obviously don't spend it on the décor." Morris looked around dubiously at the peeling wallpaper and dusty window ledges.

Sheila was Chinese, and she would have hated it here. But he took a spoonful of soup, not wanting to be impolite. He was surprised by how good it was.

Jerry leaned forward. "So, I thought you'd like to know that my friend was able to hack into your fiancée's computer."

Morris stopped eating. "And?"

"We found some interesting things in there."

"Like what?" Morris couldn't meet Jerry's gaze.

The private investigator took another mouthful of noodles, then put his chopsticks down. "Did you know that Sheila was a member of an online dating service called Montgomery's Den?"

Morris let out a breath. "No, I didn't."

"It's geared specifically to married or 'attached' adults. In fact, you can't sign up for it unless you declare that you are married or have a full-time live-in partner." Jerry sipped his tea, looking uncomfortable. "The point of it is to meet people for sex."

Morris slumped back in the stained upholstered chair. "So it's a site that helps married people cheat?"

"Exactly. And it's popular because it preaches discretion. The people you meet on the site would never rat you out because they don't want to be caught themselves."

"Fantastic. Where was this fifteen years ago when I was thinking of cheating on my wife?"

Jerry snorted. "Gotta love technology. Anyway, we were able to get into Sheila's account. My friend has a password-retrieval program. It seems she was quite active until about three years ago. Almost nothing since."

Morris put his spoon down, his appetite gone.

Jerry looked sympathetic. He took another bite of his noodles and chewed slowly before swallowing. "She's talked to a large number of men. A lot of the exchanges, as they're called, were saved on her hard drive. It would appear that her main interest on this site was webcam-type stuff. It's hard to tell if she's met with anyone in person, but I'm guessing she hasn't, at least not in the last three years. We found quite a few videos she'd saved—basically peep shows that other men have done for her. I would assume she's done the same back for them."

"We met two years ago."

"So she quit before she met you." Jerry smiled. "Good news, right?"

Morris felt like kicking him. "What about her e-mails?"

"We checked, but it would seem she kept most of the Montgomery stuff in her Montgomery account. There were a couple of e-mails from men she met on the site, so it looks like from time to time she may have given them a personal e-mail address, which was a Gmail account. Doesn't look like anyone used their real name, though, and there's no way to follow up since everyone else used free webmail, too."

Jerry paused to sip his tea. "We were also able to log into her university account. Pretty standard stuff, mostly from students. Plus quite a few messages from her teaching assistants." He put his cup down and cracked his knuckles. "One in particular. Have you ever met any of the TAs that work under her?"

The look on his face made Morris uneasy. "I'm not sure. Maybe. Her department has a Christmas ball every year, and I went last year. I might have been introduced to a few of them."

"The name Ethan Wolfe ring a bell?"

Morris sat up with a start. "Actually, yeah." He pictured the cocky twentysomething who'd stopped by Sheila's office the night he'd given her the bracelet. "He's been working for her for a while now. Oh, hell," Morris said, noticing Jerry's expression. "Don't tell me. That's the student she was screwing around with?"

"You knew it was a student?"

Morris said nothing.

The PI looked annoyed. He was clearly about to say something, but then he appeared to change his mind. He speared a dumpling with his chopstick instead. "Look, I don't know anything for a fact. Some of the e-mails were suggestive, but there's nothing definite."

Morris struggled to process this news. "Son of a bitch. That arrogant little prick." It took a moment for the information to fully sink in, and when it did, he couldn't temper his rage. "Goddammit! This just confirms I know nothing about this woman. She told me he was a student, but *that* guy? Are you kidding me?" Morris's voice was loud, and several heads turned in their direction at the outburst. The old lady pushing the dim sum cart frowned at them.

"Easy now." Jerry smiled reassuringly at the patrons around them and leaned in. "There's something else you should know." He paused again, uncomfortable.

As if it could get any worse.

"I'm pretty sure she's a sex addict."

Morris blew out a breath. "Yeah. I knew."

"Jesus Christ, man!" Jerry stared at him in disbelief. "Have you ever heard of the term *pertinent information*? This would have been important to know earlier. I thought you hired me to help you."

"Have you ever heard of the term *need-to-know basis*?" Morris's face was hot. "You didn't need to know. It's *her* issue. She's worked hard at keeping it private—from me, from everyone. I did tell you about the affair," he said defiantly, but he knew he sounded stupid and illogical.

"Man, are you serious? Sheila was a regular member of Sex Addicts Anonymous. I checked the calendar in her computer, and it looks like she's been going to meetings for three years. Can you imagine the kinds of people she's come into contact with? Who knows what issues these people had? She could have been stalked." It was Jerry's turn to get loud and he was breathing hard, food forgotten. "Why didn't you tell me up front? I could have used this information a long time ago, Morris!"

Morris pounded the table. "I don't know, *Jerry*." But that was a lie. He knew why. He didn't tell Jerry because it was shameful. It hit him then how hard it must have been for Sheila to tell him. His face flushed at the thought of how badly he'd reacted.

"Hey." Jerry raised his hands in a mea culpa gesture. "It's okay to be pissed. It doesn't mean you love her any less or that she isn't worthy of finding. You can be worried and pissed at the same time."

Morris put his head in his hands. "Why'd I even open this can of worms? She left me. Why can't I accept that? She's a smart woman, she knows what she's doing. She called me, she broke up with me, it happens every day."

"Yeah, she did, and it does. But she's also gone. And that doesn't happen every day. If you think it's strange, then it's strange. I don't give a shit what the police think. They have to follow protocol. I don't, and that's why you hired me. We'll figure it out, don't worry."

Morris stared at the tablecloth. "So where do we go from here?"

"The Montgomery's Den site is probably a dead end since she's been inactive, so I'll start with her Sex Addicts Anonymous meetings. Someone there might know something. Maybe she had a sponsor."

"I'd like to be there."

Jerry didn't look thrilled with the idea, but he nodded. "I checked online. There are three groups that meet in the greater

Seattle area, two in Northgate, and one all the way out in Renton on Thursday nights. Which is tonight. I'll start there, though I'm guessing she's probably a member of one of the Seattle groups—"

Morris shook his head. "No, I bet it's the one tonight."

"How can you be sure?"

"Because Renton is the farthest away from the university. And because she was never once available on a Thursday night."

Jerry looked impressed. "Okay, good. The meetings are held at the Front Street Methodist Church. I can meet you there at seven. The meeting starts at eight, so that should give us enough time to find the meeting leader and talk to him. Or her."

"I'll find it." Morris sighed heavily. "A church? That's interesting. Can you imagine discussing sex addiction in a church? Christ," Morris said, and Jerry smiled at the pun.

The PI ate the last dumpling and pushed his plate away. "So, what was the other thing you wanted to discuss?"

Morris looked down at his soup. It was cold and unappetizing. He thought briefly of the mysterious Tom Young, then shook his head. "You know what, it can wait. Let's see where tonight goes. By the way, I don't know if I mentioned this, but I really want to kill that little son of a bitch."

"The student? Ethan Wolfe?"

Morris nodded, his face grim.

"Be careful there, my friend." Jerry sounded serious. "Stay cool. You might only be half-joking, but in this business, you'd be amazed at what I've seen. Let me handle it, okay? I'll talk to him."

"Plan to do it soon."

CHAPTER : 29

It was hard to imagine Dennis Fisher as a sex addict. He was so . . . ordinary. And he looked so young. Until you got a look at his eyes. Morris was curious to know what kind of sexual behavior the meeting leader was addicted to, but of course it would be rude to ask.

Morris, Jerry, and Fisher were sitting in a cramped office in the basement of the Front Street Methodist Church in Renton.

"I'm sorry, guys, but I don't know anybody named Sheila Tao."

Jerry plucked a photo out of his shirt pocket and slid it across the metal desk. "This is her."

Fisher picked it up, his eyes widening. "This is *Stella*. She's the one who's missing?"

"Her name is Sheila," Morris said.

"She goes by Stella here, then." Fisher pushed the picture back. "Not that it's surprising. A lot of people make up fake names. There's such a stigma attached to sex addiction. It's not like other addictions, you know."

Morris was beginning to see that.

"You must be her fiancé, then? She talked about you a lot."

"Yeah? And what name did she give me?" Morris asked, bitter.

Fisher smiled sympathetically. "She told me you were a really good guy and she couldn't wait to marry you."

Morris said nothing.

"I was happy for her," Fisher continued. "And proud that she'd been honest with you from the beginning."

"I didn't find out about her addiction until about three weeks ago."

Fisher sat back. "Jeez. If I'd known she'd been keeping it from you, I wouldn't have been so supportive. It's one thing to lie about your name—that's understandable—but lying about the progress you've made in your own recovery? That tells me she wasn't ready to get hitched. So what happened?"

Jerry gave the man a quick rundown while Morris sat and listened. The office was hot and stifling. He tugged at his shirt collar.

Fisher thought before he spoke. "I wish I could tell you I knew she was planning to leave. But she never said anything to me about it."

"When did you last see her?" Jerry had his notebook in hand.

"Two weeks ago. She came to the meeting."

"Are you her sponsor?" Morris asked.

Fisher shook his head. "Cross-gender sponsorship is a no-no. She never wanted one, though—not everyone is comfortable with that component of the program. She mentioned she had a therapist. Not that it's any help to you."

"Therapists never talk about their patients. This I know from experience." Jerry scribbled something down in his notebook. "So, was Sheila acting differently that night at the meeting? Anything weird about her behavior?"

Fisher pondered the question, his fingers drumming on the desk. "I can't recall anything specific, although maybe she was a little quieter than usual. We spoke for a bit before the meeting started. I was impressed she made it in, what with the wedding coming up and all. It demonstrated how committed she was to her recovery, and I told her that."

Morris turned to Jerry. "We should ask some of the other members. Maybe someone else might know if there was anything going on with her."

Fisher shifted in his chair. "I can't allow that. The members value their privacy and we do everything we can to protect it. She didn't form any close friendships with anyone here that I noticed—and I would have noticed." He thought for a moment. "There was a new member she talked to during the break."

"A man?" Jerry's eyes shifted to Morris.

"Yes. He sat near the front so I got a pretty good look at him. Late thirties, I'd say, around six feet, two hundred pounds."

"White? Black? Hispanic? Asian?"

"Black," Fisher said firmly, then added, "but not *black* black."

"I beg your pardon?" Jerry's pen froze over his notepad. "What exactly is '*black* black'?"

Fisher flushed a deep crimson. He looked at Morris as if to plead for help.

Morris bit back a smirk and said nothing. *Good luck, buddy.*

Fisher tried to explain. "You know, like he wasn't *really* black. Like, I mean, he wasn't dark-skinned . . ."

"Like me?" Jerry said.

"Well, no, not exactly . . ."

"He was light-skinned?"

"Yes, light-skinned. As if he was . . ."

"Of mixed race?"

"Exactly."

Jerry's jaw worked, but he jotted the information down. After a moment of excruciating silence, he said, "Okay, what else?"

"He was very attentive during the meeting, not at all uncomfortable. I got the impression he was either a member somewhere else and had just moved here or was visiting and didn't want to miss a meeting. I overheard them chatting a little bit. He had a slight limp. And a funny accent."

"What kind of accent?"

"Couldn't tell you. He just sounded different."

"Name?"

"Not sure. John? James?" Fisher paused. "James, I think."

"Did she leave with this guy?" Morris asked, his throat dry.

"No idea."

"Anything else you can think to mention?" Jerry said.

"No." Fisher looked upset. "But you could see if she went to Tony's Tavern afterwards. She usually did. It's just down the street. And I'll ask some of the other members if they noticed or overheard anything. Better I do it than you guys. If I learn anything, I'll let you know."

Jerry put his card on the desk. "Just call me with whatever you learn, even if you don't think it's significant. You never know what it might lead to."

Fisher stuck the card in his shirt pocket. "Please keep me posted. Stella was a friend."

"Sheila," Morris corrected again.

Fisher's smile was sad. "She was Stella to me."

: : : :

Tony's Tavern was dimly lit, and it reeked of grease and beer. Morris's kind of place. He enjoyed his porterhouse steak and his forty-year-old Scotch, but it still came in a close second to a thick homemade burger and a pile of freshly fried onion rings. He and Jerry took a seat at the bar.

A waitress with frizzy red hair approached. "What can I get you boys?"

Morris consulted the menu and ordered the mushroom-Swiss burger with onion rings. Jerry ordered the fish and chips. Both ordered Miller Lites, on tap.

Morris felt a stab of guilt. It was officially the first time in two years he'd ordered alcohol in a restaurant.

"The one thing I love about not working for the department anymore," Jerry said as he raised his glass to his lips, "is I can drink while I'm working."

"I'll toast to that," Morris said.

The waitress smiled as she wiped the bar in front of them. "What are we toasting, boys?" Her voice matched her face, hoarse and weathered.

"Drinking on the job." Jerry smiled at her and raised his glass again. "This is Morris. I'm Jerry."

"Jean." The waitress shook both their hands. "I haven't seen you's here before. You from Seattle or just visiting?"

"We're locals," Morris said. "I don't get down this way much. I live on the East Side."

"So you're slumming it." Jean chuckled. "What, they don't have pubs on the East Side?"

"Hey, Jean," Jerry said, pulling out the picture of Sheila. "You ever seen this woman?"

Jean picked up the photo and dug into her apron pocket for her glasses. "I knew you guys was cops."

Jerry laughed. "I'm retired. I work for myself now. This guy's my client, and we're looking for his fiancée. She went missing two weeks ago."

Jean stood with the photo under one of the small halogen lights illuminating the bar, examining the picture closely. "Yeah, I've seen her before," she said, her eyes crinkled in concentration. "Buncha times. She comes in here a coupla times a month. Always gets the same thing—mushroom-Swiss, Diet Coke. Seemed nice enough."

"Was she here two weeks ago?"

Jean's face scrunched up. "Yeah, she was."

"You sound certain."

The waitress looked uncomfortable as she passed the photo back. "Well, I remember 'cause she came in at her usual time, but instead of sitting alone like she usually does, she met someone. He came in a little later, went right to her table."

"What'd he look like?" Morris's hand tightened around his beer glass.

"I don't know. It was dark. My eyes ain't what they used to be."

"Try and think." He couldn't keep the impatience out of his voice. Jerry shot him a look.

The woman bristled. "Well, now, I don't know if I want to. Not if it's gonna get her in trouble."

"Jean, she's missing." Jerry's voice was calm. "Anything you can tell us would be helpful. We're trying to make sure nothing bad happened to her."

Jean leaned over the bar toward them, focusing on Morris. "Look, it's not any of my business what kind of relationship you's two were in. I'm not one to judge. But this woman you're looking for, your fiancée, she wasn't acting like a woman about to get married. They sat right there." Jean pointed to the table in the center-most part of the pub. "And they were close. Leaning into each other, smiling. I served them. He was a real good-looking guy." She gave a description that matched the one Fisher had given them. "He wasn't from around here. He had some kind of accent."

"Like he wasn't from Seattle?"

"Like he wasn't from the USA."

Morris's stomach burned. "Did they leave together?"

Jean's wrinkled face was sympathetic. "Yeah," she said finally. "They left together. He was kind of touching her elbow, and he was limping a little. She looked tipsy, even though she wasn't drinking. I figured she was giddy 'cause she'd snagged such a handsome guy." Jean's lips tightened. "Truth be told, I was a little jealous."

"How'd they pay?" Jerry asked.

"Cash, I'm pretty sure. Separate checks," she said to Morris, as if it would make him feel better.

"This place have a security camera?"

The waitress guffawed. "You're funny."

"Any chance you saw what he was driving?"

"Sorry." She looked around and lowered her voice. "So, what, you boys think this guy did something to her?"

Morris said nothing.

Jerry shrugged. "No idea. We'll have to find him and ask him. What about a name? Did you hear her call him anything?"

"No, but he told me himself his name was Jack. Or James." Jean paused, thinking. "Or was it Jason?"

Jerry watched her, his pen poised over his notebook.

Finally she said, "I think it was James, but I'm not a hundred percent." A bell dinged from somewhere behind her and she straightened up. "That's your food. Be right back."

Morris took a long sip of his beer, suddenly wishing he hadn't come. Maybe it was better to let Jerry handle everything. The private investigator would have filtered this information for him. Right now it was almost too real. Raw.

Jean came back with their order.

"So you didn't see them drive off together, did you?" Morris said, pouncing on her again. "It's possible she got into her own car and left separately?"

"I didn't see what happened when they got to the parking lot." Jean was beginning to sound exasperated. "But, guys, I work in a bar. I have for most of my life. You think I can't tell when two people hook up?" She looked at Morris. "I'm sorry. Just telling you what I saw."

"You okay?" Jerry asked when she walked away.

Morris looked down at his food. "What do you think?"

They dug into their meals. The burger was decent.

"Listen. I think we're at a bit of a dead end here." Jerry took a long sip of his beer. "Unless Fisher's found out something from the other SAA members, we don't have anything to go on."

"What are the chances that somebody from SAA would remember someone's license plate number from two weeks ago?"

Jerry munched on a fry. "Stranger things have happened. We could get lucky. But it's not likely."

"What now?"

"I'll talk to her TA tomorrow, Ethan Wolfe, the one she seemed . . . close to." Jerry picked up another fry. He was choosing his words carefully. "He might know something. And Torrance ran her credit cards when he was investigating—I have a contact who can do it again for me. If she's used them in the last couple of days, we can track her that way."

Morris didn't reply, and they finished their food in silence. When they were done, Jerry paid the check.

"You didn't have to do that," Morris said as they walked out.

"Don't worry, you'll see it expensed in my invoice."

Morris chuckled, though he doubted Jerry was joking. "What are you doing now? Maybe we should talk to Ethan Wolfe tonight."

"Nah, I'll catch him first thing in the morning," Jerry said.

"I don't want you there, anyway. I'll call you if I learn anything interesting. For now, go home and rest. Enough excitement for one day."

Morris stopped when they reached their cars. "What if she's dead?" he said quietly. The wind was chilly and he shivered under the pale light of the parking-lot lamppost. "What if she had some kind of blackout or breakdown and she's lying dead in a ditch somewhere?"

"Don't think that." Jerry looked at Morris sharply. "You keep that shit out of your head. It won't help you, trust me. Right now the best thing you can do is stay positive. Remember, Torrance might still be right. In which case, we'll find her, and you can ask her yourself what the hell she was thinking." Jerry clapped Morris on the shoulder, then climbed into his Honda and slammed the door shut.

"I don't know if I want to know," Morris said after the PI drove away.

CHAPTER: 30

Jerry sat in the parking lot of the university's psychology building. The interior of his Honda Accord still smelled like cigarette smoke from the guy he'd bought it off last year, and Jerry's wife refused to ride in it. Which was fine, since he only used the ten-year-old car for work, anyway. Jerry's real car, a Nissan Infinity G37 coupe in titanium gray, was sitting in the garage at home, pristine. Annie said the coupe was an extension of his penis and a pathetic attempt to hold on to his youth, and she was right.

His cell phone rang. It was Dennis Fisher, calling to follow up.

"You said to phone if I learned anything new." Fisher's voice was tentative.

Jerry had his notebook ready and his pen poised. "Definitely. You never know what might help." He looked out the window at a pretty coed strolling by wearing jeans so tight he could see the outline of her crotch. What did Annie call that? *Cameltoe?* Damn, these girls today.

"I talked to a few members last night after the meeting, the ones who are on a friendly basis with Stella—sorry, *Sheila*—and some of them remembered seeing her talking with that new guy I told you about." Fisher cleared his throat. "His name was definitely James. A couple of the female members described him as good-looking."

Jerry smirked. Apparently not even sex addiction therapy could turn off your radar. He scribbled in his notebook.

Fisher continued. "Also, James left in an SUV. Another member saw him in the parking lot getting into something big and black. American-made, he thought. Washington State plates. Didn't get the plate number, though."

"Good observational skills."

"That's Kenneth," Fisher said. "He notices everything. He said for you to give him a call, but I pressed him and there's nothing else he knows."

"Give me his number just in case." Jerry jotted it down. "That it?"

"Yeah. Hope it helps. And listen, I'm sorry about that comment—"

"Forget about it." Jerry thanked him and hung up.

He looked up through the windshield at the old building in front of him. The George Herbert Mead Department of Psychology. Jerry had long forgotten what kind of psychologist George Herbert Mead was, but the man must have made a significant contribution to the field if they'd named a whole university department after him.

In light of her sudden absence, the three courses Sheila was teaching this semester had been divided among her colleagues—none of whom, according to the secretary whose voice had dramatically dropped to a whisper, had been happy about the increased course load. But the teaching assistants for each class were still the same.

Ethan Wolfe kept office hours on Tuesdays, Thursdays, and Fridays. Jerry was interested to find out exactly what the graduate student might know. The TA's e-mails were more suggestive than he'd told Morris, and considering his client's reaction at the restaurant the other day, that was probably a good call. Pulling his lanky frame out of his small car, Jerry headed inside.

The smell of the psychology building instantly brought him back to the four years he'd spent in night school studying to get his bachelor's degree. That would have been ten years ago now. Pine floor-cleaner and slightly stale air, shiny hallways with thickly painted brick walls. Nothing had changed. The two main lecture halls were in the center with several smaller classrooms dotting the first and second floors. Administrative offices were on the third floor, and the top three floors were reserved for teaching staff.

Jerry rode up the elevator in silence beside a girl with glossy brown hair who couldn't have been older than twenty. Her jeans were tight, too, and her sweater hugged breasts so high and firm they seemed to defy gravity. Did any of these girls wear baggy clothes anymore? How did the male professors resist temptation? It would be so easy to slip. He wondered if that was what happened with Sheila.

Jerry remembered Morris Gardener's fiancée well. She was attractive and confident with a healthy sense of humor that kept her lectures fresh. She had the ability to remember almost every student's name, and those damned sexy red lips—it hadn't taken long for Jerry to form a little crush on her, another tiny detail he'd refrained from mentioning to Morris. Jerry rather liked his face and didn't want Morris's ham fist breaking it.

Had Sheila Tao been a sex addict back then? It was hard to picture, but it just proved that people were almost never who they seemed. Everybody had secrets.

Ethan Wolfe's office was at the end of the hall. Jerry hadn't called in advance to let the TA know he was coming. People's reactions after the initial surprise were always telling.

The door was open and Jerry paused in the doorway. Wolfe was at his desk, typing studiously on his keyboard, eyes focused on the computer monitor in front of him. The office was nothing to write home about. A desk, a computer, two chairs, and a bookshelf stuffed with textbooks. Beige paint on the walls, a plastic plant in one corner. A Seahawks bobblehead sat on the desk beside the computer, nodding at nothing.

Jerry stood for a moment to observe the younger man, who didn't appear to notice he was being watched. Wolfe didn't look like a particularly small guy, but Morris had to outweigh him by at least seventy pounds. Not a smart move on the kid's part, getting involved with Sheila.

Jerry cleared his throat.

Wolfe, without looking up, said, "Be right with you." The student's fingers continued to type out words Jerry couldn't see from where he was standing. It seemed everyone under thirty could type nowadays, Jerry thought, noting Wolfe's perfect hand position at the keyboard. In his day, only secretaries could type.

The bobblehead nodded in rhythm to Wolfe's movements, and the spring in its neck produced a squeaking sound that didn't take long to get on Jerry's nerves. He resisted the urge to reach out and make it still. Not that he was easily distracted, but damned if that bouncing head wasn't annoying as hell.

Standing politely in the doorway, he waited for Wolfe to finish. Finally the younger man looked up. His handsome face displayed genuine surprise to see the tall black man watching him.

"Can I help you?" Wolfe asked, standing up. Jerry noticed

that his eyes, a striking pale gray, were rimmed with red. Fatigue, or staring at the computer screen too long? Or something else? His face had a hollow look, but since Jerry had never met this kid before, he couldn't tell if this was normal or not.

"Jerry Isaac." He eased into the little office and slid a business card across the desk. "Sorry to interrupt. I'm here to ask you some questions about Dr. Sheila Tao."

Wolfe shook his hand. "I didn't think you looked like a student, but you never know, do you? I'm Ethan Wolfe, but you look like you already know that."

"Mind if I sit?"

"Please." Wolfe looked over Jerry's card. "Private investigator, huh? The police were just here last week. Kind of freaked everybody out. We thought Dr. Tao left for personal reasons, but they made it sound like something bad happened. Are you working with them, or did the family hire you?"

Jerry smiled. "Yes to both," he replied, the answer rolling smoothly off his tongue. "I'm just here to follow up."

"But I thought the police weren't concerned about Dr. Tao." Wolfe seemed confused. "We called them for an update a couple of days ago and they told us they'd closed the investigation. Confirmed that she'd left of her own accord."

"That's why the family hired me. To look into it a bit further. Police investigations aren't always as thorough as my clients would like. Thank God for that, or I'd be out of business." Jerry chuckled. "I understand you've been working with the professor for about a year now."

"This is—was—my third semester with her, yeah."

"Anything you can tell me about her?"

"Like what?"

"Does her sudden disappearance surprise you?"

"*Disappearance?*" Wolfe repeated. He rocked back in his

chair and appraised the private investigator coolly. "They're no longer calling it an *absence*?"

Jerry waved a hand. "Just words. Does her *absence* strike you as weird?"

"Totally. She's not the kind of person to just take off. She was very organized, very meticulous about her schedule."

"Rigid."

Wolfe looked thoughtful. "No, not rigid. She would make time for anybody. She'd often meet with students outside her regular office hours, and I don't know many professors who did that. But she was very particular about getting things done, very committed to her work. So, yeah, I'd say it's surprising for her to just up and leave."

"She didn't say anything to you that might have hinted this was coming?"

"No. Why would she tell me?"

Jerry's gaze didn't waver. "Why do you think she left?"

"I have no idea. I couldn't say."

"If you could speculate . . ."

"I don't speculate."

Jerry chuckled again. "So you're telling me that you guys— you and the other TAs—haven't sat around talking about why you think she's gone? Come on now, Mr. Wolfe. You're a psychologist in training. Isn't that just human nature?"

"Why do I feel like I'm being interrogated here?"

"I don't know. Why do you? Is there something you're feeling guilty about?"

Wolfe's gaze remained cool. "Okay, you want my *professional* opinion? Maybe she's having a midlife crisis. She's at the right age. She's about to get married; her taking off could be a stress reaction to making a commitment. She was single for a long time. It can be hard to change your ways, settle down, when you've been on your own for so long."

"From what I know of women, they usually like being in relationships."

Wolfe shrugged. "It's a theory. You asked me to speculate."

"Was she pretty open about her personal life?"

"With me?"

"With anyone. Including you."

"Sometimes. We've worked together for a while now. It's natural that personal stuff would come up."

"And how would you characterize your relationship?"

Wolfe shrugged again. "Employer, employee. Professor, student."

"You weren't friends?"

"We were friendly."

"How friendly?"

"We had a great working relationship," Wolfe said with a smile.

"But you were more than just colleagues." Jerry stated this as fact.

"Were we?"

"That's what I've heard."

Wolfe's eyes narrowed. "You shouldn't believe everything you hear."

"So you never socialized outside the university?"

"Define *socialized*."

"Did you two have something going on?" There. A direct question. Jerry watched Wolfe's reaction closely.

The TA's face registered surprise. "You're kidding, right? You know how old she is?"

"What does age matter?" Jerry cracked his knuckles. "She's a pretty lady."

Wolfe laughed. "It matters to me. Besides, my girlfriend wouldn't be too impressed."

"No, I'd guess not," Jerry agreed good-naturedly. "But you didn't answer the question."

"Which was?"

"Were you fucking your professor or not?"

Wolfe stiffened.

"I'll close the door so you can speak openly." Jerry stood, his chair scraping the shiny floors of the office.

"No." The sudden urgency in the graduate student's voice caused Jerry to turn back in surprise. "The door stays open."

Jerry stared at him and sat back down. "Your call." He pulled his chair closer to the desk. "I'm waiting for an answer, Mr. Wolfe."

"Oh, for Christ's sake," Wolfe snapped, clearly unnerved. "No, we weren't getting it on."

"Funny." Jerry picked at a loose thread on his khaki slacks. "That's not what your e-mails would suggest."

"What e-mails?"

"The e-mails you've exchanged with Dr. Tao over the past few months. Three months, to be exact. Isn't that how long the affair lasted?"

Wolfe stiffened. "It's illegal for you to break into her e-mail. I could have your license yanked."

Jerry smiled easily. "Who says I broke in? Her fiancé knew her password and gave it to me. But thanks for the law lesson."

"This is bullshit. You've totally misinterpreted."

"Come on, man." Jerry sighed. "You were having sex with her. Admit it."

"That's disgusting." Wolfe's face scrunched up to demonstrate just how disagreeable it was. "She's sixteen years older than I am."

"But she had good genes. Looked younger."

"To you, maybe."

"You didn't find her attractive?"

"Not compared to my girlfriend."

"Who initiated it?"

"There was nothing to initiate."

"I heard she was a flirt," Jerry said.

The teaching assistant hesitated. "Well, yeah. But that was just her way of flattering you. Of making you feel good about yourself. It was all in good fun."

"And you never flirted back?"

"I already said. Never. And I'd really like to know who said we were hitting it, because I can confirm that we most definitely were not."

Jerry grinned. "You're right, I guess I misinterpreted. What do I know, I'm an old dog. In my day, there was no such thing as e-mail. What I might think is sexual innuendo could just be . . . friendly conversation."

Wolfe didn't respond. The two of them sat staring at each other.

A discreet clearing of the throat distracted both men, and Wolfe's eyes flickered past Jerry to the doorway behind him. A petite blonde was standing there, laptop case slung over one shoulder and a bag full of textbooks thrown over the other. She looked nineteen.

She smiled self-consciously, looking past Jerry. "Hi, Ethan. I think I'm a bit early."

"Hi, Suzanne," Wolfe said. If he was relieved to be interrupted, he didn't show it. "Can you give me five minutes? We're nearly done here."

"Sure." Her eyes skimmed over Jerry. "I'll grab a coffee. Want anything?"

"Coffee would be great. Cream and sugar. Need change?"

She shook her head, closing the door behind her firmly.

Before Jerry had a chance to react, Wolfe was up and out of his seat, maneuvering his lean body toward the door. Flinging it open, he practically fell into the hallway, his breathing heavy. Jerry saw that beads of sweat had formed at the younger man's temples.

Strange.

"Are we done here?" Wolfe was still in the hallway, struggling to compose himself. "As you can see, I have a student waiting."

"I guess we are." Jerry stood up, looking at him closely as he ambled out into the hallway. "Thanks for your time, Mr. Wolfe. You have my card. Let me know if you think of anything that might be helpful."

Wolfe raised an eyebrow. "You know, that's the exact same thing the police said. Who am I supposed to call—them or you?"

"Me," Jerry said cheerfully. "Definitely me."

: : : :

Detective Mike Torrance met Jerry at the Golden Monkey a few hours later. Jerry could easily eat here five days a week. They had the best dim sum in Seattle. Morris hadn't seemed too impressed, but Jerry was convinced.

"I think something's definitely up with this Ethan Wolfe guy," Jerry said, peeling the paper off his *char siu bao,* a wonderful doughy delight that opened to reveal tasty barbecued pork inside. The steam poured out and he let it breathe on his plate so he wouldn't burn his tongue. "He rubs me the wrong way. Something about him is off. You know the type?"

"I am the type," Torrance said, spearing a *siu mai* with his fork. Torrance couldn't use chopsticks to save his life. "So he lied about the affair? Did he not think there'd be evidence somewhere? Not that I blame him. He admits they're fucking, it looks bad if she turns up dead. But it is sort of hard to picture. He's a good-looking guy, young, and she's what, thirty-nine? Not your average hookup."

"But she's attractive," Jerry said. "You wouldn't think it was so far-fetched if you'd met her. There really is something about her. She's got a certain je ne sais quoi."

Torrance stopped chewing. "Oh, shit. Don't tell me you slept with her?"

"No." Jerry gave his former partner a dirty look. He took his first bite of the *siu bao,* savoring the flavor. "But the thought did cross my mind. If I was single, I wouldn't have thought twice about it."

Torrance snorted. "I'm sure Annie would be happy to know that," he said, referring to Jerry's wife. He looked over the selection of food on the table and speared a shrimp roll. "But what if Tao was, say, sixteen years older than you? The same age difference between her and Wolfe? What if she was seventy? Would you still find her attractive?"

Jerry laughed. "That's not the same thing and you know it. She and Wolfe definitely had an affair. That's a fact. Sheila admitted it to Morris."

"It's only half a fact. She never told him the name of the student."

"You didn't see the e-mails. It has to be Wolfe."

"You mean the e-mails you illegally hacked into?"

"No, the e-mails that I paid someone else to illegally hack into," Jerry said with his mouth full. "Asshole."

"I thought you said there was nothing specific in them."

"Not in so many words, no."

"You can't prove anything. People flirt all the time."

"I can read between the lines, Mike. She told her fiancé she had an affair with a student." Jerry waved to a passing waitress and pointed to their empty teapot. "I'd bet my left nut it was Wolfe."

"Tao's a sex addict, isn't she? God knows how many students she was screwing. Flirty e-mails or not, you need proof. I know you don't like this guy, but stay objective." Torrance forked another pot sticker. "I still think the lady took off. There's just no evidence otherwise. And Gardener's kind of . . . big. She could still attract a twentysomething, but she was gonna marry *him*? I'd have second thoughts, too."

"That's mean," Jerry said, mildly offended. "Morris is a nice guy."

"Sorry, didn't mean to insult your friend."

Jerry ignored the jab. "My *client* is a nice person. Good job, makes a lot of money, lives on the East Side. Used to play for the Packers. He's a catch."

"Maybe you should date him."

"Fuck you."

They ate in comfortable silence for a minute, then Jerry said, "I'm at a dead end."

"I figured." Torrance sighed. "I hate to say it, but I told you so. Tao freaked out, and she walked. I never really thought this would go anywhere—you know I don't hand you live cases. So you tell Gardener you tried, collect your big fat fee, and go on your merry way. What's the problem?"

"Speaking of fat fees." Jerry pulled a small white envelope out of his jacket and slid it across the table. "Here's your cut. Thanks for the referral. But I'm telling you, something doesn't feel right about this."

"Thank you kindly." Torrance eased the envelope into his

shirt pocket. "But don't think you're not paying for lunch. I'm not spending my money to eat in this shithole."

"If I'm buying lunch, you need to do me a favor."

"Depends." Torrance's mouth was full of dumpling.

"Can you run a detailed background check on Wolfe?"

Torrance almost choked. "Are you nuts? That would be a violation of Wolfe's privacy. He's not officially a suspect in her disappearance because she's not officially missing. And you want me to tap into the department's resources to find out who he is? Why don't you do it?"

"I can access only so much. That's why I called it a favor, moron."

Torrance stifled a belch. "I'll see what I can do. No promises."

They ate in silence for a moment.

"So how's the investigation into the St. Clair murder going?" Jerry asked. "Any juicy details you can share with me?"

"You fishing for inside info?"

"Always."

Torrance wiped his mouth with a paper napkin before speaking. "You know she was killed before she was dumped in the water, right?" His voice was low.

"I heard she was stabbed a bunch of times."

"Forty, to be exact." Torrance glanced around. "But according to the autopsy results, she was actually dead before that. The fucker sliced her throat, cut her carotid. She likely bled out in three, four minutes. You won't see this in the paper. Not until we catch the guy."

"So the stabbing was postmortem. That's a lot of rage."

"Oh, yeah." Torrance nodded, sipping his tea. "Somebody hated her. Or loved her."

"Or both," Jerry said.

CHAPTER: 31

"**I**'m starving," Sheila said when Ethan entered the room.

And she was. She'd spent the entire day watching chick movies on the WE channel—*Pretty Woman* was on now—and she hadn't seen Ethan since early that morning. Her stomach growled as if to punctuate her words.

Ethan reached into his satchel and pulled out a plastic bag knotted at one end. He tossed it to her on the bed, where she caught it with both hands. She peeked inside. Half a roast beef sub on whole wheat, hold the mayo. Good.

"Six inches enough?" he said.

She gave an impish grin. "Usually. But it depends on what the guy does with it."

Her joke brought a small smile to his face. Reaching into his bag again, he tossed her a bottle of Diet Coke. It landed in front of her on the crumpled blanket. She almost couldn't remember what it felt like to eat a proper meal at a table.

"Did you eat?" She muted the television and sat cross-legged on the mattress. She twisted the plastic cap on the soda and it hissed. Still sealed. He was no longer drugging her.

"Not hungry."

"Want half my sub?"

"I would think three inches would be supremely unsatisfying," he said, and she laughed because she was supposed to.

 He was still a monster, and she was still kidnapped, but she was making progress, and she wasn't about to do or say anything to change that. Things had improved significantly over the last few days and she didn't want it to regress. She had free rein of the basement, no more chains, no more handcuffs. She was allowed to use the toilet by herself and take a shower. Ethan had even brought her a few books to read—romance novels, not her thing, but better than nothing—and they were on the nightstand.

It was bearable. But she still had a lot of work to do.

He slumped on the leather sofa, seeming completely out of energy. His eyes were lost inside the dark circles surrounding them, and he hadn't shaved in days. She watched as he stifled a yawn.

She took a bite of the sandwich. He'd remembered to ask for extra cucumbers and green peppers this time. "Yummy," she said. "Thank you. Let me know if you want some."

She had learned it was better to pretend things were normal, that she wasn't being held against her will, if she wanted things to stay smooth between them. Ethan was still wary, but he was more engaged and more willing to talk. The gun still had a home in the waistband of his jeans, but he no longer kept his hand constantly poised over the butt to remind her of it. Getting it away from him entirely was her next goal.

"I have a surprise for you," he said.

"A surprise?" She feigned curiosity, though her stomach tightened at the word. She put her sandwich down and wiped her mouth with shaky hands. The last surprise had been a necklace belonging to a dead girl and a wall full of dismembered corpses. Ethan reached into his satchel again and his demeanor perked slightly. He pulled out several items, reciting the names of each as he laid them neatly on the cushion of the leather couch. "Shampoo, conditioner, body wash, moisturizer, facial soap, body lotion, shower puff, toothbrush, toothpaste, deodorant. Even got you dental floss and lip balm." He glanced up at her. "You like Aveda products, right?"

Sheila almost choked on the last bit of food still in her mouth. "They're all I use."

"Good. I also brought you some antibiotic cream for your wrists and ankles, and, uh, some pads." He dug into his bag again. Indeed, he'd bought her a travel pack of Stayfree maxi pads. "I couldn't remember when your time of the month was, but I figured it was coming at some point."

"Thank you." She stared at the items, her voice faint. "That's very thoughtful, Ethan. I appreciate it." No way was he going to kill her. He wouldn't buy her all this stuff and then kill her, right? Something had changed. The question was, what?

"You're welcome. I know you've been showering with bar soap, but Abby always says that stuff is drying if you wash your hair with it."

Abby. It was the first time he'd mentioned his girlfriend since Sheila had been here. Were they even still together?

She pointed to an unfamiliar blue-and-white tube. "What's that?"

Ethan held it up. "Diaper rash cream. I noticed before that you're pretty red . . . down there." His face had a funny expression. Embarrassment? Another first.

There was also a change of clothes—two pairs of Puget Sound State University sweatpants, two T-shirts, and a sweatshirt, all brand-new, tags still on. A few pairs of cotton bikini panties. Socks. For a kidnapper, he was being quite considerate.

Her mind reeled as she tried to make sense of it. He was showing kindness? *Now?* What did that mean?

"Thank you," she said again. The roast beef sub lay half-eaten on her lap and she pushed it away, appetite gone.

Ethan settled back into the sofa and nodded toward the TV. Julia Roberts was laughing at something Richard Gere had just said. "Turn up the volume, will you?"

: : : :

An hour later he was snoring, splayed out on the couch with his arms up over his head and his mouth hanging open. She hadn't noticed exactly when he'd nodded off, but a loud snort had gotten her attention. When she glanced away from the television to look at him, she was shocked to see him passed out.

She was wearing her new clothes. There was no reason for Ethan to have bought her all these things unless she wasn't going anywhere anytime soon. Whatever his plans had been, they had obviously changed. When she'd first arrived, she was chained and in diapers. He'd told her he was going to kill her. Now a neatly folded stack of clean clothes was beside her, with a month's worth of toiletries in the bathroom.

As if she was going to be here awhile.

She watched him from the bed. His body was relaxed and unmoving, his nostrils flaring in and out in rhythm with his snoring. The butt of the gun poked out about three inches from the top of his jeans, covered slightly by his T-shirt, which had pulled up to reveal the brown patch of hair that trailed from his belly button to his crotch.

Her captor was asleep.

Her mind flooded with possibilities.

If she was jackrabbit quick, she could have the gun out

and pointed at him before he was fully awake. She could keep it trained at his head, as he'd done with her so many times, and she could make him tell her what the code was to get out of this room. With a gun to his temple, surely he'd give it to her.

But what if he refused? Sheila frowned. Of course he'd refuse. Should she shoot him in the leg? The arm? Leave him immobilized on the sofa, writhing in pain? He'd have to tell her then, wouldn't he?

She swung her legs silently over the edge of the bed, her mind made up, then stopped as another thought occurred to her.

How many bullets were in a gun that size? Was it fully loaded? Was there some kind of safety mechanism she had to turn off before it would fire? She cursed herself for not taking Morris up on his offer to teach her how to shoot a gun. Then again, Morris had hunting rifles, which probably didn't work the same way at all. Was she supposed to just point and pull the trigger? What if she missed? Did the gun reload automatically or would she have to do something to . . . chamber it? Was that even the right word?

The questions swirled around her head like ingredients in a recipe doomed to fail. The longer she stared at Ethan's motionless body, the more desperate she felt to make a move, but she couldn't decide if the risk was worth it. What if he came at her? She wouldn't hesitate to put a bullet between his eyes. Assuming she could hit her target.

Then what? With Ethan dead and no code to get past the door, what next? The gun looked so small and the door was heavy—she had banged on it plenty of times when he wasn't around. It felt thick and impenetrable. Could bullets that small blast through it? If they couldn't, she'd be stuck down here with his dead and rotting body. Oh, God. She'd die a slow, painful death from starvation because nobody knew where she was. Hell, *she* didn't know where she was.

Unless . . . unless there was a phone in Ethan's bag somewhere. She had never seen one, but that didn't mean one didn't exist. Her own phone might be in there. Wherever this place was, it had cell phone reception—he had made her call Morris's answering machine from her BlackBerry and the message had gone through just fine.

Yes, it was definitely worth the risk.

She planted her bare feet on the floor and stood up. She eased toward Ethan, afraid to breathe.

Three steps in, he opened his eyes.

"Don't even think about it."

His voice was perfectly clear. His hand moved to the butt of the gun. Her heart sank. "What are you talking about?" she said, backtracking. "I was going to the bathroom."

He sat up slowly, never taking his eyes off her. "Don't fuck with me, Sheila. You should see the look on your face. You were going for the gun, weren't you?"

"Of course not. I wouldn't even know how to use it."

He took the gun out of his waistband and rested it on his thigh, keeping his finger on the trigger. "I thought things were better between us. Why do you want to fuck that up?"

"Okay." She relented immediately. Ethan's face was pink with anger and this was not the time to play stupid. "Okay, I was looking at it. It makes me nervous, Ethan. It scares me."

"I thought we were building trust. This really disappoints me." His bleary eyes were sad.

Sheila stood her ground. "Trust? You want to build trust? You can start by getting rid of that thing. What do you need it for? I can't overpower you, and even if I could, I don't know the codes to get out. I've done nothing since I've been here to make you not trust me. You could cut me a little slack and get rid of the gun."

Ethan seemed to be listening. He slipped the gun back into the waistband of his jeans. "I'll think about it."

"Think harder."

He chuckled. "You sound like my mother."

"I thought your mother was dead," she said, taking advantage of the opening. The tension had passed. They were okay again.

"She is."

"Did you kill her?"

Ethan didn't blink. "Ha. Right. I was just a kid when she died."

There was a minimum age requirement for monsters? "Sorry," she said, attempting to sound sincere.

"I know you don't give a shit. That's okay. Neither do I. She died in a house fire."

"What happened?"

He snorted and settled back into the sofa. "You want to know this stuff? Fine. My father left us when I was five and my mother went batshit crazy. She died when I was ten. Burned the house down."

"I'm sorry."

"I'm not."

"Why not? The death of a parent is one of the most damaging things that can happen to a child." Or an adult. Her father's face flitted through her mind. She pushed it away.

"You trying to headshrink me, Dr. Tao?"

"Just making conversation. Were you in the house?"

"Yep." His voice sounded robotic. No anger, grief, or bitterness. His jaw stayed relaxed. "I was locked in the closet, as usual. Neighbor smelled the smoke, heard me screaming, pulled me

out. It was all very dramatic. Would have made a great after-
school special about the dangers of playing with candles."

"They couldn't save your mother?"

"Her dress caught fire." The corners of his mouth twitched
and she realized with horror that he was trying not to smile.
"She died in the hospital three days later. Third-degree burns
over eighty percent of her body." His face looked dreamy. "I
like to imagine that she was in great pain when she finally
went, but she was unconscious and never woke up."

Sheila shuddered.

"I got a nice, fat inheritance when I turned eighteen," he
continued, his eyes blank and staring into nothing. "Insurance from the house, the trust she had from the grandparents I
never met. Came to just over two million bucks."

Sheila's shock was genuine. "That's a lot of money." And it
explained a lot. The souped-up vintage motorcycle, for one. A
thought occurred to her then. "Do you own this place? Whatever this is?"

"This is my house, yes."

"So why pretend to be a poor, starving student?"

"When did I ever pretend?" Ethan shrugged. "People assume. I don't correct them."

"You're awfully young to be a millionaire."

"You think so?" He finally turned his gaze toward her. "How
much money does Morris have, anyway?"

Somehow their conversations always drifted back to Morris, which frightened her. "I don't know, I've never asked him.
It never mattered. I make my own money, you know that."

"Just making conversation."

Silence filled the room and she felt a desperate need to say
something before Ethan retreated inside his head. Taking a
deep breath, she blurted, "So why do you do what you do?"

His blank gaze became more focused. "Which is what, exactly?"

"You're a master's student in psychology." She cleared her throat and spoke in her best professorial voice. "Why are you the way you are? What possesses you to do the things you do?"

He laughed, his face a picture of delight. "What, you want me to headshrink *myself*? That's a first. Planning to teach a course on antisocial personality disorder, Dr. Tao?" He saw her expression and laughed again. "What, you don't think I can diagnose myself?"

"That's your diagnosis?"

"I was being facetious." He rubbed his head, his eyes bright with amusement. "*Au contraire,* I would say I'm a highly intelligent, highly motivated individual with good impulse control."

"So you don't think you're a psychopath?"

"Psychopath," Ethan repeated. "Let's see. The definition according to the Hare Psychopathy Checklist is 'a predator who uses charm, manipulation, intimidation, sex, and violence to control others and satisfy his own needs. A psychopath lacks empathy and conscience, takes what he wants and does what he pleases, and violates social norms and expectations without guilt or remorse.'" He finished his recitation with a raised eyebrow, his gaze fixed on Sheila. "That's half the people I know. Including you."

"I don't—"

"Ever bumped a car in the parking lot and not told the owner? Ever sweet-talked a salesclerk into giving you a better deal on something? Ever seduced a guy to get what you want? With no feelings of guilt afterward?" Ethan raised an eyebrow. "We all do it."

"There are limits. We don't all rape, kidnap, and murder."

"Is that what you think I do?"

Sheila stared at him. "Isn't it? I am here, after all."

"You don't know why you're here. You think you do, but you don't."

Time to make a move.

She slipped off the bed and stood in front of Ethan. "I'm pretty sure I do know." She stepped out of her new sweatpants, then pulled her T-shirt over her head. She stood in front of him wearing just her panties, the ones he'd bought for her.

His eyes moved over her bare skin, taking it all in.

"You care about me," Sheila said. "You might even love me, though you can't admit it to anyone, let alone yourself. If you could admit it, if you could have let your guard down with me, we wouldn't be in this situation. Because there'd be no need."

She hooked her thumbs into the sides of her cotton underwear and began inching them down. "I'm tired of playing games with you. That's all we've done since the moment we got involved. You want me? You want to be with me? Guess what, you don't have to force me."

Her panties fell to the floor and she stepped out of them and moved closer to Ethan. He couldn't take his eyes off her. She knew she looked good. She'd lost weight since she'd been in the basement. Those pesky five pounds she couldn't lose in time for the wedding had finally come off.

"Now who's the psychopath?" he said, but his breath was coming a little faster. He placed his hands on her naked hips, drawing her closer.

She felt his arms move around her waist as she stepped toward him. Still seated, his lips were on her belly button and she felt his tongue tracing its outline.

It didn't feel good. It didn't feel like anything. But she plunged her fingers into his short hair and allowed a small moan to escape her lips.

He pulled her down and she straddled him. He was still fully dressed, but through the scratchy coarseness of his jeans, she could feel his erection right under the handle of the gun that was digging into her thigh. She kissed his neck, trailing her fingers slowly down his chest toward his crotch and the weapon. She began grinding her hips and his breath came faster.

"You sure you want to do this?" His voice was hoarse.

"I want you. You're the only one I've ever wanted."

"Do you love me?"

"Yes." It came out a gasp, and not because she was overwhelmed with emotion. The word had stuck in her throat because she was forcing the lie. Her fingers brushed over his stomach. Another inch or two and she'd be touching the gun.

"More than Morris?" he said.

"No comparison." Her fingers closed around the handle, already warm from being so close to his body.

"Tell me why you love me more than him."

Sheila couldn't pull the gun out of his jeans just yet. She continued nibbling on Ethan's neck, grinding her hips down a little deeper. With her free hand, she pulled down his zipper and was inside his jeans in one smooth motion. "Because you're smarter, younger, sexier."

She had his penis in her hand and she began massaging. His breath came faster and a grunt escaped his lips. She remembered that sound, remembered what it meant. Her right hand gripped the butt of the gun tighter. He was getting close. Another minute, maximum, and he'd be incapacitated for at least five seconds, enough time for her to pull out the gun and point it at his head.

Her hand worked expertly.

"Sheila," he said, his face buried in her neck.

"Yes," she said in his ear.

"I've always loved you."

"I know."

She could feel it, he was about to reach orgasm. She worked faster, her other hand tight around the handle of the small silver gun.

"But here's the thing . . ." he said, his voice strangled through his rapid breathing.

"What's that?" she said, working faster. *Come on, come on, let go already.*

His hand suddenly gripped her wrist and twisted. The pain was intense, a flash of fire. She had no choice but to let go of the gun with a whimper.

With his other hand, he shoved her off his lap. She fell over, her back slamming into the thick industrial carpet.

"I've never trusted you." Looking down at her naked body, Ethan stood and zipped his pants. "I know now I never will."

CHAPTER : 32

Morris couldn't put his finger on it, and that was what was bothering him.

He was a solutions guy. He liked to fix things. He liked to take a problem and, using a combination of research, experience, and good judgment, figure out the best answer, the best plan, the best course of action. He'd had two careers in his life—football and banking—and both relied on well-thought-out strategies and their proper executions. And, of course, great instincts, which he normally had. How could his instincts have been so wrong about Sheila?

He should have been relaxing over SportsCenter, as he usually did after a long day of work, but instead he was going over every event of the past few weeks in his mind, like an instant replay he couldn't shut off. Every conversation with Sheila, everything they'd talked about, everything they'd done or hadn't done. But the analysis wasn't getting him anywhere. He was a fat hamster running on a little wheel.

He was stuck.

With every passing day, the chances seemed to grow slimmer that Sheila would ever turn up. There were no real leads. Jerry Isaac hadn't said as much, but Morris knew the PI was running out of ideas. There was nobody left to interview.

Sheila had left him, willingly, just as her phone message had said. Why couldn't he accept that, instead of throwing money at a guy who was probably only too happy to keep looking so long as Morris kept paying?

His beautiful son was the only bright spot at the moment. Randall had swept back into his life, and it appeared that whatever chip had been on his shoulder all these years had finally been knocked off. Morris knew he had Sheila to thank for that. Regardless of the pain and anger and worry she was causing him, he knew he would love her the rest of his life for what she'd done.

He poured another shot of Johnnie Walker and pushed away the guilt that came with every ounce he downed. So far Randall hadn't mentioned Morris's drinking, but it was probably par for the course as far as his son was concerned. He'd never known his father sober.

The thought saddened him.

His BlackBerry rang. He stared at it until it stopped. It was after 8:00 p.m. and they could call back tomorrow. Then he heard his home phone. Not a work call, then. He reached over and picked it up.

"It's Jerry," a voice said on the other end. "You busy? You didn't answer your cell."

"Oh, yeah, I'm on a hot date right now." Morris's laugh was bitter. "Got a cute blonde with me. Hang on while I remove her from my lap." He looked at the bottle of Johnnie Walker Gold, still in his hand. Close enough. "What's up?"

"I met with Ethan Wolfe today. I meant to call you earlier but my wife wanted to go out to dinner. It's our weekly date night."

"Let me guess, you took her to the Golden Monkey."

"Don't knock it, man. Best Chinese food in Seattle."

"Do Chinese people agree with you?"

"Bite me. Do you want to know what happened with Wolfe or not?"

"Let me hear it."

Jerry cleared his throat. "I definitely think he was the one Sheila was having an affair with."

"He actually admitted it?" Morris felt a stab even though the news wasn't surprising. He thought once again about the night they'd met in Sheila's office. The way Wolfe had taunted her, and she didn't even bust his balls. It all made sense now. He poured himself another shot of whiskey, wondering if the PI could hear it through the phone line.

"I have a very strong hunch. After thirty years as a cop, that ought to mean something."

"So they were screwing. No shock there." Morris kept his tone light. Holding the phone away, he downed his whiskey in one gulp. "What does this mean?"

"It might not mean anything." Jerry paused. "But the guy's a bit weird, you know? Squirrelly. Freaked out when the door closed. Guess he didn't want to be stuck in a room alone with me." The PI snorted. "Logically, I can't blame him for not copping to the affair. Why would he admit it?"

Something Jerry said rubbed at Morris. A pang of familiarity, a twinge at the back of his neck, but it dissipated as soon as he tried to chase the thought.

"Thing is," Jerry continued, "he was adamant that he didn't know what happened to her."

"You believed him?"

"No reason not to."

"Does he have an alibi for the night she disappeared?"

"And which night would that be?" Jerry sounded annoyed. "We don't even know when she left town. You were in Japan, remember? She didn't call you until Sunday. She could have been anywhere by then. In any case, Wolfe doesn't need an alibi because as far as we know, there's been no crime." Jerry sighed heavily.

"What?"

"I don't know," the PI said. "Something's off. *Wolfe* struck me as off. He was wound way too tight for a guy who grades papers for a living."

"So what do we do now?"

"I could follow the kid around for a couple days. Seems to be the only option left. But I'll be honest with you, Morris, I don't expect anything to come of it. There's nothing to go on here. It's more about me wanting to squash the weird vibes I got, if that makes any sense. And it'll be expensive."

"Not exactly the same price point as the Golden Monkey."

That got a chuckle out of Jerry, but then his voice was serious again. "Listen, there's something else I want you to think about. It's looking like a long shot, but let's say that, miracle of miracles, we do find Sheila. She's now all pissed off you tracked her down. She's gone somewhere to start a new life and now there you are on her doorstep demanding answers and reminding her of the person she doesn't want to be anymore. She tells you to get lost. Is that the reunion you envisioned? Is that what you need to move on?"

"I don't know what I need anymore." Morris drank straight from the bottle this time. "But I'm not ready to let this go. I need to see her face, Jerry. She needs to tell me it's over in person. At the very least, I deserve that."

"Okay then. Just making sure. I'll keep you posted."

"Hey," Morris said before the private investigator could hang up.

"Yeah?"

"About Wolfe. What did you think of him?"

"I already told you. Kind of a weasel, jumpy."

That twinge again. "No, not that." Morris hesitated. "Did you think he was good-looking?"

"I don't know, he's a *dude*," Jerry said, exasperated. "And you've met him already."

"Yeah, but I want to know what you think."

"I don't know." Another sigh and the sound of knuckles popping. "I guess he's good-looking. My wife is addicted to this soap opera, *The Young and the Reckless*—"

"*Restless*," Morris corrected. "My ex was into that, too."

"Whatever, it's all crap. He looks like he could be on that show. He's a handsome guy. Probably gets a lot of attention from the ladies because he's young, fit, got a nice face."

"Fantastic." Morris took another swig.

"You asked." A short silence. "Seriously, man, think about what I said about letting her go. You could spend your whole life wondering, 'What if?' The stress could kill you."

Morris looked at the bottle in his hand. The deep amber liquid glowed in the dim light of the living room. "It already is killing me."

: : : :

He rode the elevator inside Puget Sound State University's psychology building, armpits damp and fists clenched, feeling like a kid on the first day of school. Morris had checked his messages after he'd finished talking to Jerry the night before, and one of the office assistants from the university had left a voice mail. The department wanted Morris to clear out Sheila's personal effects. They wanted to make room for a new professor who was currently sharing an office with someone else. Space was at a premium, so would he mind coming down at his earliest convenience to pack up Dr. Tao's things?

Morris minded. But what choice was there?

The elevator doors opened and a small sign with a red arrow pointed the way to the psychology department's main office. After a few short steps, Morris found himself standing in front of a long counter where three middle-aged women were working. All three heads popped up at his arrival.

The lady on the far right with the short, curly brown hair spoke first. "You must be Morris." Her voice was girlish and she favored him with a smile. "I recognize you from the pictures in Dr. Tao's office."

They shook hands. The other two ladies exchanged a knowing glance, then went back to their computer screens. The office wasn't busy. Morris would bet ten bucks they were playing FreeCell.

The secretary's name was Dolores. She couldn't have been more than five feet tall. Looking down at her from his height of six feet four, Morris could see graying roots and the spot on the top of her head where her hair appeared to be thinning. He managed a smile and followed her out of the office. On her wrist, she wore a bracelet made of keys held together with some kind of stretchy telephone cord. The keys jangled as they made their way back to the elevators.

"I had Maintenance bring by some boxes." She punched the elevator's up button with a short, unpolished fingernail. Glasses hung around her neck and rested on top of her embroidered sweater. "We could have packed up her office ourselves, but I thought you might prefer to do it. There are some personal items in her drawers you might want to bring to her. Or to her house, anyway."

The elevator arrived and Dolores looked up at him. "How is she?"

Morris felt his face flush. "I'm sure she's fine."

The small elevator felt tinier than ever. He had no desire to fill it with talk of Sheila or the weather or the hundred other small-talk items that people saved for moments like this. All he wanted to know was where that bastard Ethan Wolfe was, but he couldn't bring himself to ask.

They stepped out of the elevator, and he followed Dolores down to the end of the hallway, where she unlocked the last door with her master key.

She turned the knob, then hesitated. "Dean Simmons was wondering if you knew when she'd be back. He was surprised—well, we all were—by her abrupt departure. She said she was ill from stress, but . . . do you know if she's found another position?"

"I really couldn't say." His tone was abrupt. "I know as much as you do."

"I'm sorry. That was insensitive."

"Don't apologize. This is weird for everyone."

He stepped inside the office and stifled a sigh. Despite her absence, the room was filled with Sheila's presence. Traces of her perfume, a light floral blend, still lingered in the air. On her desk in a crystal vase was the bouquet of roses he'd given her the night he proposed, dried and preserved to perfection. Her favorite Pottery Barn mug sat near the computer. Its rim still had a lipstick stain—deep red, her color. Flattened boxes and a pile of newspapers were scattered on the floor.

"I'll leave you then." Dolores watched him with a sad look on her face. "When you're done, dial extension two one two on the desk phone and I'll have someone help you bring the boxes to your car. I believe everything here is hers, except the furniture and the computer."

"Thank you."

She closed the door behind her. Morris took a moment to

compose himself before getting to work. It all seemed so sur-
real. Sheila loved her job—how could she have walked away
from it? She'd said once that the university was the only thing
that kept her going after her divorce.

He plucked her diplomas from the wall and wrapped them
carefully in newspaper, stopping when a framed photograph
caught his eye. He'd been in Sheila's office only a handful of
times, so he couldn't say how long it had been there. It was a
photo of him.

He was smiling, standing beside his giant stainless steel barbecue wearing a red plaid shirt and blue jeans, a soda in one
hand and a pair of tongs in the other. This would have been
early last summer. They'd eaten steaks and salads on the patio
and talked for hours. Afterward, they had watched a movie on
pay per view. He couldn't remember the name of it now, but it
was a comedy. He could still remember the way Sheila had felt
snuggled up in his arms, and the light in her eyes when she
laughed.

Morris blinked back tears, appalled at the thought that
someone might catch him crying in her office. He grabbed a
box from the stack and methodically began to fill it.

: : : :

After the boxes were brought out to his car, Morris went back
inside the office to speak to Dolores.

In a low voice, he asked, "Do you know where I can find
one of Sheila's teaching assistants? Ethan Wolfe. He, uh, might
have something of Sheila's that I need to bring with me."

"Let me check." Dolores typed something into the computer. "Yes, he has office hours today. Room six oh six. Make a
left when you leave the elevator."

Morris thanked her one last time.

Two minutes later, he was standing outside a small, sparsely decorated office, staring at the back of Ethan Wolfe's head. The grad student was seated behind his desk but was turned toward the window, his back to the doorway. Morris rapped his knuckles hard on the doorframe.

"It's open," Wolfe said, spinning around in his chair. His face froze.

Morris stepped inside.

The kid was better looking than he remembered, but then again, he hadn't looked at Wolfe too closely the night they'd met. Morris had been too focused on whether Sheila had liked her diamond bracelet. Feeling self-conscious, he sucked in his gut and stood up straighter.

Wolfe was on the phone. "Gotta go," he said quietly into the receiver. "See you at home." He placed the handset back in its cradle.

"Howdy." Morris was trying for pleasant, but it came out gruff. "Don't know if you remember me. I'm Morris Gardener."

"Sheila's fiancé. Of course." Looking less than enthused, Wolfe lifted himself out of his chair.

They shook hands and Morris found himself pressing harder on the younger man's palm than was necessary.

"What brings you by?"

"The lady in the office asked me to pack up Sheila's things." Morris gave the smaller man a deliberate once-over. "Guess they need the office space."

Wolfe nodded and sat back down. The Seahawks bobble-head on the desk vibrated. "Office space is like gold around here. Sheila had the best spot in the building, with the best view."

"Mind if I sit?"

"Go ahead."

Morris reached for the door.

"Would you mind leaving it open?" Wolfe said quickly. "It gets pretty stuffy in here."

That pang again.

Morris shut the door firmly behind him. "I think you'll agree that what we need to talk about is best kept private."

Wolfe stiffened.

Morris eased himself into the small chair across from Wolfe and studied the young man, who was sipping something from Starbucks and watching him with a furtive expression. Christ, Ethan Wolfe was still a kid. And he looked completely uncomfortable. It was a total one-eighty from the last time Morris had seen him, when he was all cock and swagger.

Something about the way the kid sat in the chair was familiar. The thought nagged, and Morris allowed himself to ruminate on it for about five seconds before reminding himself that he and Wolfe *had* met before.

The TA finally broke the silence. "Is there news about Dr. Tao?"

"I don't have any answers for you, son."

Wolfe bristled at the condescending term. "Well, if you talk to her, let her know we miss her. I'm working under Professor Easton now, and just between you and me, I'm afraid to pick up a pencil, if you know what I mean." Wolfe's chuckle sounded forced. A bead of sweat was at his hairline, though the room was cool. He stood up suddenly. "Mind if I open a window?"

"Not at all."

As Wolfe tugged at the small pane, Morris couldn't help noticing the bulge of the younger man's biceps below the short sleeves of his T-shirt. The last time he'd been that lean, Morris was sixteen and playing high school football. A moment later a blast of cool air filled the room.

Wolfe sat back down, his face a little brighter than before. His lips turned up in an arrogant smile. "So, Morris, if there's no news, what is it you want to discuss?"

"How long have you been working with Sheila? A year?"

Wolfe's expression was cool. "Just about. She was my mentor. I'm really disappointed she left because this is my last year. I would have loved to finish under her."

And over her, and from behind, and any other position you get her into, blowhard.

"She's the best professor at this school," Wolfe continued. "Hands down. Her lectures were incredible, as I'm sure you know." He sipped his coffee again, no longer rattled.

"I wouldn't know, actually."

"You've never heard her lecture?"

"Never had the privilege."

"Wow." Wolfe leaned back in his chair, smug. "I'd have thought being engaged and all, you'd have taken an interest in her work. She was the most dynamic—"

A knock at the door interrupted Wolfe midsentence. Morris realized he was breathing hard and forced himself to calm down. Turning his head, he saw Dolores in the doorway.

"Hi again, Morris."

She gave him a warm smile and he forced himself to smile back. The woman had no idea she'd just saved Wolfe from getting his face smashed into the desk.

"What's up, Dolores?" Wolfe sounded breezy.

"I'm sorry to interrupt you gentlemen, but, Ethan, Danny Ambrose is here. He's really upset. He said Dr. Tao told him he was getting a B, but you entered a C into the system and now he's having problems with his scholarship. Can I steal you for a quick sec?"

"This might take a few minutes," Wolfe said, standing. He seemed amused for no reason Morris could see.

"I'll wait," Morris said.

Alone, he looked around at the dismal office, much smaller than Sheila's and lacking personality. He poked hard at the Seahawks bobblehead to make it nod faster and contemplated how he was going to ask Wolfe about the affair. Should he come straight out with it? Or dance around it and try to make the kid squirm?

The bobblehead's abnormally large cranium fell off its skinny body with a clatter and rolled around on the desk a few times. Morris made a grab for it before it could fall over the edge and hit the floor.

Shit, it was broken. Holding the plastic head in his hand, he allowed himself a smirk at the sight of the headless body. It was a nice parallel for what he felt like doing to Ethan Wolfe.

Fumbling with large fingers, he worked at reattaching the head. As he fiddled with the springs, something small and shiny rolled away from the base. Morris picked it up, assuming it was another broken part. But it wasn't, not even close.

He knew exactly what this was, because it belonged to him.

Stunned, he traced the engraved initials on the platinum face. *MG.*

It was the missing cuff link he'd been looking for. What the hell was Wolfe doing with it? Morris's mind raced.

Had Sheila given it to her boy toy? No, that made no sense. What would have been the point of giving Wolfe just one cuff link? Besides, they were personalized with Morris's initials.

Had he left it at Sheila's house and Wolfe had swiped it from there? No, impossible. Morris had never worn the cuff links to Sheila's house.

Wolfe would be back any minute. Slipping the cuff link into his pocket, Morris made his way out of the office.

Six minutes later he was in his Cadillac. He closed and

locked the car doors. In the privacy of the vehicle, he pulled out the cuff link and stared at it in disbelief.

What the hell did it mean? *Think, damn it.*

The last time he'd worn these cuff links was when he was working on the Okinawa deal. He'd had an early-morning breakfast meeting with two of the investors and had worn his charcoal suit with his favorite cerulean blue tie. Then he'd had a conference call with another investor in Japan. Afterward, if he wasn't mistaken, he'd met with Randall's friend Tom Young for a preliminary interview. They'd gone out to dinner later that evening.

Christ. Tom Young. The pieces fell into place.

He knew he'd remembered Ethan Wolfe from somewhere. The desire to leave the door open at the interview, the posture, the cocky grin . . .

Tom Young was Ethan Wolfe.

The hair was different, the skin lighter, but the voice, the mannerisms . . . Morris would bet his life on it.

He grabbed his phone. Jerry answered on the first ring.

Morris didn't bother with pleasantries. "We got a problem."

CHAPTER : 33

It was a bonehead thing to do," Jerry said for the fourth time. "You're getting way too involved in this. You shouldn't have even talked to him."

"You lectured me yesterday."

"You're quite possibly the most thickheaded person I've ever known. And that's saying a lot 'cause I know a lot of people. The idea was for him *not* to know we're watching him." Jerry's expression was pained. "When he can't find the cuff link, he'll know you took it."

"Nah, he'll probably think he lost it. Happens to me all the time."

"Because you're old."

"So are you," Morris finally snapped. "Quit busting my balls, it's done now. What I want to know is, why get into disguise and pretend to interview for a job? What the hell's the point?"

"Scoping you out, probably. Ballsy, but he's good at it, too. You wouldn't have put it together if it weren't for the claustrophobia thing. Jesus, he took the cuff link right off your wrist." Jerry whistled. "And brought it to the office like it's some kind of trophy."

"What does it all mean?"

"We might never know, but I do know you shouldn't have talked to him. You should have kept your distance."

Morris kept his eyes on the building in front of them. They'd been sitting outside Ethan Wolfe's apartment for the past four hours and both men were getting irritable. Morris was starting to wonder why he'd insisted on tagging along. He should have been at work. So far Wolfe hadn't gone anywhere interesting—besides the university for a few hours—but, according to Jerry, that was the way it went sometimes.

Morris felt nauseated in Jerry's tiny car. He stretched his legs out as far as they could go, longing for the roominess of his Cadillac, and complained again that his head was actually touching the roof of the Honda.

"Oh, let it go already." Jerry's voice was gruff. "I get it, the car's small. But might I remind you I normally do this alone? You invited yourself."

Morris stifled a chuckle. He enjoyed getting a rise out of the private investigator. It provided some comic relief to what had so far been a dull day.

The background check Jerry ordered had turned up some interesting information about Ethan Wolfe. He was twenty-three, born in Omaha, Nebraska. His Social Security number showed a dozen past addresses all over the United States, with not one but two current residences. The first was a rental apartment in the university district, which he co-leased with a female named Abby Maddox, also twenty-three. The other was a house in Lake Stevens, ownership in Wolfe's name only. No mortgage. He'd paid over half a million dollars for it.

Wolfe had been a ward of the State of Nebraska from age ten onward and had lived in several foster homes before he was released at the age of eighteen. His mother, Cheryl, had died in a house fire. There was no record of his father's current location, but the man had spent a year in prison for assault and battery when the boy was two years old. His mother had been the victim.

Wolfe had attended three other colleges in addition to Puget Sound State, two in California and one in Oregon. Aside from his TA gig at PSSU, he'd never held another job of any kind. DMV records showed two speeding tickets in the last three years—both paid on time—and the ownership of one 1968 Triumph motorcycle.

There was also a sealed juvenile criminal record. There was no way to unseal it without a subpoena, and since Wolfe wasn't under official investigation, Jerry wouldn't be able to get one.

Not exactly the standard record of a twenty-three-year-old graduate student.

"Where do you think the money came from to buy the house?" Morris asked.

"Inheritance would be my guess."

"What do you think he did to get the juvenile record?"

Jerry shrugged. "Could be anything. He grew up in a violent home, bounced around in the foster care system, couldn't have been fun. Probably assault, or drugs. Those are the most common." The PI yawned.

Morris was learning that investigating was not nearly as interesting as people thought. It wasn't like it was on TV. Jerry had explained to Morris that a lot of the so-called investigating happened on the phone and over the Internet, and sitting in your car in dark corners waiting for something to happen. There were few face-to-face interviews, and almost no drama. Adultery tended to be more interesting than other cases since sometimes you got to take pictures of the action. But missing persons? Nope. Morris was disappointed to see that today was no different.

They had been following Wolfe on his ultracool motorcycle and it appeared to be a day of errand-running for the graduate student. Jerry, who knew nothing about motorcycles, was shocked to learn that the vintage Triumph Wolfe was riding—perfectly maintained with custom modifications—would have cost more than Jerry's Honda Accord . . . if he had bought the car *new*.

Morris's eyes were getting heavy, and he finally stopped fighting and closed them.

He woke up to Jerry's elbow in his side.

"Up and at 'em. They're moving."

Morris sat up and looked at his watch. It was just after 6:00 p.m. He'd slept for an hour. Wolfe and his girlfriend were climbing onto Wolfe's motorcycle.

"You have to admit, the girl looks good on the bike." Jerry waited ten seconds before starting the ignition. "Could her jeans be any tighter?"

Abby Maddox had her slender arms wrapped around Wolfe's slim waist.

"You know, I don't get it." Morris rubbed the sleep out of his eyes. "The kid gets to come home every day to her. What did he want with my Sheila?"

Jerry snorted. "You know damn well men don't cheat because the other woman's better looking. We cheat because we can." He glanced sideways at Morris. "Don't sell your fiancée short. She's attractive, and an authority figure. That bodes well for a young man's fantasies."

"You ever cheat on your wife?"

"Not this one. But I've had my share of temptation." A funny expression crossed Jerry's dark face. "I love my wife. Annie's a good woman. Been married twelve years now and she still rocks my world, as my niece Keisha would so eloquently put it."

"This is your second marriage?"

"Third, actually. It took me that long to learn that one woman really is enough for me." Jerry smiled ruefully.

"Kids?"

"You're a nosy dude."

"Don't answer if you don't want to."

"She couldn't have kids with her first husband, and it never happened with my first two wives." Jerry's voice held regret. "We're too old now. It's okay, some things aren't meant to be."

They followed the couple about a mile to a soup kitchen called St. Mary's Helping Hands. Morris had read about this place in *Seattle* magazine. It had a great reputation, thanks to its tireless staff of volunteers who did everything from raise money and solicit food donations, to cooking, cleaning, and serving.

Wolfe left his motorcycle out front, and he and his girlfriend entered the worn building holding hands. Jerry parallel-parked on the other side of the street where they had a clear view of the entrance. It was a no-parking zone, but if Jerry noticed, he wasn't deterred. He turned the engine off.

"What now?" Morris asked.

"We wait."

"This is what I pay you for? To sit around in front of buildings?"

"It requires great instincts and superb observational skills."

Morris snorted. "Hard to believe those two are volunteers." He settled back in his seat and yawned.

"After thirty years as a cop, I've learned there are no rules when it comes to human behavior." Jerry looked out the window at a group of homeless men hovering by the soup kitchen's door. "You know those FBI shows on TV? Where they do the profiling?"

"Yeah."

"Cops hate that stuff. While it's all well and good to sit behind a desk and have *assigned characteristics* and *fancy medical names* for criminals," Jerry said in a prissy voice, "at the end of the day, you just don't know what anybody's gonna do. You gotta prepare for everything. Human beings are unpredictable. After three decades with PD, I still get surprised."

"Did you like being a cop?"

"Yeah." Jerry's voice was rueful. "Mostly I did, but the job was stressful and the money was shit. You like being a banker?"

"Yeah. Mostly I do, because the hours are good and the money's fantastic." Both men laughed.

Three hours later, they were still in the car, listening to sports talk on the radio and drinking the hot coffee that Morris had gotten from the street vendor down the block. Jerry wasn't much of a football fan, and Morris was enthusiastically explaining the finer nuances of the game.

Someone rapped sharply on the driver's-side window.

Startled midsentence, Morris jumped, splashing hot coffee into his lap. He cursed as Jerry rolled down the window slowly. A parking-enforcement officer was staring in at them through the tinted windows, her hawkish face against the glass.

Jerry got the window halfway down then stopped. "Hey there." He reached into his breast pocket and flashed a Seattle PD detective's badge. Morris was surprised—he didn't think retired officers were allowed to keep their badges.

"And that means what to me?" The woman was not impressed. "Move on. You're in a no-park zone. Or I'll have to ticket you." She tapped her clipboard to make a point.

"Don't you have anything better to do?" Jerry snapped, but he put his badge away. "Go bug the tourists who park illegally in the shopping district."

"So you're saying you want me to write this up?" Her ball-point pen was poised over a pad of yellow tickets.

Jerry finally gave a stiff nod and started up the car. He drove down First Avenue, grumbling under his breath.

"No respect," the private investigator muttered. "If I'd been on active duty, I'd tell her where she could stick her mother-fucking ticket."

"They let you keep your badge?"

"It's a replica." Jerry sounded sheepish. "They let you order one when you retire, to keep as a memento. Sometimes I use it to help with this job." He looked at Morris and put a finger over his lips as if to say, *Shhh.* "Like I said, most days I don't miss being a cop. All things considered, I transitioned well from public servant into private life. But I'd be lying if I said I didn't miss some of the perks. Like the goddamned respect."

Jerry drove around the block a few times, and after the fourth or fifth time—Morris had lost count—the silly little parking-enforcement vehicle was gone. Jerry edged right back into the spot where they were initially.

"The motorcycle's gone," Morris said.

Jerry was distracted as he straightened the wheels of the Honda. "What?"

"The motorcycle? The whole reason we've been sitting in this hole of a neighborhood for the past three hours listening to the radio when we could have been in a nice warm bar hav-ing a cold beer?" Morris pointed. "It's gone."

Jerry looked around. "Shit. We lost them."

"You think?"

"You shut up or I'll frigging leave you here."

There was another tap on the car window, this time on Mor-ris's side. In the dark it was hard to see who it was, but Morris was guessing the damn meter maid had come back.

He rolled down his window. It was harder than it should have been because Jerry's piece-of-crap car didn't have power windows. The handle groaned in protest.

A face blacker than Jerry's stared in at Morris. The man was covered in grime and he smelled like a garbage can, only much worse, because he also smelled like feces and urine. His hair, a snaked mess of dreadlocks, hung down inside the Accord's window. He was smiling.

"We got no money. Move on now." Jerry elbowed Morris, not bothering to lower his voice. "Roll the window back up. It stinks in here."

"I ain't ask for none." The homeless man's breath could have killed an elephant. His voice was a deep baritone.

"What do you want?" Morris asked.

"I got some information for you."

"About?"

"About the white dude you was followin'."

Morris and Jerry exchanged a look. "Who says we were following anyone?" Jerry said.

"Man, shee-it. I ain't got no home, but that don't mean I got no eyes." The man stared at them.

Finally Morris's curiosity got the better of him. "Okay, what information?"

"That white dude, his name is Wolfe."

"And that means what to me?" Jerry was staring hard at the homeless man.

"He a hunter. You best watch yourself before he hunts you."

"And you know this how?" Morris asked.

"I just know," the man said with a shrug, backing away from the car. He lifted up his tattered shirt and scratched his stomach with soiled hands. "And his woman? The pretty white girl he with?"

"What about her?" Jerry asked.

"She the leader of the pack."

"Hey—" Morris called out, but by the time he got out of the Honda, the man had disappeared.

: : : :

Ethan rode just under the speed limit, taking comfort in Abby's arms wrapped tight around his waist. In the bike's side mirror, the unevenly dulled lights of the black Honda Accord finally caught up to him. His stalkers had guessed his route correctly, and knew he was heading home. Clearly the big black dude and Morris the fat fuck weren't going to give up.

Ethan had first noticed the car idling by the curb as he and Abby were leaving for the soup kitchen. He had no idea how long they'd been following him, which bothered him. It meant he wasn't paying attention, and that was not good. He'd been losing focus. The drive to Lake Stevens and back every day, often twice a day, was taking its toll and he wasn't sleeping. But that was no excuse for getting sloppy.

Ethan couldn't see their faces, but he could imagine the two men sitting inside that ugly car, talking about him, talking about Sheila, thinking they were onto something by following his every move. They were persistent fuckers, he'd give them that. It might have been flattering had it not been so completely inconvenient.

He dropped Abby off at the apartment, explaining that he had some work to finish up. She hopped off the bike and pecked him on the cheek.

She wouldn't wait up. She never did.

On the highway, Ethan accelerated and moved into the passing lane. Sure enough, the Honda sped up behind him.

There was only one place to lead them to, only one place where things could happen the way he needed them to with the least amount of risk.

Let them come.

It was what he'd built his kill room for.

CHAPTER: 34

The vintage Triumph took the exit off I-5 for Highway 204. Jerry followed suit, his face scrunched in concentration as he carefully wove his way through the light traffic. Rain was making the road slick, and Ethan Wolfe wasn't going slowly.

"This guy's nuts." The PI had not taken his eyes off the bike's taillight. "Who drives a motorcycle in this weather?"

"Rides," Morris corrected. "You don't *drive* a motorcycle, you *ride* it."

"Whatever. The kid has a death wish."

Morris looked out the window, but the Honda's tinted glass made it too dark to see much of anything. "I think we're in Lake Stevens. I haven't been here in years."

"It's a nice area. Me and Annie looked at a place here after I retired. Thought we'd get away from the hustle and bustle of Seattle life." Jerry grinned. "The thought lasted about a day."

The streets were quiet and Jerry was forced to drop back a good distance from the Triumph. They followed for about ten minutes until Wolfe made a left into a gated subdivision. A stone half-wall engraved with fancy lettering proclaimed it THE BRIAR WOODS RESIDENCES.

Jerry didn't turn left to follow Wolfe through the wrought-iron gate. Instead he continued straight at five miles below the speed limit. Straining his neck as they passed, Morris watched as Wolfe punched in an access code at the metal box next to the gate, which opened to let Wolfe inside. He saw Wolfe give an easy wave to whoever was manning the guard's booth before the gate swung shut behind him.

Jerry made a right at the next street, parking at the curb of a small neighborhood, not as ritzy, with no gate or fancy sign to proclaim its exclusivity. He cut the lights.

"We're stuck," Morris said. "We can't get through the gate without an access code."

Jerry smiled. "O ye of little faith."

The two sat in silence for a few minutes, then Jerry turned the lights back on. In less than thirty seconds they were back at Briar Woods.

The security guard lifted his head at their approach. Jerry rolled down his window.

"Good evening, sir. Can I help you?" The guard didn't seem the least bit suspicious that two visitors had pulled up to the gate at eleven at night. He had a wrinkled, spritely face and a full head of neatly combed white hair. An ill-fitting brown polyester uniform displayed a name tag that read HENRY, and an embroidered shoulder patch said BRIAR WOODS SECURITY. Morris pegged the man as a part-time worker in his late sixties, trying to supplement his pension.

Jerry flashed his replica detective's shield through the open car window. Unlike the meter maid they'd met earlier, Henry was suitably impressed.

"Detective Isaac." Jerry was all business.

"Yessir." Henry put down the magazine he'd been reading. "Did one of the residents call you? Is there a problem? They're supposed to let me know as well."

"There could be." Jerry sounded just like a cop and Morris

suppressed a grin. The tactic worked well, even in the business world. If you sounded authoritative enough, people believed anything. "Do you know the man on the motorcycle who went through here a few minutes ago?"

"That's Mr. Wolfe." The guard's eyes widened. "He's a resident. Why, what'd he do?"

"I'm not at liberty to say." Jerry's face was stone. "I can't discuss an ongoing investigation."

"Of course." Morris could practically read the guard's mind. *Ongoing investigation* sounded wonderfully ominous.

"What can I do to help?"

"For starters, you could let us in."

The man pushed the button for the wrought-iron gates. They opened slowly to a low buzzing sound. "Mr. Wolfe lives at three five one three Maple Lane," he said, though Jerry hadn't asked for the address. "Straight ahead, first left, then a right."

Jerry nodded. "Thank you, Henry. I'm sure you already know this, but do not under any circumstances let Mr. Wolfe know that anybody was asking about him. Is that absolutely clear?"

"Yessir." Henry swallowed and adjusted his shirt collar.

Jerry's gaze was focused on something attached to the side of the guard's booth. Morris craned his neck to see what the PI was looking at.

"Say, Henry. Does that camera work?"

The security guard nodded. "It does now, but somebody broke it last year. The residents didn't want to pay to get it fixed, so I asked my son to tinker with it and he got it working again. He's an electrician. I didn't bother to bill the HOA. They're cheap and I doubt they'd pay—" Henry's face reddened. "Not that I don't like my job, I do, it's just—"

Jerry put up a hand. "I'm with you. Does the camera record?"

"Sure does. I keep it rolling constantly."

"Nobody knows it works?"

Henry lowered his voice. "Don't think anybody cares."

"Good work." Jerry sounded genuinely impressed and the security guard looked delighted. "Mind if I take a peek at the tapes you've got?"

The guard looked doubtful. "I only have a few weeks' worth of archives. I have to recycle the tapes—"

"That's fine."

"Come on in."

Morris had his hand on the door, but Jerry turned to him. "Just me. You stay here."

Jerry was in the booth for ten minutes.

Morris fidgeted inside the Honda, wondering what the hell was going on. "So?" he said when Jerry finally eased back into the car.

The PI was carrying a video cassette, which he placed on the backseat.

"Was Sheila on the tape? Has she been here?"

Jerry started the car, and the guard waved as they entered the subdivision. "I'll tell you what I saw, but I don't want you to go crazy."

Morris felt his heart lurch in his chest. "Goddammit. She's been here."

"Yes, I think so." Jerry's jaw was tight. "The video's time stamped for just after midnight on the night she was last seen at Tony's Tavern, so the timing fits. She's in the passenger seat, asleep. The image is grainy and I'll have to get someone to clean it up before I can be sure, but I'd bet my ass it's her. We're lucky the security guard keeps the tape running when he's not in the booth. If not for that, we'd never know she'd been here."

Morris's hand gripped the door handle as Jerry followed the guard's instructions to get to Maple Lane. "And the driver?"

Jerry looked grim. "It wasn't Wolfe. From what I could make out, he was darker, older, more heavyset. But he definitely fits the description of the man she was talking to at the SAA meeting and Tony's Tavern. Same with the car. Big black SUV, just like Dennis Fisher said. Couldn't make out the plate number."

Morris frowned. "So Wolfe has a friend in SAA who picked her up and brought her here?"

"Don't know. But she was here, and that's what matters."

"It could be Wolfe in disguise," Morris said, thinking of Tom Young.

Jerry's dark eyes flickered. "Doubtful. It would have to be a pretty elaborate disguise, which would suggest a whole other level of . . ." He didn't finish his sentence. "Shit, I suppose anything's possible."

The streetlamps on Maple Lane were dim and it was difficult to read the house numbers. All the homes were dark, as most suburban neighborhoods would be at this time of night. Morris found the quiet unsettling.

Jerry slowed in front of 3513. Other than the porch light, the house was completely dark. The motorcycle was not in the driveway, which meant Wolfe had parked it inside the garage. Morris wondered if the black SUV was in there, too, but the garage doors didn't have windows, so there was no way to check.

Jerry passed the house and continued down the street, looping around the block twice before stopping across the street from Wolfe's place. He shut off the engine.

"Big-ass house," he commented, looking at the sprawling

rambler through the car window. "Must be nice to be young and rich."

There was no movement on the street, though Morris thought he might have seen a curtain inside Wolfe's house ruffle slightly. Impatient, he opened the passenger door. The car's interior lights came on immediately.

In an instant, Jerry's arm was on his. "Shut the door!" he hissed. "Are you stupid?"

Morris glared at him, closing the door as Jerry reached up and flicked the light switch off. "What the hell? We came all this way but we're not going in?"

Jerry searched the street carefully before turning back to Morris. "What the hell were you gonna do, walk up to the front door and ring the bell at eleven o'clock at night?"

"Sounds good to me." Morris's face was hot. He kept one hand on the door handle. "Sheila's in there. I need to talk to her. I need to see her face and make sure she's okay."

"And then what?"

"What do you mean?"

"I mean, what if she *is* okay?" Jerry said. "It's likely she's in there because she wants to be, Morris. She wasn't struggling on the tape. She was sleeping."

"Or passed out from drugs or something."

"That's a stretch." Jerry's frown deepened. "You're jumping to conclusions, my friend. For all we know, she and Wolfe are still having an affair. There's nothing to suggest he hurt her. Or that he would hurt her. From what I could see, she wasn't harmed."

"Now who's stupid?" Morris said, huffy. "You saw her on the tape going in. I haven't heard from her in three weeks. What if that guy's done something to her? Did you see her come back out?"

"No, but—"

Morris opened the door again. This time the car stayed dark.

"Morris, *please*." The urgency in Jerry's voice caused Morris to stop. "Listen to me for one second." Jerry reached across and closed the passenger door firmly. "We can't just bust in. You're not thinking this through."

"You're a civilian. You don't need a warrant."

"I'm a civilian so I can't *get* a warrant, blowhole." Jerry was exasperated. "Which has nothing to do with anything. Whoever the guy is that drove her here, Sheila was seen talking to him. Flirting with him. I know you don't want to hear that, but that's what we know. You ring the bell and start harassing people, especially at this time of night, they'll call the cops and arrest you. Do you get that?"

Morris gritted his teeth so hard his gums ached. "Jerry, every bone in my body is telling me that Sheila is inside that house right now. I need to talk to her and ask her to come home. She might not like that I'm here—she might slam the door in my face because she wants to be with that goddamned kid—but I can't go back home without knowing. And if we have to wrestle before you let me out of this goddamned car, so be it." Morris's breath was coming out so fast, the windows of the Honda were fogging up. "You're a big guy, but I was offensive lineman All-American for four fucking years and I *will* take you out if I have to."

Jerry stared at Morris for a full three seconds. Then he burst out laughing.

He laughed so hard tears appeared in the corners of his eyes, glistening in the streetlights that shone through the windows. "I'm sorry," Jerry said, gasping. He threw up a hand, struggling to control his laughter. Then he started all over again. "You should see the look on your face. 'Take me out'? Jesus Christ, that was funny."

Morris didn't see the humor. "You finished, asshole? I meant what I said."

"I could take you."

"No, you couldn't."

Jerry shook his head as his laughter subsided. "You're worse than a five-year-old."

"Okay, let's go," Morris said, pushing down the door handle again.

Jerry placed a hand on his shoulder. "Wait." His voice was gentle. "Just wait. Give me five minutes. Let me call Torrance. At least let him know we're here, in case something goes wrong. Hell, it's a long shot, but maybe I can convince him to reopen the case based on the tape. Sheila was with a strange man the night she was last seen, possibly drugged, as you said. Who knows, it could be grounds for a search." He looked dubious, but he flipped open his cell phone anyway. "Just calm down and give me five stinking minutes."

Morris sat back in his seat and made a show of checking his watch. "Four minutes fifty-five seconds," he said, but only because it made him feel better.

: : : :

Ethan watched the black Honda Accord from a window at the front of the house, peering between two curtains. He knew they couldn't see him; all his lights were off and the house was dark. The car door had opened for a second, illuminating two faces in heated discussion. Then it had closed again.

His instincts told him they weren't coming inside. Not to-night, anyway. The PI was an ex-cop, and no doubt he was explaining to Morris right now that they had no cause, no justification.

Ethan turned away from the window and walked back toward the basement door. It bolted automatically behind him.

If they wanted to come after him, they'd have to shoot their way in.

CHAPTER : 35

Jerry spoke in serious tones before finally hanging up the phone. Morris had been listening to one side of the conversation and needed no explanation.

"This is bullshit and you know it," Morris fumed, his hand back on the passenger door. "You both have your heads up your asses. I knew Torrance wasn't gonna help." He was out of the car before Jerry could stop him.

Morris dashed across the street, crossing Wolfe's front yard in five long strides, and rang the doorbell without hesitating.

Nobody answered. He rang the bell again, holding his ear to the door. Unable to make out any sounds or movements from inside the house, he rang the bell once again and listened to the echo of the chime within. Frustrated, he pounded on the thick door with his fist.

A light went on in the house next door.

Jerry had been hovering on the sidewalk, seemingly unwilling to set foot on Wolfe's property. But when Morris shouted at full volume, Jerry was on the porch in three seconds.

"Sheila!" Morris bellowed, banging on Wolfe's door several more times. His deep baritone rang out in the sleeping neighborhood.

"All right, all right." Jerry grabbed Morris's arm. "Enough!"

"Go to hell." Morris wrangled his arm away while continuing to bang on the door with his other fist. "Sheila!"

Jerry made a move to grab Morris's other arm. Before Morris could stop himself, his clenched fist socked the private investigator right in the eye.

Jerry fell backward over the steps and onto the wet grass. He landed on his ass, legs splaying out awkwardly in front of him, pants hiking up to expose white athletic socks stuck into black running shoes.

"Aw fuck," Jerry said, his hand at his face. "You ass. I can't believe you hit me."

Morris stared at Jerry in horror, the knuckles on his right hand aching from where he'd struck hard orbital bone. He staggered down the porch steps and reached out a hand. "Jesus Christ, man. I'm sorry."

Jerry touched his eye gingerly with one finger and ignored him. Even in the dim light, Morris could see the man's face scrunched up in pain. Morris felt a wave of shame roll over him.

The sound of a door opening caught the attention of both men.

An elderly lady stepped out onto the front porch of the house next door. She was dressed in a long flannel nightgown, her hair in rollers and tucked under some kind of net cap. Bony arms crossed defiantly over her chest, and her eyes darted back and forth between Jerry and Morris. "What's going on out here?" Her voice was shrill. "I've called security!"

As if on cue, a small, white car with a familiar green logo pulled up. Henry the security guard stepped out. He shone his flashlight at Wolfe's house.

"What's going on, guys?" Henry kept his voice low, but another light flickered on from a house across the street. "I've received a noise complaint."

Jerry got to his feet. His jeans were dark where the wet grass had soaked them. "Everything's fine, Henry."

The security guard stared at the PI's swelling face. "Everything doesn't look fine."

Jerry waved a hand. "Just a misunderstanding."

Henry looked at the two men. "Did something happen with Mr. Wolfe?" he stage-whispered.

"Nothing to be concerned about." Jerry used his best cop's voice. "We're leaving. Sorry for the disturbance, ma'am," he called to the elderly lady, still watching them with birdlike intensity. "Please go back to sleep. Didn't mean to wake you."

The woman ignored his apologies. "Everything okay, Henry?" she asked.

"Everything's fine, Mrs. Hoffer." The guard tried to smile, but it was clear he was as rattled as she was. "It's under control, ma'am."

"I told my son and his floozy wife not to move to this ghetto neighborhood. If it weren't for my grandchildren, I wouldn't step foot here." Grumbling, the old woman started back inside. "But no, he says, the East Side's too expensive. Too uppity, too crowded . . ." Her voice trailed off as she went back into the house. The door slammed behind her.

Henry looked uncomfortable. "Did you guys get what you needed? Because you should get going now. If you're not visiting anyone here . . ." He nodded toward Wolfe's house.

"We're done," Jerry said, more to Morris than the security guard.

It was a long ride back to Seattle. Morris tried to apologize several more times, but each attempt was met with icy silence. When Jerry pulled into the empty parking lot where Morris had left his car earlier, he gave it one more shot.

"I'm really sorry."

Jerry's eye had swollen considerably since they'd left Lake Stevens. Morris knew his words were probably meaningless, but he forged ahead anyway. "I went a little nuts. You didn't deserve it, God knows."

Jerry cut the engine. "I'd say it's okay, but you know what, man? It's not. I was trying to help you back there, trying to stop you from doing something that might get you arrested, not to mention embarrass you and push Sheila away, but—"

"I was too pigheaded to listen. I know. I can be a total ass."

Jerry shook his head. "I can't stop you from going back there if that's what you're gonna do. You're as stubborn as a bull, Morris." Jerry touched his face and winced. "But I hope you don't. You hired me to find Sheila and I finally have a solid lead. But she's not found yet. Do you want me to keep doing my job or not?"

"I do." Morris felt terrible about hitting Jerry. The god-damned alcohol was making him crazy and paranoid and stupid.

"From now on you stay out of it. I'll call you if I learn anything, but I work by myself. As I always have."

Morris tried to think of a polite way to say what he needed to say. He chose his words carefully. "I understand that. I'm too close to this, I get that now. But it's really difficult for me to back off. I can't take feeling this helpless. There's gotta be something I can do." He rubbed his head. "Maybe I should call Sheila's therapist. She's not supposed to tell me anything, but I never did ask her about Ethan Wolfe. I'm sure Sheila's talked about him—"

"It's late. You have her home number?"

"No." Morris's frustration swelled again.

Jerry sighed and pulled out his notepad. "What's her name? I'm sure I can find it for you. Don't get your hopes up, though, because these people take doctor-patient confidentiality very seriously. I doubt she'll give you anything."

"It's worth a shot." Morris reached for his BlackBerry. "Her name is Chang. Marianne Chang. I have her office number here in case you need to cross-reference—" Morris stopped when he saw the PI staring at him, his pen poised over his notebook. "C-H-A-N-G. What, you want me to spell out *Marianne,* too?"

Jerry tucked his notebook back into his breast pocket, his face the picture of amusement, even with the swelling eye. "It's your lucky night. I know the lady. Personally."

"You do?" Morris grinned with relief. "Finally, something's going our way. Maybe you can get something out of her."

"If anyone has a shot, it's me." The private investigator gave Morris a sideways glance and cleared his throat. "Of all the therapists in all the towns in all the world . . . craziest thing, Morris. Dr. Marianne Chang? She's my wife, Annie."

CHAPTER : 36

The house was dark when Jerry let himself in, but he knew Annie might still be up. In a hurry, he kicked off his shoes and raced up the staircase, his leather jacket still on.

He was glad to see his wife wide-awake when he entered their bedroom, but was dismayed at the pissed-off look on her face. He moved in to kiss her but she turned her head at the last second. Instead of her lips, he got a freshly scrubbed cheek.

"Are you nuts?" Annie had a book in her lap and her dark eyes glared at him behind thin reading glasses. "Keisha's sleeping. You sounded like a gorilla coming up those stairs." His niece and part-time receptionist often slept over.

"Sorry," Jerry whispered. He shrugged off his coat and flopped next to her on the bed. "We gotta talk."

"I figured." She wasn't amused. She bookmarked her page by folding in one corner, a trait he'd always found strange since she loved books and otherwise took good care of them. She took in his face. "What happened to you?"

"Tell you later. Right now I want to talk about Sheila Tao. She's your patient, yes?"

Annie removed her glasses. "Yes," she said warily. "And how, exactly, would you know that?"

"Because her fiancé, Morris Gardener, is my client. He's hired me to find her."

Annie's jaw didn't quite drop, but her mouth did open slightly. "You're shitting me."

Jerry couldn't help but grin. His wife didn't swear often.

"I had no idea he was going to hire a PI." Annie's voice grew faint as she processed this information. "Since he hadn't called me, I assumed he'd let it go and was moving on. He said Sheila had made it very clear . . ." Her face clouded over.

Jerry put a comforting hand on her thigh. "You're not a babysitter, honey. If a patient wants to take off, what are you supposed to do? Assume the worst every time? You deal with adults who need therapy, not children who aren't allowed to run away. And by the way," he said, his eyes narrowing, "when did you start treating sex addiction? That's news to me."

His wife gave him a look. "And when did you start handling missing persons again? I thought all you'd been doing since you went civilian is catch cheating spouses."

She didn't know about the deal Jerry had going with Torrance, so he quickly changed the subject. "What can you tell me about Sheila?"

Annie frowned at him. "You know I can't tell you anything about our sessions."

"Give me a break." Jerry stifled a sigh. "You're not on trial here. I'm not going to do anything to make you lose your license. I'm your husband. I just need some information."

"About?" Her tone was careful.

"Ethan Wolfe."

She exhaled slowly. "You think he had something to do with her leaving?"

"So he is the one she cheated on him with. I can tell by the look on your face."

His wife didn't respond.

"You're seriously going to play this game?" Jerry said, exasperated.

Annie's frown deepened. "This is my job we're talking about. What I do is confidential. Just like what you do is confidential."

"Yeah, and how's that working out for us?" Jerry didn't bother to rein in his sarcasm. "Sheila Tao is missing, her fiancé's going crazy wondering if she's okay, I'm discovering all kinds of skeletons in her closet like sex addiction, online cheating, an affair with her teaching assistant, and you, my wife, might have been able to provide answers to this whole thing days ago if we were the kind of couple who actually talked to each other about our goddamned jobs. She's your patient. You care what happens to her, don't you?"

"Of course I do." Annie's eyes misted. "I also consider her a friend."

"And she was my teacher."

"What are you . . ." Annie's face showed confusion, then she blinked. "Oh, right. You took that night class at PSSU way back, when she was teaching under her married name. I can't believe I never put that together. Mind you, in the past couple of years, we talked a lot more about her personal life than we did mine."

His wife was quiet for a long moment. Then her mouth twitched. He had her.

"You used the word *missing*," she finally said. "Is she *missing* missing or did she *leave*?"

Jerry told her about the tape he'd gotten from the Briar Woods security guard. "She looked fine, like she was sleeping, but the driver wasn't Wolfe. Her phone message to Morris when she canceled the wedding—"

"You heard it? How did she sound?"

"Like a woman breaking up with her fiancé. Upset, crying. Said she was leaving town to go to rehab. Didn't want Morris to follow her. Apologized a bunch of times."

"Shit," Annie said again, thinking hard. Finally she looked at Jerry. "All right, I don't care. I need to know Sheila's okay, and right now I don't know that she is. So screw confidentiality. Ask me whatever you want and I'll tell you what I can."

Jerry kissed her hand. "I would never let this jeopardize your career, you know that."

Her smile was anxious. "I know."

It was his turn to think for a moment. "Okay, so I've met Ethan Wolfe. I didn't like him—something about him seemed off. He was twitchy. He maintained eye contact but he was trying too hard to convince me they weren't having an affair. Were they getting it on?"

Annie's nod was firm. "The affair lasted about three months, but he pursued her long before that. It ended when Sheila got engaged to Morris. Ethan flipped out when she suggested he work with a new adviser. Threatened to release a sex video they'd made. It would have ruined her career."

Jerry felt a flutter in his stomach, something that always happened when his instincts were right on the money. "Release it how?"

"Internet."

"So he is an asshole." Jerry grinned, triumphant. "I knew it. What'd she do then?"

In contrast, Annie's face was grim. "At first she played along, gave him what he wanted. Didn't transfer him." Annie looked as if she were about to add something more, but then stopped. "He dangled that video over her head. After a while, she became convinced he didn't really have it, because they did quarrel a couple of times. If he had it, he'd have used it."

"But what about her job?"

"She was prepared to risk it. If Ethan didn't have the tape, he wouldn't have proof, and she thought the university would back her if it came down to he said, she said. She was waiting it out. Though she did come clean with Morris about her sex addiction and the affair."

But not about the tape, Jerry thought. Not that he blamed Sheila. The big guy wouldn't have been able to handle it. "Was she scared of Wolfe? Did he threaten her physically?"

"She didn't mention anything like that to me. If I'd thought she was in any physical danger, I'd have told her to call the cops. But there was psychological abuse for sure." Annie's eyes fixed on Jerry's face. "Ethan might not have threatened to harm Sheila physically, but make no mistake—his threat to ruin her career and her relationship was terrifying."

"So she wouldn't have left town with him."

"No chance in hell." Annie reached for her little tube of cherry lip balm and rubbed more on her lips, something she did when she was contemplating. "She hated him. She wanted him out of her life."

"So in your opinion, she'd have no reason to be in a car, sleeping, heading to his house, three weeks ago?"

"None whatsoever. It's been hell ever since she ended it with him. She loved Morris—she couldn't wait to get married. We speculated . . ."

"What?" Jerry prompted.

"It's not an official diagnosis, so don't take my word for it, okay?" Annie shifted her position, stretching her legs out in front of her. Jerry placed her bare foot in his lap and began massaging it, eliciting a sigh of contentment from his wife. "We thought he might have some kind of antisocial personality disorder. On the surface, he fits the criteria. A lack of empathy for others, poor impulse control, a sense of entitlement, the inability to form meaningful relationships."

Jerry had come across a lot of people like that in his time with Seattle PD. "So he didn't love her?"

"He might have. Antisocials can feel love. But if they're rejected, they don't take it well. Ethan lashed out in a big way. He seemed intent on ruining Sheila's life."

Jerry cracked his knuckles, trying to process this information. "Okay," he said finally. "I'd better go call Torrance. And Morris." He kissed the top of her foot and got up off the bed.

Annie's eyes widened. "Mike Torrance? At this time of night?"

"Yep." Jerry threw his jacket back on and headed toward the door. "Going to see if he can reopen Sheila's case."

Annie's face held both relief and concern. "When are you coming home?"

"Don't wait up, hon."

"Hey, you never told me what happened to your face!"

Jerry shut the door behind him and pulled his cell phone out of his coat pocket.

Up until now there hadn't been anything to convince him that Sheila hadn't left Morris of her own free will. But that tape, combined with what he'd learned about Sheila's relationship with Wolfe, certainly indicated that Morris's instincts were right. Sheila had no business being in Lake Stevens. And even if the tape didn't show her in the car with Wolfe, that she was in Wolfe's neighborhood the night she was last seen anywhere was way too much of a coincidence for a woman who hated her ex-lover and was looking forward to her wedding.

He scrolled through his phone for Torrance's number. Once

he was in the car, he made the call. His former partner answered after five rings. "Mike, it's Jerry. Did I wake you?"

Torrance's voice was hoarse. "This better be good."

"I have some new information about the Tao case. I think we have enough to reopen it. Can you meet me at PD?"

"You're not serious."

"As a heart attack."

Jerry could almost hear the wheels in Torrance's brain turning. Jerry would never have requested a face-to-face if he didn't have something compelling, and Mike Torrance knew that.

"Give me fifteen minutes."

Jerry ended the call, then scrolled through his phone again until he found Morris's number.

CHAPTER : 37

Sheila watched Ethan pace the room.

He hadn't said a word since he'd arrived an hour before. Instead, he was muttering to himself, going in and out of his workroom, clearly trying to work something out in his head.

Her instincts told her he was beginning to crack. What had happened—or almost happened—between them a few days ago was proof of that. She had gotten close to him, and she was certain she could do it again.

It was her only hope.

Her feet dangled off the bed, not quite touching the floor. She watched as he came out of the workroom for the tenth time, and her heart lurched when she saw that the small silver gun was tucked into the waistband of his jeans once again. She hadn't seen the gun in days. He made no move to wave it in her face. Instead, he lay on the sofa and closed his eyes.

"What's going on with you?" Sheila asked, tentative. "Something feels different."

"Nothing. Just tired."

"Is somebody onto you?" She kept her voice light. She knew he'd only talk if she provoked him a little. But not too much. "You seem really tense."

Ethan didn't move. "Nobody's onto me. Nobody's looking for you."

"I'm not talking about me. I'm talking about you. Your girl-friend has to suspect something by now."

He opened one eye. "Don't you fucking talk to me about Abby."

Ah, she'd hit a nerve. That was good. But she had to be careful not to push him too quickly. "If I see the changes in you, then so has she. You're exhausted and stressed. She's not stupid, Ethan. You can't keep the hours you keep without her noticing."

He opened his eyes all the way. "Your point?"

"Whatever your plan is, it's time." Sheila paused for effect. "You *do* have a plan, don't you?" She allowed the smallest bit of accusation to seep into her voice.

"Things have changed." His voice was clipped.

His body language was more telling than his words. He had grown stiff, his hands clenched into tight fists; thankfully they didn't move toward the gun.

She took a deep breath. Her next move was risky. "Ethan, if you wanted to kill me, I'd be dead by now. Just like if you wanted to destroy my career, you'd have released the video. So let's stop pretending you want to hurt me. We both know you don't. You brought me here because you were pissed off and trying to teach me a lesson. And God knows you have." She leaned forward. "We still care about each other. You know we do."

Ethan shook his head slowly. "You're trying to mind-fuck me."

"Have I tried to escape?" She hoped she sounded sincere. "Have I given you a hard time about anything? I know how smart you are. I know I can't bullshit you."

"You tried to take the gun from me. When we were, you know . . ." His voice faded, his eyes darting to her face briefly before flitting away.

"I already told you, I wasn't trying anything." Sheila forced just the right note of exasperation into her voice. "I had to move it, it was digging into my leg. Ethan, you can trust me."

He stared at her, then grinned. The smile did not touch his eyes. "Impressive, Dr. Tao."

"I mean every word I say."

"You're making me angry. I suggest you shut up right now."

"But, Ethan—"

"Shut up!" he roared, standing up.

Startled, Sheila cringed into the pillows.

He took a few steps toward the bed and pointed a shaking finger at her. "You—all of you—you make me fucking crazy, you know that? You all think you're so intelligent, so unique and so exceptional, but you're all the same."

"Who, Ethan?" She kept her voice steady, wishing she had something to hide behind. She pulled a pillow to her chest. "Who are you talking about? Me and who?"

He ignored her and started pacing the room again, his hand moving to the butt of the gun. "You want to get out of here so you can go back to your perfect little life, with your perfect job and your perfect man. Well, why should I let you? Why do you get to be happy, Sheila? What makes you so fucking special?"

"I never said—"

"Shut up!" he shrieked, clapping his hands over his ears like a little boy. "Shut up shut up shut up!"

Sheila snapped her mouth closed. She had no idea what he was ranting about, but he was completely uncorked. It was time to back off.

"We had a good thing going, you and me. And then you

had to go and ruin it by getting engaged to that fat fuck." He was talking to her but not looking at her. "And, okay, I could have dealt with it, no big deal. You want to marry him, marry him. What the fuck do I care, I have a girlfriend, what does it change? But then you ended it with me. You wanted me out of your life completely. *For him.* How was I supposed to take that? I'm supposed to just shrink away, act like it's all okay? I had feelings for you." His fingers tightened around the base of the gun.

She cowered on the bed, not sure what he was going to do. "I had feelings for you, too."

"You're lying."

"Ethan, I'm sorry." She was beginning to sweat. "I handled it all wrong. I see that now. I . . . disrespected you and said things I shouldn't have. It was my fault. If I could go back and change it, I would. But I didn't think you cared. If I'd known you did, I never would have made the decision I made." She took a breath and looked up at him. "I loved you, Ethan."

He stopped pacing. Sheila had no idea if he'd heard her.

His jaw worked. "When I graduated, I thought . . . I thought we could have made something of it."

"We still can. It's not too late."

He started pacing again. "No, you picked Morris. Morris with the big-ass Cadillac and big-ass house and big-ass bank job and big-ass bank account."

How did he know all that? It certainly hadn't come from her. Ethan's obsession with Morris was scaring the shit out of her. Every conversation seemed to lead right back to him.

"Do you still love him?" Ethan asked.

Sheila couldn't think of an answer fast enough and his face transformed into something ugly.

"You do. Your hesitation says it all."

"God, Ethan, I'm not a robot!" She got up off the bed and approached him. "I don't have switches I can turn on and off. Ending it with you was agonizing. It was the hardest decision I've ever made. But I thought Morris was the sensible choice. Think about it logically, from my perspective. I'm telling you the truth." She reached her hand out.

"I'm sorry, but you can't have your old life back," Ethan said, ignoring her hand and taking a small step back. "Nobody misses you. Nobody gives a fuck that you're gone. They already replaced you at the university. Got some hotshot professor they snagged from the University of Washington to fill your big shoes. Oh, what was her name again . . . ?" He snapped his fingers several times in succession, like a jazz musician feeling the beat. "Linda something or other. Brennan. Brandon."

"Branson," Sheila said, deflated. "Linda Branson." She had no idea if what Ethan was saying was true, but it was definitely plausible. Dr. Linda Branson was indeed a hotshot professor who'd left the University of Washington to write a bestselling book on childhood phobias. Of course PSSU would have snapped her up, especially now that Sheila was out of the picture. What timing.

"And Morris." A small smile was on Ethan's lips. "I can guarantee Morris the fat fuck isn't looking for you, either. He's so over you. You never should have told him about your sex addiction. I'll bet he was glad as hell when you canceled the wedding, so he didn't have to do it. He probably thinks he dodged a bullet."

"Well, that's where I'll have to disagree," Sheila said, despite her fear. "You don't know Morris. He's very loyal. Maybe he hasn't yet, but he *will* start looking for me. He'll want answers, and when he starts digging, he'll figure out that something bad happened. He won't let it go until he finds me. And he's a juggernaut when he gets going." She felt her chin jut out defiantly. "You won't be able to stop him."

Another nerve hit. Ethan stopped pacing and turned to her, his gray eyes completely devoid of the flecks of light that made people look human. The hairs on Sheila's neck stood up and she cursed herself for opening her big mouth. Oh, God. What was he going to do now? *Stupid, stupid, stupid!*

"Morris is dead," Ethan said calmly. "I already killed him."

"No." Her heart started hammering so hard she couldn't breathe. "You're lying."

"Why do you think I'm so sure he's not looking for you?" Ethan's lips curled up in a sneer. "I made it look like an accident. He started drinking again when you left him, no surprise there. So I fucked a little with the brake pads on his big, shiny Cadillac. Five nights ago when it was raining really hard, he veered off the freeway and wrapped himself around a utility pole. Died instantly. When they pulled him out, they could smell the whiskey on him. There was an open bottle of Johnnie Walker on the passenger seat floor." Ethan smiled, pleased with himself. "The good stuff—Red label, I think. Or was it Black? I can't remember."

"You're lying," Sheila said again, feeling dizzy. "I don't believe you. Morris was innocent. He hasn't done anything to hurt you, and I've been cooperating, haven't I? There was no reason to kill him."

Ethan stepped toward her. "You don't believe me? You don't think I'm capable?" His smile was frosty and knowing. He tilted her head up with his finger. "After all the planning I did to get you here, and after all this time keeping you here, *you don't think I can do any fucking thing I set my mind to?*"

His words were nothing short of a scream. His spittle sprayed her face.

Sheila struggled to keep calm, but her insides felt like mush.

"The funeral was yesterday." He was calm again as he took her arm and led her back toward the bed. She didn't protest. "Remind me to bring you the obituary from the *Times*. They used a nice photo, the one from your office—he's in the red plaid shirt barbecuing something? Hate to admit it, but he looked quite handsome."

It couldn't be real. No, please, it couldn't be. But God help her, she was starting to believe him. Ethan's words rang true, right down to the brand of whiskey Morris liked. He was right— why *wouldn't* he have killed Morris? He hated Morris, and he'd killed before. It was all in a day's work.

She felt her mind spin out of control.

If Morris was gone, truly gone, then she was on her own. Just as Ethan said, nobody would be looking for her, nobody would care where she'd gone. And it wouldn't matter anyway, because a life without Morris was too horrible to contemplate.

She had nothing left to lose.

Sheila's voice was steady despite the stream of hot tears running down her cheeks. "Ethan, make love to me."

Ethan's head snapped toward her in surprise. "What did you say?"

"You brought me here to get me away from Morris. And then you killed him. As much as that hurts me, and it does," she said, pausing to lick the salty tears that had landed on her lips, "I know you've done this out of love. So make the hurt go away. Make what you did worth it."

Ethan saw her heartbreak, saw her pain, saw her desire. This is what she wanted him to see. She was offering herself to him, despite the horrifying news about Morris.

It worked. He believed.

He took her in his arms. It took all of her strength to let

herself melt against him, to touch him, to kiss the lips of the man who personified the word *monster*.

And when his urgent hands roamed her body, she closed her eyes and lay back on the bed, retreating to her happy place, where the sun was shining and Morris was waiting for her.

CHAPTER : 38

The coffee at Seattle PD's East Precinct was bitter and strong. Jerry suspected it was because nobody ever bothered to rinse out the coffeemaker, which had been a staple in this office ever since he could remember.

Jerry sipped the awful coffee, then hit redial on his cell phone. It rang exactly five times before going to voice mail again. Morris wasn't picking up. Had he gone to bed, or back to Lake Stevens? Jerry finally left a message and snapped his phone shut.

It had been awhile since he'd been in the precinct's control room, but everything looked—and smelled, for that matter— exactly the same. Same beige walls, same gunmetal-gray desks, same beige linoleum. He watched the computer monitor in front of him, which displayed a clear shot of Interview Room 3.

Torrance and his partner were about to begin an interview with Abby Maddox, Ethan Wolfe's girlfriend. Jerry wasn't officially supposed to be here, but considering how closely he'd been working with Morris, Torrance knew better than to shut his ex-partner out.

The young woman was sitting at the table in the middle

of the small room, her shoulder-length black hair sleek and shiny under the harsh fluorescent lights. Her skin was so pale and translucent, she appeared almost ghostly in the monitor. Jerry had gotten a glimpse of her as she passed him in the main hall and was struck by how beautiful she was up close—supermodel gorgeous. Not Jerry's type exactly, but undeniably good-looking—tall, slender, with deep blue eyes and full lips. A striking contrast to the other woman in the interview room, Torrance's new partner. The very blond and very perky Kimberley Kellogg was steadfastly staring at the interviewee with her notebook open and pen ready.

"You sure you don't want any coffee? Soda? Water?" Torrance asked Maddox.

"I'm fine," she answered in a husky voice, though it was obviously a lie. She was sitting up straight in the metal chair. "I just don't understand why I'm here. Why couldn't we have done this at my apartment? Two police officers show up at my door in the middle of the night and they wouldn't tell me what's going on—"

"Thank you for being so cooperative." Torrance's tone was pleasant. He was sitting directly across from Maddox, his smile friendly. "We need some information from you. You're not under arrest or in any kind of trouble."

"Do I need a lawyer?"

"Of course not," Torrance said. "You can leave anytime you like. We just want to ask you a few questions about your boyfriend."

"Ethan?" Maddox's pretty face was troubled. Her gaze shifted back and forth between the two detectives. "Why, what'd he do?"

"Who says he did anything?" Kellogg said, and Torrance shot his partner a look.

"We think he might know something about the disappearance of Dr. Sheila Tao." Torrance drummed his fingers lightly on the table. "Do you know who she is?"

Maddox's eyes were wide and frightened. Jerry felt sorry for her. "She's his graduate adviser. He works for her. She left town, I thought. Ethan said she was sick."

Torrance and Kellogg said nothing.

"Oh, God." Maddox's hands shook and she clutched her large purse, which was sitting on the table in front of her. "Oh, God, I knew something was up. I knew it."

Torrance glanced up at the camera. Alone in the control room, Jerry turned the volume up on the monitor.

"What can you tell us, Miss Maddox?" Torrance's voice was soothing. He was using the tone he always did when he thought the witness might get squirrelly. "Did you suspect something?"

Maddox hung her head, her ebony hair falling over her cheekbones. "He was cheating on me with her. He didn't think I knew, but of course I did. I'm not stupid."

"How'd you find out?"

"I caught them once. They didn't see me. I stopped by his office and she was sitting on the edge of his desk and his hand was up her skirt—" Maddox blinked, but the tears trickled down her face anyway. She dug into her purse for a wad of tissue and blew her nose.

"Has he been acting strange since Dr. Tao disappeared?" Kellogg asked as she scratched notes into her pad. "Anything that might indicate he knew her whereabouts?"

Maddox shook her head. "No, but he's been gone a lot. I don't know where he goes, he doesn't tell me. I work the late shift at Safeway, and sometimes I get in at three, four in the morning. And he's not home. He's been distracted for the past few weeks. And difficult."

"We've learned he spends a lot of time up in Lake Stevens." Torrance watched her face closely. "Any idea why?"

Maddox shook her head again and wiped her eyes. "Is that where Dr. Tao lives?"

Torrance glanced up at the camera again and Jerry knew what the look meant. Abby Maddox had no idea about her boyfriend's Lake Stevens house.

She started to sniffle, and it wasn't long before a torrent of sobs escaped from Maddox's slender chest. Torrance watched dispassionately, but Kellogg, the rookie, obviously felt bad.

"I should have known something was off. I should have known." Maddox struggled to contain herself, digging into her purse for another tissue.

"We don't know anything for a fact yet." The female detective attempted to sound reassuring.

"I should have known," Maddox repeated, looking across at the two detectives. "I should have done something the moment I found it."

"To what are you referring?" Torrance asked with a frown.

Maddox reached into her purse. It was hard to tell from the camera angle, but she appeared to be unzipping something. Women's purses mystified Jerry—they had so many zippers and flaps and compartments, he was amazed women could find anything they'd stashed away. She dug for a bit, then pulled out a wadded-up tissue, which she placed on the table in front of the female detective.

"Open it," Maddox said.

Kellogg hesitated, and Wolfe's girlfriend said, "It's not used or anything. I put something inside it. Something I found a couple of weeks ago in Ethan's pocket."

Kellogg looked at Torrance, who gave her a nod. The blonde

put her notebook down and reached inside her jacket pocket for a pair of latex gloves. Snapping them on, she unfolded the tissue with the points of her fingers. Something shiny rolled onto the table.

It was a woman's diamond ring.

Kellogg picked it up and examined it under the lights. Even watching on the computer monitor, Jerry could tell the diamond was huge.

"I found it when I was doing laundry. I'm pretty sure it's Professor Tao's. I remember admiring it from a distance when I went to meet Ethan at his office. I don't know why he'd have it. I thought . . ." Maddox's voice choked as another sob racked her. "I thought she'd left it behind and he'd stolen it. We're broke and I thought maybe he was going to pawn it. Now I'm not so sure."

Torrance put on a pair of latex gloves as well and took the ring from his partner. Turning it so he could see the inside of the band, he read the inscription aloud. "'Now and forever, Morris.'" He dropped it into a plastic bag and looked at Maddox, his face grim.

"There's something else," the young woman said, her voice faltering.

Torrance and Kellogg exchanged a look. *What now?* Jerry thought.

Maddox rooted around in her purse again and pulled something out with shaking fingers. "I know I'm going to get in trouble because I found this and didn't tell anyone . . ." She was barely coherent as she tried to speak through her tears. "It's just, I didn't want to believe it. I couldn't. I couldn't believe he might have—"

Torrance's face turned to stone as he took the object from her.

Kellogg looked confused. "What is it?"

Maddox's hands shook. "Diana St. Clair's gold medal."

Jerry's mouth dropped open.

Maddox's husky voice lowered to a whisper. "From when she won the Nike Cup last year. I'm sorry. I should have told somebody. But he—I love him. I didn't want to believe it."

Diana St. Clair. Holy shit. This was worse than Jerry could have imagined. Morris's instincts had been dead-on.

"You just happened to have these items in your purse, Miss Maddox?" Torrance said in a neutral voice.

"I knew . . . I needed . . ." A giant sob escaped her and Maddox collapsed, her ramrod posture folding under Torrance's hard stare. The look of terror on her face was heartbreaking. "I wanted to tell somebody, but I . . ."

He beats her, Jerry thought suddenly. His gut clenched at the thought of Wolfe's fists punching that beautiful face. He'd seen many battered women in his time, and though Abby Maddox displayed no obvious bruises at the moment, he'd bet his left nut that Wolfe smacked her around. And often. *Bastard. Coward.*

Torrance put the medal in another plastic bag. His expression would have been unreadable to anyone but his ex-partner. Jerry knew exactly what he was thinking. "Is there somewhere you can stay tonight, Miss Maddox? We'll need to search your apartment."

Torrance didn't mention searching the house in Lake Stevens, which Jerry thought was a good call. No point in upsetting the poor girl further.

Maddox shook her head and started crying again. "I don't have anywhere to go."

"We'll get you a motel room," Kellogg said. She touched the

top of the other woman's hand lightly. "Just for tonight until we get things sorted out."

All three left the interview room.

A few seconds later, Torrance poked his head into the control room where Jerry was sitting. "Consider your case re-opened."

CHAPTER: 39

"We need to get out of here," Ethan said. "But before we go, I want to tell you about my first time."

Sheila's fingers traced slow circles around his nipple. Her face looked the way it always did after sex, flushed and lazy. Her naked body was contoured against his, covered in a light, musky sweat. If Ethan closed his eyes, he could almost imagine they were back in room sixteen at the Ivy Motel.

Finally, finally, Sheila was his. The thought filled him with the deepest sense of contentment he'd ever known. Abby's face drifted into his mind then, but he pushed it away.

"I don't like thinking of you with other women," Sheila said.

Her frown told him she was sincere. He pulled her closer and kissed the top of her head. It smelled like wildflowers from the shampoo he'd bought her. "Do you love me, Sheila?"

"Yes," she answered without hesitation.

"All of me?" He pulled away slightly and looked into her dark eyes. They were soft and full of promise. "Even the bad parts?"

She intertwined her fingers in his. "Do you love me, even with my bad parts?"

She was right. Nobody was perfect. Maybe that's why, with

Sheila, it felt so easy. Unlike with Abby, where he always felt he had to pretend.

"I need you to hear this," Ethan said, looking at the television. It was tuned to CNN and muted, but the time was displayed on the lower right-hand corner of the screen. They didn't have long. They'd be after him soon; he could feel it.

But this was important.

"I want you to know everything about me," he said. "I want you to be sure about me. Because once we leave here, we can't come back. And then it's just you and me."

"I'm already sure. I can't wait to start my life with you."

She settled into the crook of his arm, and he began to speak.

: : : :

He was sixteen when they met.

She'd been sitting under a tree in front of their high school, bare legs tucked under, long hair glistening like silk in the thin rays of sunshine that filtered through the leaves above.

He had noticed her immediately, partly because she was beautiful, but mainly because she was alone, like him.

She caught him staring and met his furtive gaze with a steady one of her own. His mouth went dry. Before he could lift a hand to wave, the bell rang.

Weaving around the swarm of students trying to get to class on time, he followed her, making sure to stay a few paces behind. Her short, flared skirt topped a pair of coltish legs, and her cropped sweater revealed a hint of tummy. Her beauty set her apart from everyone else at this bum-fuck school. She didn't belong here.

He wanted to know her.

He made it all the way to her classroom door, trying desperately to think of something funny and clever to say. Before he could put it together, she abruptly turned to face him.

"Are you following me?" Her cat's eyes flashed, narrow with suspicion.

"No," Ethan said indignantly, despite being caught off guard. "This is my class."

"Since when?"

School had only started two days before. "I enrolled late. Is that okay with you?"

She blinked at his tone.

"You're very suspicious, you know," he said. "Do you really think you're that good-looking?"

He moved past her shocked face and into the classroom, taking a seat at the very back of the room. She sat a few rows ahead, and he stared at the back of her hair, imagining what the silky strands would feel like in his fingers. He had no idea what class he was in and didn't particularly care. It turned out to be American history, a class he'd already taken at another school. It didn't matter. As soon as the bell rang, he headed straight for the guidance office to officially register.

He saw her every other day for five weeks before she spoke to him again. The class had just received their midterm papers back and her eyes were on him when the teacher reached his desk. He'd received an A on his paper, the grade marked in red at the top corner of his title page.

"Nice work, Ethan," Mr. Bristol said with a smile. "You're writing at college level. Keep it up."

She was waiting for him by the door after class.

"Walk me home," she said. It wasn't a request. It was a command.

"Walk *me* home," he said, and she smiled.

Ten minutes later they were at his house.

"Are your parents here?" she asked as they entered through the side door. She shrugged out of her light cardigan and looked around the small but well-decorated space.

"George and Helen are my foster parents." His eyes darted to her face to gauge her reaction. "They both work till seven."

She smiled a smile he couldn't interpret. "Wish I had foster parents. I'm staying in a group home."

He knew that already but nodded politely. "You want something to drink?"

"Not really. Where's your room?"

Thirty minutes later, books open and cast aside, she was naked from the waist up.

She lay underneath him on his bed, her long hair fanned out over the pillow. She smelled of lilacs and rain forest and he couldn't stop kissing her. Her lips were a wonder all to themselves, at times soft and yielding, at times hard and demanding. In the background, the radio was tuned to a rock station.

He was propped up on top of her, eyes squeezed shut, humping her with his pants still on. He didn't ever want to stop kissing her. His palms massaged her bare breasts and he was delirious with joy and desire. When he opened his eyes a moment later, he saw that she was staring at him, a small smile on her face.

"Are you okay?" he whispered, slowing down.

She nodded, but her expression hinted at something different. Placing both her hands on his chest, she pushed him gently off her.

He sat up on the bed, confused. Had he done something wrong? Were they finished? Had she changed her mind?

"Don't worry," she said, as if she could read his thoughts. "Just getting into position. I want to get closer to you."

She pulled her jeans down, then her underwear, motioning for him to do the same. He couldn't take his eyes off the dark thatch of hair between her legs as she climbed on top of him. When he tried to lie back on the bed, she shook her head.

"No, stay like you are." She sat on him, reaching down to help him slide inside her. A groan escaped his lips. The wetness and warmth were beyond words.

Sitting up, locked together like this, his face was right against hers. He kissed her deeply and another groan escaped him as she started moving her hips. Her hair was so long that the soft ends tickled his thighs.

He wasn't sure what to do with his hands—at the moment, they were around her waist, pulling her to him, but did she want them somewhere else?

She stopped kissing him long enough to ask, "Is this your first time?"

He nodded. "Should we—I can go see if George has condoms . . ."

Without slowing down, she reached behind her, taking both his hands in hers. Her eyes were fixed on his when she placed his hands around her throat.

"Squeeze," she said.

He stared at her, his hips still rocking under hers. "What?"

"Squeeze."

He obliged her and closed his fingers around her delicate neck, but gently. He understood what she wanted, but he didn't want to hurt her.

"A little harder," she said. "It's okay."

"Are you sure?"

"Trust me, I'll tell you when to ease up." Her eyes were focused on his and she kissed him, her tongue searching his mouth urgently.

There were no words for the exquisite pleasure, no words to describe the incredible feeling of connectedness he had with her at this moment. It was better than anything he could have imagined. She threw her head back, thrusting into him faster. Almost without thinking, his fingers tightened.

A few seconds later, he pulled his hands away from her throat, scared he'd hurt her.

She took his hands and put them back. "Don't worry." Her eyes were locked on his and her voice was patient. "I'll tell you when it's too much. Really, I like it. It intensifies it for me."

She tilted her head back again, placing her hands behind her, palms resting just above his knees. Her thrusts were long and deep. Leaning forward, he devoured her breasts. His hands stayed around her throat as she wanted, squeezing. It wasn't long before he began to lose himself in her again, and he only vaguely heard the DJ on the radio announce the next song.

"Creep," by Radiohead.

"I love this song," she whispered, extending an arm toward the stereo to turn up the volume. "It makes me feel so . . ."

She didn't finish her sentence, but he didn't need her to because he knew what she was trying to say.

"Creep" was about obsession, unrequited love, and self-pity . . . feelings he understood all too well.

She didn't slow her rhythm and his orgasm quickly approached. He tried to hold it off, tried to think of something else so it wouldn't be over too quickly. He conjured up images of the foster father who smacked him around, the kids at school who snubbed him, the home for boys he'd lived in for two years after his mother died.

And all the while he kept squeezing. But inevitably, an incredible warmth began to spread throughout his body and he gave up. Sighing deeply, he closed his eyes and went with it, squeezing her delicate throat harder and harder.

He dimly felt her writhing in his hands, bucking and smacking at his face and scratching at his arms, but between the heady music and his approaching orgasm, there was no way to stop.

He felt himself let go, felt the pent-up release of weeks of watching her, waiting for her, dreaming of her. He came so hard he shook. Thrusting his hips upward into hers, he milked every moment, the pure bliss washing over him, controlling everything, controlling nothing.

When he opened his eyes a moment later, she was slumped in his arms, her forehead on his chest, still as a rag doll. He kissed the top of her head, spent and exhausted, but she didn't move, didn't speak.

He said her name gently, rubbing her back, feeling a small sense of pride at having tired her out this much. Not bad for a first time. She didn't respond. He spoke her name louder twice more, but still, there was no movement.

Tilting her head back to look at her, he saw that her eyes were closed and her lips were slightly parted. A line of saliva ran down the side of her mouth to her chin. He wiped it away, confused. Then he saw the two deep red marks around her throat.

Thumb-size marks, made by *his* thumbs. He'd squeezed so hard he'd bruised her. Alarmed, he shook her, but her head lolled back onto his chest with a thump.

Pressing his index and middle finger to the side of her neck as he'd been taught to do in health class, he tried feeling for a pulse. He couldn't find one. When he placed his head against her breast, he couldn't hear anything.

If she was breathing, he couldn't tell. If she had a heartbeat, he couldn't hear it.

The music reverberated through his bedroom as "Creep" reached its climax, falsetto voice against heavy guitar.

He pushed her head back again and moved her hair off her face, which was slack and unnaturally pale in the late-afternoon light. Her naked torso was shiny with sweat, no doubt a mixture of both hers and his. Her naturally rosy lips were almost colorless.

He stared at her in shock. Silent and limp and unmoving and . . . *dead*. And he was still inside her.

She was the most beautiful thing he'd ever seen.

And as he traced the line of saliva that trailed slowly out of her mouth with his finger, he felt himself begin to grow hard again.

: : : :

He stopped speaking.

Sheila lay beside him, unmoving, not saying anything. After a few minutes, the silence in the room was more than he could bear, and Ethan opened his mouth to say something. Anything. But she beat him to it.

"You liked it," she said, but her voice held no trace of accusation. She was simply stating a fact.

He looked at her. "Yes. I liked it. I liked how it made me feel. Powerful, in control, dominant. Do you know what I mean?"

She nodded.

"Do you think I'm sick?" He found himself afraid of her answer.

"Yes," she said, and her eyes closed for a brief moment. Then they opened again. "But it's okay. I can help you. If you want my help."

He nodded, too overcome to speak.

"But you're right, we need to get out of here." Sheila's fingers brushed his cheek. "We need to start over someplace new."

He nodded again, then rolled on top of her. Her lips met his eagerly, full of passion and desire, and a surge of bliss went through him.

Sheila accepted him. She loved him despite everything, and it was all going to be okay. They were going to have a new life together. His hands moved down her naked body and she moaned. Sighing, he closed his eyes and allowed himself to get completely lost in her.

He didn't realize she had the gun until he felt the cold steel barrel press against the base of his throat.

He felt his eyes widen in surprise, and he looked down at her.

Sheila's face had changed.

"Get the fuck off me, motherfucker," she said. Her eyes were black and cold. "Or I'll blow as many holes in you as it takes to *make* you get off me." Her eyes never wavered from his face, and they were serious. *Deadly.*

He rolled off her in disbelief, never taking his eyes off the gun. Sheila sat up, pointing the weapon at his face, the light from the muted TV flickering over her naked body. Her cheeks were flushed, and not from the kissing.

He couldn't help but think she looked magnificent.

"Don't look at me like that," she said, her flush deepening. "Don't admire me, you sick fuck. You think I can help you? I can't. I want to shoot you so badly I can't stand it. You're a monster, and you've always been a monster, and you deserve to rot in hell." Her free hand pointed toward the door. "Even if I don't do it for me, I would do it for all those women you killed, you twisted son of a bitch."

Ethan stared at her. She had played him. She had totally had him believing that she loved him, that she wanted to be with him forever. She had won. Checkmate.

She was going to kill him, and she didn't care if that meant she'd starve to death in the basement. She wanted him dead.

He found himself strangely aroused.

"But I didn't kill any of them," he said calmly. "I'm not a killer, Sheila. Never have been, and don't plan to be."

She frowned. Those weren't the words she'd been expecting him to say, and in her moment of confusion, the gun wavered slightly.

He went for it.

CHAPTER : 40

Jerry was trying not to fall asleep. He was doing the best he could to stay alert by sitting at Mike Torrance's desk and playing solitaire on the computer, and by drinking cup after cup of putrid coffee.

The East Precinct was quiet, even for 3:00 a.m. A bunch of cops had gone with Torrance to Lake Stevens, and the ultra-perky Kim Kellogg had snatched another bunch to accompany her to Wolfe and Maddox's apartment in the U-district. Another handful had been called away on a possible gang-related shooting in Volunteer Park. Jerry had worked quite a few of these shifts during his time with PD and didn't miss them one bit.

The officer on duty looked as bored and tired as he did. Jerry had tried to make small talk with him as the guy worked his way through a stack of papers, but the younger man wasn't interested in chatting. He was probably thinking Jerry should just go home, but Jerry couldn't bring himself to leave. While he had no official reason to stick around, this was his case in every way that mattered. He needed to know if Sheila Tao was still alive. He wanted to be here when they brought Wolfe in. He felt a sense of personal responsibility to Morris to see this through. The big guy had had a tough few weeks, and he deserved some finality, whatever the outcome.

Jerry sat back in the springy, ergonomic desk chair at Torrance's desk and wondered where the hell Morris was. He'd called him several times, unable to fight the feeling that his client had gone back up to the Lake Stevens house. He hoped not—it was ridiculous to think of the investment banker, untrained and unarmed, snooping around the house of a probable killer—but Morris was so stubborn that Jerry couldn't put it past him. Because, frankly, it's what Jerry would have done if the situation had been reversed and the love of his life had gone missing.

A husky voice interrupted his thoughts. Jerry glanced up from his mindless computer game to see Abby Maddox standing there. She didn't look bad at all considering she'd just found out her boyfriend might be a murderer. Her shiny black hair was tucked behind her ears, and without makeup, she could have passed for eighteen.

"How're you holding up?" Jerry closed his solitaire game and looked up at her. Her pale skin was luminescent under the fluorescent lights. "You must be tired."

She sat on the edge of the desk. "Too wound up."

"Maybe you should have gone to the motel."

Maddox shook her head. She'd declined Kellogg's offer to drive her there earlier, preferring instead to wait until her apartment was cleared and she could go home.

"There's a sofa in the break room if you want to lie down," Jerry said. "But I can't guarantee how clean it is. More than a few cops have slept there over the years and I'm pretty sure it smells."

This got a small laugh out of her. "Thanks, I'll pass." Maddox looked at him closely. "Listen, this might sound weird, but . . . I've seen you before, right? You followed us."

Jerry grimaced. "Yikes. Guess I wasn't as sneaky as I thought."

"No, you were pretty good. I wouldn't have noticed you at all. It's just that Ethan was always really paranoid about stuff like that." She averted her eyes. "I guess now I know why."

The young woman looked so sad that Jerry had to restrain himself from putting his arm around her. "Hey, how about some coffee? It tastes like shit, but it's hot and fresh. Just made a pot."

She peeked into his mug and wrinkled her nose. "Tempting, but do you know if there's any tea?"

"There wasn't anything in the break room?"

"I wasn't sure if I was allowed to look. I don't exactly work here."

Jerry stretched his arms over his head and yawned. "I don't either, but it didn't stop me."

"I saw a twenty-four-hour diner a couple blocks down." Maddox leaned on the edge of the desk and Jerry got a whiff of her scent. She smelled fresh, almost tropical. It was rather inviting, even under the circumstances. "Think it'd be okay if I went and grabbed something there? I could use some food, too."

Jerry gave her a sympathetic glance. "You're not supposed to leave without a police escort. Did Torrance explain that to you? You're a material witness now. They have to keep an eye on you, for your own protection."

"Yeah, he told me."

"You have a place to stay in case they don't clear your apartment tonight?"

She blinked and her face sagged a little. He noticed her eyes were moist. "No."

Jerry mentally kicked himself for upsetting her. "Don't worry, we'll get it figured out."

"You used to be a cop, right?"

"Used to."

"Can they charge people for being blind, deaf, and stupid?"

Jerry smiled and reached out to pat her knee, but snatched his hand away before he actually made contact. His hand on her leg would not be appropriate. Slightly embarrassed, he said, "It's not a crime to believe in your boyfriend. I'm sorry it turned out this way."

"Diana St. Clair and Professor Tao weren't the only times Ethan cheated, you know. There were others. I just didn't want to face it." Maddox looked down. "There were women at the soup kitchen we volunteered at. He took a close interest in some of them. For his thesis, he said. But some of them . . . some of them never showed up again. I always wondered—" She bit her lip, struggling to control her emotions.

Jerry sat up, alarmed. "You didn't tell Torrance this yet, did you?"

"They're just suspicions." Maddox finally crumpled. She put her face in her hands as a sob escaped her throat. "I loved him. I still love him."

Nothing made Jerry feel worse than to watch a woman cry. Especially one as beautiful and as vulnerable as this one. "Easy now. It's going to be all right, you'll see." He stood up and took her gently by the arm. "Come on, let's see if we can't rustle you up some type of drinkable beverage. And this is a cop shop, no way there's not a doughnut or muffin somewhere. If we can't find any tea, maybe we can put our heads together and figure out how to make a cup of coffee that doesn't taste like sewage."

The young woman lifted her tear-streaked face. She took a few breaths to calm herself until the sobs subsided. "You're very sweet. Thank you." She turned and headed for the break room. Jerry followed, trying not to stare at her ass, firm and ripe and perfect under the tight jeans she wore.

"It's quiet here." Maddox looked back over her shoulder, and Jerry averted his gaze immediately. "Is it normally like this?"

"Depends. A lot of the available officers are assisting in your boyfriend's arrest."

"Oh. Right."

They entered the small break room and Jerry looked around with a sigh. The smelly old couch sat against one wall, and an old television was mounted in the corner of the ceiling. The volume was low and it was playing a late-night infomercial for an exercise machine that was guaranteed to flatten your stomach in only six weeks. The sink was filled with dirty mugs, and crumbs were all over the counter. To the right of the sink, a soiled bread knife lay beside an opened bag of bagels. The room was a pigsty, not much better than a frat house.

"Sit," Jerry said, pointing to the small table and chairs in the corner. "I'll make the tea."

He started opening the cupboards, his back to her, pawing through the mounds of crap inside. He could swear some of it was still here from when he'd retired three years ago. "Bingo!" He reached for a box of Earl Grey tea. A name was scrawled in black marker on the side. "You're in luck. This is Detective Kellogg's, but I'm sure she won't mind."

Behind him, Maddox sighed. "She felt sorry for me, I could tell. I bet she'd never fall for someone like Ethan. She's too smart for that."

Jerry thought it best to keep his thoughts about the perky Kellogg to himself. He reached for the kettle and turned on the faucet. "Ethan Wolfe is a smart guy. And a very good liar. He strikes me as the kind of person who could fool anyone."

"You're being kind. It's pretty obvious I was an idiot. Looking back now, there were so many signs. I just can't believe I didn't see them for what they were."

Jerry plugged the kettle into the outlet and bustled over to the fridge to look for some milk. "Like what?" he said, bending over. His nose wrinkled as he pushed some of the contents around. The fridge didn't smell too good.

"Like when Diana died," Maddox said. "He was her TA, but he didn't even seem bothered by it. Considering he was the one who sliced her throat, you'd think he'd have reacted in some way. But he was like stone. It was like he felt nothing. That should have told me something."

Jerry froze, his hand on a small container of milk he'd found stashed near the back of the fridge. *Did she just say that Diana St. Clair's throat was slashed?* His mind flew back to his conversation with Mike Torrance at the Golden Monkey the week before, when his ex-partner had specifically told him that this detail had been omitted from all their press releases.

So how could Abby Maddox know about it?

The kettle whistled. He straightened up slowly, clutching the milk container in his hand. Heading to the counter, he unplugged the kettle and went about the business of fixing them both a cup of tea. His back to her, Jerry said casually, "Where'd you hear that? About her throat being slit?"

A full five seconds of silence.

Then in a soft voice she said, "I think I read it somewhere."

Bullshit.

Jerry rapidly dunked the tea bags into both their mugs, his mind racing. The police definitely hadn't released that detail to the media. No way in hell Maddox could know about it. Unless Wolfe had told her. Unless she'd been there when he'd done it. Did she know more than she was telling? What was she hiding? Maybe she knew all along that Wolfe had committed the murders, but she was afraid for her own life if she told anyone. Maybe—

Before his thoughts could fully form, Maddox was right behind him.

Her slender arms encircled his waist and he could feel her head leaning softly against his back. "Jerry." Her voice had dropped to a throaty whisper and she pulled him closer. "Thank you for being here with me. You're really helping me through this night, and I appreciate it more than words. I don't know what I'd do if you weren't here."

Jerry stiffened in surprise, almost knocking over one of the mugs. "Uh . . . Miss Maddox . . ." He put his dark hands on top of her milky white forearms. "I don't think—"

Before he could finish his sentence, her hand was under his chin. Her wrist jerked hard, just once.

As the bread knife slid into his throat, like a Ginsu cutting into a steak, Jerry had one last thought before he lost consciousness.

How could I have been so fucking stupid?

CHAPTER : 41

Sheila sat naked on the bed, staring into the barrel of the gun she'd had in her hands only moments before.

She had risked it all, and lost. Now he was going to kill her.

Ethan stood over her, his feet planted firmly on the floor. With one hand he pulled his jeans up. "You'll never win, Sheila. You see that now, don't you?" His jaw was tight as he pulled up his zipper. "But well played, my love."

"Ethan—"

"Shut up." With his free hand he grabbed his T-shirt and worked it over his head. "I admit, I believed you. You had me going. But I should know better, shouldn't I? I'm a liar, too. Except about the killing part." His face was unreadable. "You *will* be my first time. And I have to say, after everything we've been through, I'm actually glad it's you."

God, he wasn't even making sense. He'd already told her about his first kill, about the sick, perverted, horrifying way he'd accidentally ended that girl's life, and how he'd liked it. How it had spawned what he'd become.

He was watching her. "I know what you're thinking, but I haven't finished my story." He lowered the gun an inch. "The girl didn't die."

Sheila stared at him, incredulous. What did he want her to

say? It seemed as if he actually wanted to convince her of this new absurdity. "But you just finished telling me—"

He laughed, and it was genuine. He really was amused. "She didn't die, Sheila. She was unconscious for a little while, that was all. She was groggy for a minute after she woke up, and her throat was killing her, but she was okay." His eyes grew distant at the memory. "But holy shit, was she mad. She smacked me across the face so fucking hard I saw stars."

Sheila stared at him, feeling as if her brain were swelling inside her head as she tried to process what he was saying. "I don't understand."

"She was mad because I'd gone too far. I hadn't let go when she wanted me to. Believe me, I never made that mistake with her again." He shook his head. "Eventually we found . . . other ways to satisfy my need for . . . that. And we haven't been apart one single day since then. It's been over seven years."

Sheila didn't get it. She couldn't see the connection.

"Hold on," Ethan said. "It'll come to you."

It did, an instant later, after she had done the math.

"Seven years . . . oh God," she said, shocked. "Of course. Your girlfriend, Abby. You've been together all this time?"

He nodded.

"And you've kept it from her all this time?"

"Kept what from her?"

"That you're . . . a killer?" The words sounded absurd, even here, even after all the days locked away in this godforsaken basement by this godforsaken monster.

Ethan's jaw tightened. "Excuse me? I'm not a killer."

It was dizzying trying to keep up with him, and Sheila felt as if she were the one losing her mind. She worked hard to keep her voice patient. "Ethan, those bodies in the next room. Those dead women—"

"I didn't kill any of them, Sheila." Ethan frowned, then stood up and began to pace the room again. "I'm a lot of things, but I'm not a murderer. I admit I fantasize about it . . ." He looked at her, a guilty expression on his face. "But I haven't acted on it. Yet."

Sheila tried to make sense of it. It was hard to figure out where Abby fit into all this. Maybe Ethan had dissociative identity disorder, also known as multiple personalities. It was the only explanation that fit, not that it mattered now.

Ethan frowned again, the lines in his face deeper. "I might have had fantasies, yes, but I also have *restraint*. Those women, they come with me willingly. I have . . . sexual needs. And they're willing to play along. Sometimes I give them money. But I don't force them."

Stepping toward her, he raised the gun high again. "I resent that you think I'm a psychopath." His face turned pink with anger. "Apologize, Sheila." He pressed the gun hard to her forehead, just between her eyes, and it hurt.

"I'm sorry." The words came out a whimper. There was no point in arguing with people who were delusional. There was no way to win—their logic defied reason. She folded herself against the headboard. "I misunderstood. I'm sorry."

"How could you misunderstand?" Ethan looked down at her with what appeared to be genuine hurt and confusion. "I'm not a killer. I only clean up the mess. *Her* mess. Always her mess. Not mine. She plays games. How can you not get that?" He shook his head in disbelief, the gun never moving from the spot in the center of Sheila's forehead.

Once again, she had no idea what he was talking about.

"This house is where I hide her mess. Remember Diana St. Clair? We were hooking up, I'm sure you knew that. It was your class and not much gets by you."

He started pacing again and Sheila crumpled when the gun was removed from her forehead. "Did you know Diana was stabbed forty times?" Ethan's face was pained, his eyes moist. "Forty fucking times. It was in the papers. But instead of putting her in there"—he pointed toward the workroom with his free hand—"she made me drop Di's body into Puget Sound. The cruelest way for her to be found. And poetic, you know? But it was a lesson for *me*, for stepping out of line. I'm not allowed to have feelings for them. Feelings fuck up everything."

Sheila tried to make sense of his words. Something in them rang true, but who was the *she* he was referring to?

Ethan stared at her, his gray eyes dull and sad. "She lets me have them. She points them out at St. Mary's. Lets me have whoever I want. Then she kills them. That's why I brought you here. She's wanted you dead for a long time. Because she knows I care about you. The way I cared about Di." He shook his head. "But I never wanted this. I thought I could buy us time, but Morris just won't give up—"

Sheila's head snapped up. "Morris is alive?"

Ethan stopped talking immediately. His eyes flickered away.

The son of a bitch. He'd been lying the whole time. *Morris was alive.* Sheila's heart surged with so much joy she thought she might faint.

"Yes, I lied," Ethan said bluntly. "But it's too late now. You can't go back to him. I don't know that I want to go back to her, but she's all I know. I don't know who I am without Abby."

Abby. Abby was the murderer? Holy shit. Sheila tried desperately to process this, to figure out what it all meant, but she was still reeling from the news that Morris was alive. In the end, that was all that mattered. *Oh, Morris . . .*

Ethan clicked off the safety. "I want you to know, Sheila,

that you were special to me. I really did love . . ." His voice trailed off.

Forcing herself to focus, Sheila gave it one last try, even though she knew it wouldn't do any good. "Then please let me go."

"Get on your knees." His voice hardened. "Don't make me ask you twice."

The harsh truth washed over her. She wasn't going to survive this. It was going to end, right now.

But somehow, it was bearable. Morris was okay. He was safe. Sheila hadn't caused his death. He was out there somewhere, and he would live a long, healthy life. He would be happy.

She did as she was instructed, feeling a sudden numbness pass through her. It was almost as if she were dissociating from herself. A protective mechanism, she knew. There was nothing left to say. No amount of pleading would change this.

Sheila closed her eyes and tried to prepare for the end, hoping that by the time she felt the bullet rip through her skull, she'd be dead.

CHAPTER : 42

The last time Morris had felt this scared was during a football game—and not even one he'd played in the NFL.

December 31, 1980. The Bluebonnet Bowl. If he could get through that, surely he could get through this. Closing his eyes, he forced himself back to that night.

Longhorns versus Tar Heels. Fourth quarter, two minutes left, down by three, Texas had the ball. A twenty-one-year-old Morris in the huddle, listening to the quarterback call the play. His stomach burned with a mixture of fear and ferociousness, and he was hyperaware of the NFL scouts sitting in the first three rows of the Astrodome near the fifty-yard line. He'd vomited, some of it landing on his own shoes. It hadn't mattered. All that had mattered was winning.

This felt like that, multiplied by a hundred. Sheila might very well be trapped inside Wolfe's house, and Morris was so sick with worry he thought he might vomit right now.

He wondered what he must look like at this moment—a hulk of a man standing in front of a big black Cadillac, scoping out Wolfe's house in the middle of the night. Morris had made it past the old security guard at the gate without any trouble—Henry thought he was a cop. But if anyone saw him, the Remington 700 hunting rifle tucked under his arm, surely they'd call the police.

Let 'em come. Anything to get their heads out of their asses and over here, where they belonged.

Morris approached the rambler at 3513 Maple Lane. He took the three steps up to the front door quickly, knees creaking in protest. Hesitating for only a second, he rang the doorbell and got his weapon ready. The rifle was loaded, though he didn't want to have to use it. But he would, if it meant saving Sheila's life. Or his own. In that order.

Like the last time he'd been here, he heard the bell ring clearly through the stained-glass window panels on either side of the door. And, like the last time, there was no movement from inside. The house was dark. He rang the bell once more, waited another moment, then gave it a good bang with his fist.

Still no motion he could detect. Either nobody was home or Morris had just alerted Wolfe that he had a visitor. Shit. He was at a loss as to what to do next. He'd honestly expected someone to answer the goddamned door.

What now? Should he shoot the lock with his rifle? Break the glass panels and reach through with his hand to unlock the door from the inside? Neither option sounded appealing. As it was, he was trespassing. If he got inside, it would be breaking and entering. And with a weapon—well, what would that mean? Home invasion? Attempted something-or-other?

And what if there was an alarm system? A house this size, there had to be. Would it scream silently or wail like a banshee? Would the neighbors come running with their guns to shoot him, the intruder? Or would Wolfe hear the alarm, panic, and hurt Sheila?

He hadn't thought this through. For a split second he found himself wishing Jerry were here—the man was sensible and would know what to do.

Morris really did feel bad about punching the PI, but, goddamn it, Jerry had no balls. And, for an ex-cop, no instincts. Something about Ethan Wolfe stank to high heaven—how was it possible that Morris was the only one who could smell it?

He didn't care whether it had been Wolfe on the security tape or not. Sheila was *here*. He could feel it.

Before he could overthink it, he slammed his body into the door with all the force he could muster. If this didn't work, he'd blow the door open with the rifle, neighbors be damned. But under his weight, the bolt ripped from the casing and the door swung open. Surprised, he stood frozen, waiting for the alarm that was sure to sound.

But nothing happened. No beeping or screeching announced Morris's entrance. No red or green lights flashed anywhere on the walls to acknowledge his body movements. On the contrary, the house was eerily quiet. He was breathing fast and he tried to calm down so he wouldn't give himself away. A warm trickle of sweat ran down the nape of his neck to the curve of his spine.

It was too easy. What kind of guy would put such a flimsy lock on the front door with no alarm system? In an upscale neighborhood like this, burglary was a legitimate concern. Maybe Wolfe had a silent alarm, but the point was to scare intruders away, not let them ransack the house before they got caught.

Morris raised the Remington and entered the house, shutting the battered door behind him. A small amount of light filtered through the stained-glass panels from the streetlamps outside. Otherwise, it was dark. The shapes from the glass cast strange, dim patterns on the hardwood floors. He stopped again.

What if Wolfe was watching him this very moment? Crouched in a shadow, ready to pounce?

Feeling around on the wall perpendicular to the door, he found the light switch and flicked it on. A stretch of hallway that ran straight to the back of the house was instantly illuminated. Morris clutched the rifle, fully expecting to see Wolfe coming at him with a gun or a knife or some other awful instrument of death designed to kill him where he stood.

But there was nobody. Just the tasteful entryway of a big house.

"Sheila!" Morris stage-whispered. It sounded ridiculous somehow. "Sheila!"

He walked down the hallway, his finger hovering over the trigger. The Remington's trigger pull was heavy. It minimized the possibility of unintentionally firing a shot. He was especially happy about this since his hands were shaking. He moved swiftly from room to room, continuing to whisper Sheila's name. Nobody responded.

The door to the master bedroom was open, and he entered. Turning the light on, he let out a breath when he saw that nobody was waiting for him, ready to blow his head off. In actuality, the bed was neatly made, the furnishings surprisingly nice even though the large room was minimally decorated. He crossed to the bathroom ensuite, but nobody lay in wait there, either. The room was spotless and smelled faintly of disinfectant.

Three more bedrooms yielded nothing—two were empty, and one held a desk and nothing else. Another bathroom, also pristine. At the back of the house, the enormous kitchen displayed state-of-the-art appliances, gleaming as if they had never known the joy of cooking.

Something was off about this house, and Morris couldn't put his finger on it. It came to him a moment later.

The entire space was completely devoid of personal items.

No photos on the walls, no clothes in the closets, no dishes in the sink.

Did Wolfe even live here? Why buy a house like this and then rent a crappy one-bedroom apartment in Seattle? What was the point?

Back in the main hallway, he spied a connecting door to the garage. He opened it and poked his head inside, his eyes widening at the sight of Wolfe's vintage Triumph motorcycle.

The kid was here somewhere. But where? Morris had checked the whole house. Frustrated, he shut the connecting door and stepped back into the main hallway.

Something flashed in the corner of his eye and he turned toward it. A little green light was blinking on a keypad that was mounted to the wall a few feet away. Beside the keypad was a door he must have passed earlier, but apparently hadn't noticed. It looked out of place. Keypads belonged on the outside of the house, to keep folks out, but this one was *inside*. Frowning, he walked toward it and tried the handle. Locked.

His heart, already well into tachycardia, kicked into an even higher gear. No locked door had ever seemed so sinister. The goddamned front door had a crappy lock and no alarm system, but this one was bolted with a keypad? Why? What was behind it? Closet? Crawl space? It was impossible to know without either looking at the blueprints or looking inside. Morris wished he had the blueprints.

He rattled the handle again but it didn't budge. There was only one way to find out what the door was concealing. Insanely, Monty Hall's voice from that old game show *Let's Make a Deal* echoed in his head. *What's behind door number one?*

Damp with sweat, Morris stood back as far as he could before hitting the wall behind him. Aiming the Remington, he took a deep breath and pulled the trigger.

The sound was louder than anything he could have antici-
pated. Bits of wood flew everywhere, one fleck hitting Morris's
cheek just below his eye socket. The rifle's crack was scary and
exhilarating. Obviously, he'd never fired a rifle inside a house
before; it was crazy to think he'd just done it in Wolfe's house in
the middle of the night. The neighbors had to have heard *that*.
The old biddy next door was probably ripping out her curlers.

The door handle was gone. In its place was a huge, gap-
ing hole. Morris kicked out his foot and the door swung open
easily.

It was a basement. Morris was stunned. Nothing on the
outside of the home indicated the house even had one. A set of
stairs covered in gray industrial carpet led straight down to the
bottom. His heart accelerated once again. Nothing good could
be down there.

"Sheila!" he yelled at the top of his lungs before fear could
overtake him. Trotting down the stairs as fast as his stiff knees
would allow, he felt half out of his mind with panic. A few
steps down, he yelled again, the rifle cocked and ready. He
had three rounds left. If Wolfe was holding Sheila captive, he
wouldn't hesitate to pump all three of them into the bastard's
body. "Sheila, are you down here?"

As if to answer his cry, he heard a whimper, a small sound,
a pitiful sound, but it pierced his heart.

Sheila.

Turning the corner into the main room, not waiting to fully
process what he was seeing, Morris aimed the rifle and fired.

CHAPTER : 43

Unrecognizable voices were speaking in hushed tones when Sheila awoke, but it was the strong smell of antiseptic that told her she was somewhere new.

"I'm telling you, Kim, it was the creepiest shit I ever saw," the man said in a low voice. "All these masks, like real human faces, lined up neatly. A whole shelf of them. At first I thought they were actual heads with the eyes gouged out. I didn't think they could make masks that looked so real. Sick motherfucker."

"What about the wall?" The female was whispering, but there was no mistaking the horror in her voice. "Jesus, they think there could be a dozen women inside there. And those are the ones he *kept*. Who knows how many others there were?"

Sheila blinked, her eyes crusty with sleep. A pretty blonde was sitting at her bedside, wearing a fitted jacket, a small black notebook in hand. Her young face was expectant, and she was staring at Sheila with an intensity that was frightening.

"Stop looking at her like that." The dry, male voice came from somewhere in the corner of the room. "You're gonna scare the shit out of her."

Too late. The panic of not knowing where she was had already begun to ball up inside her. What was this place? Was Ethan here? Where was Morris?

The blonde put her hand gently over Sheila's fingers. "It's okay. You're safe." A smile lit the younger woman's pretty features. "Welcome back, Dr. Tao."

Sheila turned her head and saw the medical equipment, the light-mint-colored walls, the large window with the blinds rolled all the way up. A snippet of sunshine streamed into the room through a hole in the clouds. Her hand was stinging and she looked down. An IV needle was burrowed into the back of her hand near her bruised wrists. The tears came then.

"I'll give you a minute." The blonde retreated into a shadow before Sheila could say anything.

A nurse clad in cheerful pink scrubs entered the room. She headed briskly toward Sheila, checking the monitors. "She's awake? How wonderful. Hi, honey." She dabbed gently at Sheila's cheeks with a warm, moist cloth. Turning to the man and the woman in the corner, she said, "You two wait outside until the doctor's had a chance to look her over."

They didn't move fast enough and the nurse jerked her thumb. "Out. *Now*."

: : : :

The story came out in a steady stream, though Sheila honestly didn't feel there was much to tell. She was so, so tired, and she thought at one point she might have actually fallen asleep midsentence. If she had, the police detectives who had come to take her statement were polite enough not to say so. The young, kindly doctor—Sheila couldn't remember his name—had explained that her crushing fatigue was normal after such a stressful experience, and he advised her to sleep as much as she needed to. They'd given her a mild sedative, which helped stave off the bouts of panic. There were no dreams.

The doctors had left, the detectives were gone, and the nurse had dimmed the lights in the room. Visiting hours were over and the hospital was quiet. The clock on the wall told Sheila it was 9:00 p.m., but time felt meaningless to her. She lay on her side, her back to the door, staring out the window at the moon. She wished to God the sun—which she hadn't seen for three weeks until earlier today—would come back out. The darkness was awful.

It was coming back to her in bits and pieces. Ethan was dead. Morris had come for her. And Morris had killed him— he'd shot Ethan in the back with his hunting rifle. If he'd come a second later, it would be Sheila downstairs in the morgue.

It would be weeks before the bodies encased in cement at the Lake Stevens house could be removed and identified, as- suming they *could* be identified. Sheila had told the detectives what she knew about Marie, the homeless woman, and also about Diana St. Clair. It turned out they already knew.

They also knew all about Ethan's girlfriend, Abby Maddox. Abby had cut the throat of the private investigator Morris had hired, the man who'd been instrumental in helping to find her. Then she'd escaped the police station. Amazingly, Abby had missed Jerry's carotid artery. The officer on duty at the precinct had found him only a few minutes later and was able to stop the bleeding before the paramedics arrived.

Why she had tried to kill him was anybody's guess.

Thinking about the private investigator now, Sheila choked back a sob. Poor Jerry. He'd been her student a long time ago and she hadn't seen him in years. A hard worker, juggling school with career. She and Marianne had been meaning to get their men together for a double date for a while now, but it had never happened. Careers got in the way, and there'd been no time for socializing beyond therapy sessions and cups of coffee. And now Marianne's husband was in critical condition because of Sheila. The guilt was consuming.

She had done this. She had brought Ethan Wolfe into their lives.

The door to her room opened. Surprised, she rolled over to see who it was. A police officer was posted twenty-four hours outside her door, so it was probably just a nurse coming to check on her, but her palms were already sweating. Abby Maddox was still out there. While the police weren't convinced that Ethan wasn't equally or even totally responsible for the dead bodies in the basement of the Lake Stevens house, Sheila believed everything Ethan had told her. Abby had killed those women. There were many unanswered questions, but about this, she was certain.

But it wasn't Abby in her room. It was Morris. In the dim light, he was just a shadow, but she would know the outline of his face and body anywhere.

It was the first time she'd seen him since that day at her house before his business trip, the day before she'd been kidnapped. A lifetime ago.

"I didn't think you'd come." Her breath caught in her throat, and she was ashamed at how pitiful and small she sounded. "I can't say I'd blame you."

She'd put him through hell. She'd put them both through hell. Morris had never asked for any of this. The only thing he had ever done was love her.

He stood at the foot of the bed, shadows and moonlight playing against the contours of his face. He looked exhausted. She wanted to cry.

"Been here all day," he said. "You've been either asleep or

with the cops or doctors. Busy woman, as always." He managed a smile. "Did I wake you?"

She shook her head. "I wasn't sleeping. Though I guess visiting hours are technically over."

Morris walked around the bed and took a seat in the chair near her pillow. "I won't tell if you won't." The lightheartedness in his voice sounded forced, and she was disappointed when he folded his hands neatly in his lap.

She ached to touch him. Her heart broke at the sight of his face, clearly visible now that he was inches away. His eyes were bloodshot and framed with lines she hadn't seen before, his complexion blotchy and covered in three-day stubble. His hair was tousled. The strong scent of Listerine on his breath told her he'd started drinking again. Yet another thing that was her fault.

Still, he was beautiful.

"How are you?" she asked.

"I'm good." Another tired smile. "More important, how are you?"

She tried to match his smile but her lips wouldn't turn up. "I'm fine. They said I'm dehydrated but otherwise okay."

"I talked to the doctor. You can go home tomorrow morning. Sleep in your own bed."

"Can't wait." Sheila felt no enthusiasm whatsoever. Unable to restrain herself any longer, she reached for him. "Morris, I'm so sorry."

"Shhh." His voice was soft, and she was glad when he finally took her hand. "There's time for all that later."

"We need to talk about it."

"We will. But not tonight. You need to rest."

Was he angry with her? It was hard to tell. Before she could say anything else, a discreet cough came from the corner of the room near the doorway. They both looked up. Sheila could see the shape of a tall man but couldn't make out his face. Instantly, her stomach tightened again.

"It's okay, darlin'." Morris squeezed her hand, careful not to touch the IV needle stuck there. He waved the stranger closer. "Were you able to get it?"

The man nodded and passed something to Morris that Sheila couldn't see. Morris looked at it and grinned, and it was a typical Morris grin, ear to ear. It warmed her.

"Sheila, I'd like you to meet my son Randall. I believe the two of you have been in touch via e-mail?"

A younger version of Morris stepped closer to the bed. His hair was longer and straighter and there were fewer pounds on his tall frame, but there was no mistaking the resemblance, right down to the grin that lit the young man's face. "Hey there, Sheila. It's so nice to meet you finally, circumstances notwithstanding."

Sheila stared up at Morris's oldest son in surprise. "Randall!" Holding out her other hand, she grasped his wrist. "I can't believe you're really here. I'm so glad."

"It's because of you." Randall bent down and kissed her cheek. Placing his free hand on his father's shoulder, he said softly, "Thank you."

Morris looked at his son with so much love that Sheila thought her heart would burst. Then Morris turned back to her, his eyes watering. "He's right, darlin'. You did a good thing."

Randall gave her hand a gentle squeeze before letting it go. "I'll wait for you outside, Dad."

"No, stay. Please." Morris looked at Sheila and cleared his throat. He seemed nervous and she felt a stab of alarm. "I have something that belongs to you. I know we have a lot to work through, and I know it will take time, but I'm hoping . . ." His lip trembled slightly. "I'm hoping you'll say yes again."

He slipped something shiny onto her finger. In disbelief, she lifted up her hand and gazed at it in wonder. Though her wrists were still bruised and a needle was stuck in her vein, she felt a smile light her face.

Morris had given her back her engagement ring.

oseburg, Oregon, was chilly in November. But something about the crisp air and the misty skies cleared Sheila's head. She sat on the veranda of the large ranch house, a thick wool blanket wrapped over her coat, looking out into the gray day and feeling better than she had in a long time. It was Visitor's Day. She was probably the only person dumb enough to sit out in the cold waiting for her visitor, but she wanted to be the first person Morris saw when he pulled up to the New Trails Treatment Center for Addiction.

The front door to the left of Sheila opened, and Melanie Rudder, one of the ladies in the administration office, poked her head out.

"Holy cow." Melanie wasn't even all the way outside but her arms were already wrapped around herself. "It's freezing out here."

Sheila smiled at the younger woman from her rocking chair. "It's not so bad once you get used to it."

Melanie shook her head in disbelief, shivering. She held out what looked like a postcard. "Here, this came for you. I must have missed it when I was handing out the mail this morning. Quick, take it before my arm freezes and falls off. Looks like it's from your work."

She dashed back inside once Sheila took hold of the glossy postcard. Melanie was right; there was no mistaking where this was from.

The front of the card showed a picture of the grounds of Puget Sound State University in the autumn, specifically the quad in the middle of campus where the huge water fountain sprayed mist into the air. In the background stood the old, brown-brick George Herbert Mead psychology building where Sheila had worked for the past fifteen years.

She smiled to herself; she hadn't even known that PSSU *had* postcards. It was sweet of her colleagues to think of her. Dean Simmons, especially, had been very understanding. Her job would be waiting for her whenever she was ready to return.

She wasn't sure if she wanted to go back. But it was nice to have the option.

The sound of snow crunching under tires made her look up. A big, black Cadillac was making its way up the long drive- way toward the ranch house.

She waved happily to Morris, who grinned and waved back. Turning the postcard over in her gloved hands, she smiled in anticipation of the kind words.

Her hands began to shake and it wasn't from the cold. This note wasn't from anyone at the university—at least not from anyone there *now*.

Dear Professor Tao,

Saw you the other day. You seem to be doing well.
Enjoy it while it lasts.

Best,
Abby Maddox

Sheila heard the roar of a motorcycle from somewhere behind Morris.

Looking up, she caught a glimpse of tight jeans on a Triumph before it sped away.